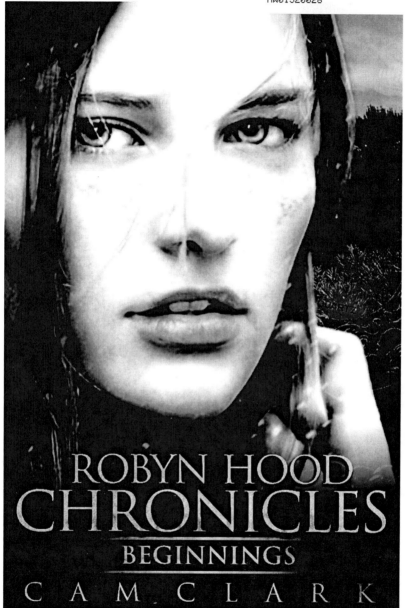

ROBYN HOOD
CHRONICLES
BEGINNINGS
CAM CLARK

For more information, visit
www.CamClark.com

Chapter 1.

I'm standing on the deck of the ship, staring over the bow at the tree-covered hills in the distance; lost in my thoughts. The last few days, I've spent a lot of time out here watching the water and thinking. Most times, the mission ahead is top of mind. Today my thoughts are on the past and that one day when my life turned completely upside down. It was just over a decade ago, yet a lifetime away. Had someone asked me that morning *"what will you be doing ten years from now,"* I would never ever have guessed the truth. Not in a million years. *How did I get here? How did my life get so turned around that I wound up exactly where I always wanted to be?* Destiny, I guess. I suppose I believe in destiny. Certainly my parents did. *Why else would they have saddled me with the name "Robyn Hood?"*

Grandma and Grandpa Curtis, my mom's parents, were on vacation when I put in my appearance some two weeks early. I'm a little ADD, and I guess I just couldn't stand waiting any longer. Even today, I still have trouble waiting. When they saw me for the first time at the age of three days, first words out of Grandpa's mouth were *"You named your daughter – MY granddaughter – 'Robyn Hood'?"* Apparently, mom looked shocked – she hadn't put the names together – and dad explained that they'd watched a nature program on TV about birds a couple of days before I arrived, and somehow the segment on robins made an impression on both of them. So much so that when they saw my red hair, it was an immediate word-association. I'm sure dad said it with his famous lopsided grin, so no one really knew whether it was the gospel truth or a minor work of fiction. He always had this gleam in his eye when he'd tell a story so you'd never quite know whether or not to believe him. They were usually hilarious and never meant to hurt anyone, so I always hoped they were true.

Of course, that story I heard much later in life. When I was younger, mom and dad both tried to convince me that I got my name because we really were descendants of the original Robin Hood. I think they felt a little guilty. At least, Mom did. Dad – I'm not so sure. I think he knew exactly what was going on when they named me. But they did try to make up for it – *how many parents give their daughter a bow and arrow set at the age of four?* I stuck with the archery right through high school – even came in second in a regional competition one year.

I was never consistent enough to be really, really good. Some days, I could fill the bulls eye with arrows. Other days, I was all over the place. I guess that was my ADD showing up again.

One thing about my name – no one ever, ever forgot it. That was – and is – a mixed blessing. From grade school to basic training – *guess who was always the first one called on from the very first day?* I think most people were a just little curious about this girl with the legendary name. On the plus side, it allowed me to be lazy when it came to choosing a costume for Halloween. Every year that I can remember, I dressed up as me – Robyn Hood. My little sister Kim was usually Maid Marion. Except for that one year we made a bunch of puppets and she went as the Merry Men.

My name also kept me out of trouble in my teen years; I was terrified that if I was ever caught, and had to give my name to a cop, it would just make everything worse. But I never, ever liked wearing green right through my teen years. That thought now makes me laugh. If only my parents could see my current wardrobe. Almost everything is green. Mostly camouflage. I know my Dad would have been proud.

But ... back to that day. It will always be "that day" in my memory. *How could it ever be anything else?* It started as a daytrip to the mountains to celebrate the end of school. Mom and dad in the front seats of our SUV; me in the back with Kim – 15 at the time – and my boyfriend Jon Smith – yeah, maybe the fact that we both had such original names helped to draw us together.

Actually, my fiancé Jon, but we hadn't told anyone yet. That was to be the surprise at dinner that night. He was seated in the middle as usual – he claimed it was so he could take advantage of the gap between the front seats for more legroom. Some truth in that, I guess, since he was by far the tallest of the three of us. I think it really was to keep Kim and me separated, because if we sat together, we'd be talking to the point that poor Jon wouldn't have a chance to get a word in edgewise. We got along pretty well for sisters.

The pickup coming toward us took a curve way too fast and swerved into our lane. Dad had no time to react. Our truck was struck and spun around in the collision; I got thrown out of the car. I remember as I flew through the air, seeing the fence I missed, and the trees, a pile of stones, and a power pole, I was on my way to execute a high-speed face plant into a freshly-seeded cornfield. Lots of scrapes, bruises, a couple of cracked ribs, a sprained ankle – and a large mouthful of dirt. Those were my injuries, along with a badly broken heart that has never fully healed, because no one else in our truck survived. And me? I could have walked to the ambulance, but they insisted on putting me on a stretcher. I wondered later if it was mostly to keep me from seeing the burnt-out wreck with the bodies still inside.

The couple in the other truck were hurt, but they survived. It turned out their teenage daughter had just been in an accident – they just got the call and were driving to the hospital at top speed. She didn't make it either and they were too late say goodbye. But, maybe that fact helped me to move on. I'm not sure. The sadness, the grief, my survivor's guilt – that was all there. Still is at times. But not anger – at least, not directed at them. *How could I be angry when, like me, they were so grief-stricken?* That at least was something I *could* understand.

Anger at myself? Now that was different. It was more than just typical survivor's guilt. Jon and I were horsing around, being a general distraction. Dad had just finished telling us to settle down seconds before the crash. Maybe if his attention was on the road, instead of his bratty daughter in the back seat, he might have had time to react. Maybe the accident wouldn't have happened. Or maybe my seatbelt would have been too tight and I would have been trapped in the burning wreckage along with everyone else. The accident reconstruction officer told me that based on the speeds of the vehicles, the curve in the road, and the skid marks – there was no way that dad could have avoided the accident. It made me feel a little better at the time, but even all these years later I still ask myself *"what if?"*

Of course, I only feel better until I close my eyes, that is. Some say we dream in black and white. I know I dream in full color. I still see the blue sky, the green fields, Jon's bright yellow shirt, Kim's hazel eyes. I see the orange flames and the red blood. I hear the sounds too. Screeching tires. My mom's scream. Sirens. I still remember waking up in a sweat, flat on my back, staring up in confusion at an unfamiliar ceiling. Slowly, the noises and antiseptic smell of the hospital began to register and I knew where I was. When I tried to move, the pain in my ribs brought me back to reality! Was I screaming? No one came running in, so I guess not. Slowly, I started to remember the ambulance ride to the trauma center; followed by a litany of cat-scans, x-rays, monitors, people asking questions, checking me for broken bones, internal bleeding, head injuries. I got a glimpse of Grandma's worried, tearful face through the window of my room. There was a seemingly endless stream of doctors, nurses, technicians and cops going in and out of my room. Then I heard my dad's lawyer friend saying that I'd be okay. I heard they would keep me overnight and release me in the morning. Then the rest of the news – mom, dad, Kim, Jon – were all dead at the scene! A counseling team will see me before I'm sent home. Then I remember feeling all alone, lying in the hospital bed, with tears rushing down my cheeks.

Here I was two months away from turning eighteen, just finishing grade twelve, with my whole life ahead of me – and all alone in the world. The next morning I think I remember the counselors showing up; I honestly don't recall. I guess they didn't make much of an impression on me. Grandma and Grandpa Curtis picked me up and took me to their home. For the next two months, they'd be my official guardians. Sometimes I lived with them, but most of those first few weeks I spent at home. It was easier to go through the motions in a familiar environment. Mom was an accountant, dad an engineer; both worked long hours so I was used to looking after Kim and me. Now it was just me. My parents' life insurance paid off the house and left me some funds to live on so I could afford to take some time to heal and figure out what I really wanted to do with my life. The lawyer told me there would be further settlements from the accident, but that could take months; or even years. "Don't wait up" was the message that came through loud and clear.

Attending university was always in my parents' plan for me. It was no accident they bought a house four blocks from their Alma Mater – the campus they both attended and where they met. The intent was for me – and later Kim – to attend the university, so we could live at home and walk to school just like we did when we were six, going to elementary school. My problem was, I really didn't have a clue what I wanted to study – or what I wanted to be when I *grew up*. I wasn't even sure that I wanted to go to university – and particularly not the one literally around the corner from home.

For years I had just wanted to get out of my parents' shadow. There was always an expectation for me to succeed ... in everything. School of course, math in particular, since both parents were numbers people. I did okay, but never quite enough to meet their expectations. At least not my mom's. Somehow that carrot was always just out of reach for me. I alternated from desperately hungering for acceptance ... and pretending that it didn't matter. When it came to schooling, failure was not an option. High school was bad enough. University would be a completely different matter. Even if I got good grades, failure could come in the form of not finding a good job on graduation. *What program to choose? What did I want, as opposed to what did my parents want?* One false step and all my attempts to live up to their endless expectations would explode in my face. The possibility terrified me. Somehow, I managed to work up the courage to complete an application and submit it about fifteen minutes before the deadline. The 'accepted pending receipt of final grades' letter came two days before the accident. Something else we were going to celebrate.

I was always in Kim's shadow too. She was the shining star. Her grades were consistently better than mine, but her real forte was dance. She was about four when she first saw ballet on TV, and she was hooked. She collected a wall full of medals and trophies in ten years of competitions. My lonely silver in archery was buried in a drawer somewhere. After the accident, they all went in the trash. I really wasn't angry at her or jealous of her success. They just reminded me too much of her and I couldn't handle the reminders.

Since I wasn't hooked on any artistic endeavor, mom chose for me. Piano. After four years of lessons, my teacher ultimately moved across the country, mercifully putting an end to that experiment. I switched to judo – definitely a better fit for me, but it didn't earn many bonus points with mom.

Jon's family lived two houses away. We'd been pretty much inseparable throughout grade school. His mom was a teacher, so I spent a lot of time over there summers and school holidays. As we got older, we drifted apart, with different interests and social networks. Then, that last year, we reconnected. His parents' marriage was falling apart and he started coming over after school just so he could stay out of his house as much as possible.

I remember his funeral being filled with family drama, making it very uncomfortable. His mom and dad could barely stand to be in the same room with one another, but they managed to put on the masks long enough for the service. His dad stormed out right afterward – not bothering to show up at the graveside service. His mom acted like everything was fine with her and everything was his fault. His older sister Kate didn't try to hide anything – not her tears from the loss of her brother or the anger at both parents. She's four years older than me. When I was six, that seemed like a lot. She was someone I looked up to and emulated. Partly for me and partly for her, I managed to get myself to the funeral. I think she was shocked that I came, given that I'd faced three coffins at the funeral for my own family just the day before. *But how could I not?* I told her about our engagement – she's still the only person I've ever told. The hug she gave me – I thought she'd never let me go. One week later, a For Sale sign went up on the lawn in front of their house, and the parents went their separate ways. I continue to keep in touch with Kate. We started meeting for lunch or coffee a couple of times a year. Now both of us are on the same campus, so we get together a couple of times a week. When her boyfriend dumped her and their six-month old son out on the street a few years ago, I was the first one she called. Now she has a condo and both feet firmly planted on the ground. But we don't talk much about family. I suspect she has little to do with either parent, but I don't know for sure. She's moved on, got a Computer Science degree, works as a data recovery specialist for the University, and is raising her child on her own.

I moved on too. After the accident, university took a back seat. My future was this great black hole ahead of me. I was in no position to make any decisions, but after a month or so I hired an agent to rent the house and moved in with Grandma and Grandpa Curtis (mom's parents). My dad's parents were much older – he was the youngest of four, and they were both over forty when he was born. They'd farmed a couple hundred miles away and were both now in a seniors' home in a nearby town. The last time we'd visited, neither one remembered me. Grandma remembered Kim, but only when she danced. As soon as the music stopped, the question was "who are you again?" They died six weeks apart about a year after the accident.

Mom's parents were a lot younger. Both retired, still full of energy and life. Grandpa Curtis did four years in the army, then became a cop. Made it to Senior Detective in Homicide by the time he was pensioned. He was always full of stories of his time in the army and behind the badge. His army stint fell between wars, so he didn't see any combat. His stories reflected that. He spent a year driving a tank in Germany and then he rotated around various bases across the country being trained, training others, and driving more tanks. And drinking beer – somehow he always managed to wind up in a tavern, pub, or saloon! Odd how that worked. But somewhere in the bases, training and drinking, he found himself and turned out to be a pretty good man. Grandma agreed. Finding myself ... *exactly* what I needed at that time. So a week after my eighteenth birthday, I headed down to the local recruiting office and joined up.

In basic training, the army discovered I was a pretty good shot, so I got shipped off to sniper training. I guess the years of firing arrows into a target in the backyard paid off. Maybe not, since I didn't make the cut and was in the end, returned to my unit. Like the archery, I was good, but not consistent enough to be top of the class. But I loved the Army; the training, the routine, and the camaraderie. Those things were exactly what I needed at that time to get my mind off everything else. And to find myself.

It also turned out I was reasonably good at languages. That was a surprise to me, although I did take French and Spanish in high school – they weren't my best marks, but they weren't bad either. So they stuck me in a class on Pashto, one of the main Afghani languages. *Guess where I'm off too?*

I wound up doing two tours. It's hard to remember all the details, but I'll never forget the faces: I see them nearly every night as I drift off to sleep.

It was just weeks into my first tour, based in Kabul at the time. Intelligence learned that an attack was planned, so our unit was on high alert. Then another unit hit an IED (improvised explosive device) and we were called in to secure the scene. I watched a young woman astride a scooter stopped at the side of the road talking on a cell phone. She ended the call, stuffed the phone in a pocket in her robe, and started the scooter. Through my scope, I could see she still had something in her hand and what looked like a wire running into a pack on her back. As she started to ride in our direction, I had her in my crosshairs. She looked up, and we locked eyes. What I saw was not fear, not anger ... it was sadness. Bottomless, hopeless, sadness. My unit commander told me to take her out – to incapacitate, not, however, to kill. As I aimed for her shoulder, I realized I was seeing her through a 50-power scope. I could see her eyes, but she couldn't see mine. But she caught the movement. I saw her eyes grow big just as I squeezed the trigger. The bullet went right through her and into the pack; I watched her melt into the explosion as the bomb she carried detonated. I don't know whether it was my bullet, or her hand that triggered the bomb. Still, she counts as my first kill. And those wide eyes still haunt me almost every night.

But she's not the only one. There are others. Insurgents who died within my sight; the friends who didn't make it back to base; the comrades blown to smithereens by an IED right in front of me. They also have places in my recurring and colorful nightmares.

It was between my tours that I fell in love. Not with a person – with the accident, and then watching friends and strangers get blown up in Afghanistan, I haven't let anyone anywhere near close enough for that. I fell in love with a place and a history. I was sent to take an advanced Pashto course in England. Since the British Army has been mucking around in Afghanistan for two centuries, they are very good at the languages of the country. We were at a base not far from the university town of Cambridge – and I loved it. Weekends, when most of my classmates were searching for the best pubs, I was touring the back roads in a rented car and finding hidden corners of history.

Yes, of course I took the A52 north to visit the remnant of Sherwood Forest and the city Nottingham. Fortunately I didn't run into any evil sheriffs. But I did spot an archery range just on the edge of the forest. I guess that's a pretty obvious location. I couldn't resist, so I stopped, paid my twelve pounds to shoot, and picked up a bow for the first time since the accident. In the weeks immediately afterward, when I wanted to forget and archery might have been therapeutic, I couldn't pull a bow because of my cracked ribs. By the time they healed, I was in the army and had far more powerful weapons to distract me.

I pulled the string and remembered. Okay, it took a bit. The first three arrows were a little random, and then I hit my stride. I pretty much tore up the bull's eye. As I pulled that bow and fired arrow after arrow at the target, I could feel the stress melt away. It was like all the pain, all the tears, all the nightmares of the past years were reduced to the bow, the arrow, and that little dot in the middle of the target. And each arrow took a little extra with it. After an hour, I was exhausted yet fully relaxed for the first time since that life changing day. Yeah, the owner got a good laugh when he saw my target and I told him my name. He wouldn't believe me until I pulled out my ID. Then he called over his journalist buddy who happened to be nearby. I guess it was a slow news day, because even the BBC picked up the story.

When I got back to base that night, my roommate was all over me. "What happened to you? You should get on TV more often – it does you a lot of good. I think that's the first time I've seen you smile."

I slept like a log that night; no nightmares. I thought maybe they were gone. But the break didn't last. They were back with a vengeance the very next night.

The archery was only a passing distraction from my growing passion for earlier times: Norman; Anglo-Saxon; Roman. I kept going further back. Pre-Roman – that was where I stopped. The tribes inhabiting this area now known as East Anglia at the time of the Roman invasion are in the very shadows of history. They had no written language, so we know them only through the scant records left by the Romans. The word "scant" is not really adequate to describe the dearth of information. Virtually non-existent is closer to the truth. The Romans first reached this area about 45 AD, shortly after they founded London, but they pretty much bypassed these tribes as they pushed north into the midlands. Then about 63 AD, the Iceni, led by Queen Boadicea, revolted. Accompanied by some other tribes, they pushed the Romans out of their territory and burned London to the ground before they were finally defeated. The Romans responded with great force and over the next two years, most of the tribes in the area just disappeared. It's not known if they were slaughtered, pushed into other areas, or incorporated into the Roman population. What is known is that those near the coast also faced incursions from the north as the Saxons and other tribes from the continent pushed their way south, pillaging and burning as they came. Until they collided with the Romans, that is, who managed to push them back to the north – again crossing the same territory that had just been ravaged. The low, fertile land was devastated and the inhabitants nearly annihilated over the entire area by the conflict. It was centuries before the population recovered; it was really not until the Angles settled here late in the fourth century that this region was again highly populated.

It is thought the people who lived here before the Romans arrived spoke a Brythonic language – a Celtic language related to that of Gaul across the Channel and the basis for modern Welsh – but that is only an educated guess. They built largely with wood, on land that has been long been cultivated, built on, and otherwise reshaped by successive inhabitants, so the archeological sites have almost all been disturbed, forever destroying much of the evidence. The artifacts that remain are fragmentary – tiny pieces that raise more questions than they answer.

The only written descriptions available are those by the Romans. They wrote through the filter of their role as invaders and conquerors. Their words were limited by their experiences and colored by their culture. Roman records give a one-sided view of the cultures and peoples that they conquered. The records of the peoples of what is now East Anglia in England were further compromised by two factors. First, the Romans only had contact with these people for a comparatively short time. They conquered the area about A.D. 45; the population was virtually wiped out only twenty years later. And during much of that period, the Romans almost ignored this region. They focused their attention on the parts to the west and north where they found mineral wealth in the form of tin, copper, iron, and lead. This was a land of farmers. Here, the Romans built few works. Certainly they did nothing on the scale of the roads, walls, and cities that survive in other parts of the country. They did build roads and a few bridges over some the larger rivers where they needed to move troops in numbers too great for the existing fords. Most of the road-building happened after the original populations were gone. In the early years, the established tracks linking key settlements that served for generations also met the needs of the invaders. Perhaps the Romans had little to say about these people because they had little contact with them.

Second, almost all Roman documents of the period were written on papyrus – a form of paper produced from rushes that grew along the Nile in Egypt. The rushes were harvested and sliced into strips. The strips were placed side by side, a second layer laid at right angles to the first. It was pressed and dried, producing a smooth, cheap, and reasonably durable writing surface. Papyrus was convenient, but suffered two grievous defects for the modern historian. If it is kept dry, after a couple of centuries, it becomes extremely fragile and falls to pieces at the earliest opportunity. Important documents were copied by hand to new material and the originals tossed or burned. Apparently ancient papyrus is perfect kindling for starting fires. Of the documents that have survived, few are intact. Most are fragmentary, forming a massive jigsaw puzzle with some of the pieces missing – and no picture on the box cover to serve as a guide. Scholars have spent entire careers in this slow and painstaking process. There are thousands of fragments that were collected a century ago and are in still waiting to be reassembled and interpreted.

The documents that were exposed to moisture fared even more poorly. A little water and the documents just fall apart; the natural glue which keeps the strips together is water-soluble. Dampness also leads to mold – which eagerly consumes papyrus given the chance. Since England is renowned for its chronically damp climate, it is no surprise that very few Roman documents survived here. It is only the few that made their way back to Italy that might have survived, but almost certainly all are now in fragments.

I knew there had to be more to the story of the people of this time and place. *What was life like? How much did they interact with the Romans and other tribes? Did some survive the upheaval?* All questions for which I had no answer. Eventually I had to leave the history and return to the twenty first century in my mind, long enough to complete my course. And as I prepared to return to Afghanistan, for the first time since that fateful day, I felt a sense of purpose beyond the army.

Who were these people? I had to find out.

Chapter 2.

My name is Muirenn. I live in the settlement of Tordur located on a slight rise along a river, about a two-hour walk from the sea. This is a low, flat region. Even though our hill is not much higher than the great trees in the nearby forest, it is the highest point anywhere in the surrounding lands. The hill and the river which bends, gives us some protection and keep us safe.

In recent years, my father, the chieftain, has given us even more protection by strengthening the walls that surround us. Where once woven branches and mud was enough to keep out the wild animals and occasional raider, he foresaw that something stronger was needed. We dug a deep ditch around the sides not protected by the river, and used the soil and rocks to build up a high dyke all around the edge of the settlement, inside the ditch, and along the bank of the river. Each year, we build the dyke a little higher and dig the ditch deeper. Soon it will be below the level of the river – then we can allow it to fill with water and turn our little hill into an island. On top of the dyke, a strong wall of vertical logs gives more protection. Inside the wall, there is a walkway all the way around, so we can look over the wall to see anyone approaching and rain down destruction on any attackers: stones, spears, or anything else we can lay our hands on.

Our wall has two gates. The large gate is in the wall farthest from the river and faces the setting sun. It is wide enough for three horses abreast to pass and high enough that even a tall man on horseback can enter without ducking his head. On both sides of this gate, we made the wall extra tall and strong, and continued the wall right over the top of the opening. It was our Roman friends who suggested that we strengthen the gate, since it is the weakest part of the entire wall. The path leading to the gate crosses the ditch on a wooden bridge – another idea from the Romans. My father's idea – we built the bridge offset from the gate, and made the path to run parallel to the wall on a narrow shelf between it and the ditch. That way, anyone trying to attack the gate will be exposed to our defenders on the wall. There is also a second gate – a small one barely big enough for one person – at the back corner, facing the river, almost hidden from view. When that gate is closed, it is very hard to see it unless you know it is there.

Within the walls are thirty round huts that are the homes of the nearly two hundred people who live here. Surrounding the huts are gardens and structures that serve as stables, granaries, and other purposes. In the very middle of the compound is our hall – by far the largest and tallest structure in the entire settlement. The hall is a rectangle nearly forty paces long and fifteen wide. The side walls are higher than I can reach. Like all our buildings, its steep roof is thatched with reeds harvested from the river to keep out the rains. The entrance door faces the gate. In fine weather, it usually stands open to allow in light and air. Light also enters through windows high up in the side walls, just below the eaves. The roof has an opening just below the peak so the smoke from the central hearth can find a way out. Most of the inside is a single large room. There are two small rooms along the back wall, away from the entrance, where we keep some of our most precious treasures.

Near the hall, close to the wall is a shed open on one side that we use for much of our cooking. A brick oven for bread stands nearby. There is also a fire pit large enough to roast a whole ox, although that is a very rare event. Lamb and pork are our more usual fare those times we do have meat. Not far from that is our latrine, so all the smells stay in this one small area. Across the settlement, on the other side of the hall, is the water well. Close to the well is the home I share with my parents and my older brother. My grandmother – my mother's mother – also lived with us until her death last winter.

Outside the walls, mostly to the west, away from the river, are the fields of crops and the pastures for herds that keep us fed and clothed. Since the fields are outside the walls, open to attack, we are vulnerable. So we watch and guard. I suppose at one time, all the land around us was forested. Over the years, much has been cleared – the wood is used for building or the fires that cook our food and keep us warm in the winter. The cleared land is cultivated for fields or becomes pasture for our livestock. The crops are near our walls – mostly wheat and barley with a few beans and oats thrown in. Further away are the pastures for our herds of sheep, cattle, swine, and goats. The most distant pastures have huts for the herders, and fenced enclosures for the animals. Now that it is summer, they live full time in the fields. Unless there is a threat of attack –they then will try to bring the animals back to safety inside the walls. A pack of hounds for the hunt and a few cats to keep the mice down round out our population.

We also have a few horses. My father has six – two stallions, three mares, and a new colt that arrived this spring. There are another eight horses owned by other families. They are used for riding – on the hunt, or when traveling further than a day's walk. Very rarely do we ride to war. Our warriors usually fight from behind our walls – we are a peaceful people who do not seek out battle. Not that we can't. We have some very able bowmen who are both strong and accurate. Over the years, the Sea-wolves have learned to their cost that we are not an easy target. Our bowmen would far rather exercise their skills at putting meat on the table than fighting off people. But they are not afraid to defend us.

Our settlement is one of twelve that make up our tribe. The largest is nearly a day's walk away to the west. Most of our people have never traveled that far. It is the home of the king of our whole tribe, so as chieftain, my father visits there often, and he sometimes takes my mother with him. I have never gone with him, but he's promised to take me the next time he goes. Mother's father was the chieftain here until his death when I was very young. Since he had no sons, when my parents married, my father was named his heir and grew into the role as grandfather aged.

There is another town only a couple of hours' walk away. It is situated on a river as well, nearer to the sea than we are. They are mostly fishermen and we often purchase some of their catch for a change from our normal food. Many of our families have kin there for there has long been much traffic between the two places. My mother's sister lives here – wife to the chieftain and mother to his son and two daughters.

At sixteen years, I am old enough to be married, but have not yet found anyone. Usually, the woman moves to her husband's settlement when she marries. But I desire to stay at Tordur. That makes it harder, for few men are like my father and willing to make the move to his wife's home. In his case, he was the third son of a chieftain, and although a warrior, hunter, and respected leader of men, he could not become chieftain for his oldest brothers were both equally capable and had the advantage of greater experience, for he was considerably younger.

His moving here to wed my mother let him become chieftain here, and solved my grandfather's problem of the lack of an heir. Since one of my brothers will almost certainly be chieftain after my father, I don't have the same advantage my mother had. Sometimes I feel so old, that life is passing me by and that I'll need to give up my dream of staying here in order to find a husband suitable for my status.

This morning I stand by the well and look around. Some call where we live a village, others a hill-fort. I'm not sure that either really describes the place. I know that I call it home. I feel safe here, safer than I do in the other places I've visited. Even though we are near the sea, we can't easily be seen from the water, so for many years, the Sea-wolves from the north would pass us by in their search for plunder. Or maybe it was our archers who kept them away. Now that they rarely come this far south for fear of the Romans, I feel even safer.

Most who come to our gates, do so in peace. Some are merchants who travel the land with goods for trade. They are most welcome. Our tribe has long worked in iron, acquiring raw iron from the north, and turning it into finished tools and weapons. We still have a forge and smiths who work in iron, but it is no longer our main source of income. The other settlements around us rely far more on the ironwork tradition for their trade, and we are glad to leave it to them.

During our winter, with the short days and constant rain – almost everyone spends as much time as possible inside. It is during such times that wanderers of a different sort arrive and are welcomed. They are the bards and minstrels, and wanderers who bring tale and song. When darkness comes early and the dawn tarries forever, a harp and a ballad help pass the time.

Others come to our gates for a completely different reason. We are known across the land as a place of healing. Our great hall is not for the gathering of a war host or to increase the pride of a chieftain. It is a hall of healing, with cots for the sick and wounded. Our gates are open to any who come seeking healing – at least any who comes and can afford our price. And we take most who cannot. Some of our neighbors fear us, or at least distrust us because of our art, for it seems to them like magic. It is not, it is a learned skill, passed on from generation to generation and kept a carefully guarded secret. Not all who come to our doors can be healed – some come too late or have illnesses beyond our skills. But enough of those who walk, crawl, or are carried here leave healthy, so that our reputation now extends far and wide.

Even some of the Romans, the conquerors who arrived on our shores before I was born, have come to us for healing. About ten years ago, a lady arrived at our gate – the wife one of the Roman leaders. She did not come alone, for she was in the back of cart and guarded by six soldiers on horseback. She was deathly ill, with a disease that was fast stealing her life. Her Roman doctors had given up, and told her to go home and die. But she was a fighter, so when she heard a merchant speak of us and our reputation for healing, she decided that she had nothing to lose. So she made the trip. And she arrived in time. Just in time. It was months before she was able to make the trip back home, alive and well, long after she was supposed to be dead.

From then on, we always had a couple of Romans staying in our hall. I learned their language and something of their ways – mostly from the soldiers and slaves who accompanied those who came as patients. Since they had time on their hands as they waited for their charge to either get well or die, I would often talk to them and hear their stories of far-off places. As I listened, I started to dream of visiting these places – Londinium; Gaul; maybe even Rome itself. But reality and my love of the life here has kept me from actually taking leave.

Our secrets give us power. Our secrets of healing include our knowledge of plants and herbs, passed down from our ancestors. The gardens within the walls are devoted mostly to our healing plants. Only a small area is reserved for food crops. Other plants will not be confined within our walls, and only grow in the surrounding forest. Gathering them is my job. I love the time I spend in the forest, seeking out the plants, the hidden fungi, and other ingredients for our medicines.

In the past year, things have changed. The Iceni, a tribe to the north, revolted against the Romans. Queen Boudicca led them to victory in several battles; they even burned much of Londinium. So more soldiers came and in the end, the Iceni were defeated. Of those Romans who had been our friends, many were killed. Others fled south before Boudicca's wrath reached them. The governor who knew and *trusted us was recalled to Rome and replaced. A new governor arrived, and we fear he will use his forces to subdue the remaining tribes – all the tribes, without exception. It was last fall that he came, and the Romans stopped coming here. They were busy last summer repairing the damage and building new encampments for troops. This past winter, when the rain, cold and dark kept everyone close to home, they quietly increased their troops and prepared for war.*

Traders and other wanderers were paid well for information about the people. Whispers around the fire spoke of a campaign planned for the spring – a campaign that will leave no one with the strength to launch a future rebellion against the power of Rome. We fear that even those who have been friendly to the invaders in the past will be targeted, and that none will be safe. We fear even as healers, we will not be immune when the war comes. Of course, if we are not attacked, the wounded will come. War always means that we have our hands full.

Already we have seen wounded pass through our gates. The Romans are sending out small patrols on horseback. A dozen or so men armed with swords and spears ride the roads, testing our strength, and learning the land. They are the vanguard of things to come. So far, they do not attack the fortified settlements. They avoid them when they can, and ignore them when the road brings them near. Anyone who crosses their path as they travel does not fare well. Men are attacked on the road. Most die; some are left injured. Few of those wind up at our doors. Women fare worse, for those who are captured are taken back to the encampment. The few who survive are gravely wounded in spirit and body. We have had some; they may still live, but their full restoration is beyond our skills.

Those who till the land are terrified of being caught. They spend as much time listening for hoof beats as they do working the fields. This spring brought considerable rain at the time for planting, so much work still remains to be done. And much will be left undone. So, the crops may be less than normal this year. If war does come, the crops that did get planted may well be trampled, burned, or stolen. It could be a hungry winter.

The travelers from the north also bring troubling news. The Sea-wolves stayed on our shores this winter. In past years, the Iceni were strong enough to drive them away. Rather than face constant attacks through the winter, they returned to their homes across the sea each fall, and only returned in the spring when the weather was fair and the sea calm. They come to pillage, then leave. Last year, with Iceni weakened by their war with the Romans, were no threat to the Sea-wolves. So the invaders stayed last winter, still far to the north of us, but far too close. Close enough that their boats have already been seen this far south. And it is only spring. My father thinks it is only a question of who will arrive first – the Romans or the Sea-wolves.

But today, there is no sign of either. Being spring, there are many herbs in the forest for me to gather for our medications. I spend most of my days in the woods, searching and collecting. My mother gets worried that I'll be in danger, but I am not afraid. The Romans with their horses stick to the roads, and avoid the forest paths that I travel. Besides, they are not silent in their approach. The hoof beats, the rattle of harness and armor – I will hear them long before they are near enough to see me. But they won't come, for the paths I travel are not for a man on a horse. And the Sea-wolves look for open fields and settlements; they too avoid the forest. If any threats do appear, I will simply fade into the forest until they pass. The narrow ways and low branches on the roads I travel ensure my path will not cross with any invaders.

Chapter 3.

There is little I want to say about my second tour of duty. I spent most of it Kabul, part of a team tasked with building relationships with the Afghani people. With my now fluent Pashto, women came to trust me. Once they learned that I'd lost my family, like so many of them, the walls started to come down. That was something we shared in common. Nearly everyone in that war-torn country has lost someone. Some are like me and have lost everyone. I know them by the vacant look and the eyes drained of all tears. I remember seeing that same look in the mirror. The rage I felt against whoever did this. They could tell I knew it from the inside and not from reading some book. So, I was one that they trusted.

As people responded to me, I started to respond to them. Little by little, I let down my walls too. I started to let these broken, wounded, frightened women get to me. Then along came Fatima. Just a couple of years older than me, she lost her brother-in-law, husband, and young son in a market bombing. She was left with a newborn baby and not much else. They had been living with her husband's parents – after the explosion her in-laws kicked her out onto the street. Don't blame them. They lost the breadwinners of the family – without them, there was no money to feed all the mouths. They had little choice but to bury their grief, and find some way to survive. So she was turned out. She came to us starving and freezing – hoping that maybe somehow we could help to keep her daughter alive.

We got them food, warm clothing, and a place to live. We helped her find a job. And she became my friend. I came to know her as a caring, intelligent woman, passionate about her people, her country, and her child. She was a woman who understood the challenges ahead of her and had the courage to face them head on. Through her, I saw myself in a new light – not brave, but a coward who ran to the army for comfort and belonging when everything fell apart. Brave behind a gun, but a complete chicken when it comes things that matter, and never ever trusting anyone. Slowly, as I taught her to survive, she taught me to live. And I slowly and gradually cracked open the door to my heart.

Three weeks before I was scheduled to rotate back home, and dreading having to say good-bye, there was another bomb in another market. Fatima was killed instantly. Her daughter died before they got her to the hospital. A whole family exterminated by the violence. And the light that had started to grow in me, a light of trust and hope, died with them.

But now I knew that I couldn't face another tour. As soon as I got back home, I took my discharge, moved back to my home town, and applied to the Department of Anthropology at the university. *Keep my distance, turn people into scientific experiments. Data points on a graph. Keep my distance. Keep safe. Study people who are already dead, so they can never disappoint me by dying again.* Unlike the living. Grandma Curtis was diagnosed with Leukemia during my second tour. She died in the spring of my first year of university – just as I was studying for my final exams. I buried myself in books, while Grandpa's heart was shattered. I shared his grief, comforting him and still managed to pass all my courses. But he never recovered from her loss, and followed her in December the same year. I was left alone, with one more inheritance – just what I didn't want for Christmas.

The next spring, I fled back to the army and signed on with the Reserves. Got my commission. "Captain Robyn Hood" ... kind of has a nice ring to it. I got my undergrad and masters' degrees, and was accepted into the Ph.D. program. "Doctor Robyn Hood" – that sounds okay too.

After Grandpa died, I moved back home – my real home, the house I grew up in. Maybe I was just trying to hang on to something from my past – as there really wasn't anything else left. But it was too big and too quiet, so I rented the extra rooms out to other students. There are five of us living here now – and 'quiet' is not the issue. Denise's room is across the hall from mine. She's short girl with long dark hair and has this incredibly expressive face that can speak entire paragraphs with just one raised eyebrow. She wants to use her endless energy to save the world, so her Ph.D. will be in disease prevention among refugees and other displaced populations.

Down the hall is Michele. She's a quiet, blonde, botany major with a wicked sense of humor that mostly comes 'out of hibernation' when she's stressed. Her way of dealing with the pressure is to crack a joke and get everyone laughing. Either that or play some freaky practical joke on someone. She's also pretty talented with styling hair and is a licensed scuba diver.

The basement is occupied by Don, a post doc in theoretical physics, and Max, who is a professional student, currently working on an applied mathematics degree to go along with his degrees in computer science, mechanical engineering, and a couple more which I can't remember just now. I think he hopes to do something in advanced robotics. Or maybe he'll just stay in academics. Don looks like someone you'd really hate to run into in a dark alley. Big and bald, with a goatee. You'd expect him to ride a Harley and drink straight whiskey. He actually drinks soda water and drives a white minivan that he inherited from his grandfather, when he drives at all. Usually he's in one of only three places – home, university, or the pizza joint down the street. And walks in between those places. I think he's made the trip there so many times that he's worn a rut in the sidewalk. Max looks so quiet, with a neatly trimmed beard and short greying hair. Give him a tweed sports coat and a worn briefcase – he's got that associate professor look down pat. Appearances are so deceiving. He's the drinker and the one who will flirt with almost any girl who crosses his path. And is the life of any party he chooses to attend. He's the one who you can never pin down because he is very cautious about who he will let see behind his facade. Even though he's working on his 6th degree, he still doesn't have a clue what he wants to do when he grows up.

So that's the gang I share my life with. At least in theory. I spend summers training with the Reserves. The rest of the year, my life mostly revolves around the university. Not very exciting, but after so many years of watching the people I love die, boring is good.

It was just last year at the end of August when boring got interesting. The day was blazing hot, even at six am. It started with the long bus ride back to our base from the training camp. Of course, I got a bus with an air conditioner which barely managed to keep the interior just below "broil." That was followed by a summer's worth of goodbyes and – thanks to a crash on the Interstate – a three-hour crawl through grid-locked traffic to my home. On a good day I can make the trip in twenty minutes. I was totally exhausted, grubby, and seriously grouchy when I finally pulled into the drive. I was so looking forward to a bath, home cooking, and wearing something that's not military green. I walked in the door and my jaw dropped. In the ten weeks I'd been gone, the living room had been totally transformed. Six racks worth of equipment covered one wall. I could see through to the dining room, where the table was pushed over against the wall and covered with monitors, keyboards and other gear. The middle of the living room was occupied by a cage-like collection of metal tubing, covered with a seemingly random collection of unidentified bits of equipment and connected to the racks with dozens of cables snaking across the floor. I was totally speechless. I dropped my duffle on the floor and stepped into the room, staring at all the apparatus. I thought I recognized a few lasers, maybe a camera – I wasn't sure what anything else was. I did recognize my coffee table carefully centered within the cage.

I sensed someone behind me and slowly turned, totally unprepared for anything after the shock of seeing this maze of technology in what was once my home. The sound I was hearing was coming from below me, near the floor, so I looked down. Max was face down on the couch, totally zonked out. I got the feeling the couch has received lots of use this summer, because it was the one spot in the room which somehow managed to escape being buried in equipment. Then I noticed the white metal box on the floor. The box that belonged on the kitchen counter. The box was missing a keypad and apparently had been stripped of most of its components.

"MAX!" I used my best drill-sergeant voice. "WHAT did you do to my microwave?"

I swear, it seemed like Max jumped at least a foot off the couch and was stumbling to his feet by the time I finished spitting out my words. That's the fastest I've ever seen him move in the five years I've known him. Argh! How do you stay mad at someone at the same time as you're doubling over with laughter at the sight of him trying to get himself upright, while looking appropriately befuddled? At least I had his attention.

"Sorry Robyn. Uh, welcome home." He stammered like he almost forgot how to form the words. "We needed the timing circuit last night – early this morning, really – to get this working. We didn't think that you'd be home this soon. Don's out now picking up a new one for you as we speak."

My being more upset about the microwave, but not the redecorated living room, does kind of expose my culinary skills. The microwave is the one cooking appliance that I actually know how to use. I'm excellent at nuked mac and cheese. I'm pretty good with frozen pizza, too. I suppose that reheated frozen entrees don't exactly qualify as "home cooked," but that's about as close as I can get. Besides, they still beat army food. Without that magic box, I'm joining Don at the pizza joint. Since a new one was coming, I decided to let it go. I didn't even bother to ask where the money was coming from. I assumed from the next month's rent, based on previous experience with these two.

I slowly turned back to the middle of the room. I admit – I was more than a little curious about the apparatus.

"And what is 'this'?" My tone was whole lot softer than I used for my previous blast. I managed to get it almost down to my normal voice.

"Jess – do you mind explaining?" Max asked as he looked over my shoulder toward the dining room. I turned to follow his line of sight to see a vaguely familiar-looking woman – I guessed we must have crossed paths at some point on campus.

"Hi. Doctor Jessica McKenzie," she said, approaching and holding out her right hand in greeting.

With the name, I made the connection. Last year Don convinced me to go to this lecture on the multi-dimensional universe. I insisted we sit near the back of the room so I could slip out if it got too boring. Not that it really mattered, since there were only about 30 people there – it was mid-January and one of coldest nights in years. A bitter wind came in from the north carrying a large deluge of snow and most people wisely stayed at home. Don really wanted to go and convinced me that he'd feel a lot safer walking with someone with survival training under their belt, given the miserable weather.

My initial response was "Yeah, Don. You've walked this route at least a couple thousand times – you won't get lost."

But his pleading worked. We went. I suspect everyone else who showed up lived in residence, right on campus, and got there without stepping a foot outdoors. Most of the lecture went way over my head, so I pretended to pay attention while in fact, studying the handful of people around me and dreaming of warmer climates. We stopped for pizza on the way home and talked. Don is actually pretty good at explaining complex theoretical concepts in plain language. Once we left the math behind, I actually enjoyed listening to his description.

The space-time universe consists of more dimensions than the four we normally perceive – the three dimensions of space ... plus time. But there have to be more dimensions – the most recent theories predict at least eleven. With any fewer, the math just doesn't work. Jessica presented a mathematical model showing one dimension – the seventh in her theory – acting as a lock. This dimension is believed to be circular, and if an object were to rotate through that dimension, it would be able to move through any of the first four dimensions freely and with very little energy.

Things clicked for me when Don explained that what Jessica really presented was a hypothetical framework for time travel. That night I lay awake, unable to sleep as I mulled over the possibility of travelling through time. I knew where and when I'd want to go – to the people of England's east coast, at the time just before they disappeared, we assume wiped out by the Romans. To be fair, Don did warn me as we trudged back home through knee-deep snow that practical time travel was still decades away. Still, I couldn't help dreaming. My thoughts eventually wandered away from time travel and back to Don as I realized that in all the years I've known him, tonight was the first time we'd ever sat down over a meal, just the two of us. It felt good – almost like a date.

But now with Jessica in the room, I became even more curious about the strange equipment in my house. Even so, for some reason I was also a little ticked that she tacked the "doctor" onto her name. "Captain Robyn Hood" I replied, taking her hand. I was willing to be friendly, but I wanted to remind her she's not the only one who can tack a title on to her name.

"Thank you so much for letting us set up here," she said. "When they found asbestos in the lab building, we thought we'd be shut down for the entire summer while they removed it. And we were so close to success. Then Don suggested we move our equipment here. Since both Don and Max are on the team and it is so close to campus, it made perfect sense. Three months ago, we made a breakthrough and were actually able to send a paperclip back a few nano-seconds in time. But in order to go further through time, we needed to be able to establish our location in three dimensional space so we could maintain a fixed location on the Earth during time travel. This cage is our second-generation experiment, which puts us one step closer to a workable time machine."

She explained that time travel itself is a bit of a paradox. "Traveling through time is actually the easy part. Once we worked out how to make that 90-degree rotation in the seventh dimension, moving through the time dimension becomes possible and the physical equations involved are relatively simple. The difficulty is the need to simultaneously move very precisely through three-dimensional space so that you arrive not just when you want, but **where** you want. We all know the earth rotates once per day – which means the earth spins a little over a thousand mph at the equator. The earth also revolves around the sun, taking a full year for the trip. This requires an average speed of nearly 70,000 mph. The sun, earth, and the rest of the solar system rotate around the center of the Milky Way galaxy at about 500,000 mph. Consider also the Milky Way is blasting through space over four times that speed – and you begin to see why the "where" is absolutely critical to time travel. The smallest miscalculation in your position and time travel will leave you literally lost in space.

"The breakthrough Max and Don came up with is what they call geo-locking. Geo-locking freezes the time machine on a specific point on the surface of the earth and uses a feedback loop to constantly measure and adjust the position relative to that point during time travel so it moves with the Earth and remains in the exact same point on the surface during the travel through time.

"One of the first problems they needed to solve was how to measuring that location. The usual 21st century solution of the global positioning system is simply not an option. GPS is based on time signals from satellites that orbit the Earth. Since time travel is all about messing around with time, GPS also gets messed up. Then, if you travel to a time before the satellites were launched, then you'll have no signals, therefore no position information, turning you into instant space junk.

"Fortunately, they found another option. An Inertial Navigation System (INS) relies on lasers and prisms to calculate changes in location. Far bulkier and more expensive than a GPS receiver, an INS is even more accurate and has the huge advantage of being completely self-contained. It requires no signals from outside, and depends on minute changes in wavelengths instead of external time signals. It works at any time, any place. And fortunately for us, it even works during time travel."

I was in absolute awe as I circled the room staring at the cage. There was a time machine in my living room! I was speechless, which those who know me will attest is a very rare occurrence. "Have you made any further progress?"

"Yes," Jess replied with a smile that reminded me a bit of my dad's lopsided grin. "A week ago, we were able to send a set of winning lottery numbers back in time, and secured the funding to move forward without having to mess around with research grants. It was either that, or apply for funding from the Department of Defense. But they would have wanted us to move to Area 51, and Arizona is just too hot."

I wondered if she was serious or not. I never could figure it out with dad; I decided I probably wouldn't have any more success with her. It turned out she was serious.

"I think we will need some support from the Department of Defense anyway. I was wondering if you might be able to use your connections to help us there."

I rolled my eyes. Not long after I got home from my first tour, the rumor got out that a certain General and I had an affair going. We really were just friends. I was rather convincing in the media scrums that followed and the matter was soon dropped. My medal came shortly after that, supposedly for taking out that bomber before she could take out our patrol, but I've always wondered if it was really for bravery under fire from the media. Now, said General holds a very high position in the Pentagon and people assume I have some influence with him. I might – we still keep in touch.

Jess continued. "The solution to the problem of staying on earth during time travel opened up another problem. Time travel is not like travelling through empty space. While you are actually moving through the time dimension, you don't occupy any space in the normal three dimensions. Because you are actually in a different dimension, you only occupy a single point in three-dimensional space. Since this point is smaller than an electron, any other object which happens to pass near that point won't interfere with you. But as soon as you complete the journey through time, you rotate back into three-dimensional space. Now the space that you need to occupy had better be filled only with something that can move aside to make room. Air is a good choice, but creates a problem. Either you arrive really close to a surface capable of supporting you, or you arrive prepared to fly. Arriving close to a surface opens the possibility of having an object in the way that is reluctant to move suddenly – trees and rocks immediately come to mind. An aircraft would be an option, but there will be a period of time after you rotate into three-dimensional space before the airflow over the wings stabilizes to provide aerodynamic lift. During that time, the plane will not be flying, so will drop like a rock and have absolutely no control. We calculated a plane would lose nearly twelve thousand feet in altitude until it is able to fly. *That's survivable, but once the plane is flying – where do you land it? And take off again?* Because of the need to have a sizable team and to bring in all the gear needed to accomplish the mission, it would need to be something on the size of maybe a C-130. Even then, the supplies and fuel that you can carry are very limited. Plus you need a good place to land. And take off again to get back home. An airplane doesn't sound like a good choice.

Or, we could travel on a surface that has the give we need, but can also support a structure large enough for our needs. Water! We eventually concluded the ideal time machine is a ship. A ship doesn't fly through the water, it floats on the surface. As it rotates into three-dimensional space, it will simply push its weight in water out of the way so that it will float. Fish, floating logs, and everything else will go with the water. As long as it is deep enough for the ship, you don't have much to worry about. If you are in the ocean, you do need to calculate the state of the tide, so the water level at your arrival is close to the same as it was at departure. But close is good enough. If you're off by a bit, you just make a bigger splash. And the calculations involved are simple compared to those required to get you there in the first place so we should be able to handle them.

In terms of supplies, a properly-sized ship will serve as a base and have plenty of room for the food, fuel, and equipment to support a fair-sized team – and bring everyone home safely. The equipment can even include a helicopter, drones, and weapons – whatever is required. It's also portable – you're not stuck in one place. Add in radar and sonar to look for hazards above and below the water, and you're pretty much covered. On the downside, a ship is a little hard to hide. Once you complete your time travel, you become instantly visible to anyone who happens to be looking in your direction. One could use a smoke screen – or stay far enough off-shore to avoid being really obvious. Staying off-shore has another advantage: no one can sneak up on you. And if you need to impress the natives, size does matter, and a ship is big enough to get attention."

"Sounds like you've done a lot of thinking about the practicalities of time travel – not just the physics," I said.

"We have. Don has handled much of the physics, but Max headed up the logistics."

I'm sure I sound a little puzzled in my reply. *"Logistics? What kind of logistics?* I thought this was all very theoretical and that it will take decades for time travel to become a reality."

Jessica smiles as she answers. "Six months ago, I would have said the same. Our progress this summer has been far beyond anything I imagined in my wildest dreams. If our next series of experiments goes well, we could be ready to send a team through time within the next year. So logistics is totally relevant. Just working out the people we need and getting them together is a huge job. The equipment and supplies are another huge job."

Then Max jumped in. "Many who foresee time travel postulate sending a small team who can fit seamlessly into the existing culture

– taking no modern tools or weapons with them. That just isn't practical. According to the math, travelling through time will create ripples in space-time that will impact the return journey. It's possible to adjust in advance for these ripples in the calculations, but we think it is safer to delay the return home until enough time has passed to be clear of them. The greater the mass you send through time, the larger the ripples, so that is a downside of our plan to use a ship. With what we propose, we need to remain in the other time for at least three months before attempting to return. We *think*. So that means we need a team that can be totally self-supporting for at least that period of time. To be safe – to allow for delays, losses, and the unknown environment we will face – we plan to send enough supplies to last for at least 18 months."

"Have you thought of when or where you will send the team?" I knew what my vote would be, but I doubted it would count for much.

"We hope you might have some ideas. And I might add, we also hope to convince you to join the team. We need an anthropologist."

Inside, I was jumping for joy because I just landed my dream job. Outside I managed to keep calm. "I am most familiar with my area of study: what is now England in the late first century, at a time shortly after the Boadicean Revolt. That is my first choice. There are many unanswered questions about that time, so a visit to that time would have great scientific value to me. Further, since Latin was spreading across the land at the time, communication in that language should be possible."

Jess asked. "Do you know Latin?"

"Most of the original documents I study are in Latin, so yes. Max is pretty good at it too."

We didn't make the final decision right then, but when I got to my office I found two items in my inbox that clinched the deal. The first was from an anthropological journal specializing in the Roman Empire. A document covering the early years of the Roman occupation of Britain was recently discovered in Italy. A colleague noticed the article and forwarded a copy to me knowing this era to be my specialty. The original document was in Latin from the middle of the first century AD. It was a personal report from the governor of Britain at the time to a friend in Rome. Of course it was found in fragments and some of the pieces were missing so the analysis was necessarily incomplete. One segment in particular caught my eye. It reported a settlement to the north east of the Roman capital of Londinium where the people were widely known as healers. Many Romans had gone there for treatment, and had been welcomed. Most returned healthy, even some of those with sicknesses beyond the skills of the Roman doctors.

I excitedly scanned the article for more details. There was only one settlement that had this skill – a hill fort located at a bend in a river, near the sea about a three-day journey from Londinium. The fort belonged to a small tribe – the name was missing – occupying a small area of the island. Some of the people living in this fort were fluent in Latin, learned from the Romans who came through their gates.

The location would them right in that corner of England that draws me, the people who are almost invisible to history. These people are the very reason that I got into anthropology in the first place. Now, I had in my hand a very interesting piece of the puzzle. And the technology to research them in a way that was never before possible.

Later that morning, I found a second interesting piece in the form of a preliminary report from an archaeological dig conducted by an English university that summer. A historical survey conducted on the site of a proposed car park in East Anglia revealed an early Anglo-Saxon settlement. During the dig, they also found an even earlier settlement at a deeper level – late Iron Age, dating from early in the Roman occupation period. This settlement site showed signs of being burned. Even so, it is the most intact site from the time ever found in the area. Exploratory pits exposed parts of a kitchen, a corner of a hall, and part of a typical circular iron-age home. The car park had to find a different location and this site will be more fully excavated next summer. I quickly wrote a letter of interest asking to join the dig and sent it off to the lead archaeologist before my coffee got cold. I also noted the exact latitude and longitude coordinates printed on the aerial photos of the site. That could be a very useful bit of information.

Chapter 4.

The summer solstice is less than a moon away, so the sun rises early and far to the north. Even so, I arise at the first sign of light because I want to take full advantage of the long day to travel further than usual, to a hidden spot in the forest where I can find a fungus that we need. It only appears in the spring, and only in very few places, and is so potent for healing some illnesses that it is well worth the journey. So, I make the trip at least once a week at this time of year to replenish our stocks. I have my collecting bag ready, beside is another bag with some cheese and bread for my lunch that my mother prepared last night. Both bags are dark leather, soft and supple, well-worn from long years of use. No one else in my family is awake, so I silently get dressed in drab trousers and tunic, grab my bags, and head out. Just before I leave, I also grab one of our precious iron knives – both for protection from any wild animals I might meet on the path, and to harvest the plants I am seeking. I don't bother with a water bag, since there is plenty available from the creeks and rivers along my planned route. I cross the open center of our little village. None of the other huts show any sign of life at this early hour, but a thin wisp of smoke rises from the cooking shed at the far side of the hall, where someone else is already at work. I know I could stop there and maybe get some fresh bread for my breakfast, but I have other things on my mind for today.

Instead, I turn in the opposite direction and walk past our great hall toward the wall which protects us. Here, near the front of the hall, the wall is pierced by a gate large enough for horses and carts. In the gate is a small door, just big enough for the passage of single person. With the threat of war on two sides, we keep a guard posted at all times. As I approach, one of the sentinels quietly greets me, and after telling me there has been no sign of any danger, opens the door, and I disappear through it into the early morning mist.

I cross the river that runs past our walls in one of the little coracles we keep for that purpose. The skin-covered boat handles easily in the lazy current, and I soon reach the far side bank. I can swim the river as I've done many times in the past, but today I'd rather stay dry, for I plan a long walk. Once I reach the shore, it is easy to lift the light craft and conceal it some nearby rushes for my return journey this evening. Then I climb the riverbank to the path that parallels its course. If I turned to my left, I would soon strike the road leading to the north, which leads past the nearby settlement of my kin. I know it goes beyond there – how far I do not know. But the traders who come from that direction speak of great forests, mountains, and strange peoples. Someday I may go that direction to learn what lies beyond the borders of our little land, but today I turn to the right, following the river in the direction of the sea. After about half an hour, I leave the river and enter the forest. My search takes me to a small tree-lined stream which I follow downstream. Experience tells me that I will find what I am looking for along its banks, near fallen trees, among the moss and lichens, where the sunny banks meet the deep forest. My plan is to follow this stream until just before it reaches the sea. Near the shore, just before I leave the forest behind, I'll cross a low ridge to another stream a little further on, and follow it back up, gathering more. Once my bag is full, I'll cross that stream and walk a little further to a hill that overlooks the sea. There, I will rest and eat my mid-day meal. On the way back, I will fill the bag which held my lunch some moss, ferns, and other plants that we need. I know the path and the plants I will find there, for it is my favorite route home. I should get back just about the time the sun sets, exhausted, but with both bags stuffed full of much-needed supplies. This is familiar ground to me, for most days I gather in the forest or along the banks of one of the many streams that wind their way through it to reach the sea.

As the sun rises, the mist begins burning off. I can feel the day grow warm, and see the sun through the forest canopy. On the ground, there is not a breath of wind and the air under the trees start to feel muggy. I soon reach the stream and cross on the rocks, because I know there are several spots on the far side where I am likely to find plants we need. The trees spread their branches to almost cover the stream like the roof of a giant green hall. Where there are gaps in this living roof, I can see blue sky and only a few clouds. We've had a lot of rain this spring – more than usual, so a day of sunshine is most welcome. Not that I'll be able to see much of it for the forest is dense with few clearings.

Today, the collecting goes well – the rain has produced lush growth on the forest floor. I manage to find several of the precious fungi sprouting in the shade of fallen logs. We think they feed on the old fallen wood, so each time I find one I use my knife to slice off a few slivers of wood from a nearby log and press them into the ground nearby. It seems to work, for the places where we get our greatest harvest are surrounded by our bits of wood. Of course, this was not my idea. It's one that I learned from my mother, who learned it from her mother – we've been doing this for many generations. This is only the second year that I've been going out gathering on my own. From the time that I could walk, I helped – or tried to help – in the gardens. As I grew older, I went out to the forest with my mother or others to learn the secrets of finding the plants we need. Early last year, I started making some gathering trips by myself. This year, mother generally stayed at home, preparing supplies and medicines for the sick and wounded, so I gather on my own.

As the sun passes noon, my first bag is full, my feet are tired, and my stomach is grumbling for a meal. Finally I reach my hill and eagerly climb the slope. I call it "my hill" but in truth, it is no more my possession than is the sun or the rain. It is simply my favorite place, and has been since my mother first brought me here about five years ago. Near the crown of the hill, the woods thin to a clearing on the very top, like the bald spot on my father's head. It stands on a bit of a point, so on a clear day I can see miles up and down the coast and across the choppy water of the sea. Today the view should be fantastic. I love to sit here, stare out over the sea and imagine what it would be like to cross to the other side. Some of the Romans who visit us tell stories from across the sea – stories of strange people and great cities. I love hearing them, even though I don't quite believe everything that they say could be true.

When I reach the top, I go right to the far point of my hill, to the very edge where it falls away to the beach below. There, I drop to the ground and open my lunch. As I eat, I sit and watch. I watch the gulls play in the air and hear them squawk as they fight over some morsel of food. I lean back and look up to the sky. Far above I can see a hawk turning in lazy circles, barely moving a wing as it glides through the air. I find myself imagining – what fun it would be to fly like a bird. What wonders could you see from way up there? Soon, in my mind I am soaring through the air, feeling the wind in my face, looking down and seeing the tiny people far below. I nearly drift off to sleep, but instead I drag myself back onto my feet and stare out across the water.

Far to the south, I see something that shouldn't be there. A boat. I blink, hoping that it will disappear. But it doesn't. It's far from shore, shrouded in the remains of the mist, but undoubtedly, it is there. No boat on these waters is good news for my people. Those who arrive on our shores come only to plunder or conquer. The Sea-wolves plunder – take what they want and leave; the Romans conquer – take what they want and stay. This boat is coming from the south, so it might be Roman. I'm not sure. I've never seen a Roman boat before, and this one looks very different from those of the Sea-wolves. Not that I'm an expert in their boats either, but this one is different. I look again – and that's when it hits me – it has no sail. It looks to be big – very big from what I can see. It looks kind of lumpy – something is sticking up, but it is not big enough to be a sail. This boat can't be moving very far because even though there must be enough breeze to fill a sail, they haven't raised one. Even I know enough to guess that whoever is on that boat would rather let the wind push them along than man the oars. Sails or oars – there are no other choices to move a boat that I've ever heard about. This one is a long ways off and since it's not moving, I don't think it's a threat to us. But I will tell my father about it when I get home.

Before I leave, I turn and look to the north. Now, just past the next headland, I can see them. Sails and masts. Lots of sails. Sails on boats that I recognize, even though I've seen them only once before that I remember. The Sea-wolves we call them – Northmen who come to attack and pillage. They are close in and heading toward shore. Some are very close – they may have already reached land. Others are still at sea, but heading toward shore. There must be twenty boats – maybe even more. Possibly a thousand warriors. And they are far; too close to our homes. Do they know? Are they prepared? I turn, grab my bags and start to run. No more collecting today; I'll run and hope I am home in time to give a warning.

I'm not too worried about my home. Not yet. Instead I will head first to Dubri-tun, the home of my mother's sister, her husband and children, and other more distant kin. Their settlement is near the sea, much closer to the Sea-wolves than we are. And they have fewer people than we do – they have perhaps fifty able-bodied warriors at most. Their wall is not as strong and their location is more exposed. They will face the enemy first.

As I run, I think back to the lone boat – the one I first saw sitting still. It is pointed directly toward the fleet from the north, yet not moving in that direction. Why? Do they know the fleet is there? They're not running toward them, so they're not Sea-wolves. I guessed as much – the boat looks very different from theirs. They're also not running from them – they showed no fear, sitting still, clear from land. Like they are waiting. I wonder "for what?" Are they enemies to the Sea-wolves? Waiting perhaps for others boats to join before attacking from the sea? If that is the case, then these people are our friends. Perhaps they are heading further north, and are waiting for dark to slip past. Would they not then be trying to hide near the shore? Or making their way further to sea, to be out of sight of land? But this boat is just sitting there, almost daring an attack. I don't understand. Why?

Chapter 5.

I feel the deck of the ship gently roll under my feet in the light chop, and I stare into the mist, searching for the first glimpse land. Now, just a few miles of water – and this fog – stand between me and history. I feel the salt spray stinging my face, driven by the wind caused by the motion of the ship, and the pre-dawn chill makes me shiver. But nothing could drive me inside this day. The deck tilts as we swing slightly to starboard. Captain Johansen must have seen something. I know he's on the bridge, watching the display screens that tell him where we are, and what is around and beneath us. The inertial navigation system gives him our exact location. Two high definition radar units constantly search above the water, looking for land or other boats; our forward-looking sonar probes beneath it, searching out bars or reefs in these uncharted waters; the infra-red scanners are another set of eyes, seeking heat from a fire, a sun-warmed rock, or a living human. As the ship turns, I feel something else – warmth from the sun. I glance at my feet to see a long shadow trailing off to my left. The morning sun is rising, burning off the mist. And to the west, I see the dark line of land, grey in the mist. The fog is starting to lift, so I will soon have my first clear view of the land. But it also makes us visible to any watchers.

We chose to arrive in early June, 64 CE, just a year after the Iceni and related tribes led by Boadicea revolted against the Romans, burning their capital at Camulodunum to the ground, before moving on to attack and burn the commercial port of Londinium. Apparently the damage to Londinium was not as extensive, for after this date, the Romans moved their political and military capital there, making it the leading city of all Britain. We chose early June for our arrival to give us a full summer of long days and generally good weather. Our goal is to remain here for about four months so the ripples we created in the space-time continuum during our outbound journey won't disrupt our trip home. For better or worse, we are stuck until late September. When we do come back, we will return to the exact point of our departure and just a few seconds later so we don't freak everyone out by disappearing from the sea without a trace.

The land here is low, with wide shingle beaches rising to rolling hills covered with forests. Further north, the land is even lower. There, too wet to support trees, it is covered with grass and reeds. To the south are the famous white cliffs that attracted Caesar and his Roman legions a century ago, and will still be there 2,000 years from now. Roman ships likely have not yet come this far along the coast, which is fortunate for the people who live here; the wide beaches make ideal spots landing an invasion fleet. The Romans may not have come this way, but other invaders have. The Saxons and others from the European mainland have pillaged this coast for centuries. Rarely do they come this far south, since there are rich pickings closer to home. But they come often enough that the few settlements near the coast are strongly fortified and alert for the arrival of strange ships.

So our plan is to remain about four miles off the coast – far enough to not cause alarm should anyone spot us. We will be visible from land, but we hope that we'll not be seen as a threat. With no sails, we expect anyone who spots us will believe we are just drifting with the tide, which is exactly what we plan to do today. Once we are in position, we'll launch a drone to scope out the land. It will climb to about three thousand meters – too high to be seen or heard from the ground. We have two drones specially equipped for this mission. They have high resolution cameras, radar, and infra-red imaging and the transmission equipment to stream the detailed images back to the ship or directly to our team on the ground.

I feel the change in vibration as the engines slow. *Are we here? In our planned position?* I'm just starting to turn to face the bridge as I hear the scuff of a shoe on the deck behind me.

"Captain Hood, Ma'am. We are ready to launch a drone. I thought you'd like to know. The team will be meeting in Mission Control for the first images in about 15 minutes."

"Thanks Andrew, I'll come in now."

Andrew is one of our deckhands. Like us, he has no strong ties to home and is not afraid of hard work or adventure. All characteristics which are pretty much obligatory for this mission. He's twenty-something, with short blond hair, average height, thin build, and surprisingly strong. He grew up in a small east-coast town, working on the family fishing boat from about the time he could walk. I guess his home life was pretty rough since he left the sea for the oil rigs inland as soon as he turned eighteen. Now, he never speaks about home. But a few years far from the coast and he was ready to see salt water again. I'm glad we convinced him to join us – he's a natural on board the ship with the confidence and skills that we need. Except he seems a little afraid of me. He knows that I used to kill people for a living, so that could have him intimidated. It's happened before. Or maybe he has a crush on me. Maybe both.

I turned and walked back toward the deck house, climbed the stairs to the level of the bridge, and headed for the door that leads to the passage behind the wheelhouse. I admit – I'm so excited I feel like I must be in someone else's body. This can't be actually happening to me. But the reflection glancing back from the window beside the door was definitely mine. Staring back is the familiar round face with blue eyes, a few freckles framing a nose, I always think is a bit too big, all topped by the straight dark-red hair I keep just long enough to pull back into a pony tail when it gets in the way. All are attached to a very fit body, if I do say so myself. I flash a smile which the reflection returns, then open the door and step inside.

To my right is a passage leading directly to the bridge. I stay away from that part of the ship. I may carry the army rank of Captain, but on board it is Patrick Johansen who is THE Captain. And the bridge is his domain. He's got to be nearly seventy, with a face worn by a life-time at sea. After a stint in the navy, he spent the rest of his career running ferries across the English Channel. He stuck to the ferries because he couldn't stand the thought of being away from his wife, the love of his life, for months at a time. So he shuttled to ports on the continent and was home every night. But not long after he retired, she died from cancer and the cottage they shared for forty years became too big and too quiet. The sea was drawing him back at the same time we were searching for a mariner experienced in these waters. He came to us full of questions, but in the end convincing him to join us was far easier than I thought possible.

He came with one condition: the bridge and wheelhouse were his domain. He agreed to take responsibility for the safety of the ship, and we promised to keep out of his way – nobody who is not ship's crew enters the bridge unless invited. I'm okay with that. I'm pretty careful about who I want on my landing team, so I understand his demand.

Passing the forbidden door, I head further down the passage to the room that serves as our Mission Control.

Newly christened 'MV Voyager,' our ship is a former naval supply vessel we chose primarily for its vast capacity for fuel and supplies. And being built to military standards, it has the strength to handle any rough treatment we dish out during time travel. The forward half of the ship is occupied with a three-story superstructure, with the bridge, wheelhouse, and Mission Control at the top. Quarters take up the second level. The lower level is the galley, lounge area, gym, storage lockers, and sick bay. Machinery, fuel, and storage take up the space in the hull. Behind the superstructure is the hanger for our helicopter and drones. The flat deck at the stern holds the helipad and a catapult to launch the drones. We don't have quite the space for the drones to land, so we installed two masts with a large net. The net is on shock absorbers, so we just fly the drone into it at landing speed. The net catches it and brings it safely to a stop. The masts are on hydraulics so they and the net can be lowered out of the way when we need to use the helipad. Pretty slick system.

The time travel equipment doesn't take much room, so we installed it in an extra cabin on the B deck. We even brought a second backup time machine just in case anything goes wrong with the primary. We have lots of extra cabins, since the ship is designed to handle a crew of over one hundred. We only have twenty-one on board so everyone gets private quarters, and even then we have extras. I took over one of the extras for a sitting room and private office, but several others remain empty.

We bought the ship at a surplus sale, but did get defense department's assistance with weapons. The team had a lot of heated arguments about what weapons we should carry – if any. In the end, we agreed that we needed to be able to protect ourselves because we could be walking into a war zone. Since one of our mission goals is to get everyone back home safely, I eventually won the weapons argument. Our success also requires establishing trust with people who are under the threat of attack, so we need to have the means to protect them if that is what it takes.

Our ship carries short-range radar guided missiles. These are small and intended for anti-terrorist duty. They are able to take out small boats, vehicles, or small structures – that sort of target – anywhere within their 35-kilometer range. The Navy found they lacked the explosive power to reliably stop an approaching target that's trying very hard to not be hit. So they ordered a new version with a bigger bang so a near miss will still do the job, and we managed to score the originals. Since our greatest threats will be wooden sailing vessels manned by crews with no idea how to avoid a supersonic missile, the older version should meet our needs.

Most members of our landing team will carry a side arm, and at least two on each mission will have assault rifles. Our helicopter carries air-to-ground rockets and we have a heavy machine gun we can mount in the side doorway, just in case. Also, just in case, it is equipped with a rescue winch, so we can pull people out of spots where we don't have the space to land. The crew is trained and we all work well together. Most of the time. I think we are covered for pretty much anything.

The chopper will be on standby today. We will map out our area of interest from a drone before we send in a team by boat to get a view from the ground. The goal today is not to make contact with anyone, so we will be in full camouflage. Today we will try to avoid people, and will disappear into the forest if anyone comes too close. But, we will still be armed in case we need to protect ourselves.

The drone is our advance eyes. Our helmets have built-in displays so we can see images from the drone, even when we are on the move. We also have full voice communication with each other and with the ship. The drones carry radio relays to ensure our communications will not be interrupted by hills or other obstacles. Each of us also carries a transponder that sends out a unique identification code. The radars in the drones and on the ship can pick up the signal and identify the location of each member of the team. This way we always know who's got our back and we can find someone if they get separated from the team. I also carry a tablet which gives us a larger display we can share, and allows me to control the drone cameras – zooming in on details, panning, or changing between visible, infra-red, and radar images. The drone itself is controlled by a pilot on the ship.

I turned to my left and entered the room. Four others are already here. Michael and Kelly will be on my landing team today. Michael was a warden in a park in Virginia. He's an expert in forest navigation. Even though the terrain here is much flatter than what he's used to, we expect the forest to be similar. Kelly is a paramedic from Detroit. Trees are not his thing, but he's the one I want around if anyone gets hurt.

Trace is sitting at a control desk, facing a bank of displays, with her hand on a joy stick. She's one of our three pilots, and is flying the drone today. Her real name is Tracey, but she's so tiny – barely five feet and probably not even ninety pounds soaking wet – that her name was long ago shortened to just Trace. She flew crews to off-shore oil rigs in the Gulf of Mexico. Of our other pilots, Jerry flew survey work up in northern Canada and Jack did forest fire fighting out west. All are highly experienced in pretty demanding flying – these are three excellent pilots. All three are also trained on the drones – they in turn trained others on the crew.

Lance will also be on the landing team today. He's ex-navy, handy with boats, and built like a tank. He's a few years younger than me and even though he managed to make it through a four-year tour without any actual combat time, I trust him. I think in part it that he has this way of telling stories of his time afloat that reminds me just a bit of Grandpa Curtis. Not sure that he'd consider that a complement, so I keep that little fact to myself.

A couch at the back of the room is occupied by our photographer/videographer par excellence. I first met Taylor during my second tour in Afghanistan. He was working on a news team that did a special on our work with the Afghani people. After my return to civilian life he did a couple of follow ups on returned veterans and sort of made me a poster child for a successful post-military career. We kept in touch – I provided some input as an anthropologist on a documentary he directed on the long-term impact to people displaced by war in the Balkans. He was between projects when I came looking for someone to document the mission. It took a while before I admitted to him that when I called, I was just hoping that he might know someone ... and never dreamed he would be available. But I'm so glad that he was. He was totally invaluable during the preparations for this journey – we wound up spending a lot of time together as we finalized the details. He's organized enough trips to various parts of the world to have some very good insight into what to bring and to expect. Today, he'll cover our mission from the ship, but if things go well, will join us on the ground tomorrow.

Andrew didn't join us in the room. Instead, he headed to the stern platform to prepare the 16-foot inflatable boat that he will use to take us to shore. It's equipped with a powerful electric motor so our approach to land will be virtually silent. We don't want to draw attention to ourselves today, and we are heading to a land without the noise we are so used to in the 21st century, so quiet is the order today.

Don and Max wander in together a couple of minutes behind me, with a very pensive Martin right on their heels. Martin is our mission controller. After a stint in the Air Force in Air Traffic Control, he wound up in the media, producing a local news program. He was laid off a couple of years ago, and was seriously under employed until we ran across him serving drinks in a bar.

"Martin." I said, "You look worried." A worried Martin is probably not good news.

He doesn't even look at me. "Trace, can you put the drone and radar images on the screens?"

The room darkens, and the two large screens that take up an entire wall, light up.

"The screen on the left is showing the live image from Little Bird One. On the right, we're showing an enhanced radar and infrared view from the ship." Little Birds One and Two are, of course, the drones. I focus on the left screen, watching the forest drift slowly under the camera.

Martin continues "We launched the drone and climbed to altitude over the water, and are just starting our first pass along the coast. We're directly west of our current position and will follow the coast north. Our coverages extend from the shore to about eight hundred meters inland. This pass we're looking for possible landing sites and potential threats – or even people who might be in a position to see us. Trace will continue to fly the track and will let us know if she spots anything interesting. Now, I want to focus on the right display. Robyn, this is what has me worried."

"About fifteen kilometers north of us and close to shore, there is a fleet of at least twenty-three longboats. Four look to be already drawn up on the beach while the others are still approaching the shore. One hundred ten kilometers out and closing at about four knots is another fleet of at least thirty boats. Those are not an immediate threat because if they are headed toward the same spot, they won't arrive until midnight, unless the wind picks up. In another hour the tide will turn and be against them, so their speed will drop to about three knots. The boats close in are just beyond a headland, so we don't yet have a clear view of exactly how they are positioned or the size of the crews. We'll know better in a few minutes when we have visuals from Little Bird. I doubt they've spotted us." As soon as we picked them up, Captain J turned the ship bow on to them, so we presented our least-visible profile. With the headland only our radar mast was visible from the ground and the remains of this mist should keep it concealed."

"These boats typically carry a crew of about fifty, so with twenty-three, that makes give or take eleven hundred ten warriors on the ground. I'm concerned about putting in a landing team with those warriors so close. And I'm concerned that some of the approaching fleet is headed further south. As soon as they come around that headland, we will be visible to them. We will probably have to engage them to protect ourselves and discourage them from getting too close. I'm not worried about us. Even though the boats are wooden, they carry enough metal that our missiles won't have any problems finding them. I just don't like the idea of taking out people who don't have a chance against us."

I'm staring at the right screen now. I can make out sails and masts, but can't see the hulls or the beach. Even though the radar and cameras are mounted high on our mast, the headland blocks the view. As I'm working through this new situation in my mind, I start to talk it through so I bring the team up to speed on my thoughts. "Let's take a look at them before we get too excited. I think we can select a target zone for the landing team that steers clear of them. I'm more worried what they may do to the sites we came to study – I don't want them to destroy anything before we can even identify our primary sites. We may need to move faster than we'd planned and we may need to engage them on land to protect the study area. One piece of good news by taking the side of the locals in a battle should help us to quickly gain their trust – and they are the people we're here to study. As far as the approaching fleet goes, we'll need to blackout the ship tonight – no lights showing in any direction. And get the chopper ready to hit the air just in case things get ugly. But once we launch it, there will be no point in trying to hide – everyone within miles will see and hear us. But we may be able to chase them off without getting into a firefight. We have so much strength that I'm hoping we can discourage the invaders without actually having to exercise it. If we have to, we could take out those boats and everyone in them in about sixty seconds. I've seen enough people die; I don't want more blood on my hands."

I turn my attention back to the other screen. A small clearing right on the shore is drifting by. From the shadows, it looks to be at the top of a low hill. The elevation readout puts the ground nearly fifty meters above sea level, but that's the highest point we've seen so far. Once we scout the coast, our plan is to fly a grid pattern and create a detailed 3-dimensional map of the entire area. We will need that for our mission, and it will be an incredible resource for historians when we return. "Have you seen any good landing places yet?" I ask Trace. "We know the site we are seeking is on a river or stream and not far from the sea, so if we can find a site near the mouth of a watercourse, I'd like to come back and make a run at it and see what's there. Finding a landing place is at least as big a priority as checking out that flotilla."

Trace updates us. "There was a good sized river mouth right after I started my run. There were three sizable streams and five small creeks visible since then. I marked a couple of potentials. The others aren't big enough for anything much larger than a canoe. There's a lot of water down there, but it's divided into a lot of little streams. Wait ... here's one that's a possibility."

Together we watch as an inlet drifts into sight and Trace turns to the left to follow the shoreline. I see the mouth of a stream almost immediately, coming into the inlet almost at the point it reaches the sea. Here and there between the trees that grow thickly along the banks, I can see the stream snaking away out the picture. Lance pipes up. "That looks like a decent landing spot. Let's mark it." Trace

46

pushes a button, then and a thumbnail pops up on in a column on the left side of the screen, directly below the images for the sites she already marked.

The inlet proves to be the mouth of a rather sizable river. Trace banks the drone to the right, picks up the other shore, and points it back out toward the sea. "Far side of this river forms the headland that's blocking our view of the longboats" she adds by way of explanation. We watch as the drone flies over the headland; the beach with the long boats swings into view. Trace sets the drone to circle, clicks on the autopilot, and comes to join us. Five boats are drawn well up on the shore. We count eighteen more arriving. Three more reach shore and we see the men piling out and wading to land. As we watch, two more grind onto the beach and disgorge their crews. The men then line up along each side, and drag the boat up onto the shore, creating a space for the next boat to arrive.

Martin walks up to the screen and touches an icon on the side. The image freezes. Using his finger, he draws a box around the area with the boats and the beach. Another touch opens a menu, and he selects "Warm Bodies." "103" pops up in response. The "warm bodies" app to count people in the image is the creation of our tech guru Steve. He is this largely nocturnal presence on the ship who keeps everything running and normally only becoming visible at meal times, except for those few occasions when someone manages to talk him into joining the rest of the gang for a movie. But he knows his stuff and we'd be lost without him.

More thinking out loud ... "Not quite as many as we thought. Some may have left the beach already, but these boats are a little smaller than the later long boats. It looks like they each hold about forty."

Martin touches the screen again and the display jumps back to the live feed.

"No horses," I observe. "So they'll be travelling by foot." I notice something and walk toward the display. "It looks like they plan to stay here for a while. See these guys here?" I say pointing to a group of one hundred or so piling supplies on the beach well above the high water mark. We can see they are carrying swords and spears – Trace has a radar image overlaying the visual, so the metal in their weapons is clearly visible. "Look at that pile of weapons – they are obviously getting ready for a fight." The drone continues on, they leave the picture as another group appears further up the beach. These men are standing in smaller groups – about twenty in each.

"They are carrying weapons and look to be ready to move inland. Raiding parties, I think. They'll probably head out in several different directions to gather food or scout for targets." As I speak, the drone reaches the end of the beach and banks into a turn to the left. The route back will be over forest, so Trace switches to infrared so we can spot anyone hiding in the trees. We spot the odd one here and there in the bushes. Eighteen by the warm body counter. Just before we hit the river and turn for another pass, we spot a group in the trees, heading back toward the beach. Thirteen more.

"Wonder where they're coming from?" I ask the room. "A party of scouts who discovered a target and are coming for reinforcements? Or maybe a foraging party that was raiding some nearby fields? Can we stay over them?" Trace rolls Little Bird into a turn to keep them in view as they break out of the trees onto the open beach. Watching them meet the men on the beach is almost like watching an old silent movie. We see them greet, see the gestures, watch them point back the way they came, but there is no sound, no words. Not that any of us would understand them, anyway. They are probably from what will be Northern Germany, the ancestors of the Saxons who will conquer this land in about four hundred years with their allies the Jutes and Angles, bringing with them their Anglo-Saxon language, which will eventually evolve into modern English. Possibly, they may have come from as far as Denmark. Not likely would they be from further afield.

Many of the men gathering in small parties are now joining the group that returned. Even the men unloading the boats stop their work to join the crowd. The counter tells us three hundred ninety-one are now on land, with more piling out of the boats just now reaching land.

"Looks like they are gathering a party for a major attack," I guess. "Those scouts came back along this path that parallels the river. Let's fly up and see what's there."

The image stops turning as Trace rolls the drone back into a straight path, and navigates along the meandering route of the river. It doesn't take long before we again pick up the path through the forest roughly parallel to the north bank. The path is pretty clear on the infrared image, but no people appear. "Can we zoom out to see a wider area?" I ask.

The path and river shrink as Trace pulls back on the zoom. The south bank also comes into the image. Looking with the wider view proves to be the right decision. In about five minutes we come across a group of men hidden in the trees. Across the river is a walled town. The group grows on the screen as Trace zooms in. Twenty-two. She pans across to the town. The infrared won't pick up anyone in one of the buildings, since the thick thatched roofs are too well insulated. We count twenty-five people wandering across the compound, staring over the wall or through open gates across the fields, tending animals, cooking. More people are in the fields and gardens outside the walls, going about their day, oblivious to the army concealed only a short distance away. The fields extend about two kilometers away from the town to the south and west. Just outside the walls to the east along the river, several small boats are drawn up on the shore. As we scan the surrounding area, we spot a road – wider than the paths we've seen before – running north and south about a mile to the west of the town. This is truly a road, wide enough for four horses to travel abreast. It winds around the hills so probably wasn't built by the Romans, since they tended to build their roads as straight as possible. A little to the south, separated from the fields by a narrow belt of trees, we spot an open meadow and a path connecting the town to the road.

"Let's follow this north, and see where it goes." Ripples in the water reveal a line of stepping stones and a shallow ford for horses where the road crosses the river. It continues north, past the point where the path we saw earlier joins from the east. We follow the road for another ten minutes until we come to another town that is somewhat larger than the first. "Looks like this one is better defended. Those walls look pretty solid," I said.

I look up at the top right corner of the screen where a box shows the current latitude and longitude of the drone. Of course, we don't have

GPS, so the drone picks up the range and bearing to the ship. The navigation computer makes the calculation.

I speak up again. "The first town we saw – that could be the one we want. This one seems too big and is a little far away. Let's go back to the first town and map out the area to the south and west so we can plan an approach. We may need an intervention here. We've come too far to watch our target get burned to the ground on the day we arrive."

We follow the road south. It runs through a belt of forest, across another ford and then extends a considerable distance through fields and pasture. Some sections are completely open, while in others a band of trees on one or both sides separates it from the fields. After a few miles, the road crosses yet another river on another ford. Not far beyond is another hill fort.

"This one is bigger than the first – but smaller than the second one that we found. I count thirty-eight round huts. The first had only twenty-one. Population here could top two hundred, where the first was probably around one hundred, thirty. One thing we do know for sure – this town is the location of the dig in our time. The lat-long coordinates are an exact match. We'll certainly want to come back here. But for now, let's keep mapping the area between the road and the sea. We need to find a ground route to Town A." I don't need to explain that Town A is the first on we spotted, the one threatened by the Saxon invasion force. I am on my feet, thinking this through as I approach the board. Trace captured a still showing a broad area to south of the town, the fields, road, and river.

"This river is a possible route in. I think it's the one we spotted earlier; the one Lance saw a landing spot at the mouth. I can see a path along the bank here. I start drawing on the image. The trees offer good cover all the way to the road, but if we cut through here" – I draw a line through the trees less than a kilometer before it reaches the road – "we will come out to the open at the closest point to the town. It's only about eight hundred meters to the gate. I'd like to try for some high ground, but there just isn't any. From there, we can guard the approach. They may attack as soon as their forces are gathered or they may wait until nightfall. Just in case it's earlier, I want to be in place as soon as we can."

I go back to the live image just as Trace announces "I just spotted someone – only one I've found in the forest on this side of the river. Here in the clearing by the sea that we spotted earlier."

I look to see a small figure that quickly grows larger as Trace zooms in. A girl or young woman with long dark hair and pale skin is lying on her back looking up. Trace comments "She's a long way from home – she's nearly ten kilometers from the nearest settlement. I wonder what she's doing there."

Far below us, but still far from the ground, I see a hawk cross the field of view. "I think she's watching the hawk."

Trace ignores my comment, but continues her report. "I ran the facial recognition on her, just in case we run into her again."

Thanks to our defense connections we were able to get a copy of facial recognition software developed for anti-terrorist applications. We hope to identify individuals to establish population levels and track their movements. I am most interested the degree of travel between sites. She's the first in our database, so gets tagged F0001.

We finish mapping the area, grab our equipment and a quick lunch, and head to the boat. Four hours later, our team is tracking along the river, fully armed, and ready for action. The drone keeps us updated, so we have a good idea what we will face. Shortly after we landed, a group of seventy of the invaders crossed the river at the ford, and approached the town from the west. They were spotted, the alarm raised, everyone pulled inside and the gates closed. Now, they have established a siege – spread out through the fields watching the town and the forest. These first arrivals are in no hurry because they know more will arrive before sundown. Trace has been tracking them. It took them a while to get organized and move out and the large group is taking a longer route away from the river bank so they can't be seen from the town. The bulk of the forces are still about three hours away.

We followed the girl as she also took the path we planned to take. Likely this is her home; if so, she is caught outside the walls for she arrived after the Saxons besieged the place. Little Bird could see her standing just in the edge of the forest for about fifteen minutes, like she was trying to decide what to do. When she finally backed away, one of the attackers must have spotted the movement, for he came in her direction. He came right to the edge of the trees and stood there, watching. She was back on the path by then and he didn't see her. A sound assumption as he didn't follow her; but we did, all the way to the road. As soon as she reached the road, she turned south and started to walk toward the ford. On the far side, the road curves as it passes through the trees lining that bank. Beyond is a long stretch of open fields with little cover.

By the time she nears the ford, we're already at the road. All four of us are on the path when Martin's voice crackles in my ear.

"You've got company. Twelve men on horses are coming fast toward you along the road. Romans, I think. You should hear them soon."

I step off the path into the brush; the rest of the team follows. Here we can see the road, but should remain invisible in the shadows. I watch the girl and see her stop dead in her steps just as she reaches the river. She's heard the hoof beats. She turns and runs away from the ford, back toward us. *Is she headed for the path?* The bushes near the river should provide cover. Then I realize – these men are mounted so are much higher than men on foot would be; they will be able to see over the bushes and grasses and spot anyone hidden there. She knows that, and that is why she's headed to the denser trees of the forest where there's better protection in the shadows. Exactly where we are concealed.

But the road is rough here. There's obviously been recent rain that left the road muddy; the surface has been torn up by passing feet, hooves, and wheels. Now the sun is baking it hard. Just as she's nearly beside me, I hear her squeal and watch her drop to the road. Just then, the first of the riders burst through the trees on the far side of the ford. She hears the splash as the horses enter the water, and turns in fear. I see her try to rise as the first two riders spot her and spur their horses to a run. I know what Romans do to women they capture and I can't let that happen to her. I make my decision and step onto the road beside her. The first rider draws his sword. I raise my rifle and take aim.

Chapter 6.

When I left my hill, I took the path that leads to the northwest in the direction of Dubri-tun. This is not my usual road – I've only been this way twice before, and never alone. But these are my woods, and I am not afraid of losing my way. I am a little afraid of the Sea-wolves, but I don't think they will be on this side of the river yet. Their boats were all beyond the headland that is on the far shore, and the river here is too deep to ford. If they are coming this way, they will come by boat. I didn't see any boats on this side of the river, so I'm pretty sure I'm safe. I stop in my tracks when I remember – except for that one boat sitting alone. That one was on this side of the headland so could make for this side of the river. But that one was so far out and not moving, so I don't think I need to worry about it. I find myself wondering about the people on it – why were they here? Why were they sitting off our shores? And why is there just one? I admit that I don't know much about boats and armies, but I think they usually travel in fleets – at least three or four together. This one was alone and not hiding or moving. I think that how the boat was sitting pointed directly at the invading fleet. I suddenly realize – they'd be hard to see from the beach because the boat is so much narrower than it is long. They know the fleet is there, they aren't running away, but they are trying to not attract attention. Why?

There is something else that bothers me, but I don't quite know what it is. It confuses me and I don't like being confused. I compare the image of the boat in my mind to the images of the others. And I realize – it's gigantic. It must be many times the length of the Sea-wolves' boats. No wonder they're alone – that one boat is the size of their whole fleet. I think back to the winter before last. Some of the Romans who visited talked about the boats they arrived in. I listened because I was interested in learning their language, not really because I was interested in the boats. The boats they described sounded a lot like those of the Sea-wolves. Open, room for maybe fifty people, with oars, and sails. A bit bigger, but not much. Nothing like what I just saw on the water. If not Sea-wolves and not Roman, then who? Someone else looking to steal our crops, our land, our freedom? I'm scared now that maybe there is someone behind me. I start to run again.

I've come to the stream that runs near the settlement and start to follow it upstream. I'll need to cross it before too long. In a dry summer, the water would be low enough to wade at many points. But with all the rain we've had the stream is full. I don't know how deep the water is so I'm not going to try wading. The current doesn't look very fast, but I know from experience how deceptive that can be. Last year, when I was gathering in the woods, I tried to cross a stream after a rain. I was right in the middle when I slipped. I went under and when I got to the surface, I was far downstream. By the time I managed to grab a tree that had fallen into the stream and pull myself to shore, I was shaking like a leaf in a windstorm. Partly because I was cold, but mostly because I was so scared. Fortunately today I don't need to wade through the river. Before I get much further, I come across a tree fallen so it lies across the stream. It's a bit of a climb to get up on it, and the surface is slippery with moss but I manage to cross without falling.

As I get closer, I start to get scared. Will I be in time? I try to run, but the path is still muddy in places and that slows me down. Where the sun has reached, it is even worse. There the mud is getting baked hard and in places it is rough. I can't afford to take a spill and get hurt – I need to get through. At least this path isn't much used, so it doesn't get all torn up like the main roads do. I've heard that the Romans cover their roads with flat stones, so they don't get soft in the rain and horse hooves and wagon wheels don't make a mess of them. I wish they'd do that here, but that would take a lot of stone.

Finally I have to slow to a walk; I can't run all the way. At one point I think I hear feet pounding on the path behind me, but that could just be my own pounding heart. I hope it's my heart. This path seems endless today, but I can tell by the sun that it really is only about three hours after noon when I finally near the edge of the forest. This path runs in a wide band of trees that follows the stream all the way to the main road. There are several small paths that cut off to the right and will take me to the fields that surround the walls. Now I need to be careful – which one to take? I'm not sure, so when I think I've gone far enough, I take a path. I should see the light of the open fields after a short distance, but this path soon curves to the right, into the deeper forest. I turn and make my way back, and travel further. It is the third path that I try which finally brings me to the corner of the open field. Here, I have to be careful. I don't want to startle someone and get an *arrow in the chest. There is heavy undergrowth here, so I step off the path and work my way through the bush to where I can see, but not be seen. I am so glad that I did. Scattered around the field are Sea-wolves. Most are looking at the walls, but some are looking toward the forest. One is looking almost at me. I freeze, and stay frozen until his attention wanders elsewhere. He didn't see me.*

Now what do I do? I slowly fade back into the deeper bush to think. I can't get through to warn them of what I saw, and they obviously already know that an attack is coming. They may not know how big the attack will be, but what good would it do if they did? No one can get in; no one can get out. Go home, I guess. Bring the plants that I gathered today. Tell my father, so we can prepare. We might be their next target; their next victims. They won't stop, and with the size of their force, I don't know if even the Romans can defeat them.

I realize I've been standing in the woods for some time when I notice my breathing has slowed to normal. I'm tired from my run, but it will only take me a couple of hours to get home from here. I turn and head back to the path. From here it is only a short distance the road. The road is dangerous for a lone walker because the Romans and others are known to travel this way, but there is little choice until I get closer to home. Only a short distance from where the path reaches the road, the road crosses the river at a ford. On the other side is a narrow belt of trees, then open fields. There is a line of trees along one side of the road for some of the distance, but in many places there is not enough cover to hide from a man on a horse. And this early in the year, the crops are barely out of the ground so a field mouse wouldn't find cover there. But that is the way I must go if I am to get home, so I follow the path to the road and turn toward the ford. Just as I reach it, I hear the sound that strikes fear in my heart – horses. Several horses, coming at a steady trot. From the metallic jangle, I'm sure they are Romans. Across the ford there's no place to hide and anyway I'd leave tell-tale wet footprints that would lead them right to me. So I turn and run back up the road, toward the safety of the trees. Here the surface is rough, torn by the traffic during the rains. Now the sun is baking it. It's not easy, but I run because my life depends on it. I'm at the forest, almost to the path, looking for a place to hide instead of at the road. I catch my foot in a rut and go down. I try to rise, but the pain is too great. I start to crawl. Maybe I can get to the bushes, and maybe I won't be noticed. But it's too late. I hear the horses splashing through the ford; hear a voice call. I've been seen.

I collapse on the ground. There's no escape for me. Then I hear a rustle of leaves, and look up. The most extraordinary person I've ever seen is standing over me. He's wearing clothes that are mottled greens, browns, and grays – like the pattern of sun falling through leaves. And I realize how hard it would be to spot him in the forest. On his head is a helmet – I think it's a helmet, but it's completely different from those the Romans wear. This is also green, and rounded to fit his head. The face that looks down at me looks young – no trace of a beard, but I see the smile. It's not a mean smile, it's a kind one. Even so, my panic is rising. He is facing a Roman patrol, and I can't see any sign of a weapon – no spear or bow. Not even a sword. He carries a long odd-looking stick, black in color, with all kinds of bumps and bulges. I can tell it is crafted by hands, but I don't know to what end.

The Romans had stopped to size up this new arrival, but now they decide to move. The first two spur their horses to a trot. The one in the lead draws his sword and starts to raise it when I hear a loud crack – like two stones hitting each other. The man lets out a cry, drops his sword and leans forward in the saddle as he reins his horse to a stop and rolls off to the ground. The second is now at a gallop, spear in hand, and rising to throw it. A second crack, and he stops dead, drops his spear, and pulls back on the reins as he flies over the back of the horse. The horse rears to a stop about the time that he hits the ground.

The remaining Romans are still gathered at the ford, trying to figure out what to do next. The one standing over me speaks, clearly, loud, and in Latin. "Who wants to die next?" One, clearly the leader, pulls his shield off his back and starts to approach, shield in one hand, sword in the other, guiding his horse with his knees. Another crack. As his shield flies back, he is close enough that I can see the pain in his face. He turns his horse in the road, sheaths his sword, and heads back. The men make way for him as he splashes through the ford; they also turn their horses and follow. The horses of the two fallen soldiers turn and bolt after their companions, leaving the men lying in the road.

As soon as they disappear, my saviour drops to one knee beside me, and reaches up and removes his helmet. Her helmet, I should say, for now I can see the face of a woman! Her short hair is a reddish color, something I've never seen before. Women in our tribe wear their hair long, as do the Romans, so I'm not quite sure what to make of the short hair. And the color – I've heard stories of red-headed people, but have never before seen one.

"Are you hurt?" she asks in Latin, but with an accent that I've never heard before, then adds "Do you speak Latin?"

I nod and point to my ankle. The panic is gone, but I'm still shaking too hard to actually form words.

She speaks again "My name is Robyn. What is yours?"

"Muirenn" I manage to get out.

"Muirenn – that's a pretty name. I will let you rest for a minute while my friend Kelly and I check the two Romans. I will be back soon." I look up and notice for the first time three more people dressed in the same green clothes as Robyn have emerged from the trees. Two carry sticks just like Robyn's and are watching the road. Another carries some sort of bag in one hand.

Robyn gets up, takes her helmet in one hand, pulls her hair back with the other, and puts the helmet back on her head. I hear her speak to the one with the bag and they head down the road to the fallen Romans. I guess he must be the one she called "Kelly." They check the one with the spear first. Clearly, he is dead, because they roll him to the side of the road and walk away. The other is leaning up against a tree clearly still alive with his left hand clasped over his right shoulder. He's alive for now. I'm told warriors don't have much time for wounded enemies, and I wonder how Robyn will deal with this one. I watch as Robyn kneels down, and again removes her helmet. I can't hear what's going on, but I know they are exchanging words. Kelly opens his bag and gently starts to work on the wounded Roman. I stare in recognition. He's a healer. They're not about to kill this man – in fact they're making sure he doesn't die. Robyn rises, puts her helmet back on, then reaches down to the Roman. She pulls him to his feet, and with his arm around her shoulders, guides him down the road toward us.

Kelly, meanwhile, comes to me. He – no doubt, this is a man – helps me to rise to a sitting position, and starts to examine my foot. He gently removes my soft leather boot and probes my ankle. I can see the swelling and bruising – I hurt it quite badly. It might be broken, but I think not. For sure, I won't be walking for a while. And I'm stuck here, far from home, with an army behind me and four strange people surrounding me – and I don't know what they're going to do with me. I grab my bags, the full one with the plants that I gathered this morning, and the empty one which held my lunch, and pull them in front of me. I notice for the first time the scrapes on my hands from my fall and realize I also scraped my face. Kelly has finished checking my foot and is sitting back. I can hear him talking in a language I can't begin to recognize, but he's not talking to me. I don't know who he could be talking to for the others seem too far away to hear. It seems like someone is responding because he stops like he is listening but I can't hear anyone else.

A shock of understanding I realize something – could these be the "green men" of story and legend? Have I stumbled upon the other worldly keepers of the forest who are occasionally seen in the deep woods? Not that I've ever seen one before in all my journeys, but I've heard tales of them all my life. In some stories they are cruel, but in others they are kind, protecting the weak or those who lose their way in the woods. I didn't know they travelled in groups and I didn't know they speak the Latin we learned from the Romans. But here they are. And they saved me from the Romans.

I guess I should feel safe, but I can feel the anxiety start to rise in my chest. My mind is swirling with questions. What will happen to me? How will I get these plants home? How will I warn them of the Sea-wolves in time? Will I get home? The tears start to flow. Kelly moves over beside me and puts an arm around my shoulder and I bury my face in the rough fabric of his clothes. I'm mostly cried out when I feel a touch on my other shoulder. Robyn is beside me. I turn and throw my arms around her. Somehow, I feel safer with her. Maybe because she's a girl. Maybe because we can talk. Maybe a little of both.

"Muirenn, we need to get you patched up and back home. Do you live here?" She points behind us at the surrounded settlement.

I shake my head. "Tordur – that way" and I point toward home. "I saw the Sea-wolves' boats, and came here to Dubri-Tun to warn them because I have kin here but I was too late. I was going home when the Romans came and I hurt myself trying to get away from them."

"Then you probably saw our boat, too. We saw you on the hill by the sea, so we guessed that you might have seen us."

It was their boat I saw? In all the stories I've ever heard, Green Men never come from the sea. But no one seems to know where they do come from, so maybe they are from across the sea. And they saw me? I'm not very big compared to the boat; how did they see me? Who are these people? They don't want to see me harmed; I am sure of that. They're not Romans, and aren't afraid of taking them on. Most people on foot would flee from a whole mounted patrol. Robyn didn't. That stick must be a weapon of some sort, but I can't guess what it does. One Roman is dead; two more are wounded, without any of them getting close enough to harm us. I guess she has no reason to be afraid. They didn't finish off the wounded Roman that was left behind. Why not? Anyone else would. That's the way these things work – wounded enemies are killed.

I hear Robyn speaking in a language that's completely foreign to me, but she's looking away from me. Now she turns to me and asks "You're not afraid of birds, are you?"

I shake my head, and give a bit of a smile. I kind of like birds.

Robyn continues. "We need to get you off the road. The Romans we chased off will soon join a larger group and will likely come back. We've got time before they get here, but we need to get to the trees that line the fields surrounding the town back there. We have a huge bird that we'll use to push those attackers away, and then we'll hitch a ride back. There is a big group headed for the ford; they should arrive about the time that The Bird does. I want to be in the trees before then, in case they start to head in our direction and we have to turn them back. The Romans – well they may decide not to come this way after all. We have a little bird keeping an eye on them to be sure they don't get up to any mischief."

"You have birds? Is that how you saw me? I always wondered what it would be like to fly like a bird."

"You will soon have the chance. We will fly you out to our boat to get you cleaned up and take a better look at that ankle. Then we will take you back home. But first we need to get off the road and take care of those invaders. Michael is the big guy over there, and this is Lance. The guy over there is Kelly. The Roman is Marcelus – he's a little bruised from falling off his horse – and pretty sore where I winged him in the arm, but he'll be okay. Since you can't walk and we have the need for speed, Michael will carry you."

With that she helps me to my feet. Michael comes over, hands Robyn his stick and squats down in front of me. Robyn takes my boot from my hand – I've been holding it ever since Kelly took it off – I can't lose it as I only have one pair, and sticks it in my bag. Then she grabs both bags from the ground, throws them over her shoulder, grabs a bag that I hadn't noticed before, that Michael had on his back, and we all head off. Lance in the lead, then Kelly helping an unsteady Marcelus, Michael and me are next, with Robyn last. We turn onto the path I came in on, the path that leads to my hill, then take a side path to the open fields occupied by the Sea-wolves. I get a little scared that Michael will forget about my really painful foot hanging out there as we push through the forest, but he carefully pushes branches aside or dodges around them. I think he's done this before.

It doesn't take long for us to reach the edge of the forest. Michael sits me down with my back against a tree, still concealed in the bushes, but where I can see most of the field. The rest of the group spreads out along the edge of the forest. Robyn hands Michael his stick and bag, then positions herself between Marcelus and me. She gives back my two bags and says "Hang on to these. When The Bird comes, we'll need to move out quickly."

When we reach the edge of the trees, I can see the number of Sea-wolves has grown. There must be two hundred surrounding the walls now. I am so scared for the people inside. They are only about one hundred, and not all can fight, so they are badly out numbered. The Sea-wolves are still just out of bowshot from the walls, so there is nothing the people inside can do about them anyway. They have several fires going and are roasting animals they captured. And they aren't paying as much attention to the fields and forest as they were earlier. Then I look at Robyn and remember how she drove off the Romans. "Maybe we're not so outnumbered, after all," I think.

Robyn pulls the bag off her back, and reaches in. "Do either of you want water?" She asks both Marcelus and me.

We both nod yes. She pulls out what looks like three blocks of clear ice, but I can see liquid water inside. She quickly takes each one, makes a little twisting motion and removes a piece from one end of each. One she hands to me, one to Marcelus, and keeps one for herself. She lifts hers and pours water into her mouth. We both do the same. I've never seen anything like this. It's not ice because it's not cold, but it's hard and clear but thin – I can feel it bend in my hand. Now Robyn pulls something else out. It looks like a flat, thin stone.

Robyn speaks to both of us. "I want you both to know what is going to happen, so that you're not completely terrified." She touches a spot on her stone and it lights up. "Come close so you can see. This is called a tablet, and with it we can see what is happening around us." I look, and don't recognize what we are seeing. Robyn explains "We are looking straight down on this field. Here are the trees where we are now. Here is the town, with its walls and the people inside. There are two hundred, fifty-eight Sea-wolves surrounding them, with more on the way. You can see them gathered around their fires here. There are also at least one hundred in the trees across the river, so there is no escape by swimming the river. We can only find one hundred, sixteen people in the town. If they are going to survive, they're going to need help. We are going to give them that help."

"What we are going to do will badly scare the people in the town. I don't want to do that, but I have no choice if I am to save them. Soon, you will hear a distant thumping. In about five minutes, the biggest and noisiest bird you've ever experienced will come over the tree tops about here, and cross the fields this way." She points out a location on the stone. "It's not really a bird. It is more like a wagon that flies through the air. As it gets near, we expect the Sea-wolves will run away. To add a little extra incentive for them to move, you will see

fire streaking from it toward them and their fires. When our fire reaches theirs, we'll see logs, sparks, coals, all fly in every direction. That will get them to clear out and we'll chase them across the ford. Some may try to come this way. If they do, we'll need to take them out. I don't want to do that – I want to chase them all the way back to their boats and leave them so scared they never bother these shores again. But I may not have the choice. Once it is safe, The Bird will land as close as possible to us. We need to get out to it quickly, because we don't want to be on the ground any longer than we can help. Muirenn, Michael will carry you again, but he'll probably just pick you up in his arms. Marcelus, Lance will help you. Once we are all onboard, there are seats. We'll get you strapped in and give you helmets like these. It gets really loud and you'll need them so we can talk. You will see what I mean when we get there."

"The Romans are close enough that they will hear The Bird and maybe see it too, but they won't have a clue what is happening. We're not sure what they'll do. They may come flying up the road, thinking that there are enough of them to counter any threat. Or they may turn and run. If it looks like they're headed toward Tordur, Muirenn, we will turn and head them off. Then we will take you both out to our boat where we can get you cleaned up. There is a thunderstorm building to the west, so we'll need to reach the boat before it gets here. We'll get you some food and then bring you back. Muirenn, we'll bring you to Tordur – they must be wondering where you are. Marcelus, what should we do with you?"

I hear Marcelus speak for the first time. "I am not Roman, my family is from Gaul. My forefathers were brought over to Britannia when the Romans first invaded, for our language is similar to the tribes in the south of this island. Even though we have served loyally for generations, we still have to prove our trustworthiness far more than do those who were born Roman. I am young and am not fully trusted. They know that I was wounded and fell into the hands of the enemy. Because you let me live, they will believe I am one of you and will never again trust me. At best, they will send me far from here. More likely they will torture me to find out what I know."

He looks in Robyn's eyes, "If you send me away, you will kill me." I smile. I've seen that look before. What he said may very well be true, but there's something else entirely behind his words. She drops her eyes, and gives a classic response. She changes the subject.

"Listen! You can hear The Bird coming."

I can hear a faint thumping sound in the distance.

"Now watch." She touches her tablet, and I see the image change so we can see a larger area. Coming from the bottom is what looks like a dragonfly. I think it is, until I realize that it is covering whole trees as it goes by. The thing is huge. The thumping is getting louder. The Sea-wolves hear the sound now; I can see them turning, looking, pointing at the sky. Some are running, but most are staying put. I look up as this massive grey object blasts through the sky in a thunderous roar, travelling faster than the wind. I watch as a streak of fire extends from The Bird toward the nearest of the Sea-wolves fires. Fire explodes in every direction. I watch the cow carcass they were roasting fly through the air and land on a fleeing Sea-wolf. More streaks of fire, more fires explode. It is total chaos in the field now. I see some running our way and reach out to grab Robyn to warn her. She's gone. I look around in a panic, but then I look down. She's lying on the ground face down, legs spread and with her stick up to her face. Even over the roar of The Bird, I hear the crack, and see a man fall. Lance and Michael are standing, also pointing their sticks at the approaching hoards. I watch as Robyn rolls slightly to her right, pulls a black block from the bottom of her stick and throws it aside. She then grabs a different one, and puts it into the stick. In one motion she rolls back down, and the cracks start again. I notice little bits of metal flying out of the side of her stick, and want to ask her about them. I watch and start to make a connection. Crack. A bit of flying metal. A Sea-wolf goes down. I don't think I should disturb her right now, but I am so curious.

Most the Sea-wolves that were coming in our direction are lying on the field now. Those that are still standing have realized there is something very bad in those trees and are trying to back away, but those behind them continue to push them in our direction. More cracks and more Sea-wolves fall to the ground. Now The Bird is coming across the field, driving the remaining Sea-wolves toward the road. I see it rise up as it reaches the road, and turn around to come back over the field, slowly this time, lower, and close to the ground. Robyn is rising to her feet now. She grabs all the blocks lying on the ground and stuffs them into a bag or pouch on her clothes. I've never seen that before. All of them are now on their feet, with all their sticks and bags. As Michael comes to me and bends down, Robyn also leans down.

She asks "You have your bags?" I nod – they are hanging around my neck. "Put your arms around his neck."

I do, and he lifts me with one arm around my back, the other under my knees. My father sometimes carried me like this when I was little. I'm not very big even now, but I can't believe he is running flat out toward The Bird while carrying me!

As we approach The Bird, an opening appears in the side. Someone inside reaches down to grab Lance, the first to reach The Bird. Michael and I are next. He hands me to Lance and the new person. Inside there is a large open space. Beyond, I can see chairs. We have one in our house that belongs to father. Only rarely have I sat in it. We have little stools, or we sit on the floor. They carry me to a chair by the wall. There is a hole in the wall – I reach out and touch it and find that it is not open, but is hard and clear, like the water Robyn gave me. There are cloth straps attached to the chair which the new person fastens around me. I start to panic until I remember what Robyn told me. Kelly hands me a helmet like the one he wears and motions me to put it on. I do. Instantly the thumping of The Bird becomes quieter. And I can hear voices. I can't understand anything that is being said. The other man – the one who was in The Bird when we arrived, hands me a little bag make from some thin material. I wonder what it is for.

I hear a voice in my ears that I recognize as Kelly's; then I hear Robyn speak to me. Even though I can see that she's still a long way from me – she's outside The Bird, it sounds like she's right beside me.

"Muirenn, are you already to fly like a bird? If only we can get our Roman friend aboard, we can get out of here."

I look out of the opening – I'll call it a door, but it's not like any door I've ever seen – Marcelus is standing staring with wide eyes at the scene, and not moving. Lance is beside him with a hand on his back, trying to urge him forward. He won't move. I see Robyn walking backward, watching in case any more Sea-wolves come in our direction. She gets beside him, and turns and hisses into his ear a single word; I hear it clearly.

"Coward."

That works. She puts her hand on top of his head and the three of them run forward. Michael pulls Marcelus in with his good arm. The other two climb in on their own. Robyn closes the door and walks to the front. I see the backs of two chairs – past them I can see the fields and trees. The new man squeezes between the two and sits facing the front. I can see there is someone already in the other one. Michael and Lance get Marcelus settled in a chair, and then strap themselves in. Marcelus also gets a little bag. Kelly and Robyn are already in chairs. I hear the noise level increase, and feel us start to move. I hear Robyn's voice again, with another one that I don't recognize. Now she speaks again, this time in Latin "Marcelus, Muirenn: we're going to push the Sea-wolves back across the ford before we head for home. We don't have much time, because that storm is moving fast and we want to get down before things get bumpy. Don't want any one getting sick on their first ride. The bag is just in case you do."

I'm not sure what most of what she said means – except the part about getting sick. The noise level rises, I feel the floor start to move, and my stomach suddenly feels like it dropped. I look outside to see the ground drop away, then tilt so all I can see is the sky. Oh! I see what she means about getting sick. I am determined not to surrender to this sick feeling. I glance across to Marcelus. He has actually relaxed a bit, and is looking out his side. I look back outside just in time to see the road come into view. We are flying along it toward the ford. It doesn't feel like we're moving very fast, but I think it will have any Sea-wolves running for their lives.

I hear a constant chatter of voices, and start to tune them out since I can't understand anything.

Then there's a bit of a pause and I hear Robyn speaking in Latin. "Marcelus, Muirenn, the Sea-wolves are all back across the ford now.

I'd like to push them a little further, but with this storm coming, we need to clear out. I think the town is safe for now. That Roman patrol met the larger group and they're all coming this way. They stopped when they heard The Bird, but think once we leave they will continue on, so they and the Sea-wolves should keep each other busy for a while. But we won't be able to help or even see what happens until after the storm passes."

I feel us turn again, then find myself looking straight down beyond the walls into Dubri-tun. Just like a bird! I see people huddling near the wall, looking up in terror as we pass. I hope they realize the Sea-wolves are gone, that we chased them off. Then the town is behind us and I watch the trees pass underneath. I can't imagine how fast we are moving now, but the trees are just a blur. The trees end and now we are over water. That took me half the afternoon to travel on foot but in The Bird I barely had time think, and we're already here. I'm trying to look for the boat, when I feel us slow down. A turn, and I can see it now. It's big – this huge grey mass sitting like a rock in the water. We turn again and I watch the boat rise up to meet us. I feel us hit the boat and the thumping noise fades away. In the relative quiet I hear a loud whine. But that also soon fades away. Robyn comes over to show me how to remove the straps that hold me in the chair. I give her the empty bag with a bit of a smile. As she gently takes off my helmet I see there is some sort of rope that holds it to the chair so no one can take it with them.

When the door opens, there are a couple of people with what looks like a cot, but it is as high as the floor we are standing on. Robyn has her helmet off too, now.

"We're going to put you on this cot, and take you inside so we can clean you up and bandage your foot. Then we'll get you something to eat, if you are hungry. Don't be afraid, I'll be right behind you, but we also need to move Marcelus. Let them help you, don't try to fight. You might think they will hurt you, but they won't."

Michael and Kelly carry me over to the cot and help me lie down. I watch one of the people standing beside the cot reach down and pull up this stick that runs like a branch along the side of the cot, just where my hand can reach it. I grab on as I feel the cot start to move. We go through a doorway and are inside the boat. A couple of turns, and we go into a large room that seems like it is outside, because it is filled with light. There's a woman there who takes a little white tool and sticks it on one of my fingers. It is tied to a sort of a string – I guess they don't want to lose it. Beside me is a box that makes odd noises and has little lights on it. There's an area that looks sort of like Robyn's tablet with little lights in different colors that move and form interesting shapes, but I don't know what it does.

The woman comes back with a bunch of things in her hand. I see a bag of water, and a many other things that I have never seen and don't understand. In one hand I see her holding a shiny piece of metal. It's very thin and about as long as my little finger. She touches me on the inside of my elbow with the other hand – I notice that her hands look odd – they're white and no nails or hair. I feel a prick and see the bit of metal that she had is now sticking in my arm. She puts a little bit of cloth over it, and then attaches a string. But it's not really string, I can see through it and it looks like water is running down and into me. I start to get scared until I remember Robyn's words.

"Don't be afraid."

Just then, another cot comes into the room with Marcelus; I see Kelly and Robyn by his side. The lady comes over to Marcelus, and I watch as both she and Kelly surround him. I think they are doing the same things to him as they did to me. Robyn is standing by his head, with a hand on his cheek. I can hear her telling him that it will be okay. He seems to relax, and Robyn rises, gives him a little pat, and comes over to me.

"He'll be okay now. He's lost some blood when he opened up his wound again while we were in the trees, but not enough to harm him. He's been in a lot of pain for several hours now, and they want to get him taken care of first. I've told him what's going to happen, and I think he'll be okay. I also apologized for calling him a coward earlier. I know he's brave – I just needed him on that bird, and I couldn't think of a faster way to get him to move."

"I want to tell you what is happening. When I was about your age, I got hurt – the same foot as you just hurt, plus a few other things. I was pretty scared too and I knew a bit of what to expect. So much has

happened to you today, you must be scared. This," She points to the little thing on my finger, "tells us that you're okay. It talks to this box through this." She holds up what I thought was a string. I can see it goes to the box. Pointing to the thing in my arm, she says, "This helps you stay okay. We are giving you water, a little salt, and something so your foot doesn't hurt so much." I almost forgot about my foot. "Sandy is the lady looking at Marcelus. As soon as she's done, she will come over and take care of your foot, and the scrapes on your hands and face. I'm going to have to leave for a little bit, but I'll be back. We need to keep an eye on those Sea-wolves to be sure they don't attack again."

Chapter 7.

As soon as I leave the Sick Bay, I tear up the stairs to Mission Control. This day has not gone anything like we'd planned. Those invaders really threw a wrench into the works. But, in a way, things couldn't have gone better. We have made contact with a local who knows that we're on her side and who knows Latin so we can communicate. We saved a Roman who might just have more influence than he thinks – maybe we can help him with that. I know he's got a crush on me – I'll try to nip that one in the bud. Maybe I should get some of the team to call me 'Tribunus' – about the closest rank to mine in the Roman Army – and he'll get the idea that he's aiming a little high.

I try not to think about the sixty-three Saxons Martin says I killed today – oh yeah, the Roman too. That's sixty-four. But there was no choice. We hoped they'd head away from the chopper toward the river. But a whole mass came straight for us and I had to stop them. I wasn't the only one. A few died from flying debris after Jerry fired the rockets into their bonfires. Lance got a few – five according to Martin. Michael got two. Considering none of them has ever shot at a person before, I'm surprised they even stayed. It wasn't a pretty sight and I dread revisiting it in my dreams – I hope they will somehow manage to escape that fate.

Not all the men who attacked Dubri-tun are now dead. A few headed for the road when the chopper showed up, though at least some of those were wounded. Most of those pushed north back across the ford when we did a pass up the road. Those that stayed south of the river will have to deal with the mounted and armed Roman patrol that is headed in their direction. Not a good day for the Saxons all around. *But will it be enough to send them away and save the settlements we came to study?* Only time will answer that question. They are a large force, but got very little from their efforts today and left many in that field. Oh great – now my mind is already back on those dead men.

Instead of reminding myself of those I killed, I try to focus on Muirenn. I like that kid. She's probably about sixteen or so and is amazing. What a day it has been for her, facing all these things that are completely outside any frame of reference that she could possibly have and she just accepts them. I wonder ...I'd like to get Michele to look at the plants she has in her bag, but I need to ask her permission because I want her to trust us. I wonder if any of them have medicinal value. If so, she may be from the town of the healers; if that's true, then we've identified our primary target on the first day.

Michele, of course, has been having fun with my name since we first chose the destination for this mission. Actually, she's had fun with it since the day we first met. I've told her repeatedly that we're at least eleven centuries too early for the historical Robin Hood, but to no avail. The team is my "Merry Persons" and now she's tagged Muirenn with the nickname "Maid Marion." Which got everyone laughing until Muirenn got upset because she thought she did something wrong and people were laughing at her. It took a while for me to explain enough of the story that she realized we were really saying something good about her – comparing her to a hero from a tale.

Another good thing that came out of today – we all worked amazingly well together. Everything went right and worked perfectly. I had the information I needed on the ground when I needed it and the landing team held up when faced by the Saxon hoards. Martin was phenomenal at keeping us organized and on track, while all three pilots sure earned their stripes. I honestly didn't think we would need close air support on our first day, but then I didn't expect to be outnumbered eight hundred to four, , with two wounded locals to manage at the same time. But they all came through with flying colors. But, I wondered for a moment, if we were the origin of the dragon stories that float around in myths and legends from this region through the centuries.

We hoped we could remain undiscovered for four or five days so that we'd have time to map the region and get comfortable working together. But once that chopper hit the air, that plan was gone. Truthfully, just as soon as I decided to intervene and save Muirenn, all our plans went out the window. I'll have to take some heat for that.

Now the room is filling up with the team. I talk with Jack, who took over for Trace on the drone not long after we landed back on the ship. We recovered the drone about fifteen minutes ago so he is indexing the images he captured on the way back. It looks like the town residents are recovering since they are coming out of hiding and probably realize they are safe for now. The Romans continued on and ran into the Saxons just as they were gathering to renew their attack. More bloodshed, and this time the surviving Saxons are scattered along the north bank of the river and look to be returning to the beach and their boats. The chopper is in the hanger so the deck is clear until the storm passes. Already the wind is howling and the rain is starting. Captain Johansen thinks the worst should pass over us in about two hours. The radar shows the heaviest rain from the storm should track just a little north of us – right over the Saxons' beach. This is not their lucky day.

Kelly just came in so the full landing team is in the room and we can get started. I rise and walk to the front of the room, forming my words as I go.

"Wow. Talk about a trial by fire. When I stepped out of the bush to save Muirenn from the Romans, I know I brought this all on. And I apologize to everyone on the team for putting each of you in a difficult position which none of us ever wanted to face. I am completely amazed with the skill and professionalism which each and every one of you displayed today. You act and work like a fully trained and experienced team; I have no fear placing my life again in your hands."

"There is a reasonable chance that Muirenn is from the town of healers that is our primary target for this mission. I hope to find out more when we take her back to her home tonight. Dinner is almost ready, but I need to give you an opportunity to discuss today."

I remain standing at the front of the room with twelve sets of eyes staring at me. Silence. Finally Martin speaks up. "Robyn, when you first stepped out of the trees, I think every one of our hearts stopped. And they didn't start again until Don explained what usually happened to a woman caught by the Romans. She would have been taken back to their camp and gang-raped. He told us why you couldn't let that happen. Neither could we. We had to help you save that girl."

Don knows. I had shared with him that when I was fourteen and on a visit to the farm where dad grew up, two older cousins took me out behind the barn. I tried to hide what happened but my mom noticed right away something was wrong. She took me immediately to the hospital in town; they called the cops. Since I was only fourteen – the age of consent in the state was sixteen – and they knew my age, with the DNA evidence the case was a pretty much a slam-dunk. Both pulled long jail terms. I showed up for their parole hearing not long ago in full dress uniform. The younger one got parole but the older one didn't. I guess that experience explains in part the judo and maybe contributed to my decision to join the army. I wanted to be prepared if anyone ever came at me again.

"I am humbled. I think I'd better sit down before I start to cry. If any of you have anything else that you'd like to say, we have a few more minutes before dinner."

I somehow make it to the back of the room and collapse onto a sofa. I pull in my feet, feeling for some reason more vulnerable than I have in years. Suddenly, I feel like I'm fourteen again. Taylor is back here beside me – I didn't even notice him come in. He's slender with short blond hair with a scruffy beard. He always looks like he has a great tan, but that's his natural skin color. He throws an arm around my shoulders as I sit down and I feel a couple of tears slide down my cheek for probably the first time since I buried my family. We sit without talking until Martin's voice brings me back to the present.

"The second fleet of Saxons – we think they are more of the same group we fought today – are still coming. We sent up Little Bird Two for a look at them earlier this afternoon. Based on their current course and speed, they should reach the beach near midnight. One of the questions I have is, do we continue with our plan to black out the ship at sundown, or do we let our presence be known?"

I get back to my feet and start to walk toward the front, trying to distil everything I know about the Saxons and the army we faced today into a reasonable plan. "They have to know that we're here. The chopper is just too big and noisy for them to not notice. If any have made their way back from today's action, they will have done the math and connected us to the attack. They will come tonight, lights or no lights. No lights will mean nothing to them – it is what they'll expect. The moon is nearly full, so if these clouds move out it will give enough light that they will see us, no matter what we do. We show a few lights and they'll know we're not hiding, and may be a little cautious. Every light on the ship on – I have no idea how they would react because that's outside their frame of reference. I'd suggest that we light up the ship like a Christmas tree, but that's mostly because I'm very curious how they will respond. But all that that light would interfere with our night vision. My vote is for night operations lighting. And be ready with the missiles."

Night operations lighting means just the required navigation lights with subdued red lights for stairs, doors and interior passageways for safety. The red lights have less impact on night vision than other colors, so they won't hamper our ability to see if they approach. The team is okay with the lighting, but no one really wants to use the missiles. We need to fire them when the targets are at least one thousand meters away so the missile has time to stabilize in flight and home-in. That distance also protects us from the resulting explosion and debris. A wooden ship manned by men armed with spears and swords is hardly a threat to us. We have a top speed of twenty-three knots versus their six, and we are way bigger than they are. And the fact that we're made of steel also presents a serious challenge to their weapons. And we have rockets, a heavy machine gun, and small arms. We're not worried about us. I agree that if only four or five boats come, we use our light weapons to discourage them. However, if a larger fleet approaches, we will need to break out the heavier weapons because our small crew could be overwhelmed by a large force. There is a lot of discussion as we formulate a plan to handle such a situation. We finally come to a consensus just as we hear the announcement for dinner.

On the way to the mess room, I drop in at the sickbay to check on our wounded. Muirenn and Sandy are nowhere to be seen, but I hear noises coming from the shower room. Marcelus is sitting in a chair, right arm in a sling, staring out the window across two miles of water to the land. He seems rather subdued. It might be the drugs – Sandy would have given him pain killers and a local to stitch up his arm. Maybe a sedative if he started to panic. But I think it's something deeper.

I walk over toward him, grabbing a chair on the way. I plop down on it backward, arms crossed on the back. "Hi."

Marcelus doesn't look up, but starts to speak. "Why didn't you kill me? You could have. I thought at first I was just lucky and Antonius wasn't, but I when I saw what happened to the Saxons – what you can do – I realized that you could have killed the lot of us. I know you could kill every Roman on this island if you wanted. But you didn't kill me. And I wonder why?"

Antonius. That is the name of the man we left lying on the side of the road. I wonder where he came from, and where his family is. If he had a wife or girlfriend. And how long it will be before they learn that he is dead.

I answer. "You only had a sword – I only had to stop you before you could reach us. Antonius had a spear – I had to be sure he went down before he could throw it. That's why you lived and he didn't. You may find this hard to believe after today, but I don't like killing people. But I do know what often happens to girls who fall into the hands of the Roman army, and when I saw Muirenn,

I just couldn't let that happen to her. I also couldn't leave you on the side of the road to die when your unit abandoned you."

"I'm not here to lead an invasion. I am here to learn as much as I can about the people. To do that, they have to trust me. They have to know that I am on their side. I have to protect them while doing the least damage possible. The Saxon attack today wasn't planned. We just happened to be here."

"What is going to happen to me?" he asks.

"I don't know. What do you want to have happen? We can send you back to your unit. I think if we fly you in with our bird and drop you off, they won't kill you. They'll want you to tell them everything you know about us. We want to be left alone – if your army does, we'll leave them alone. If not, many Romans could die. Can you convince them of that? If we let you stay here, I know you can help us. But one day, we will leave and go back home. What then? We can't take you back to our land. It would be completely strange to you. For a start, I am among the very few who know your language, so you would need to learn ours. Think about what you want. But we don't need to decide anything right now.

Just then, Muirenn and Sandy come in from the shower room. Muirenn is wearing a pink t-shirt and black track pants – I think the clothes are Michele's, which makes sense since they're both about the same size. She's been patched up and cleaned up – I'm pretty sure Michele's had a hand in styling her hair. Her right foot is in a plastic walking cast, but she's already learning to manage it. She's still looking a little worse for the wear – a bad scrape on one cheek and bandages on both hands. I see her scan the room with a worried look until she spots her bags on a table. She hobbles over to them and is all smiles when she throws the straps over her shoulder. Sandy explains to me that her clothes are in the laundry, so Michele gave her something to wear. I was right on that point.

"Are you hungry?" I ask. "Let's all go find something to eat."

I lead them both down the passage to the mess hall. The room is way bigger than we need, so we turned half of it into lounge space. The original crew lounge and the gym are also on this level – just through a set of doors past the cafeteria line. We barely ever use that lounge, but the gym is another story. I spend at least an hour there every morning and usually have a few others to keep me company. To our left as we walk in the door is the long cafeteria counter stocked with food. We use less than half of it for our small crew. Behind the counter are our chief cook Candice, and Francois – our jack-of-all trades and kitchen helper. He helps in the kitchen, keeps the place clean, and generally makes himself useful. I just hope he washes his hands well between cleaning toilets and chopping carrots.

Almost the entire crew is already eating, so I lead my little entourage to the food line in front of an audience. We eat well on board. Candice was chef in a restaurant who got tired of the stress so didn't lose a lot of sleep when the recession cost her job. But she couldn't stay away from the kitchen so she jumped at the opportunity to cook for a small crew where she could have a free hand on the menu. Today it's a choice of Chicken Cordon Bleu or prime rib, roast potatoes or wild rice, fresh steamed veggies, and a salad bar. And pepperoni, mushroom, and onion pizza. A promise of pizza at least once a day was pretty much a condition to get Don to come on board. Tonight is a special dessert: birthday cake and ice cream in celebration of Taylor's thirtieth. Maybe we'll have a Taylor's Turning Thirty party every night unless we can find something more original to celebrate.

I let Sandy go ahead, and then put Muirenn in front of me, Marcelus behind. I show them how to grab a tray, plate, and cutlery then start down the line. I have to explain each dish to them. For Muirenn, beef is reserved for really special events, so that is her choice. Marcellus goes for the chicken. Neither one has ever had either potatoes or rice, so I suggest they try both. Veggies and salads they both understand, but I have to explain about the dressing. Beverages are a whole other discussion. I introduced them to bottled water earlier today, but now there is milk, juice, soda, coffee, tea, beer, and wine. Marcelus takes a beer – no surprise, since it is popular in the Roman army. Muirenn follows my lead and grabs a coffee. I drink mine black, but I explain the sugar and cream to her. I'm sure the caffeine will keep her wide awake for hours, but my guess is she probably wouldn't sleep much tonight even without it.

We carry our trays over to an empty table – we replaced the original long tables that were crammed together with small round ones that give us more room and make it feel homier. The tables are securely fastened to the floor so they won't move in heavy weather, but the chairs are loose. I show our guests how to use a knife and fork as I dig into my dinner. Marcelus has a tough time since he only has the use of his left hand – and he is clearly right-handed. So we learn about napkins, too. Our table sits four, and the extra chair gets filled with a series of guests over the course of the meal. Max comes over and starts to try his charms on Muirenn, until I point out that she doesn't speak English and is only about sixteen. I don't bother suggesting he try Latin. As soon as he leaves, I have to explain to the others what I told him. And why. Marcelus laughs for the first time – it's good to see him relax a bit.

Muirenn just gives a shy smile and says "Thank you."

When Michele comes over – she's met Muirenn already; it turns out I was right about the hair, too – we talk about plants. I tell Muirenn about Michele's interest in plants and ask if she will show us what she's collected. She hesitates for a minute, and then pulls out her bags while I stack the now empty plates and trays to make room on the table. Muirenn explains that the empty bag held her lunch, but the other has plants she collected this morning. She was going to fill the empty one with more plants on her way home, but saw the Saxons and ran to give the warning instead. The full bag contains a number of different plants, but is about half filled with what appears to be some sort of fungi. Michele recognizes most the plants – many have known medicinal properties. She takes pictures – we have to explain what a camera is – and carefully returns them to the bag. The fungi she doesn't recognize, so after we take pictures, I ask if we can take a sample. Muirenn looks a little confused, but gives her okay. Michele whips out a small core sampler and sample bottles – she came prepared – and takes samples from three different spots, then carefully returns the remainder to the bag and gives it back to Muirenn. She still has this odd expression, so I ask if everything is all right.

She sounds upset when she speaks "Why did you ask before you looked in my bag? You could have just taken it and I couldn't stop you. I don't understand. You saved me, brought me back here, took care of me, fixed up my foot so I can walk, cleaned me up, and brought me to a feast. You killed other people, but you protect me. Then you ask if you can look in my bag. You're way stronger than me – I'm just one girl and there are so many of you. You could have taken it any time, but you wait until you've taken care of me, and then you ask. I don't know why!"

With that, she starts to cry. I'm sitting right beside her and as I put my arm around her, she buries her face in my chest and lets out everything that has happened to her today. The terror, the pain, the fatigue, all the new people and things, the hope. She probably is afraid that these people who seem so nice will turn on her. It's all way too much for her to process. It takes quite a while for her to cry herself out. Marcelus looks really uncomfortable until he remembers the napkins and grabs a handful and hands them to her. By this time, Michele needs one too. And I'm dangerously close to crying for the second time today. By the time she finally comes up for air, all three of us are blowing our noses.

"I know it's just been way too much for one day." I tell her. "We are not here to take from you or hurt you. We are here to learn about you and your people. We want to be your friends, and part of that is helping you when we can and not taking from you. So we didn't go through your bag until you let us. Besides, I like you. You seem to be a really kind, smart young lady."

She cracks a bit of a smile.

"Dinner isn't quite over yet. This is a special day for Taylor, so we are going to sing a song for him, and serve up some special treats."

We all gather in the lounge, get Taylor standing on a chair and sing "Happy Birthday." Candice wheels out a cart loaded with bowls and spoons, a chocolate cake, and a tub of vanilla ice cream. As soon as the song ends, Taylor gets out of the spotlight and disappears into his comfort zone behind a camera. We dish out the dessert – the cake is incredibly good – but I can't help keeping my eye on the clock. We still have several hours of daylight, but I'd really like to get Muirenn home early enough so we can visit her town for a while before dark.

Suddenly Taylor is at my elbow. "How about I get some pictures of Muirenn with the crew and print them out while you're getting her back into her own clothes so she can take them home. I know you well enough to know you'll want to visit the town tonight. And we need to get going while the light is still good." I guess I give him a questioning look because he adds, "You're not leaving me behind again."

I know Taylor well enough to know that arguing will be useless. Not that I would. I kind of like the idea having my favorite photographer beside me to capture the sights.

Chapter 8.

There are still about three hours of daylight left when Robyn leads us back to The Bird. I got to watch them start the one they call Little Bird a while ago. It is still bigger than any bird that I've ever seen, but it is so much smaller than the one we ride in that I can see how it got its name.

I almost wish that I didn't have to go back home, but Robyn has promised to come back tomorrow. And that I am welcome on their boat anytime. Before we left, they moved much closer to land, almost to the mouth of the river that runs past Tordur. If anything bad happens, I can take a coracle down the river. They'll see me and pick me up. I think they also moved because they expect the Sea-wolves to attack tonight and they have a plan to drive them away. I can't understand why they are so reluctant to kill them – they would kill all of us given half a chance. Robyn explained that she sees every person she's killed in her dreams every night and she doesn't want to add any more to that list. I think I understand that.

The bird will land close enough to Tordur that we don't have far to walk which is good because my foot is really sore. Robyn and Taylor are coming with me. Robyn told me about these boxes they have called cameras which remember everything they see. Taylor told his to copy some of the things it remembered onto some sort of papyrus and gave them to me. At least, I think it is papyrus – I've only seen any a couple of times, but it wasn't nearly as white and smooth as this is. Now I can see myself with Robyn, Taylor, Kelly, Michele and all the others any time I want. I'm glad they're coming with me because I don't think anyone would believe that I actually got to fly through the air like a bird unless they did. In fact, I'm not quite sure that I believe everything that I saw today. But I do have my injured foot. And those sheets of papyrus. And a bag of clothes that Michele gave me – clothes in colors I've never seen before. These things are real, so maybe tomorrow I'll believe the rest.

It is not long after we leave the boat that I look down on my home from the air for the first time and see it as the birds do. I see the walls, the hall, the huts that just this morning looked so magnificent, but from far above they look tiny and insignificant. I think about the people I met this afternoon and what they can do; how easily they could destroy this whole town and kill everyone in it. Maybe it is wisdom that leads Robyn to kill only when she has no choice.

I look down on the people I know scattering for cover as we fly over the walls. I wish I could tell them there is nothing to fear, but I can't. The bird makes far too much noise for them to ever have a hope of hearing me. We settle to the ground directly in front of the gate, just out of bowshot from the walls. But no arrows fly in our direction, for the walls are nearly empty of people. Only one head can be seen. That will be my oldest brother Gwyn, proving to my father and the people that he is not afraid of anything. As soon as we land, Robyn opens the door and jumps down to the ground, followed by Taylor. They help me out, and we all start to walk toward the gate. Behind us, I hear the rise in noise and feel the wind as The Bird leaves. The plan is for The Bird to go and see what the Sea-wolves are doing, then come back for Robyn and Taylor. Robyn is carrying her killing stick – what she calls her 'rifle.' She also has something smaller which fits in her hand, and does almost the same thing. She calls that her 'handgun.' Taylor is carrying several cameras. Neither one is wearing a helmet, because they don't want the people to be scared of them. The bird was enough. Robyn showed me a little thing she can stick in her ear so she can hear everyone else. Taylor also has one. They offered one to me, but I can't understand their language, so I said no.

I can see Gwyn staring at us as we walk toward the gate. As soon as are near, I call out in our own tongue "Gwyn, open the gate. It is Muirenn and I come with two friends who today saved me from both Romans and Sea-wolves." I see Gwyn call down, and before long the gate slowly grinds open. The big gate, not just the little door I used this morning when I left. Most of our people are gathered inside, eager to catch a glimpse of these two strangers. I don't get nearly this much attention when I arrive alone. Of course, everyone saw and heard The Bird. My foot is a little sore by the time I get through the gates, but I hurry to find my mother. She takes the bag with the plants I collected and hands it off to one of our assistants. I keep the one with my new clothes. I stuck my boot in there too, so I won't lose it. All three of us are ushered into the hall and followed by nearly all the townsfolk. Everyone wants to hear my story.

The fire in the hearth in the middle of the floor is small, for it is little needed at the end of this warm day. That leaves much of room in shadow. As my eyes adjust, I see the cots at the far end are mostly occupied, more than were here when I left this morning. I don't want to say too much about where I was and why, because I do not want everyone to know I was gathering plants for our medicines – the plants are our secret. I said that I was walking in the forest, when I noticed what I thought were ships. I climbed a hill for a better look and saw many masts gathered near the river that runs by Dubri-tun, so I ran there to raise the alarm. I tell the story in detail from that point on.

There is a lot of disbelief, but not quite as much as I expected. Men came from Dubri-tun this afternoon with news of the dead Sea-wolves and the fire-breathing flying creature that destroyed them. "Dragon" is the word they used. People here saw The Bird arrive and know that we rode it. I show off my new clothes and the drawings of me with my new friends. The scrapes on my face and the splint on my foot are hard to conceal. So are the two people that came with me. Robyn sits beside me the whole time. Taylor stands at the back, facing me, with one of his cameras in front of his face. I can see a little red light shining at me – Robyn told me that light means the box is remembering what it sees and hears.

When I finish, the whole hall is silent. Finally Gwyn speaks in Latin – not to me, but to Robyn. "What do you want from us?" His Latin is a little rough – he hasn't spent the time with the Romans that I have, but his is better than my father's.

"We want to be allies with you against the Sea-wolves."

"What can you offer me?

"You heard Muirenn's story, you know what we can do."

"But you – you are a woman. What do you have to give?"

"I myself killed sixty-three Sea-wolves and a Roman today. And I brought your sister home with only the hurts she sustained before we met."

"And what do you want from me?"

"I want to learn your language and the ways of your people. I am a warrior only by need, but a learner by choice."

I know Gwyn is having trouble following her words. He tries to hide it, but I can see that he is not convinced and I don't think he knows all the words she used. I tell him that I will explain more tonight, as best I can in the privacy of our home. I don't really understand why they want to learn about us. We are not big or famous tribe. Others in this island are larger and more powerful. Do they want to learn our healing skills? Maybe? But from what I have seen, their healers already have skills far beyond ours. It is far more likely I can learn something from them than they can from us.

I'm musing over these thoughts when Robyn leans over to me. "The bird is on the way back. We need to leave now, but we will come back in the morning. I'd like to take you to Dubri-Tun so we can talk to the people there and ensure that we mean no harm to them. I'm sure they are terrified from what they saw today."

We rise, Robyn says her farewell to my people, and we start to walk to the gate. Suddenly, Robyn jerks backward as someone grabs her from behind. The next thing I see is Bledwyn, my younger brother, flying upside down through the air. He lands on his back, and by the time that he skids to a stop, Robyn has one foot on his chest and her handgun pointed at his head. I see her relax when she see who is lying on the floor. She points the handgun at the sky as she pulls her foot away. With her other hand, she does something to the gun then puts it away. Bledwyn scrambles to his feet and doesn't quite look anyone in the eye as he scurries away.

Robyn looks at Gwyn with a smile. "I don't think he was expecting that."

As the oldest, Gwyn always just assumed he would be chieftain after my father. The oldest son doesn't always follow his father, for some do not have the skills or desire for the role. Gwyn has both, and everyone knew he would one day become chieftain since before I can even remember. At six years older than me, he has always been my hero. Bigger, stronger, faster – but also very protective of his little sister. I always felt safe around him – so did the other children my age. It was only recently that I realized even back then, he was already working to gain the support of those he would one day lead. I don't think it was planned on his part, for he didn't realize that even then he was a leader.

Bledwyn has never had that confidence. Only two years older than me, he has always been second place to Gwyn. He is smaller than Gwyn and less strong. He knows he won't be chieftain here, so he could do as my father did and marry the daughter of a chieftain with no sons. Except, as luck would have it, all the older chieftains in our tribe have sons. He is a fair hunter, but not as good as either Gwyn or my father. And no better as a warrior, either. The bow is his best weapon, so he often is left to guard the walls while the others hunt. He is skilled in working with iron, but that is not seemly for a chieftain's son. Now he's been laid flat on his back in front of everyone – and by a woman. Even if they don't understand the power she held in her hand, they saw the look in her eyes. Everyone knows she could have killed him. All she had to do is step down on his chest. But she didn't. Instead she chose to let him go. Now he owes her a life guild. In our tradition, if a warrior has the life of another in his hands, but spares that life, the warrior whose life is spared is now bound to the other. It is a sacred vow, and both Gwyn and my father will make sure that he honors it.

As Robyn and Taylor head toward the gate, I hear the distant thumping of The Bird. Suddenly, I am terrified that if they leave, I will never see them again. I tell my mother that I want to go with them. She gives me a squeeze on the arm, and I start to chase them down, but I can't run. I want to surprise them, but I have to call out to them. Maybe it is a good thing, thinking how Robyn reacted when Bledwyn surprised her from behind. They hear me and turn. Both break into smiles and Taylor gives Robyn a playful punch in the arm. I reach them and throw my arms around Robyn, "I want to go with you."

I feel her arms around me. "Taylor said you'd catch up to us before we reached the gate," I said, smiling.

As we cross the ditch, I can see the grey shape of The Bird as it approaches. We wait just beyond the ditch until it touches down, and *then walk down the slope. I glance behind as we walk. The wall is now crowded with curious faces, no longer terrified of this flying monster. I hope we get the same response at Dubri-Tun tomorrow. Behind us, I hear a shout; we all turn to see Bledwyn running toward us, bow in hand. My father must have had a talk with him, reminding him that he is now bound to Robyn, and will never have any honor anywhere in the tribe if he fails in this. For good or ill, Bledwyn is now with us.*

I quickly explain to Robyn as Bledwyn approaches. All the eyes are now on Robyn. I didn't have time to tell her what to do. She can push him away – which would tell him and the people that he has no value, and is of no use even as a slave. She can force him to his knees, accepting him as a servant. She does neither – she throws her arms around him, slaps him on the back, and accepts him as an equal. Robyn just earned a whole new level of respect from everyone watching from the wall. By accepting Bledwyn, she has also accepted my father, Gwyn, and everyone else. If she wants to be allies with us, she did exactly the right thing.

All four of us are now walking toward The Bird. Bledwyn is walking a little taller than he has in a long time. I can hear both Robyn and Taylor talking – and I smile as I think about communications with Bledwyn. I'll have to translate, because I think he knows about six words in Latin. All of them curses. I roll my eyes at the thought. By the time we climb into The Bird, Robyn is wearing a rather worried look. I wonder why. Maybe she's just tired.

As we get ourselves strapped in and put on helmets, Robyn starts to talk. "The Sea-wolves are still in the woods just behind Dubri-Tun. After we left, they started to move back toward the ford just in time to meet the Roman patrol. The Romans had some archers with them, who managed to drive the Sea-wolves back into the forest with very little damage to themselves. Since the Sea-wolves rely on swords and spears as weapons, the Roman bowmen could strike them while still out of their range. Now the Sea-wolves are moving back to their beach. That should be good news, unless it means they will try to attack us tonight. If they do, we'll be ready."

"You look tired." I venture.

"I'm exhausted. It's been a physically and emotionally draining day."

I'm not sure what some of her words mean, but I do understand the sigh that comes out of her next. Even Bledwyn understands that. It only takes minutes to make the trip to the boat, but during that brief time the sky darkens. I tell Bledwyn about the boat, so he knows a bit of what to expect, but when it swings into view, we both gasp. The part where The Bird lands is lit as bright as day. Around the boat are little lights of different colors – red, green, white. They don't flicker like flames – they shine like little stars. We land, and by the time we get unstrapped and are standing on the ground, it seems much darker. I ask Robyn about the light. She replies, "The light was only so Jerry could land The Bird easier. Now, we are getting ready for night. While the crew gets The Bird ready for tonight, I have to talk to the team. Then I need to get some sleep. Come with me, I will show you around, but first I need to talk to some people."

We find Marcelus – he didn't ride with us in The Bird, but appears as soon as we get back – and go to the place where we ate earlier. It looks different at night, because there is a red glow all around. I look for the fire or torches, but can't see any. The light doesn't change or move like fire does either. Robin stops at a place in the wall and touches a spot. A light appears, and the wall slides open. All four of us step into a small room. Robyn explains to me that this room moves – it will take us up to other floors. Robyn touches a spot on the wall and it starts to glow. The wall slides closed, I hear noises and feel the floor move, as I explain to Bledwyn as best I can what is happening. The wall opens again and we step out and follow Robyn. She leads us to a room with a large table surrounded by comfortable-looking chairs. I've never seen a table like this before – it is huge and smooth – I bet not even the king of our tribe has something like this. Across the room are some cots. I could stretch out and go to sleep on one right now, but I see a couple of people sitting in them. Closer to the big table, against the wall, is a smaller table with several things that look like Robyn's tablet fastened to the wall above it. There are also a number of strange boxes on the table itself. A man is sitting at the table, staring intently at one of the tablets.

The wall on the other side of the room, behind the big table, is covered with two large squares – I think they are more of Robyn's tablets, only bigger. Much bigger. I don't understand what I am seeing on them, but I can see things change and move. I glance over at Bledwyn. He is standing in the middle of the room, turning in a slow circle, like he's not quite sure whether to believe anything that he is seeing is real. Robyn and Taylor walk with us to the chairs, and we all sit down. They show us how they turn and move, and how we can make them go up or down. Robyn is beside me so she can explain what is going on; Bledwyn is on the other side so I can explain to him. Michele is on the other side of Bledwyn. Robyn explains that the two of them aren't allowed to sit together because they talk too much during meetings. Marcelus is on the other side of Robyn so she can tell him what is happening too.

Others come and sit in the remaining chairs around the table. Robyn gets up and speaks for a few minutes. I recognize my name and Bledwyn's, so I think she's telling the people about us. Then she sits down, and the room goes quiet as a man I haven't seen before, stands and starts to speak.

Chapter 9.

Martin quickly brings us up to date. "The surviving Saxons have returned to their beach, built fires, and are cooking a meal. They don't appear to be preparing to move out; they appear to be setting up camp and settling in. That not good, because the second fleet will arrive in about three hours – those on the beach must be expecting them, because they built up a huge fire that looks like a beacon and they've moved some boats to clear space in the center for the new arrivals. Once the rest of the boats arrive, we will have a fight to drive them off. They must know we are here and will probably wait to attack until after the rest of the fleet arrives with more men. Our mast lights will be visible so they will have no trouble finding us. We will have to drive them away, because we can't abandon our allies now. Yet ... there is hope.

Martin goes on to explain the plan. About the time the rest of the fleet approaches, we will move in closer and position the ship about four kilometers from their beach. We'll be sure they can see the helipad at the stern with the chopper in full view. Saxons have old traditions about dragons and we plan to take full advantage of them. We've loaded incendiary rockets, which should give a pretty good impression of a fire-breathing dragon at night. Any boats on the water, we will aim for their sails. They should be nice and flammable, and losing them will disable the boats while doing minimal damage to the people inside. We can burn supplies at the camp and some boats on the beach. Since between us and the Romans, they lost nearly two hundred people today, they can lose six or seven boats and still have enough space to take the remaining people back home.

If they attack with the full fleet, we finally agreed that we'll need to take out at least one boat. One in the second line, near the middle is our target. We don't want to take out a boat in the front row, because any one could have their war chief onboard, and we don't want them to have a fallen leader to avenge. We want to cause confusion and fear in the hope they realize they are facing a foe far beyond their power so they cut their losses and go home. If they don't turn away, we have no choice but to launch a full on attack. But no one on our team is looking forward to that prospect in the slightest.

I share what I can with whispered words to Muirenn and Marcelus. Martin gives me a look. He is obviously thinking that Michele is not at the root of the distractions we cause. "I am just updating our guests. They are very patiently sitting here, listening to a conversation where they can't understand a single word."

He sighs. I roll my eyes. We get on with it.

He briefs us on the current status. Radar shows the incoming fleet only twenty kilometers away from us – only a little over twelve from the beach. The tide has turned and the wind picked up, so they are closing a little faster than they were. We have maybe two hours.

Martin concludes with "those who will be involved and have been going all day" – here he looks directly at me – "had better grab a nap."

I agree. It could be a long night.

We break. Before we leave the room, I ask our wounded guests how they are doing and if they are in pain. Both deny it, but both are obviously hurting, so I call down to the sick bay to see if Sandy can bring something up for them. I take them down a level to the quarters. Since we have lots of spares, each will get their own. We take them to their rooms and show them the showers. Explaining the toilets initially results in some blank looks, but I finally get the message across.

Sandy comes with some painkillers. All three accept them when I explain what they do. I forgot that Bledwyn has some pretty good bruises from his landing. Good thing Sandy didn't. Finally, I get into my room, and fall into bed. It seems like I only just shut my eyes when Michele is shaking me awake.

"I don't think anyone else is sleeping. Most are wandering the ship or hanging out in the lounge by the cafeteria. Just waiting and wondering what will happen. Even the three you brought from land made their way to the lounge about half an hour ago. April got them some food, and someone put on a movie. I looked in on Mission Control just in time to get put to work giving you a wakeup call," she explains.

No time for a shower. I quickly dress and head downstairs. I wish Michele hadn't said anything about food, because now I realize how hungry I am. I head into the cafeteria and grab some bars. They'll have to do. I stop and speak to Muirenn and Marcelus.

"Is this like where you live?" Muirenn asks, pointing to the screen.

I glance at the movie. I don't recognize the film, but the scene is downtown New York. "That is my world, but not where I live. I can show you where I live later. Our town is deemed "picturesque" and has served as a background in several movies and TV series over the years. I have a few favorites in the library here. Besides, my father took lots of home videos of birthdays, holidays, and other special events. Grandma and Grandpa had them burned to DVDs for me before I shipped out. I haven't watched them in years, but always carry them on missions.

"Can we stay here?"

"Sure. You've had enough excitement for one day."

I look at the three of them, surrounded by members of my team. Michele is back in her spot in the corner of a sofa having completed her task of waking me. Kelly is here, so is Andrew. April joined them. She is also ship's crew, scheduled for duty on the helm at some point tonight. Someone found clean clothes for Bledwyn and Marcelus. Cleaned up and in tee shirts and jeans, they almost look like they belong.

I head out to the deck. John just finished fueling the chopper, and is reeling the hose back onto the spool. 'Little' John is about the biggest guy I've ever met. He went through college on a football scholarship and was headed for the pros when he blew out his back. Instead, he wound up a heavy duty mechanic, got bored of that, so switched to helicopters about ten years ago. Now at close to fifty, he's still about the strongest one in the crew. I'm not about to try flipping him anytime soon – he must weigh three hundred, fifty pounds. He looks after the ship engines and all three aircraft.

Trace is already on board – she is flying tonight. I get the right seat. Just in case we need to use the heavy machine gun mounted in the door, I put on the tether harness while we are safely on the ground. It's really uncomfortable to sit on, but I'm not about to try putting it on in a hurry, in the dark, and risk forgetting something. I triple-check each fastener. We've moved the ship to only fifteen hundred metres from the shore and about five kilometers south of the Saxons and are slowly moving closer. The night is dead clear and we're showing enough light that they know we're here. The lead boats in the arriving fleet are now a little over a thousand meters from the beach that they will reach in minutes. Little Bird One is over the beach and it looks like the boys down there are having a good time. They have some skins out and I don't think it is spring water that they're drinking. That is probably good for us. A little alcohol in their veins should nicely intensify the dragon effect and will probably keep them from generating any sort of organized response to our attack. It may even make them braver than normal, and that could turn out really, really bad for them.

As Trace finishes her pre-flight check and starts the engines, I slide into my seat. I'm not used to being up here with the view. Almost always I'm riding in the back. We did some training flights to prepare for this mission, so I am practiced with the weapon system. We couldn't actually fire the rockets, but I spent a lot time perfecting my aim using boats on the reservoir near our town for targets. Even though we have some defense funding, the helicopter carries civilian registration. And various government bodies have rather strict rules about civilian aircraft carrying live weapons. If anyone asked, they were movie props. In front of me are projected cross hairs with a joystick to move them. When the cross is on the target, I hit one of two buttons to launch a rocket. The right button launches an incendiary from the right pod. The left one launches high explosive from the left pod. Both leave a visible trail of fire in the night, but the effect on the target is completely different. The sky is clear, but the moon is still below the horizon, so the night is dark. Our dragon will look like more like it is spitting fire than breathing the stuff, but I'm pretty sure that distinction will be lost on the Saxons below.

I try to imagine the terror those on the beach face as this huge, loud, flying thing swoops down at them out of the night sky. They run long before I start to fire. I take aim at the nearest of several large piles of supplies on the beach. Incendiary into the first one. Impressive sight as the rocket streams toward the ground and whatever is in its path burns nicely. I try high explosive next. Still looks like fire streaming from the nose. I think that was a pile of wineskins, because it appears some liquid and bits of leather sprayed all over the beach. They won't be happy with me. End of the beach, climbing left turn, then back down cutting across the beach for the beacon fire. High explosive ... and there are burning logs flying all over the beach. The lead boat with the new arrivals is about fifty meters from the shore. They can swim that. My incendiary rocket sets the sail on fire and hits the mast. Mast and sails all come crashing down in flames as men go over the side.

We will see if that is enough. As we climb away, I tune in to Little Bird to see what is happening back on the beach. The pile of supplies is burning now; the boat we set on fire has drifted over and set two more ablaze. Not everyone was able to make it shore – the light of the blazing boats reveals several bodies floating in the water. The remaining boats are milling around, not sure if they will land or stay out. It looks like they are coming in. Good, let's go home. Maybe we can all get some sleep.

Trace is the newest member of our team. She joined only a month ago, after we searched long and hard for a third pilot. She is one of those people who knew from day one what she wanted to do. She wanted to fly planes. She started flying lessons while still in high school, got on with a local commuter line, and eventually graduated to a national carrier. After ten years of living out of a suitcase, with basically no friends outside the airline industry because of the crazy hours, she was ready for a change. While on vacation on the gulf coast, on a whim she walked into a charter helicopter service, and found they were desperate for pilots. She quit her job, got trained on the choppers, and never looked back. Home every night, got new friends, got a dog, and fell in love with a guy who worked on one of the rigs. Five years of happiness for them; then he's killed in an accident at work. She's the one who flew him out to the rig that day.

After her bereavement leave, getting back into the seat and heading out was really rough. She hung on there for a couple more years, but the joy was gone. When we came along, she was looking for a place where she could do what she loved, with no reminders of that day. Fire, water, death. Tonight may have been too many reminders. I'm sorry Trace.

Too many reminders for me, too. On the way back, I couldn't help thinking about all those families back home. Waiting for the sails to appear, waiting for husbands, sons, fathers, brothers. But they won't be coming, because I decided that their lives were disposable. Here I am, coming to a time where I don't belong and choosing who lives and who dies. I wonder how these thoughts will play out in tonight's dreams. I can justify it in my mind: they came to kill, and the only way to stop them before they did was to kill them first. And their targets were just ordinary people – farmers and fishermen; people just trying to scratch out a living. And healers; people who do their best to sustain life, not destroy it. I guess those are the ones I have to protect. *Isn't that the Robyn Hood legend? To protect those who have no power from those with power who wish to abuse it?*

By the time we land, we're both pretty quiet. While Trace does her post-flight shut down, I get updates from Martin. The Saxons have landed their boats. We still might get an attack in the night, but it seems less likely now they are on the beach. Trace folds the rotor and we help John get The Bird into the hanger. Andrew gets the net up and we watch as Jerry brings in Little Bird One for a perfect recovery. Little Bird gets tucked away, the net is folded and we all head inside. April and Lance drew the night shift so they'll keep watch on the radar and infrared and will call if they need help.

The lounge is still occupied. Michele, Don, Taylor and Steve are all keeping our three guests entertained. And fed. I see signs of popcorn, chips, candy, and pop. Great. They've had less than six hours of life in the 21st century, and we're already getting them hooked on movies and junk food. I squeeze in between Michele and Muirenn and grab a bowl. *Who am I to argue?*

I've never been much of a movie person, I'm ADD enough that sitting through a two-hour movie just doesn't happen. Unless I have a distraction. Like Michele whispering in my ear bringing me up to speed on the plot, or Muirenn whispering in the other ear trying to learn pretty much everything. The movie is some sappy romantic comedy – and most my friends know I have a weakness for sappy romantic comedies. Especially tonight. Anything to get my mind off the day. So I do want to get the plot synopsis from Michele, but Muirenn really wants to know what is going on. I explain that it is a story – like a ballad from a bard – only you get to see it and hear the characters.

Then everyone breaks out in laughter including me. Marcelus and Bledwyn look up from their snacks, Muirenn is in my ear trying to find out what is happening. And I'm laughing so hard I can barely talk.

I finally get my hands into a timeout 'T' and get out "please pause the movie!"

Don finds the remote, the image freezes, and I manage to get it together enough to explain to Muirenn how the guy was trying to work up the courage to talk to this girl while she was trying to get his attention, and they run into each other in a store – insert a whole explanation of a store – and they're both stumbling over their words and trying to explain the situation, thoroughly confusing each other. Other people are watching this exchange, she slips, he tries to catch her and they both wind up falling together in a heap on the floor, knocking over a huge stack of soup cans in the process. That's what got everyone laughing.

We continue the movie. Of course, just then there's this special moment and it looks like they will click. But then both their phones go off and the moment passes. I have to explain what phones are. Finally they meet again. Talk. Kiss. Walk away hand in hand, both tossing their phones into a waste basket as they pass. Roll the credits, interspersed with clips of them both tearing through the garbage can trying to find their phones. I love it. Then I have to explain the markings on the screen, how the symbols form words. Marcelus has seen writing, but does not read or write. Only very few in his culture know how to do either. Muirenn and Bledwyn heard rumors of such a thing from the Romans, but writing is complete unknown to them.

I tell them "I want to learn your language. Will you teach it to me?" Muirenn gives me an odd look, so I quickly add, "Not tonight."

"No one ever wants to learn about us. People come from outside only to take our land and crops. They don't come from far away to learn about us. We aren't strong or wealthy. We don't want to conquer our neighbors or pillage distant shores. We just want to live in peace. Why are you interested in us? I've seen what your world looks like. You have so much, we have so little. Why do you care about me? Why do you care about any of us?"

How do I explain about the science of anthropology and the "publish or perish" principle of academia? And how they are the least-known people of the Early-Roman period in all of England. And how being the first person to describe them and their language would certainly get me my PhD. Hopefully a research and teaching position at a decent University. I can't. It would take far too many words for the end of a really long day.

So I answer, "I look after the little people; those who are threatened by ones with power and wealth. That is not just what I do. It is who I am."

Marcelus looks at me. "That's why you protected her from me. I understand. But why didn't you kill me? Why care about me?"

I look him in the eye when I replied. "If you had any real power, they would never have left you behind. You deserve my help as much as Muirenn does."

"But I tried to kill you," he replies.

"You never had a chance of getting close enough. Besides, I tried to kill you, so we're even."

Muirenn has been thinking. "Could you teach me to read and write? And maybe you could teach me your language so I can talk to everyone here?"

Teaching English is not really my expertise, and writing in a totally unknown language with no alphabet? That would be an achievement. Too bad we don't have a linguist. Or has Max included linguistics in his studies? Where is Max anyway? He's been keeping an unusually low profile today. I'll ask him tomorrow.

"Yes, let's do that." I'm in no mood to tell her that would be too much work. I bet she'd find a way to learn, even if I didn't help her. "But now it is time for Robyn to get some sleep." I almost forget to repeat my last words in English for the rest of the team.

I've been putting off sleep. I am afraid of what my dreams might bring. But I can't hang on any longer, so I extract myself from the couch and head over to the stairs. I glance back to find that most the group is behind me. We all stumble up the steps and into our respective rooms. I hit the shower, find something clean and dry to wear, and collapse onto my bunk. I was right about the dreams. I see the faces of men, fleeing the terror in the air behind them, only find out too late they are running toward a greater danger – the one that will leave them dead. Watching them try to react as their comrades fall to the dirt beside them, and they have no idea where to turn or how to fight. Because by the time they see the girl on her belly in the bushes, it is far too late. For they are next in the crosshairs of her scope. Then my dream changes and I am on a beach, trying to run from fire that is falling from the sky.

The clock says it is nearly four when I wake covered in sweat and knotted up in my blankets. I don't feel rested – far from it. But I think I can face another day; so I drag my body out of bed. I think about showering, but instead I just change to track pants and a t-shirt before I head down to the gym. A few miles on a bike; then on to the weight machine for some sets. I'm surprised that I'm the only one down here. Good thing that I didn't bother to change. I'm just ready to leave when Marcelus peeks around the door. He's used to waking with the sun and came down looking for something to eat. He didn't find anyone, but heard a noise so went to investigate. I show him how the bike, treadmill, and weight machines work. Then try to explain why we go through all this effort to get nowhere and do nothing. I'm not sure that he gets it, but decides to give the bike a try. I watch him for a few minutes, then head back upstairs for a shower and change of clothes. I want some downtime before I start the day. I'm just drying my hair when the phone rings. It's Max asking for a meeting up in Mission Control. Right, that's where he's been. Since he and Don have little to do when we aren't preparing for time travel, they have other tasks. Don helps John keep everything running, and Max spells off Martin and the rest of the crew in Mission Control. Both are trained to fly the drones, and both can lend a hand to Steve, our tech guru, who sets up and runs all our imaging and communications gear.

I head up to Mission Control. Max, Martin, and Lance are all there, watching images from Little Bird. A little before three a.m., when the moon was well above the horizon, the Saxons approached with fourteen boats. Max called Martin, and between them, decided that the team was too wiped from yesterday to get everyone up. Martin made the call, and Lance fired a missile when they were just under two kilometers away. The boats were close together in sort of a diamond formation with one in the lead and with four rows of three, then a single in the rear. The missile hit the boat right behind the leader, went right through the hull and exploded under the stern. It was destroyed, one beside it capsized, and two others swamped. The remaining boats had to stop to haul the crews out of the water. The sky was already turning pale in the east, giving them light for the rescue, but also ensuring they would see us. We didn't approach so as to not interrupt their rescue. They cleared out and returned to their beach about an hour ago. Little Bird couldn't find any survivors or bodies in the water.

"What do we do now?

I don't want anyone else to die. They know we are here. Maybe if we make sure the whole camp can see the size of their foe, they will decide that this area just isn't worth the cost. Martin calls the wheelhouse: April and Captain Johansen are there and agree with our plan. They bring us even closer – only twelve hundred meters from the beach and just beyond the end of the headland. Here we are in full view of the Saxons. We stop. Most all our crew is on deck, awakened by the movement of the ship, and staring now at the men on the beach. We watch them as they stare back at this monster of the seas. Then Captain Johansen gives a blast on the horn and opens her up so they can see that we can also move far faster than they could ever hope to achieve. We return to about five kilometers out, and watch Little Bird's pictures as they get to work. We'll know in a couple of hours, but it looks like they are packing up and heading out. One threat down. I wonder if it is any coincidence that the Saxons won't land this far south again for nearly four hundred years.

Chapter 10.

I awake with a start. I feel a deep, rumbling vibration through my cot. I open my eyes and am disoriented by the strange surroundings. I am not in my home, snuggled under my favorite skins. Slowly, I remember yesterday. I wasn't sure if it was just a dream - the flying through the air, the boat, the food, the people. Is it all true? I jump out of bed and as my foot hits the floor, I realize with a shock of pain the part about getting hurt definitely is true. I reach over and grab that thing – I still don't know what to call it – and put it back on my foot the way Robyn showed me. I pull on my clothes, and wander out in search of Robyn. I see someone ahead of me, so I follow him through a doorway and find myself outside. There is a place to walk, it isn't very wide, and when I walk to the far side, I see that there is just a low wall – I can look over and see straight down into the water, far below. Bledwyn and Robyn are standing just a little ways down, so I join them, and look toward the land. I recognize the beach where the Sea-wolves landed. I see the boats, but the rest of the scene is all confusion. There seem to be more boats than there were yesterday – maybe it's because I am seeing them from so close. Some of the boats look strange – some look to be all burnt; at least one other is at an odd angle. On the beach, men are staring. You can tell they were at work, but now they are just stand and stare. I jump as there is a blast of a horn, but far louder than any I've ever heard before. The men on the beach jump too. I feel the rumbling again and realize we are starting to move.

Robyn turns and tells me "They tried to attack us last night, so we had to destroy two more of their boats to drive them off. We wanted them to see us, so they will leave these shores and go back home. Now we'll see what happens." Then she adds, "How did you sleep, and how is your foot today?"

"I slept well," I answer, "And my foot is okay as long I wear this – what do you call it?"

"It is called a brace" she answers. Then she adds, "Are you hungry? Let's go get something to eat."

With that, she opens a door and steps into a part of the boat I've never seen before. I stick close behind, because if I don't I'll probably get lost.

Bledwyn comes up beside me, and raps his knuckles against the wall beside him. "It's iron." He says. "Everywhere I look, the whole thing is made of iron. Remember the Druid last winter?"

"Oh." I had forgotten, but in a flash it all comes back. Last winter, near the solstice when the nights are long, a lone Druid came to our gates. Druids are not our favorite visitors, nor do they frequent our hall. While we welcome their tales and offer due respect, we are also somewhat afraid for they have strange powers. But this was at the end of a long day of driving rain and a bitter wind; my father would not turn away anyone into a night like this. Least of all a Druid.

So the gates were opened and the man entered with his horse. Stable and feed were found for his steed and he was welcomed to our hall. His face was not known to any of us and he did not give a name. Most Druids offer a tale in thanks for a meal, so we were not surprised that once he had finished eating, he started to speak. Most of our people gathered into the hall, for there is little better on a wet winter evening than a story. His tale that night was new to us – even the oldest of our elders had never before heard this one. He spoke of a hero long ago who came from the other world to rescue the people from an invasion of dragons. The hero traveled in a boat made of iron. I remember laughing at the idea – even I know that iron doesn't float. Why would anyone make a boat out of it?

I thought of asking the Druid how one could build a boat from iron, but never had the chance. The next morning dawned calm and misty, but the rain had stopped. He thanked us for our hospitality and wished us peace. He then rode away and has not returned.

I put the thought of the story aside while I work up the nerve to ask Robyn a question that I should have asked yesterday. "Where do you come from?"

Robyn answers, "Far to the west – across the water."

"The land of the Irish?" I ask. We have heard of a people from the west who sometimes visit this island, but never come to our shores in the east.

"Far, far further than that. Past the land of the Irish is a great water, many hundreds of leagues wide. I come from beyond that water."

One more question. "What is your boat made from?"

"Steel" She answered.

Steel – not iron. The only steel I've ever seen is in the swords of the Romans. I know it is rare and expensive. I can't imagine there being enough steel in the world to make a boat the size of this one. I think of how I'm going to tell Bledwyn the boat is made of steel, and not iron when I realize something: in our language, the word for steel is the same as our word for iron.

One more question "Steel? How do you make a boat out of steel? It doesn't float."

She raps her knuckles on the wall, just the same as Bledwyn did. "This is steel, and we are floating, so you know now that it can be done. If you make the boat right, you can make steel float."

I turn to Bledwyn and tell him. "It is made of iron. And they come from across the great water, beyond the land of the Irish."

I need to sit down. I choose a chair beside Taylor; Robyn sits beside me and Michele is in the other chair. I start to explain about the Druid and his story that night and how at the time I didn't believe that a boat could be made of iron, but now I have to because I'm sitting here in a boat made of iron. I run out of words and fall into silence.

I see Robyn glance at Michele before she speaks. "The people in your hill fort, Tordur; you are known as healers. Am I right?"

"Yes"

"I thought so. Michele knows a lot about plants and recognizes all but one of what you collected yesterday. All the ones she knows are healing plants. She tells me the variety you had is remarkable. The fungus – the soft, pale one she doesn't recognize, but she tells me that she's pretty sure it is a healing plant, too. I came to learn about your people. We chose to come to you in part because we learned from the Romans you have healing skills. We actually know almost nothing else about you."

I tell her "But your world is so amazing, I want to go there. Why would you give up all that to come here?"

I don't understand. They showed me something of their world. It's magic and exciting. Why would they come here? I think of our great hall, how big it is, and how impressive it seemed yesterday morning. Then I saw their huge halls that tower to the skies. My father is the chieftain, so our home is bigger than most. But compared to what I saw from Robyn's world, it is so small and so plain. And the food! There is lots of food, so they let me eat whatever I want. Most years, we fare well, but when the harvest is poor or the Sea-wolves plunder, we have lean times. Here, I think they always have enough.

There is silence before Robyn answers. "If we hadn't come, you and many of your people would probably be dead by now. That makes me glad that we came. I hope you understand this. We travelled more than just across a vast distance to get here. We also travelled through time to get here. We came from a time almost two thousand years away; what you see around you and the pictures you saw last night are all from that time in the far distant future. I'm not sure if telling you this is the right thing or not, but I think you can understand. I hope so. Later today, we will show you some more of our world. For now, let's get some food."

I don't understand what she says about traveling through time. I know there are only certain times when it possible to cross from the other world to this one. All the stories tell us it is at the times-between-time – dawn and dusk – when they can cross over. So maybe that is what she meant. Suddenly I have a question about the other world. I think about the forest I love and how few trees I saw in the images of the other world. I ask, "Do you have forests in your world?"

"Yes we do. Michael works in a forest. He teaches people about the forest, keeps them safe, and keeps them from harming it."

"Will you stay here forever or will you go back to your world? Will you take me when you go?"

"Yes we will go back at about the end of harvest. We don't plan on taking anyone from here when we leave. Our time is complex and can be very scary and it would be very hard for you to leave here forever and then learn everything you'll need to know to live in our time. No promises that we will let you come with us."

I think about my future in Tordur. How I will need to move somewhere else and leave the place I love to be married. Maybe Robyn's world would be okay, as long as there are forests. But I don't want to think about that right now. The aroma of food ... I'm hungry! Robyn and I both rise and head over to pick make our choices. Marcelus and Bledwyn both materialize behind us. I don't know where they've been, but somehow they manage to appear just in time for each meal. She explains all the foods that are in front of us. I recognize an apple and something that looks a little like bread – that will do for me. She takes something that looks like some sort of grain, and adds a thick, creamy substance to the top. Marcelus and Bledwyn fill their plates as we move along. Robyn gets a coffee and an opaque liquid that is a color that reminds me of leaves in the autumn. I decide to try some.

Then she asks if I want my bread warm. I nod, so she takes it and puts it in this metal box, and presses something on the side. I see markings on the box where she touches it. It makes some noises, and when they stop, she opens it, and hands my bread back, nice and warm. Of course, the boys want their bread warmed up now, too, so Robyn warms their bread up as well. Once we have our food, we carry it back to our table – since ours is now full, Marcelus and Bledwyn grab one near us and start a conversation. Apparently, Bledwyn does know more Latin than I gave him credit for. I look at Marcelus and realize he looks no older than Bledwyn's eighteen years. Not much older than me. Then I look around the room at Robyn's people - everyone is older than me.

I ask Robyn, "Are these people married. Do they have children?"

She answers, "No. Most of us are still young and never have been married. Some of older ones were, but their partner died or the marriage didn't work. No one on the team left a partner or children behind. We do have one man who is a father – Barry – I don't think you've met him yet. He's the tall guy over there. The girl with the long hair beside him is his daughter April.

She said they are young, but they look older than me, and most girls my age are married. "How old are you?" I ask.

She laughs. "In our world, you never ask a girl that! But I'm just a little younger than Taylor - you saw his birthday last night – he's now thirty. I will be twenty-nine in the fall. Michele's the baby at this table. She's twenty-five."

"Most girls in our world are married by fifteen. At sixteen, I am the oldest girl in Tordur who is not married." I add. "Men are usually a little older, but most marry before they reach twenty."

Robyn tells me, "In our world, not many people get married before they are twenty. Most wait until they are twenty-five or older. Some choose not to get married at all."

"Does the girl have to move to the man's home?"

"No, each couple decides what works for them."

I'm thinking that Robyn's world sounds better and better all the time.

I look at April's hair. It's even longer than mine. Then, I look around the room at the women's hair. It is all different lengths – some longer, some shorter. And all different colors too. Michele's hair is the shortest – as short as some of the men. In our tribe, a woman with short hair has either been sick, or has had her hair cut off in punishment for some crime.

I can't imagine that she did anything wrong, so I ask Robyn "Is Michele sick?"

Robyn tells me, "No. Do you ask because of her hair?"

I nod.

She goes on. "I thought so. No, she is not sick. She just chooses to keep it short."

I can't think of any more questions, so I finish my meal while listening to Robyn and Michele talk in their language. Once we have finished eating, we take our coffee up to the big room we were in yesterday. Robyn explains that we are going to plan our day, and the first thing to do is visit Dubri-tun so the people there know they are safe. If the Sea-wolves have left the beach, we will stop there, and then drop in on Tordur. While we are on the ground, the rest of the team will do some more exploring, to locate the Roman encampments. Robyn, Taylor, and Lance will accompany Bledwyn and me on the ground. Marcelus gets to sit here with Max –Max knows some Latin, so they can understand each other a bit. They will look for Romans with Little Bird.

We are going to Dubri-tun in a small boat, so we don't scare the people by flying in The Bird. Once they meet us and we can tell them The Bird is no danger to them, Robyn will call it to come so we can travel in it for the rest of the day. That's good for me; it will be a few days before I can walk any distance and I wouldn't want to miss this day. Then Robyn gets caught up in a discussion in her own language. I try to follow, but my mind drifts around the words I can't understand.

Was it only yesterday that I lay on my back watching that hawk, dreaming of flying through the air? And today flying seems almost normal. I never really believed the stories about the other world, but I look around the room and realize they didn't tell half the truth. The view from Little Bird catches my attention, as a settlement drifts across the wall. I watch as people wander in the direction of their cooking shed, seeking their first meal of the day. And I wrap my hands around my warm cup of coffee – a beverage I first tasted yesterday - and think about all the food that is downstairs.

But my attention is drawn back to the room as people start to leave. Andrew goes to get the boat ready; Robyn and Lance go to get their weapons. Bledwyn and I follow Robyn so we don't get lost. Bledwyn is wearing his own clothes. I wear the clothes Michele gave me because the breeches stretch to fit over the brace on my foot. Besides, they are more comfortable than my old tunic and breeches.

When Robyn arrives, she's wearing her heavy green coat and carrying the weapon she had when I first saw her step out of the woods. Right behind her are Lance and Don, carrying a box. "This coat" she explains "is my armor. We have some that should fit you. Here, try them on."

With that she takes similar coats from the box and hands one to each of us. I hear Bledwyn give a bit of a grunt when he takes his. When I mine, I find out why. I nearly drop it on the ground; it is so heavy.

"This is so heavy! I complain. "Do I have to wear it?"

"I know it's heavy, but after a while you forget you're wearing it. It will protect you from being hurt by an arrow or spear, so you should wear it. We hope there won't be any need for it, but here is something else you need."

Holding up a little black box with a string hanging from it, she says "This lets you hear what is going on and talk to us if you need to." Pointing to the end of the string, she adds "This goes in your ear. To talk so that we can hear you, just touch this spot on the box." She quickly sticks the end into my ear, and drops the box down my top. When it comes out the bottom, Don hands her a strip of fabric with an attached pouch. Robyn slips the box into the pouch, and quickly fastens the fabric around my waist. She does the same for Bledwyn.

"These boxes also let Little Bird see exactly where you are. If something happens and you get separated from the group, don't panic. We will know where you are and come find you. If you can, touch the box so we can hear what is going on, but if you are really in trouble don't call attention to the box, just in case someone thinks it's valuable and takes it from you."

I nod in response.

We also each get helmets like the one that Robyn wears, but we will take them off when we come to Dubri-tun so they recognize us. Robyn also gives other coats to wear, ones that we only need while we are in the boat. Robyn tells me that if we fall out of the boat, these will keep us floating so we don't drown. Considering the heavy armor I have, I think if I end up in the water, I'll surely sink like a stone.

The little boat is floating at the side of our big boat. We have to climb down a ladder to get to it. I'm not very comfortable on the ladder with the extra weight from the armor, but it really isn't very far. I don't think anyone sees how scared I am, but Robyn tells me when I do get down that I did well because the first time she climbed down that ladder, she slipped and fell on her back in the boat. Then she smiles ... and I wonder if it is really true.

There are some metal boxes at the back of the boat and up near the front is a sort of a table with a wheel and some other things. Some of the men on the big boat untie the ropes that hold us and throw them into our boat. Andrew then goes up to the table and does something. Next I hear a low rumbling noise coming from the boxes and we start to move.

I look toward the shore and see how far away it is, and wonder how long it will take to get there, and then I hear Robyn speak to me. "Hang on to the ropes. Get Bledwyn to do the same."

I see Robyn, Taylor and Lance are all sitting down in the bottom of the boat, with their backs against the sides, and hanging on with both hands to a rope that runs along the top of the sides. I do the same, and tell Bledwyn, too. He looks startled to hear my voice, but sees what I am doing and does the same. I hear Robyn's voice, and then I watch as Andrew does something at his table. The noise gets louder and we go fast, faster than a galloping horse. I watch the shore get closer, see the water spray past, and feel the waves hit the bottom of the boat. I'm not the only one who thinks this is fun; Robyn gives a loud shout! I know we are not going as fast as The Bird can fly, but it feels faster because of the wind and the waves. All too soon we slow down, arriving at the mouth of the river.

Robyn explains. "The water is shallow here, so Andrew has slowed down so we don't hit anything. He can see what is under the water, so we are safe. The Sea-wolves are busy loading their boats, so I don't think they will bother us. But just in case they do, I want to be ready."

It is then that I notice that Robyn isn't holding onto the ropes now. She has her rifle in both hands and is watching the shore where we saw the Sea-wolves yesterday. But nothing happens and as we arrive at the landing for Dubri-tun, Andrew chooses a low spot and points the boat to the shore. We jump out onto land, take off those coats for the boat, and then push the boat back into the water. Andrew turns and heads alone toward the sea. But Robyn watches the far shore, rifle in hand, until he is out of sight and around a bend.

We remove our helmets and walk toward the gate. Robyn shows us how to hook them onto the coats we are wearing so we don't have to carry them in our hands. A sentry is watching us over the wall and more heads appear as we approach the gate.

Bledwyn cries out in our language. "Hail, people of Dubri-Tun. I am Bledwyn of Cynbel, of Tordur. I come in peace with my sister Muirenn and guests from a distant land."

Some heads duck down behind the wall, and as we approach, the gates open and we enter in. The gates close behind us, and we are surrounded by the people, all trying to tell us at once about the excitement of the previous day. Slowly we got their story of terror – first with a few Sea-wolves appearing near mid-day. Fortunately few of their people were outside the walls, and all but one was able to get inside before it was too late. The one caught outside was in a far field was able to hide in the forest without being spotted by the attackers.

Then more Sea-wolves came. The herds that were outside the walls were slaughtered; they lit fires just out of bowshot from the walls and settled in to wait. Even more arrived. And then came the dragon, which terrorized them to the point even the bravest abandoned their post on the walls and hid. They never realized it was going after the Sea-wolves until the dreadful silence that fell after it went away. One man worked up the courage to look out. He saw that those Sea-wolves still on the field were dead. The sight gave them a bit of hope but they were still fearful the dragon would return. In all our stories of dragons, they never, ever are on our side. They are evil and dangerous. But this one was real and appeared to be good.

The story goes much slower than this, because I have to tell Robyn in Latin, then she repeats it to Lance and Taylor in their language.

Then Wynad completes the story. He is the one caught outside the settlement, who hid in the trees. He didn't see me heading toward the road, but he spotted the four strangers dressed in green. He followed them at a distance, heard the cracks of Robyn's rifle, and saw much of my rescue. He then saw most of our attack on the Sea-wolves and watched us leave in the Bird. He recognized Marcelus as a Roman and me as a member of our tribe. Once we left and it appeared safe, he made his way back to the gates. So they knew most of the story before we came today.

After we left, they watched as the Romans fought the Sea-wolves; then the rain came. Lightning struck a tree near where they last saw the Sea-wolves, but they don't know if any were still there. After the rain, they relit the fires and used them to burn the bodies left on the field. Help came from Tordur, but it still took them far into the night to finish the job.

I then fill them in on my story and then translate as Robyn gives her story.

Bledwyn adds his part, but he forgets to include the bit about being bested by Robyn. I think about reminding him, but realize he's embarrassed about this loss and might not appreciate my help. They then honor us with a meal made from the meat the Sea-wolves left behind when they fled. After we eat, it is time to leave. Before we do, we pass on to the people news Robyn just received – the Sea-wolves have left the beach and are turning their boats back to the north in the direction of their home. As we leave the gate with a promise to return, The Bird comes over the tree tops and lands in the field. No longer is it an object of terror for the people, so they watch as we climb aboard and take off toward the beach.

When we arrive, Robyn and Taylor go to work. Taylor has his camera out and points it at most everything. Robyn examines almost everything they left behind. While they are working, the rest of us wander among the stones, looking at the destruction and imagining the terror here last night.

They left the remains of four boats. Three are burned, and the other has a large hole in the bottom. Robyn tells me there are two more floating out in the sea. It doesn't look to me that there is much else except a bunch of burned wood and shredded skin. But Robyn gets excited when she finds a couple of spear points buried in the remains of one fire. She calls Taylor over with his cameras, then carefully removes them from the fire and places them in little bags which she marked with symbols. I wander over to see what is so interesting.

Robyn tells me "This is the first pile of supplies we destroyed last night. It looks like it was spears and maybe other weapons. It is hard to tell, but based on the size of the pile and the remaining wood from the shafts, there must have been three or four hundred spears here. They took most of the spear heads, but fortunately they left two behind. Now I know they were Saxons, because we have other Saxon spear heads from this period, and these are identical. Come over here." I follow her to the ashes of another fire. "This is the second pile of supplies we destroyed. Look at the hole in the ground and shreds of skin. Our fire went right through the skins and hit the rocks beneath the pile. There it exploded," – here she uses a word I don't know, it is only later that I learn the meaning – "sending rocks everywhere, turning the skins to shreds, and spilling their beer. Probably one of the rocks went far enough to hit that boat with the hole in the bottom."

"No wonder they headed for home. They were attacked by a dragon twice, a Roman patrol, and fireballs. They lost about two hundred men, six boats, many weapons, and much of their store of drink."

We continue to examine the beach, and find a few more items – weapons, bits of food, clothing, and several patches of blood. Before we leave, we use The Bird to help drag the boat with the hole in the bottom well up onto the beach, above the highest waves. Robyn wants to come back later and examine it again.

From the beach, we head to Tordur. I watch the familiar trees and forests rush beneath as we near the hill with our settlement. Suddenly, I'm anxious about heading home. I don't want to be there and I can't tell anyone why, because I don't know myself. But for the first time in my life, the collection of buildings down there feels ominous. I watch as they draw nearer and descend toward the ground. I can see the sentinels watching from the walls. Few others seem to be around and that adds to my growing fear. The constant voices in my ears, speaking words that I don't understand, does not help, either. I realize that Robyn's voice carries an edge that I've never heard before.

When we land, as we are walking toward the gate, Robyn explains. "Earlier today, two Romans on horses arrived here. They were welcomed inside, and went into the hall with your father, older brother, and many others. They left about an hour ago. They are now approaching a patrol of Romans coming in this direction. There are a hundred mounted soldiers, including archers. Whether they are coming here or not, we don't know. They could be after the Sea-wolves, not knowing that they were driven off last night. Or, they could be seeking the person who killed one of their own yesterday – and kidnapped another. What do you think, Marcelus? Can you guess why they are here?"

Marcelus' voice comes through now. "They must have heard rumors of a dragon in the sky, breathing fire down on the ground. Perhaps from surviving Sea-wolves; perhaps from the patrol that was nearby yesterday. They may even know that it came here – it is a little hard to hide. Since the dragon for them is a symbol of royalty, they would be most curious in finding the truth. If they believe that Bledwyn's father is accepted by a dragon, they might consider him king over the entire region. And that could be very good for your fortunes. And very hard on Cydyrn, who is the king."

As we approach the main gate, the sentinel calls down to people on the ground. The great gate swings open just enough for us to enter. As soon as we pass through, the gate creaks closed. From here, one of my father's warriors leads us to the back of the hall, and we enter through a door beside one of the storage rooms. As we slip in, we can see the cots at the back of the room are all full of wounded men – some of our healers are tending them. Most of my father's warriors are gathered around him at the other end of the hall. He sees us enter and calls on us to move forward and join his men.

As we take seats on the floor outside the circle of warriors, he begins to speak.

"Maximus came to thank us for caring for those wounded in the attack against the Sea-wolves yesterday. He was very grateful to see his men in such good hands."

Bledwyn whispers "Maximus came here? He is the Tribune in charge of all the troops in this region and rarely visits the smaller settlements."

I pass that news on to Robyn; then hear her speak to Lance and Taylor in their language.

My father continues "He also told me one of his patrols was attacked by the Sea-wolves yesterday, killing two men and wounding a third. Oddly enough, when they returned later with a greater force to seek vengeance, they found only a single body on the road, although there was blood where the second man fell. They did come across a large force of Sea-wolves and drove them off after a bitter battle. The wounded here in our care, came from that battle."

"He also spoke of rumors that the Sea-wolves were attacked by a dragon. Many died in that attack, so the numbers that met the Roman patrol were far fewer than had been feared. The dragon was a blessing, for the battle would have gone far worse for the Romans had they faced a much greater force. His men heard the sound of a great flying beast through the trees; they were terrified, although they never saw it. He then told of the rumor the same dragon or another like it, was seen here yesterday. He then asked for my response."

"I told him that I too heard rumors, but I could only speak to what I have heard with my ears and seen with my eyes. I told him that yesterday during the day, we heard strange sounds that came from the north, in the direction of Dubri-Tun. Some sounds were like the hooves of many horses running over stones. Others like distant thunder. Then, not long before sunset yesterday, a large beast came through the sky and settled in the fields in front of our gate. This beast also made the noise of many horses and I believe was the source of the sounds we heard earlier. I saw it breathe no fire so cannot speak to that. Three people descended from the belly of the beast. Two were

dressed in green – one had the look of a warrior, though carried no weapon that I could see. The other carried several strange boxes. The third was my own daughter, who had left early in the morning on a journey to the forest as she often does and had not returned. As they approached our gate, we could see that one of her companions, the warrior, was a woman. When they arrived, they told their stories."

"Muirenn told us that she saw the masts of the Sea-wolves' boats when she was in the forest, so ran to warn the people of Dubri-Tun. She arrived too late, for the town was already surrounded and none could enter or leave. As she turned to head for home, she injured herself and was unable to walk. Things would have gone ill for her, had not the lady in green found her and protected her from the Sea-wolves. Muirenn was carried to the home of these strange people. These are the same people who drove the Sea-wolves from the walls of Dubri-Tun, leaving so many of them dead on the fields. People from Dubri-Tun came yesterday during the rain requesting help to burn the dead. We sent six men with horses to their aid. Our men arrived back well after sunset with the report that over one hundred, fifty Sea-wolves lay fallen on the fields. The people of the settlement reported a great beast flew through the air, spewing fire at the Sea-wolves. Many died, while others fled. Many of those who fled also died. Muirenn was in the trees watching this and tells of seeing the woman in green personally kill over sixty of the Sea-wolves, for she can kill from a distance like an archer, yet carries no bow."

"We are told that she makes her home on a large boat, and uses the beast to travel through the air between her boat and the land. She is also not alone, but is the leader of a small company of warriors. I have rarely seen a warrior of greater skill, for she bested my youngest son in manual combat last night. Bledwyn has now gone with her, for he owes a life-guild because she spared his life. I rue the loss, but am happy that we are now allied."

"When he asked about their intentions, I told him that she spoke of a desire for knowledge, and not conquest or plunder. I told him that I do not know her intentions concerning the Roman people, but she does speak their language, albeit with an unusual accent."

"The tribune then asked if this wondrous warrior has a name. I told him that I had not heard one."

"Her name is Robyn." The voice came from behind me. I turn as Bledwyn spoke out. "There are many who owe Robyn for their lives. She saved me yesterday and I owe her a life-guild. She also saved my sister and my kin who live in Dubri-Tun. I can speak to what I have seen. I have seen and ridden within the great flying beast that serves as her steed and spews fire at her enemies. I also saw a boat made of iron – larger than any I have seen before and able to move at great speeds without sail or oar. I also watched as she defended against an attack by the Sea-wolves last night, driving them from our shores. We visited the Sea-wolves abandoned camp today before coming here so I can testify that they are gone."

My father now spoke again. "Maximus doubted my words; he believed that I spoke what I knew, for we trust each other with the truth. He doubted that I'd been told the truth. His words to me were 'Few warriors travel great distances for the sake of knowledge and learning. They come looking for riches or power. How do I know that they've told you the truth; perhaps she concealed her true intentions from you. I think we should attack hard, before they can raise a rebellion against the power of Rome. Once before we underestimated a woman on this island, and look what happened? Many people died. I won't make the same mistake as my predecessor'."

"This is when Gwyn spoke for the first time. He simply said 'Remember the dragon. You may find a fight in this case is more costly than you can afford'."

The room falls silent now that my father has finished his story, so I jump when Robyn speaks right beside me. "I have no argument with the Romans. We are here only to seek knowledge and do not wish to take any more lives. Maximus does not realize that, nor does he realize his danger if he does choose violence. He will not need the century of riders he leads in this direction and will be here within the hour. But we need to get into the air and take care of them."

With that, she stands and starts to the front door. We all follow. When she reaches the door and calls out "Greetings to the people of Tordur" in our language. Then she whispers to me, "Did I say it right?"

I smile. "Yes – you heard Bledwyn this morning."

She nods.

Bledwyn and Marcelus follow us out into the light. As we approach the gates, the sentinels unbar and swing them open. We walk to The Bird, and lift off into the air just as soon as we are all aboard. We fly almost over the main hall, so I can see my father standing looking up at us. Robyn is sitting in the open doorway of The Bird, with her feet on the step we use to climb in, waving as we fly past. As soon as we pass, we turn and head west, into the setting sun. I see her climb back in and reach beside the door. She pulls out a sort of a stick mounted on some sort of pillar. I never noticed it before, but I think it is a larger version of her rifle. She pulls it out in front of the door so it is in front of her when she sits back down.

I hear her speak in my ears. "We will go past Maximus, far to the north of him and then turn so the sun is behind us. We will come in low over the trees – they'll hear us, but won't see us against the sun until we are right on top of them. This gun is loaded with what we call tracers – they will be able to see the bullets coming. I hope that scares them enough that they leave Tordur and your people alone without us having to hurt anyone."

I watch out my window until I feel us turn, leaving the sun behind us. We drop until it looks like I could reach out and touch the tops of the trees as they go by. With the tree tops so close, I can appreciate for the first time just how fast we are moving. Far faster than a horse can gallop – faster even than a hawk can fly. The trees are just a blur as they fly past my window. For the first time during my rides in The Bird, I feel a little again when I think of our speed. I always thought flying through the air would be nice and smooth, but today we keep hitting bumps like we are riding fast over a rough road. When I ask Robyn why it is so rough, she tells me that between the sun, wind, and the trees, there are warm spots where the air is sort of soft. When we hit one, The Bird drops a bit and we feel the bump.

Then she adds, "We are almost to the Romans, so I need to be ready."

I am looking out over her shoulder when we suddenly tilt and I find myself looking straight down onto the road full of more Roman soldiers than I have ever before seen in one place. I can't help it – I scream. They are looking up as if they expect us – of course we make a lot of noise, so they heard us coming. Here the land near the road is quite open, with fields on both sides, so the men are brightly lit by the sun. I can see some of the men shading their eyes with their hands as we pass over them. I can see a group of archers, bows in hand with arrows loaded, ready to fire. I can see them trying to aim at us, but their horses have different ideas. The horses are rearing and trying to get away from this huge beast in the air – I bet most of the men are of the same mind.

Then I see streaks of light coming from Robyn's gun, and see puffs of dirt where they hit the road just in front of the lead horses. This is too much for them – they turn and bolt, running away from Tordur back toward their encampment. I can feel us pull up in the air and slow down as soon as they break in a run. Now it feels like we are barely moving, but we are keeping pace with the horses. Some of the men were thrown from their horses, and now the rider-less horses are running with the rest, leaving the men on the road far behind. Once in a while I can see streaks coming from Robyn's gun, but they go just over the heads of the riders. Then we hit a bump just as she fires, and one of the rider-less horses goes down right in the middle of the pack. Other horses and riders swerve around it, hitting each other as they try to avoid the pileup. I see at least three more horses fall – two with riders.

We chase the soldiers just a little further, then swing away and turn back to look at the men and horses that went down. There are three men, all up looking a little dazed, and running for cover as we approach. I can see four horses on the road – three look to be dead, but one is struggling to get up. Robyn fires, I see the streaks going toward the horse. It collapses on the road and lies still.

She swings her legs in, pulls the gun back, and slides the door closed. I see now that she has straps wrapped around her that are fastened to the floor. She takes them off, hangs them on a hook just inside the door, and comes and sits beside me. "Martin spotted the wounded horse; the men there tried to finish it off, but it was struggling so much they couldn't get close enough. Now it is done. He reported that all the men who were unhorsed when we first flew over them are on their feet and walking home. They look to be okay, so now we can go back to the boat and see what Maximus does."

Chapter 11.

During the flight back to Voyager, I watch the view from Little Bird on my helmet display. Maximus and his lackeys have finally gained control of their horses and are nearing their encampment as we are landing on the ship. Those that are on foot still have a long way to go in the dark. They are not my concern – they're big boys and can look out for themselves. Maximus is the question on my mind. *How will he respond? Will he try a peaceful approach, will he attack us, or will he go after our friends?* Their encampment is close to the town of Wynt, the main center for the tribe and home of the king. Like all the towns we have found so far, it is located on relatively high ground near a river. It also stands beside a main road to the north, one used by Romans and Britons alike. Here, the Romans built a wooden bridge to replace the ancient ford across the river. Already the major center before the Romans came, it has since prospered from their attentions. It now has close to a thousand people by our count, making it by far the most populous place in this entire region.

The area inside the walls is tightly packed with homes, stables, workshops, and a large marketplace. The walls have not expanded as quickly as the population, so the town is mostly filled with structures. Now the only green space is in front of what is clearly King Cydyrn's great hall. The only other open area is the main market street near the west wall. The rest of the town is a jumble of buildings separated by a maze of narrow lanes. More people now also live and work outside the walls, mostly on land to the north and east. What was once farmland is now covered by homes and industry – it reminds me of the urban sprawl of our time. To the west is an open field; the Roman camp is to the south across the river. The camp looks to hold maybe three hundred soldiers plus support workers, so close to four hundred people will call it home.

That night I again watch the faces of men as they fled from the flames, only to run right into my sights. Then the people change in the scene, and it is my family that is running toward me as I spray them with bullets. Once again, I wake covered in sweat. I know I won't get back to sleep without some help, so I twist the cap off the bottle I keep on my nightstand and pour myself a glass. I down it in a single gulp, then stagger off to pee before returning to bed. It doesn't take long before the alcohol slows down my brain and I drift off to sleep.

In our morning meeting we try to guess what Maximus will do so we can plan accordingly. Marcelus knows something of the Roman mind and has been very helpful in teaching us the ways of the camp and the men who lead it. He doesn't think Maximus will attack Tordur – at least not right away. Maximus will try to find out more before he takes action. He will probably first try to make peace. If that doesn't work, he will wait for advice and reinforcements from the south. He saw enough last night to know he doesn't have the strength to defeat us. Instead he ended up leading his men home with his tail between his legs. He didn't lose any men, but some will be bruised and rather footsore this morning after their long walk home last night. He's smart and politically savvy – he won't act until he knows more, and is far more likely to try a peaceful approach rather than risk his men in an attack. Marcellus is pretty sure that he won't want to unleash anything that will prove embarrassing to the Romans – and thus damage his own career. I hope that's true. In any case, I hope he takes a few days to think things over, which will give us time to catch our breath and maybe actually work toward our mission goal: to learn about the people.

Jerry suggests we take some of the team to the beach vacated by the Saxons. We can't keep everyone holed up on the ship forever, so we decide most of the crew can take the afternoon off. It is a fantastic day in June, the sun is shining; the wind and sea are calm. The water is a little cold, but we have wetsuits for those who want to try swimming. The beach is more shingle than sand, but it sure beats sitting on the boat all day. Captain Johansen brings the ship to half a kilometer from the beach. Jerry will fly some sight-seeing trips and drop people off at the beach. Lance has offered to run others ashore in the boat. The bow of the ship faces south, so those who want can stay on board and sunbathe on the deck. Don volunteers to man Little Bird for the afternoon. Tonight's menu of barbeque steaks, baked potatoes, and salads won't take long to prepare, so even Candace gets most the afternoon off.

I'm not much of a swimmer, but I do want to get out of my army green for a while. Bikini, tank top, and sandals – I'm headed back to the beach. At the last moment I grab my radio and earpiece – I don't want to be totally out of touch if something happens. It fits in the cell phone pocket on my tank, so it won't slow me down. Max is going to help me set up a grid so we can document our finds. We should have done that before we disturbed the site, but the spearheads were exciting finds, and I wanted to be sure they didn't disappear. Iron is a valuable commodity in this society, and I am sure this site will be scavenged before long. We didn't find any iron at Dubri-tun and the fact that we found only two spearheads here indicates their value. The Saxons gathered most of them as soon as the fire died down. These two were buried a little deeper and were missed. I found them because the iron showed up on Little Bird's radar so I knew where to look. We've long supposed that invaders came to these shores from north-western Germany, but now we have evidence. The spearheads look to be identical to some found at sites on the continent. Of course, these are in a lot better shape than the ones in museum collections because they just went through a fire instead of getting buried in a bog for two thousand years.

Then there is the boat. I want that boat. It is by far the most intact first-century boat from Northern Europe known to science. In fact it is the earliest boat known from north of the Mediterranean. It's too awkward for the helicopter to lift, but if we can patch the hull and get it out to the Voyager, we can use her crane to get it on board and bring it home. At only thirty-eight feet long, it is only about a third the length of a Roman warship of this period or the much later Viking long-boats. It is a wider relative to its length than either as well. Eight oars to a side – two men to an oar, make a total of thirty-two rowers. Our count gives a total crew of about forty. There is a hold for stores below the feet of the rowers. Two steering oars at the stern provide control, and a single mast with a square sail gives propulsion when the wind is favorable. It is a solid, sea-worthy craft suitable for the journey across the North Sea.

I try to convince Martin that we should take it now, but he reminds me that it is so large that the only spot for it is the helipad on the rear deck – and we need that clear. I finally concede on that point. But we do drag it well up onto the beach so it doesn't get damaged by a high tide and we'll try to recover it before we head home.

We set up a grid and complete the search. The Saxons didn't leave much behind. Some remains from the supplies we destroyed and some scraps of food – that's about it. It could be that others have been here already and collected anything useful. As we are searching, I talk to Muirenn. I give a phrase in Latin, and then she gives it back to me in her language. I repeat it back until I have it down. And I take notes, spelling each word phonetically. After a while, we switch to English lessons. I'm reluctant to teach Muirenn much English because it may make it harder to leave her behind at the end of the mission, but it will make life easier for everyone on the ship if she knows a few basic phrases.

When we finish the search, Muirenn and I sit on a sandy spot and continue with the language lessons. Bledwyn and Marcelus soon join in. Max comes over, too. Early in his student career, he picked up a certificate in teaching ESL, so that makes him better qualified then me to help with the English part. I watch him relax as he starts to teach and am reminded just how much he loves sharing knowledge. He's been wound tight on board the ship, but the stress seems to visibly melt away for him, as we sit on the beach. Those who don't know him well may think it's the limited opportunities for flirting on board that's the source of his stress. True, he's already made passes at all the female crew – and been rebuffed. But the few of us who know him well, know that the truth is far different.

Down the beach I can see Michele and Kelly walking. She seems happy. I hope so – she deserves it. When we first met, she'd just been through the breakup from hell. To forget, she buried herself in her studies and has only in the last few months started coming up for air. Kelly's a nice guy.

My focus shifts from them to Taylor. He's prowling the shore-line, totally focused on capturing that next image. Taylor is one of the few people I truly trust. While preparing for the mission, we spent a lot of time together and had some long talks. He's a survivor of a family filled with addictions and violence, turning to the camera as therapy in his teens. Photography soon became more than an escape. He added film and journalism to his studies and it became his weapon to fight against the cycle of violence. His film school documentary on the success of a violence prevention program in his home town attracted wide-spread interest and earned him a commission from a well known current affairs program to film our work with the displaced people of Afghanistan. He elected to follow my work with Fatima and her son, and it was Fatima's death that turned the film into an award-winner, and forever cemented our personal friendship.

We've both often wondered if Fatima was just in the wrong place at the wrong time, or if she was targeted because she was working with the Americans. Maybe someone saw Taylor filming her, and that made her a high-value target. When she died, it nearly broke me. I don't think I would have been able to keep it together without Taylor. He since told me that I was the only thing keeping him going during those dark days. I told him about my rape and the accident. He told me about the bruises and broken bones, the fights, the constant upheaval in his life; the eighteen schools in twelve years. He cried on my shoulder while I fought back my own tears. Somehow we both managed to survive. So no, there's never been anything romantic between us; our friendship has seen too much death to ever go in that direction.

Maybe it's a rustle of leaves that didn't come from the wind or the snap of a twig, I don't know. Perhaps the whir of a startled bird or the whisper of a voice that didn't sound like an animal. But suddenly I am acutely aware that someone is in the forest behind us. I look around at the group and realize that I broke my own rule that says every landing team must be armed. There are twelve people on the beach and no one is carrying a weapon. I wanted so badly to put yesterday's violence behind me that I didn't want to consider any threats today. Knowing there might be more coming tomorrow is bad enough. So no one is carrying anything more dangerous than sunscreen. At least I had the sense to bring a radio – I don't think anyone else did.

There are five of us in a circle on the sand. Kelly and Michele are a way up the beach. Sandy and April are gathering shells. Michael and Andrew are flinging a Frisbee. Lance just left the beach with Candace and Francois – they're headed back to the ship to fire up the barbeque. I check our air-support. Jerry has Martin and John in the chopper – they're about thirty minutes south and are heading back to the ship already. Don is mapping with Little Bird to the north-west and can't give us a visual for at least twenty minutes. I do catch Lance at the ship – he'll grab a couple of weapons when he comes back to the beach. I just hope it doesn't come to fighting. I'm hardly dressed for combat, as my fluorescent bikini and white tank certainly won't offer any camouflage in the forest – or pretty much anywhere else for that matter.

I tell the group about the noise –someone is out there. Muirenn tells me the people in this area are closely related to her tribe but she has never been this far herself. Their language is almost the same, so if they are locals we will be able to communicate. Bledwyn has been to their chief town, but never to any of the smaller settlements. Most of the people are farmers and herders so no doubt are as relieved as we are that the Sea-wolves have been driven off. Now they may be curious about the victors and are probably worried that the newcomers will be just as bad.

Most important thing now is to relieve their fears so they don't launch a pre-emptive strike. We all get up and face the woods. Maybe when they see there are women here and no weapons in sight they will find it easier to believe that we come in peace.

Bledwyn shouts out "Greetings people of the forest. We are here in peace to celebrate with our women-folk a victory over the Sea-wolves. I am Bledwyn, son of Cynbel, from Tordur. With me is my sister and companions from across the Great Water who aided us in the victory. We will shortly return to our companions' boat to eat a meal. You are welcome to join us, if you wish."

Silence. I see a shadow; a bearded face. The others on the beach realize something is up and start to gather around us. I'm not sure it's a great idea, but maybe they'll see there are too few of us to be a threat or maybe that there enough that they won't risk an attack. It depends on how many there are and whether they are armed. There are three faces now, two bearded and the third hairless. They keep to the shadows, so I can't tell if the third is a woman or a youth.

Muirenn spots the faces and takes a few steps forward. "We won't hurt you"

Slowly, one steps from the shadow of the woods. She is a young woman, probably no older than Muirenn, dressed in the clothes of a peasant, and she's in trouble. Her face is grey with pain, the way she holds her left arm, I'm pretty sure it is broken. Her clothes are soaked with blood down the right side. And she looks to be about eight months pregnant.

"Lance," I shout over the radio. "Forget the weapons. Grab Kelly's medical kit and get here as fast as you can." I dash forward. Both Muirenn and I reach her just as she stumbles, we help her as she collapses to the beach. Sandy and Kelly are both right behind us.

"Kelly, Lance is on the way with your kit."

Kelly nods as he and Sandy get to work on the woman. I'd like to back off and give them room, but I need to translate their questions into Latin for Muirenn, she translates them into her language. The ragged responses come back the opposite direction. Her forearm is broken; it's a simple fracture so we'll get it set on the ship. The blood is from a bad cut on her side, just below her ribs. It's not deep enough to have hit anything vital, but she's lost a lot of blood. It has mostly stopped, but there is some oozing from the wound. She's conscious, but barely.

Just then Michael runs up with the medical kit and a rifle. I am so involved with the girl that I didn't even hear the boat arrive.

He hands me the rifle. "Lance had it in his hands when your call came in, so he decided to bring it along any way." Kelly grabs the kit and flips it open.

Now I sit back and let them go to work. Kelly gets an IV line into her and starts her on some plasma while Sandy attaches the monitor, then gets a pain killer ready, followed by a broad spectrum antibiotic. Kelly hands me the IV bag, so I stand up and play IV pole. Once the meds are in her, Kelly works on bandaging her side; Sandy works an inflatable splint onto her arm. The splint is just in place when she starts to puke. They roll her on her side fast so she won't drown in her own vomit. I'm standing, watching the waves roll in, wondering how we can bring in the chopper for a med-evac without scaring off the rest of her people, when I hear Muirenn beside me.

"Will she be okay?"

"Yes, it looks like she got here in time. Sandy will want to get her back to the boat, where we can treat her better. I'm worried about the waves; the water is getting rough, so I think we'll give her a ride in The Bird. Can you let them know so they're not scared off?"

I look past Muirenn, and realize there is another stranger beside her – a girl, younger than the one on the ground. Apart from some scrapes, this one appears to be uninjured. A definite similarity in appearance and the tracks of tears down her very dirty face make the connection. "Her sister?" I ask.

"Yes."

Beyond her are two men, older and bearded. As Muirenn explains about the huge bird that will come to take us to the boat in the distance, I ask Jerry to come to the beach on the way back. I can feel myself relax now that the crisis is over. I'm surprised to realize my rifle is hanging from my shoulder. I remember Michael bringing it, but I don't remember taking it from him. I think of my apparel – this is a rather odd combination. Oh well, at least now I can protect the team. And Taylor has pictures so I won't forget.

Slowly we get the story of the four refugees. There were six of them – four men and the two girls – working in a field yesterday morning planting a crop of beans when the Sea-wolves suddenly broke out of the forest. The man closest to them was speared immediately. The rest happened to be near far end of the field and turned to flee. Luseth – the wounded girl – was a little slower than the rest, and was just reaching the forest and diving around a tree, when a spear grazed her. She fell, breaking her arm. Her husband saw what happened and turned back to help her. He took a spear in the stomach for his efforts. Luseth and the rest got away for the Sea-wolves didn't pursue them into the woods. They were in a field distant from home and were afraid to go back to their settlement, thinking that it would be under attack. They'd heard of a settlement of healers to the south and with a strand of hope tried to get Luseth there. They were soon in unfamiliar territory, and between the fear and the grief, got lost. They spent a cold and hungry night in the woods, but kept walking this morning, because the only alternate was to give up. They heard our voices and headed our direction. They had been watching for a few minutes wondering if it would be safe to approach before I became aware of their presence. When Bledwyn gave his speech, they argued quietly among themselves the best course of action. They were trying to decide when Luseth struggled to her feet and deciding that she had nothing to lose, staggered onto the beach. They had no idea the Sea-wolves had been defeated or that this was where they landed until we told them.

I hear the chopper coming now. Jerry sets down just above the high water mark. Michael and Max run to get the stretcher – after yesterday we decided to keep one on board. All hands together lift her up so they can slide it under her. Then it's across the stony ground to the chopper. Lots of hands lift her aboard. We get all four newcomers, Taylor, Kelly, Sandy, Muirenn, Bledwyn, and me aboard. Michele, Martin, and John decide to take the boat back, so Marcelus comes along too, riding in the right front seat. The flight is only a couple of minutes; then Luseth gets transferred to a gurney for the quick trip to sick bay. I'm still holding the IV bag so I hook it onto a pole and follow the crowd. Muirenn and I can't leave yet in case we're needed for translation. Luseth is still drifting in and out of consciousness, so she probably won't be talking for a while, but our medical team will check over the other three. But first they cross match her blood and get a transfusion going.

Sandy spent years working in the ER and spent vacations doing volunteer work in clinics in developing nations. She knew what we needed to bring and right now I am so glad that we have her, and that we listened when she listed her supplies and equipment. Like the digital x-ray they are using on the arm, and the ultrasound that will check her baby a little later. By the time they finish getting her arm in a cast and her side stitched up, she's starting to come around, but is still pretty groggy.

While we are waiting, Muirenn and I talk to her sister. We learn her name is Genovea, and that they live in a settlement about twenty-five kilometers to the northwest of the beach. Their community raises crops and sheep. The wool they weave into fabric for their clothes and for trade; the crops are their main source of food. The spring rains this year kept them from planting some fields until now, so they are rushing to finish the job in the hopes of a decent harvest. That is why even the pregnant girl gets put to work out in the fields.

They think the Sea-wolves left the field in the direction of their settlement so they have no idea what they will find when they get home. Probably the group they ran into was one of the scouting or foraging parties we saw returning to the beach. Probably they were looking for food, which is why the freshly-planted field didn't interest them enough to pursue the escaping laborers. It sounds like the wall around their village is pretty flimsy; more suited for keeping sheep in than raiders out. If the Sea-wolves got that far, I am afraid their people and flocks may have paid the price. Little Bird is back on board now – after dinner we will send it up for a look in the area to see if we can spot their home.

Genovea doesn't want to leave her sister, but we finally convince her to get something to eat. I think the aroma of barbequing beef may have changed her mind. I know from Muirenn that they don't get meat very often. Since the people of Tordur are relatively wealthy, they can afford meat more frequently those in the smaller agrarian settlements such as Genovea's home. I bet they only get meat on special holidays and never beef. Considering that all they've eaten in the last two days is what they could find in the forest, the offer of a real meal is hard to resist. Luseth is barely conscious and isn't up to eating anything yet, but I feel a little mean leaving her behind as I lead Genovea and the guys out onto the rear deck. All three are dirty and have plenty of scrapes and cuts, but we'll get them cleaned up after we eat.

Sandy sends Kelly out with us. Once he's eaten, she'll come and get her dinner. He likes his steaks rare; she likes them well done, so this arrangement will keep them both happy and Luseth won't be left alone until she's stable and fully awake. Our visitors need some help loading up their plates. Steaks they understand although beef is a very rare commodity for them. Potatoes are a totally new food, but it looks like they are all getting into the idea of loading them up with butter and sour cream. Salad greens are familiar to them, but Caesar salad dressing is something else new. Fresh rolls top off the main course. Watermelon is for dessert.

I sit back and watch the newcomers interact with our team. The anthropologist in me says we shouldn't be interacting with them and certainly shouldn't expose them to our culture and technology. The soldier in me sees them as the people we are fighting for; the victims of war who need to be given safe shelter. The human in me just wants to make sure they all get home in one piece. Of course, Bledwyn and Muirenn are the only ones who can really talk with them. Max and I are both trying out our new Brythonic knowledge, but progress is slow, so Muirenn is frequently called in to help translate

Andrew is showing Elsidd, the older of the two, how to use a knife and fork. He is uncle to the two girls, and is probably about forty, but looks sixty. Nyn, the younger of the two is eating like he's afraid someone might come and take his meal from him. He has one arm protectively around his plate while he shovels his food in as fast as possible with the other. *What will he do when he learns he can have more?* I wonder how long has it been since any of them had a meal like this. April is with Genovea, learning how to navigate the mess hall. Once they've finished eating, she'll help get her cleaned up and then Kelly will to tend her scrapes. He'll also get the guys cleaned and patched up.

As soon as dinner is over, we launch Little Bird back into the sky. With the long June days, we still have a good four hours of daylight to go searching for the refugees' home. We can search just as well in the dark, but we need them to identify their settlement, and it is a lot easier for rookies to recognize features in daylight. We know they have about twenty huts enclosed by a wall, with a large sheep pen in one corner. There is a second pen outside the wall to the west. They told us they don't have a hall, but the chieftain's hut is larger than the rest. A cooking lean-to against the north wall completes the enclosure. We think they are about two kilometers east of the main road and about fifteen north of the town we spotted yesterday. Unlike the larger settlements we have seen, this one is not on a river or a hill-top. It's just a little collection of huts surrounded by fields. Jack will fly just east of the road, with the camera in wide angle, and it should be a snap to find. I just hope we got the right information from them. None of these people have ever before been this far from home, so their geographical knowledge is limited. Add in the language differences and we could be quite a bit off in our understanding.

It doesn't take long before Jack gives me a call – he found a candidate twelve kilometers north and just under three from the road. It looks to meet the description, but it's clear the Saxons have been there. The pen outside the wall is broken, open and empty. The town itself hasn't been burned, but there doesn't seem to be many signs of life. I send Muirenn to the sick bay to see if any of our guests are ready and to bring any able to come. Then I dash up the stairs to Mission Control. By the time I get there, Jack has zoomed in and added an infrared overlay. There are sheep lying in the shade of the wall and clear signs of people in the cooking area. Not many people are visible, but enough to know some are still living there. We search the surrounding area and find more people working in the fields. But we can also see bodies lying in the fields outside the wall, so clearly not everyone survived the attack. When we hear footsteps approaching, Jack heads the drone back over the town site. Let's make sure we have the right place before we let them see the bodies.

Muirenn and Marcelus rush in, followed by the three guests and Kelly, pushing Luseth in a wheelchair. She was awake and couldn't bear to be left behind. Bledwyn brings up the rear. The big screen shows the view from overhead. Muirenn explains this as a drawing, from a bird that remembers everything it sees and creates this image so we know what it saw. I point out the features – the wall, the sheep pen, the huts. Then I try out my new language skills, "Is this your home?"

Nyn is the first to say yes. Luseth, Elsidd, and finally Genovea each recognize specific things that convince them that this is home. When we fly over the bodies, I see shock and sadness in their faces. People they know are dead. They can also see the flock they rely on for their livelihood has been decimated. I see them all stare silently at the sight before them. In the silence, I slide over to Kelly and ask about Luseth – can she go home?

"She'll be okay in the helicopter, but I'd really like for her to come back so we can keep an eye on her at least overnight. We'll need her back in a month to get the cast off her arm – and she will be giving birth about that time too."

"We need to get you home tonight." That's beyond my skills, so I speak in Latin and Muirenn translates. Before we leave, I stop at my room and get changed. I'm in full combat gear this time. I think the others are starting to feel a little chilly, because each one disappears and returns a few minutes later wearing more clothing. We were able to get the blood and dirt cleaned from the clothes from the four refugees, so they'll return home nice and clean.

Jack's now flying the drone south to see what the Romans are up to. Trace is on flight duty for the chopper tonight, so she gets started on the pre-flight checks as we bundle everyone down to the pad and get them aboard. As we expected, Luseth refuses to be left behind. It's her home, her people that were attacked. Sandy checks her vitals and gives her clearance to fly. We've got a full slate on board: Kelly is coming in case there are wounded, Lance and Michael are on security, Muirenn for translation duties. Then we have the four refugees. Taylor and I complete the crew. This time, I am fully armed. I won't make that same mistake I made this afternoon.

While we are in the air, Jack comes back with the news on the Romans. Another three hundred troops have just arrived in the camp near Wynt from another garrison to the south. From the images, we are guessing this was a planned transfer of forces and not a temporary reinforcement because they came with a train of fifty wagons worth of supplies – enough to keep them for months. They are pitching tents and unloading supplies. This looks to be the start of a long-planned offensive. Probably it will take them a couple of days to get settled before they move out, so we don't need to act tonight. Good. Maybe we can come up with a plan to discourage them that doesn't involve killing people. For the rest of the flight I stare out the window in silence and think about our next steps.

I barely notice when we touch down in the field just outside the settlement. Once again, we get to approach the gates of a town full of terrified people and give them good news. Like most towns we have seen so far, the main gate of this one faces west, so is spot-lit by the evening sun as we approach. No faces appear over the wall as we approach. Elsidd is the first to speak. Nyn and Genovea follow in turn. There is no response until Luseth also speaks up. Then the gate moves a bit, but remains nearly closed. Elsidd breaks into a run, followed by the rest of the team. He and I reach the wall at the same time, and press on the gate. It swings open, and we find ourselves facing a teen-aged boy armed with a bow. Gathered in an arc on both sides of him are perhaps thirty others of various ages. A few are armed with spears; one has a sword. The rest are carrying pointed sticks or rocks.

I'm just trying to decide whether to raise my hands or reach for my weapon when the boy with the bow spots Elsidd. He relaxes the bow, drops it to the ground, and runs to Elsidd, and throws his arms around him.

As the reset of the team come up behind us. Nyn explains to Muirenn, who passes the news on to me. "This is his youngest son."

Weapons are lowered and we enter the gates. Once they are closed behind us, we gather around and get the story. The day before yesterday, around noon, a band of Sea-wolves burst from the trees armed with spears and swords. Many of the villagers were out in the fields and only a few were able to reach the safety of the walls or escape to the forest. Those that were caught were killed. They expected to be attacked, but the Sea-wolves just went for the sheep penned outside the walls. They slaughtered and took the entire flock, leaving in the direction they came. Of the people, only thirty-five escaped injury. Another ten were more or less injured – Kelly turns a little green when he learns the number of patients, but we explain that he is a healer and will look at each of the injured. One of the villagers offers to lead him. Lance goes with them to lend a hand. Our four brings the total number of survivors to nearly fifty – only about half the population that lived here before the attack. Most of the very young were in the settlement, so they survived. Most of those lost were teens and adults for they were working in the fields to plant crops – the town most of their main workers. Luseth and Genovea lost both parents, Elsidd lost his wife and daughter, but his two sons both survived. Nyn's wife is among the injured. Their two-year old survived unharmed.

They had assumed all six people working in the far field were probably killed, so seeing these four alive brings the survivors to tears. After so much loss, they almost don't know how to handle this gift of life. All four have to repeat the story of their survival several times, and Luseth has to show off her stitches. I'm a little surprised at her willingness to hitch her dress up well past her waist to expose the wound on her side in front of the entire village. No one seems to be overly shocked – I guess after growing up in a world of one-room homes, naked bodies are nothing special.

We have to tell our story, too. I explain that we came from across the Great Water in a large boat, and that we are here to protect and learn, not to conquer. I tell them we drove off the Sea-wolves so they won't be back anytime soon. And that I am so sorry that we arrived too late to save their people. I add that we are watching the Romans, and will try to keep them from attacking the people, too. Of course, it isn't quite so smooth and concise, since I am still speaking to Muirenn in Latin, and then she translates. The people have a lot of questions, about us, and our 'bird,' and how can so few of us fight off an army of Sea-wolves. I explain about the dragon – that the steed we ride can breathe down fire on enemies, and the Sea-wolves left after our fire destroyed their weapons and some of their boats.

Kelly and Lance are still treating the wounded, so we go looking for them. On the way, I hear a whimper from Luseth, and an echo from Genovea walking beside her. At almost the same time, I feel Taylor bump into me and whisper in my ear, "Time to switch out of soldier mode, and take care of them. No one knows better than you what they are going through."

The image of a destroyed truck, flames, a hospital ceiling, and four coffins flash before me. He's right. I face the girls as Taylor guides Muirenn beside me. "I'm sorry; I should have stopped and taken the time for you two." I pause as Muirenn translates. "You lost your parents, and Luseth, you lost your husband. And I, of all people, ignored you." Another pause for me to gather my words. "I was about your age Luseth, when I saw my parents, my little sister, and the man who was to be my husband, all die. I just want you both to know that I am here for you. Both of you can come and stay with me on my boat if you would like." Another pause for translation and to give me time to collect my thoughts. "Luseth, you might have some bad days with pain from your arm. If you are with us, we can help you. Sandy wants to check your arm and side every few days to make sure you are healing right. And she will need to take out your stitches and take your cast off once you are healed."

I hear Muirenn add some words of her own. I think she says "And I want you to come, so we can be friends." I'm pretty sure I'm right by the way both girls light up with smiles. Genovea throws her arms around Muirenn, almost knocking her over. I nearly forgot that is was only yesterday that she sprained her ankle. Luseth throws her arms around me, clonking me on the back of the head with her cast. I shouldn't have left my helmet in the chopper. Clearly they were both hoping they could stay with us for a while.

By the time we reach them, Kelly and Lance were nearly finished. The most seriously wounded never made it back to the walls, but were slain where they lay. Those who survived have injuries sustained while escaping – mostly scrapes and bruises, with a couple with deeper cuts from weapons. They clean and bandage the scrapes, suture the deeper wounds and administer antibiotics. There are a couple of people with more serious injuries: a dislocated shoulder and a fractured ankle. Kelly wants to take them both back to the ship. Nyn's wife suffered a bad cut, but she's okay here, so he stays with her. Elsidd will stay with his sons, so we have room in the chopper to take the two wounded.

Both are young men; the one with the broken ankle is a shepherd who tried to save sheep. But the Saxons were too close, so he not only couldn't save any of his sheep, but he managed to step in a hole while running for safety himself. Fortunately he was not alone and the others managed to drag him back within the gates before the Saxons arrived. The second was working in a field and climbed a tree to escape – and fell trying to get back down. With the loss of manpower, both are needed in the fields to finish the planting and care for the remaining animals. And both will be out of commission for several weeks, but we will do whatever we can to help them heal quicker.

Chapter 12.

By the time The Bird takes to the air to fly us back to the boat, the sun is nearly down. I've been trying to hide the throbbing pain in my foot all day, but I'm not sure I can do it much longer. I'm so afraid of disappointing Robyn. All my life I've always lived on stories from the other world. Around the fire on long winter nights someone always called for a story. Usually it was me. Even when I was very young, I loved the tales of heroes and magic. If we were lucky enough to have a bard staying with us, we might get a ballad in song. If not, my father or one of the other men would start one of their favorites. I never quite believed they could be true, but in my bed at night or during my walks in the forest, I'd dream of meeting one of the great heroes of in these legends. My favorite stories were those of the green man of the forest. I'm sure Robyn's people must be of the same kind even though they're not the least bit as I imagined in my dreams. I always thought of them as strong, arrogant, and a little mean; I dreamed of having the courage to stand before one of them without quaking. But they are so kind and gentle, yet with far more power than I ever imagined. I say "they," but I really mean Robyn. She is the one who saved me and is the leader of the whole team. But when we talk, I feel so intimidated and shy – I've never felt that way before. In my world, I'm the one everyone my age looks up to. But now I'm the one looking up. And I can't let her down by appearing to be weak. So I grit my teeth and try to ignore the pain by focusing my attention on something else.

It isn't just Robyn. All the people here treat Bledwyn and me so nicely. It's not because I'm the daughter of a chieftain, since they also treat Luseth and Genovea with the same gentleness and they are just peasants; tillers of the land. I look at them across The Bird as we soar through the air. Genovea is almost asleep, leaning against her sister. Luseth is staring straight ahead, looking like she's too terrified to move. I bet her arm is hurting, too. I go back to looking outside and watch the boat draw near in the fading light.

As soon as we land, the two injured men are loaded onto cots and are wheeled away to the sick bay by Kelly and Lance. As soon as they are safely on the way, Robyn comes over and helps the three of us out of The Bird. I can't help but wince as my foot hits the floor. I glance at the other two as I follow Robyn inside. Luseth looks like she's just barely holding together and Genovea isn't doing much better. Taylor and Robyn lead all three of us into the sick bay. A table near the door holds four tiny bowls holding what look like little berries of different sizes and colors. Each bowl is marked with some of the symbols they use for words. There are cups of water beside the bowls. Robyn grabs one bowl with two berries and hands it to me.

"Take these, don't' chew them, just swallow. Drink some water to wash them down. This red one will help with the pain in your foot, and this little white one will keep it from swelling. And here," she adds pointing to the symbols, "is your name written in our language."

The next bowl she gives to Luseth. "You'll need one for the pain in your arm and your side. You also get this big white pill. It should help your arm heal quicker. The big red one will help you recover from the blood you lost. And this green one will help to keep you and your baby healthy. And this is your name written in our language." Of course, I have to translate for her.

The next bowl is for Genovea. She just gets one of the green pills. The last one is for Robyn. She points to the symbols on the bowl. "That is my name."

I don't get how these symbols are people's names. I look at the symbols and can't make much sense of them until Robyn explains.

"These symbols represent sounds. We put them together to match the sound of the word. It's more complex than that, because there are a lot of rules and exceptions, but once you learn the letters, you can pretty much guess how a word will sound. If the Romans give us some peace, we will spend some time more tomorrow learning each other's language. But now, we need to translate for Sandy and Kelly again."

We head over to the cots with the two injured men. Robyn explains that both have been given something to reduce their pain, and now Sandy is using her special camera that looks inside so she can see the bones. She used it on me yesterday and Luseth earlier today, but today for the first time I want to watch, and see the bones too. Robyn and I gather around as Sandy points out how the bones of the arm should fit into the shoulder joint. Kelly, Robyn, and I all work together to explain to the man with the dislocated shoulder, how we will put it back. Kelly *twists, pushes, and there's a pop as the arm slips back into place. Meanwhile, Sandy is getting the other man a brace – almost the same as the one I have. Sandy saw that his ankle wasn't broken, just a sprain. A bad one even worse than mine. By the time they are done, the sun is long down and we are all so tired we can barely stand.*

I'm not used to staying up later than the sun, for when the sun goes down it gets too dark to do much more than tell stories. These people have things that create light. Not the dim, flickering light of a fire or lamp, but a strong, steady light that seems to come from everywhere. Inside the boat it is so bright that I almost forget that outside it is night. But it is. So when April comes to watch over the wounded men in case they need help during the night, we all head off to bed. Luseth and Genovea refuse to be separated, so they share one of the beds in my room. It doesn't take us long to shed our clothes and get into bed. Sleep comes quickly for me, but sometime in the night I wake to the sound of a clunk followed by a squawk from Genovea. She comes over and crawls in beside me – a tossing Luseth managed to hit her in the head with a rock-hard arm and she decides it might be safer in my bed.

I'm not used to sharing a bed with anyone so the presence of another body keeps me from sleeping well for the rest of the night. Since my father is chieftain, our house is larger than most and has two rooms – one for sleeping and the second for eating and gathering during the day. Sometimes my mother cooks food in our hut, but most cooking happens in the big kitchen behind the hall. The sleeping room is big enough that my two brothers and I each have a bed of our own – my parents share a bed of course. Now that Gwyn is married and has a home of his own, there is even more space. Most huts are much smaller with only a single room that serves for all purposes. All the huts in Genovea's village were like that, so she is used to sharing a bed. She falls to sleep right away, and I lie on my back staring at the roof.

When night is fading into the grey light of dawn, it starts to rain. I listen to the rain fall for a while, and then prop my head up with my arm so I can look across the room over Genovea's head. It's bigger than the sleeping room of my home - bigger than most of the huts in Tordur. And this is a room that usually holds only two people. There is a smaller room right beside this one that is totally amazing. There they have clean cold or hot water at a touch – whenever you need it – so you can stay clean and this sort of a chair that is way better than having to get up and go over to the latrine like we have at home. Then there are the lights – they are unbelievable. There is this little thing on the wall by the door that makes the light go on and off. Genovea kept playing it last night until I thought Luseth was going to throw something at her. There is also a little light for each bed, which have little things you turn. The lights do get a little warm but I can touch them – not anything like a fire. I don't have a clue what is in them to create the light. I just can't get over how these people from the other world have everything. I thought the Romans had a lot of curious things, but they don't have even half as much as our new friends.

Then there's the food. They have so much – and such a variety. We mostly eat what we grow and raise: wheat, barley, beans, and greens; plus milk and sometimes meat from our animals. We get fish from the river or gather eggs from birds' nests to add variety. Most years we have enough to eat, but if the crops are bad, things can be pretty lean. Somehow, I don't think these people ever go to bed hungry. But thinking about food has got me hungry, so I slide out of bed carefully so as to not disturb Genovea, and throw on some clothes. I thought I was quiet enough to not wake them, but when I look in their direction I notice two sets of eyes watching me.

"I'm going to see who is up and get something to eat. You can come with me if you are hungry."

Two sets of feet hit the floor, so I wait until they get dressed and we all head down to the place where we eat. The room is dark, but I can hear people talking just around the corner, so we head into a part of the boat I have never seen before. I find Michele, April, Martin, and another man whose name I can't remember all in this room with some really strange chairs and other things. Michele is sitting in this odd chair with rests for her feet that move them almost like she is running. Martin and the other guy are both walking on these platforms that move under their feet, so they walk without going anywhere. April is lying down on a bench, trying to push a metal bar toward the roof. It looks to be heavy, because she lets it down and has to try again. All four are breathing hard and sweating, so this can't be easy. I don't understand – it seems like all of them are doing a lot of work, but I can't tell what they are trying to do. And there's no one I can speak with to ask.

Michele stops what she is doing, and grabs a piece of cloth to wipe her face. She picks up a little box and starts touching it. Then she looks toward us and says something – I recognize the word "Robyn" but nothing else. April gets up and looks at us, then pats the bench she was lying on. I think she wants one of us to try what she was doing. I start in that direction, but Genovea gets there ahead of me. She lies down, grabs the bar – and is barely able to move it. April gently presses down on the bar, and I see Genovea relax. April then reaches behind the bar, over Genovea's head, so she twists around to see what is going on - and pulls a little piece of metal out of this big black block, and sticks it back in, in another spot. She steps away, lifting her hand off the bar, and I see Genovea try again to lift the bar. This time it moves, and I see the block is actually a stack of flat plates – some move with the bar, some don't. I think they must weigh quite a bit, because that is why it is so hard to lift that bar. But I still can't figure out why they are doing this. It just doesn't make sense.

Robyn now comes into the room, drying her wet hair with a cloth.

Luseth immediately goes to her and says "We were hungry and Muirenn thought maybe we could find some food." I'd almost forgotten why we got up, but she hasn't. But then, she was getting her side sewn together and her arm fixed when we were eating last night – I don't know when she ate last. Maybe that's why food is top of her mind.

Robyn laughs. "Well come on, let's get you something."

With that, she leads us all toward the place where we eat. We are almost there before the significance of the exchange struck me: I didn't need to translate. Robyn understood Luseth and replied in our language. I look at her and raise my eyebrow to ask the question "how did you do that?"

She whispers to me "When Michele told me you were all down here I guessed maybe you were hungry, and worked out how to respond on my way down."

The room where we eat is now brightly lit and several people are here. We help Luseth and Genovea as we gather our food and carry it to a table. Of course, Luseth can only use one arm, so she gets extra help from Robyn. I watch as Genovea boldly digs into the unfamiliar fare, while Luseth carefully picks at it while she decides what she is going to risk eating. Eventually, her hunger wins out and she does eat, but you can tell she'd really rather have something else. Or maybe it's just that she'd rather be someplace else.

After we finish eating, we all go up to the room with the fancy chairs and pictures on the wall that change where they always go when they want to see what is happening and make plans. Genovea runs into the room and stands there, staring at the pictures on the wall as they change and move. Luseth is terrified. She won't come in until Robyn takes her by the hand and whispers something to her. Only then will she allow herself to be led to one of the chairs. She sits down and slowly looks around, but still looks pretty tense. I thought maybe with the clouds and rain, we wouldn't be able to watch from the sky today, but they send up their Little Bird and we can see the Roman encampment almost as clearly as we could yesterday.

Once everyone has gathered, Robyn asks if I can translate for her. I guess she has reached the limit of the words she learned in our language. She tells us first that the men they patched up last night are still sleeping – when they awake and have been fed, they will take them back home – Luseth and Genovea too, if they want. I take a glance at them. Luseth relaxes, while Genovea looks torn, like she can't decide what she wants to do. Then Robyn adds that we will make other trips, now that we are friends we will be able to visit. And Luseth will need to come back once her arm is healed to remove the cast.

Once that is settled, we discuss the Romans and what to do with them. They are moving more men and supplies into their camp. Robyn suggests that we visit Wynt, and offer our support to the king. Someone else asks what they might do if we destroyed their supplies – would they go home like the Sea-wolves did? Marcelus responds that if we destroyed most of them, they would likely replace them by pillaging the settlements in the area. If we attacked their columns when they are moving men and supplies, it might work better. It would make them more careful – increasing the number of guards, moving at night, and changing routes. Since we will be watching them from the sky and can see them even at night, it won't matter what they do – we will find them.

As I translate the words to our language for Bledwyn and the rest, Genovea speaks up. I'd almost forgotten that she and Luseth were beside me, they were so quiet. "Instead of destroying their food, can you take some from them and give it to my people? In a normal year, we are barely able to raise enough to last until next harvest. This year with so many of our workers dead or wounded, food will be scarce. Most of those that are left are the old or very young – most of those who were in the fields that day are now wounded or dead. Many of our flocks were destroyed so we won't have much wool to trade for food. Can you help us?" The tears start rolling down her cheeks as she speaks.

I translate for Robyn and she translates to her own language for everyone else. There is a tense silence in the room until Taylor speaks and you can see the people relax. Robyn explains to me that there is an old legend in their land of a hero with her name, a man who took from the rich and gave to the poor –which is pretty much what Genovea has asked us to do. Taylor just reminded them who is in the room – that is why they're all smiling. But in the end, we decide to wait and see what the Romans do before we attack. Robyn doesn't want to be the one who starts something. But she also promises Genovea to do something to help the people in her town.

We also decide to watch Wynt and maybe visit the king there soon. Marcelus and Robyn think that if the people there are preparing to defend themselves from the Romans, we should be able to tell from the air. They may work to strengthen the walls and call up warriors from the surrounding settlements. Or they may gather supplies to prepare for a siege. We'll watch who comes and goes, and look for changes to the walls. If we can't see signs of change, we might have to go there ourselves so we can hear what the people are saying. We're pretty sure that even if the king welcomes the Romans, there are many in the town that will resist them. Bledwyn has been there several times and knows a few that he is sure will not desire any form of association with the Romans.

Before we go, Robyn wants to learn more of our language so she will better understand the people. Good, I'm tired of having to translate everything. I think Robyn is too. So we spend the rest of the morning in language lessons – Bledwyn, Luseth, and Genovea all share our language. Max, Taylor, Don and Kelly all join Robyn in trying to learn. I think Kelly is here because he's tired of the three-way translation too. I'm not sure why Taylor is here, because he has these boxes that remember everything they see and hear, but isn't using them. We learn Robyn's language is called "English" – and I think everyone is surprised when Genovea is the first one to put words together and make herself understood in the new language. That includes Genovea.

I really looked at her then for the first time. She's probably almost the same age as me – I'm guessing that Luseth is a bit older, and they must be only a year or so apart. She's actually a little taller than her sister, and her long hair is raven black – even darker than mine, and my hair is pretty dark. I grew up mostly ignoring the children of the herders and planters. There are a couple of other girls about my age in Tordur and since the place is so small we knew each other, but really didn't cross paths that much. I spent most of my time with my mother learning the skills of a healer. They were in the fields or maybe the cooking area with their mothers. Only in the evenings when we gathered in the hall for stories and songs would we meet. Sometimes we'd talk, but it was hard to find anything to talk about. Even the boys they knew were not ones open to me, so we didn't even have that in common.

There was one other girl, the daughter of another healer. Because she was also learning the art, we were together a lot. She was a year or so older than me, but close enough that we could talk for hours about so many things. She was so much like an older sister, but a couple of years ago she got a pox that we couldn't cure and she died. Since then, I haven't had any close friends. The two girls in Tordur I haven't seen much since they both got married. I couldn't even tell you the color of either one's eyes.

Genovea's are another matter. She has these brilliant green eyes – almost the color of spring leaves in the sun. Those are eyes I will never forget.

Robyn has a little box lying on the table in front of her, like the one Michele used this morning. It makes a buzzing sound, kind of like a fly. She picks it up and starts touching it. I can see that it has writing on it – I think I recognize the symbols, but I don't know what they mean – I can see they change as she touches it. Then she tells us that the men are awake, so we need to go down and help them get something to eat. Just in time too; I'm getting hungry.

Robyn leads all of us downstairs and we take the two men to the place where we eat. Their eyes get big – never in their lives have they seen such a variety of food – and we show them how to pick their meals and carry then to a table. As soon as we sit down, Michele comes over with some many-colored things in her hands. She hands one to each of us – except Robyn who grabs a brown one from her hand so fast, that she has it before Michele realizes what is happening. Then Michele says something to Robyn.

She laughs, and then tells us, "Let's see if you can figure out what these are."

I look at the one in my hand. It is about as long as my hand, but thin; bright yellow and covered with symbols. Luseth's is red and a different shape, Genovea's is also yellow and different again. Bledwyn has one with a bunch of colors – one of the others is mostly white with some silver metal. These people do like their metal. Now, I take a closer look at mine. I'm guessing it is some kind of food, since that is what we do here. It is kind of soft on the outside, but when I press on it I can feel something harder inside. The outside feels smooth and seems to be thin – I think maybe it is a covering. I've seen others here take a covering off things before they eat them, so I try that. Sure enough, the cover tears away easily and I am left with this brown thing. It is long, and kind of lumpy; it really doesn't look very appetizing, but I smell it anyway. I can see everyone else is watching me to see what I'm going to do. Some have followed my lead and are removing the covering, too.

It smells okay, so I take a bite. Just a little nibble from one end. It is so good! I've never tasted anything like it before. It is sweet but so different from honey. And there are crunchy things inside. My second bite is a lot bigger than the first. Luseth and Genovea are right behind me. Robyn and Michele are laughing, which has me a little worried, until they start eating theirs' too. The men are a little more cautious but now that all the rest of us are eating they get the idea and join in.

Robyn explains that it's called chocolate – and she guessed that the women would figure out pretty quick what to do with it. In their world, women are known for their love of chocolate. I can see why. I want more. But the rest of the meal also beckons so I turn my attention to other food. I have a kind of bread, covered with what I think is cheese, a meat I don't recognize, mushrooms, and some sort of spicy red sauce. It's all hot so the cheese is melted and sticky. Bledwyn likes it – he told me to give it a try. It's okay, but I like the chocolate better.

As we eat, Robyn asks us how we celebrate the solstice.

In our town, we rise early, well before sunrise. Most of us walk an hour or so to a circle of large stones that someone stuck upright into the ground a long time ago. Only those who are unable to walk the distance, are occupied with caring for the sick, or are preparing the feast that will follow, remain behind. Usually it is just people from Tordur, but occasionally a wanderer from elsewhere will join us. Often a Druid will come for the celebration. Once we get there, we wait for the sunrise. If a Druid comes, we also bring a sheep or goat to sacrifice as soon as the sun appears. Afterward, we chant an ancient blessing and return home. Then comes the feast. Usually we have an ox and a harvest of fresh greens from our gardens. Of course, there is plenty of mead to drink. Sometimes even wine. The day will end with stories and songs that will last until the sun returns the next morning. Not everyone will be awake the whole time, of course. But some will. By noon the next day, life will be back to normal. It isn't the multi-day feast of the winter solstice, because there is too much to do at this time of year.

Luseth tells us they have a similar celebration, except they remain in the settlement since there is not even a single standing stone nearby. But she seems almost reluctant to say more. Then Genovea asks if they can stay with us until after the solstice. Robyn and I look at each other.

Robyn answers. "Yes, of course you can."

Genovea then admits that she's scared to go back. Some of the men in the settlement when they've had too much to drink will try to have their way with a young woman. The sisters haven't had to worry in the past, since their father made it clear that any man who tried would need to get past him first. Now, they are on their own; Luseth is protected because of her pregnancy, but Genovea would be a target.

Robyn's response surprises me. "Are there any others who need our protection? We can pick them up when we return the men to your settlement this afternoon."

Genovea thinks for a moment. "No, I think everyone else who survived has someone to protect her. So many young women were in the fields that day and didn't escape the Sea-wolves."

No one knows what to say after that, so we finish our meal in silence.

Chapter 13.

After we return the wounded men to their settlement, we meet in Mission Control to decide how to manage the upcoming solstice festival and assess how the Romans are likely to play it. Marcelus agrees with me that they just might use the festival as an opportunity to launch an attack. Where they will attack is another question. The most obvious target is Wynt, given both its importance and proximity to the Roman encampment. Constant traffic crosses the bridge linking the two sites, and Wynt contains the greatest market in the region, and the Romans appear to be good customers. During the day the gates stand wide open welcoming visitors with money to spend or goods to trade. The Romans may be just browsing the shops and stalls, but they might be studying the layout of the town as they plan an attack. As the seat of the king and home to his warband, the town is the key to the entire tribe.

Cydyrn, the king, won't willingly give way to the Romans; Bledwyn is sure of that. He has been to Wynt, met the King and his warriors so he knows they have considerable distain for the invaders. But that distain is mixed with considerable fear. Cydyrn knows he doesn't have the strength to resist a determined attack. His warband is only about a hundred strong and his gates could not long withstand the Roman army. Not that it would matter – they usually attack walled towns with a siege – they surround it until the food is gone and the people are left with the choice to submit or starve. And this time of year after the long winter, food stocks are at their lowest. The new crops are far from ready for harvest and the herds are in the pastures, gorging on fresh grass. It is the perfect time for a siege.

We decide to visit Wynt in the morning to learn about the town, share what we know, and offer our aid. Bledwyn will take the lead since he is known to the king and some of his people. Rumors of our presence in the region and victory over the Saxons have no doubt reached his ears, so we may be expected. But I don't want to terrify the people as we arrive, and I'd rather not announce ourselves to the Romans stationed just across the river. So we won't fly there. There is a forest clearing about eight kilometers north east of Wynt that is away from any town. We will fly there and walk the rest of the way. Taylor and I will go. Muirenn really wants to be on the team, but will her foot be ready for a walk of that distance? I send her down to Sandy for a check-up while we finalize the details. Genovea is, of course, absolutely determined to join us. Luseth is not nearly as interested – I think her arm is sore, and of course she's carrying an extra load. She'll stay on the ship for the day. Part of me wonders about the wisdom of taking a peasant girl with us to visit the king – I saw how Muirenn and Bledwyn responded to them when they showed up, clearly treating them as lower class citizens. But in only a couple of days, Muirenn has clearly been won over.

Maybe her change in attitude comes from the way we treated them; that we accepted the girls as equals. I know she sees me as a hero and maybe that influenced the way she looks at them. Also she is a healer by nature; maybe she let down her guard a bit over Luseth's wounds. But most of the credit has to go to Genovea. That is one remarkable young lady. Several times already she's surprised me with her astute grasp of the situation, in what is completely outside of her previous experience. And I have to admit, her long, raven hair, skin tanned from hours in the fields, and jade green eyes give her a very striking appearance. We'll take the risk and bring Genovea. When we first met, she was a battered and dirty girl in a tattered and stained dress. Now that she's cleaned up and in borrowed clothes, she could pass for one of my first-year anthropology students. No, that's not quite true – she has far more presence and confidence than most of them. No, I don't think I need to worry about bringing Genovea to the king.

The rest of the day is set aside for planning. Also on the away team will be Michael, Kelly, and Bledwyn, and Taylor, of course. Marcelus wanted to come, but his arm was bothering him, so he'll stay behind and watch from Mission Control. Muirenn comes back all smiles with Sandy's blessing for the mission, and ... without her brace. We could use another armed member. I don't think we'll run into trouble, but I've been wrong on that before, so Lance decides to join as our final member.

The rest of the afternoon we pour over the images of Wynt, planning our route and identifying the buildings. The town is built on the north bank of a sizable river. Immediately to the west of the town runs a main north-south road. This road pre-dates the Romans, and it crosses the river on a three-span wooden bridge that is clearly of Roman construction. The ford that was the crossing before the bridge was built can still be clearly seen just upstream in the alignment of the road to the west. The bridge is aligned with the south gate of the town, indicating the Romans see it as a key center of population and commerce. The town itself also shows signs of Roman construction as many of the buildings are rectangular, rather than the round huts we've seen earlier. And unlike most other settlements, Wynt does not have a west-facing main gate. The gates leading to the market are in the north and south walls. A third, clearly minor, gate near the north-east corner leads to the road to Tordur and Dubri-Tun.

The marketplace is clearly visible as a wide street, lined on both sides with the homes and workshops of the merchants and craftsmen. Behind the buildings is a maze of animal pens, smaller buildings, and other structures connected to the market. Forges identify the iron-mongers; the ones with pens are most likely for slaughter. I'm a little surprised to see what looks like a tannery, too. Ancient tanneries were not known for their pleasant odor, so I expected they would be on the outskirts of town. The market street extends the length of the town, from wall to wall, with a gate at each end. Elsewhere in the town are narrow paths that wind between the closely-packed structures for access to the great hall and the surrounding buildings, but it is clear the true center of the town is the market.

The great hall of the king pre-dates the market. Though it is larger than the hall at Tordur, the style is the same. The front door faces west, the walls are timber-filled with wattle and daub. The roof is thatched. Surrounding the hall is about the only open space in the town. Nearby are the homes, kitchen, and stables we've seen in other settlements.

I'm worried about members of the team getting lost in the maze of paths of this town. Fortunately, all the buildings are single story, so the great hall and the walls are visible from pretty much everywhere, so we should be able to orient ourselves from them. The low buildings will also make it easier to keep visual contact with the team members from the drone. All of us will have communicators and trackers, so we shouldn't lose anyone. Language will still be a problem, but at least I have a little Brythonic now, so Muirenn won't have to translate absolutely everything for me.

We don't have clothing that will blend in, but Bledwyn tells us not to worry. Since Wynt is a market town and on a main road, travelers from far afield are common and we won't be the only ones that are obviously strangers. Bledwyn and Muirenn will wear their usual clothes so they will be recognized as members of the tribe.

During the planning for tomorrow the topic of archery comes up. Both Bledwyn and Marcelus suggest that carrying swords or bows would be a good idea since people recognize them as weapons, and will therefore take us seriously. The king's people won't have any idea that the sticks we carry are weapons far more powerful than anything they have in their arsenals, so they might take us for easy targets. Taylor mentions that I have a bow, so now they want to see it. They recognize it, but my competition compound bow is a long way from the wood longbows they use. A little friendly competition is proposed, so Little John gets tasked with setting up a target on the rear deck of the ship. With the target against the back wall of the ship superstructure, we can stand a little in front of the stern railing to get a regulation forty meter distance. I give Bledwyn a few arrows to get the feel of the bow, and then the competition begins in earnest. Each of us gets twelve arrows – in two rounds of six. I just beat Bledwyn. Muirenn and Genovea both give it a try – they're not bad. Marcelus can't pull a bow yet, but assures us of his tremendous skill and that he would have clearly won had he been healthy. On our team, only Michael comes anywhere close. Even though it might serve a purpose, I don't want to carry the bow. If things get tough and I need a weapon, that won't be what I reach for. It will just get in the way and slow me down. In the end, I convince Bledwyn to carry my bow and arrows. After being caught on the beach without weapons, I'm not about to take any chances. In spite of Bledwyn's promises, I'm not convinced that the king won't be more interested in pleasing the Romans than allying with strangers. Obviously, the Romans have brought a great deal of prosperity to the town and I can't see the king or his people wanting to risk losing the wealth that a busy market brings in exchange for us. Unless he knows we can offer something even the Romans can't.

We could give them some of the goods we brought for trading, things that we knew would be useful in the first century – metal utensils such as pots and knives, fabric, and the always-popular glass beads. We also have raw materials that are rare and valuable at this time – steel, copper, glass. We even brought aluminum, plastic items and solar lights – useful items that are totally beyond any price or imagining in this world.

But Bledwyn convinces me that we can also offer one thing that no one else possibly can: the ability to break a Roman siege. He saw what happened to the Saxons; we have weapons that overcame their great numbers. Besides, we could break a siege simply by flying over the attackers. Rumors of our presence must have reached Cydyrn's ears. It's not like we've been subtle. The speculation and fears generated by our huge and noisy bird must have risen to his level. Bledwyn knows the king keeps abreast of the events in his realm and will be most curious to meet the people behind these stories.

I admit that I'm also rather curious to meet the king. But that will have to wait until the morning.

Tonight we will celebrate Taylor's birthday. Again. I suppose it will get old long before the mission ends, but for now it gives the team something to help with the boredom. And Taylor likes the attention, sort of. He tries to keep a low profile, but I know he secretly appreciates the thought. As a plus, it gives Michele an outlet for her energy that doesn't involve booby-trapping my room.

Over supper, Muirenn asks how we celebrate the solstice and is totally shocked when I tell her that we don't. So the conversation rolls to what we do celebrate. They've already learned a bit about birthdays, but Christmas, Thanksgiving, and the 4th of July all take some explaining. So, I take the easy way out and pull out the DVDs of the home videos my dad took over the years. I'm wedged in between Taylor and Muirenn. Muirenn keeps asking questions – hers and those from the rest of our Brythonic guests that she's passing on. Watching the family gatherings is excruciating; I've watched them a couple of time since the accident, but they didn't affect me the way they do tonight. Maybe they just remind me how far I am from home, or maybe it is a reflection of how much I've changed over the years. Nevertheless, the grief is still there; these people who were so special to me are all dead.

Technically – that's not true. None of them will be even born for centuries. In fiction, time travelers can change the future. They go back in time, and the rest of the plot usually revolves around how they try to fix things that have gone wrong, while not breaking anything in the future. It is kind of an ego-centric view of time as if their life remains a continuous sequence of events and time shifts around them. It isn't that way at all. When we travel through time, we become part of history instead of creating history. The history that we experienced in the 21st century already includes the impact of our presence here and now. I've often wondered how dragons became such a popular symbol for this island and now I wonder if our 'dragon' is the source. *What else might we have impacted by our presence here?* My mind moves away from the pictures on the screen as I muse about what other ways we might be making history. It's a much less painful place to be.

Muirenn's voice in my ear brings me back to the present (whatever that means).

"What is this now? Genovea wants to know."

I glance at the screen. *How did that disk get in the machine? For that matter, how did it even get here?* I thought it was still buried at the bottom of my dresser drawer at home. It's one I've never watched, the one my father took of what turned out to be Kim's last dance. It was only a couple of weeks before the accident. She started with ballet, but soon changed to modern dance. Here is a solo competition, just Kim alone on the stage performing a dance she choreographed. The grace of her movements, the creative skill she displayed was amazing. No wonder she came home with a trophy that day. It brings back a rush of memories and sadness. Suddenly, I'm grateful for Taylor's presence beside me in a way I didn't expect and can't explain.

"It is a dance, moving to music. That is my little sister."

"The one who died?"

"Yes. This was just a few days before she was killed."

"She looks like Genovea."

I hadn't really noticed before. Or, maybe I pretended I didn't. Both have the same dark hair, similar slender builds and facial structures. And they're about the same age. But it goes deeper than that. She has the facial expressions and mannerisms of my little sister. Even her voice is the same. And I bet she can dance. Yeah, even now, she's moving to the music.

"Do you dance?" I ask her.

"I've never heard music like this before that makes me want to move. We don't have any musicians at home, and we are too small for many bards to come our way," she replies.

"Do you want to try? Come, I'll show you."

I'm not much of a dancer even without comparing myself to Kim. But at least I can keep time to the music and know some basic moves that I learned from her. Taylor kills the DVD – it was the very end anyway – and switches to music. Before we left, we gave everyone phones and told them to load their favorite music. Our tech guru Steve then downloaded everything to our network, so we have a huge selection of music and videos. Of course, there's no cell service here so we can't use the phones, but Steve set them all up to text over our Wi-Fi network. Each drone has a repeater and since there is no interference from other radio signals, we find the service is pretty good even for the away teams. And everyone has some really amazing photos to share when we get home.

Given the diverse people in the crew, it is hardly surprising that we have amazing variety of musical tastes. I pick first and since I lean mostly to folk, I choose a very danceable Celtic piece that might be vaguely familiar to our guests. It isn't really, but they have fun dancing. Then Taylor starts picking the music and the beat gets going. He's actually a pretty good DJ. We pull back the furniture in the lounge area and turn the mess hall into a club. Most of the crew hear the music and make their way down. Except Andrew who drew the short straw and has to keep watch. Even though we are securely anchored in a sheltered cove, someone has to keep an eye on the ship and the surrounding sea. Downstairs, I learn that some of my shipmates know how to burn up the dance floor. Barry is the one who surprises me the most. He is tall, thin, with dark, balding hair. He does not look like my idea of a dancer. Or a seafarer for that matter. He actually reminds me of my grade eight math teacher. But he can sure dance.

Captain Johansen is different. He doesn't dance. I can't imagine him ever dancing. He looks like my idea of a ship captain. Not as tall as Barry, but barrel-chested, with a face worn by years at sea. His close-cropped grey beard and turtle neck sweater complete the image. He found a table and is listening to the music, watching us dance as he quietly nurses a beer. He doesn't talk much, except to give orders on the bridge. I think he likes things quiet and ordered. That is part of why he doesn't like strangers on the bridge. He did allow me in once during our journey across the Atlantic. It was like walking into a church it was so quiet. The sun was just setting behind us, so the huge windows looked out over the gathering dusk and endless water. I stood fascinated by the view and the silence. The big wheel stood unmanned, slowly turning as the autopilot adjusted our course. The Captain sat in a comfortable swivel chair, surrounded by a display showing the ship's status and its track across the ocean. A second display showed the radar image of the surrounding sea. I was shocked to see nearly twenty ships within reach of our radar, and we were still in the middle of the Atlantic Ocean.

The Captain said, "We are seeing fifty miles in all directions, so nearly eight thousand square miles of ocean. As we approach the coast, the number of ships will grow. When we near the English Channel, there could be well over a hundred ships and boats visible at this range. At that point I'll switch the radar to a shorter range to reduce the clutter and to better see the nearby ships which might interfere with our course."

Talk then turned to our plans. "We will complete our crossing and fuel at the port of Plymouth in southern England. Once our tanks are full, we will head west back into the Atlantic. Once we have clear seas around us, we will make our time jump. When we jump back, we will return to the exact same spot, less than a minute later. We know that we will suddenly disappear from radar, but since we will reappear a few seconds later, we will be back before anyone notices."

We talked a long time that night. I learned of his life at sea, guiding ships between the ports lining these shores, and his dream of a peaceful retirement on land that was shattered when his wife died. I shared something of my quest for knowledge and the far deeper quest to find peace with myself. It is something I've never talked about; not with Kate, not with Taylor, not with anyone. Somehow, opening up with Captain J seemed so natural that it happened almost before I realized it. Maybe he reminds me a bit of my grandfather, maybe it's the wisdom that comes from years of staring over the sea with nothing to do but think. Whatever the reason, I cracked the door open for him. Since that terrible day of the accident, I've struggled to find purpose. *Why did I live when my whole family died?* Until I find an answer, I don't think I'll ever really find peace.

Maybe the talk did some good, because when it was time for a slow dance, I didn't head for the hills as usual. I find myself dancing with Max and actually enjoying it.

Too soon the evening is over. Most of the team heads to bed for tomorrow will be another early start.

Chapter 14.

I can't sleep. I want tomorrow to come. I've never been as far as Wynt, and tomorrow I will be there! The last few days have been exciting beyond my wildest dreams. How could I ever imagine flying through the sky like a bird or living on a boat made of iron? Or meeting people from the other world? Maybe because visiting Wynt is something I've dreamed about ever since I first heard of the place, it is more real to me, and that makes it more exciting. For whatever reason, I'm tossing in bed and can't sleep, so I finally decide to get up and go for a walk. The boat is dark and silent as I leave my room. In the quiet, I can hear a gentle rumble that seems to be coming from deep below me. It scares me a bit until I remember the similar rumble when the boat moves. Maybe it's related. I can hear other sounds, too. The slap of waves, the click of a door, the soft murmur of voices. Someone else is still awake somewhere above me. I follow the voices, soundlessly walking in my bare feet, past the place where we meet to make plans, into a part of the ship I've never been before. I find a door standing open; I can hear the voices clearly coming from the other side. As I step through the door, I'm awed by the sight in front of me. The room is dark, darker even than the passageway I just followed. The entire wall in front of me is clear so I can see the water and land. The light from the moon reflects off the water, and lights the beach and trees. As I step into the room, I see the old man they call Captain who was sitting with Robyn earlier tonight. With him are two others. I can hear them talking, but can't begin to understand what they are saying.

Quietly, so as not to disturb them, I walk up to the wall and touch it. Of course, I now have seen windows on the bird and elsewhere on the boat, but this is so big that I can't believe that it is real., Robyn told me that it is made of glass. We have a few bowls made of glass that we got from Romans. But they are small and white. Light shines through them, but they are nothing like this. It reminds me of ice on a still pond – clear, smooth, and hard. Nothing else that I've ever seen looks anything like this. I stand with my hand on the surface trying to imagine a world full of glass, where you can stand inside where it is warm and dry, and still see out. So unlike our homes. Only the hall has a stone floor. All the huts have dirt floors. Not even my father's house has stone. When the winter rains come, everything gets wet and the floor turns to mud. Even with a fire burning on the hearth, it's never really warm and nothing is dry.

In Robyn's world it is so different.

I suddenly realize the voices behind me are silent, so I turn to see the three men watching me. In the silence, I feel self-conscious and am a little afraid that maybe I shouldn't be here. The Captain is there with Lance and Martin, all gathered around in a little circle. The Captain looks so stern I nearly run from the room. But then I see his face relax into a smile, and I stay where I am. Then he says something that I think means for me to come over.

They are looking through one of their special windows that let them see things that are far away. This is much smaller than the ones I've seen before, and it looks very different. It looks nothing like what I can see with my eyes, but has shapes in different colors. Martin touches it, and the colors shift.

"This is rain," Martin says to me, pointing to a bright yellow blob. He spoke in English and I understood what he said! Sort of. I don't really get how this shape is rain. I touch it, and it's not wet. I guess we are seeing rain that is far away, just like we can see other things during the day.

The men go back to talking among themselves, and I can't really follow what they are saying, so I give them a smile and walk back toward my room. I'm still not really tired so instead of going back to my room, I wander around the boat. Another partly open door – this one with light shining through the crack – attracts my attention. I slowly push it open and peek in to see Robyn sitting on a soft bench. She's almost crunched up in a ball, with her legs pulled up and her arms wrapped around them. She's staring straight ahead, with a sad look on her face. I don't want to disturb her, but as soon as she hears me enter, she looks up and smiles. But it seems to be a sad smile. All the same, it gives me the courage to step slowly into the room. Robyn sees my hesitation and pats the bench beside her, so I come and sit beside her.

She drains the drinking cup she's holding and places it on the table beside her and asks me, "Can't sleep?"

"No." I shake my head. "You?"

Robyn turns and looks at me. "I was asleep, but I dreamt of all the men I killed. In my dream, they kept coming. I shot and hit them, but that didn't stop them. They kept coming, covered in blood, holding bloody swords and spears. Just before they reached me, they exploded into fire, and that's when I realized they were really my family, and I couldn't save them. All I could do is watch them burn. I woke up covered in sweat with my heart racing, and now I can't get back to sleep. So I came here to try to relax and maybe I'll get back to sleep before morning."

I throw my arms around her and remind her "You saved me. If you didn't come, I would be dead by now. And if you hadn't killed all those Sea-wolves and driven them from our shores, who knows how many others would have died."

I feel Robyn hesitate before she responds by putting her arm around me. It takes longer before she responds. When she does, her voice is quiet with a softness I've never noticed before. "Thank you for reminding me. It helps me when I remember that you, Luseth, Genovea, and many others are alive today only because we are here."

In the silence that follows, I can almost hear Robyn gathering her courage to say something more. I'm not sure how to take this – she's a hero from the other world. I've seen her face down a Roman patrol and a host of Sea-wolves without flinching. We will remember her in tale and song. Why is she so afraid of words? Maybe it's because they have so many ways to talk – with their writing and little boxes that send words to each other. Ways to speak to each other while they are far apart. The things that remember what they see and hear, and draw them back whenever they want. Maybe speaking words person-to-person is scary for them, because they never really talk to each other.

Words are all we have. We have to look someone in the face and speak to them. We can't save our words for later or send them far away. I've been jealous of all the things these people have, but right now I wonder if our way is better. Robyn is the greatest and strongest person I've ever met, but she struggles to find words.

Just as I think these things, Robyn speaks. "When Jon, my betrothed died, I felt like part of me died. Losing him and my whole family all at once left me so alone in the world. I just wanted someplace to belong. That's why I joined the army. Then I met Brad and I felt once again that he was someone who understood me, who I could trust, and was real. Then, he died in the war. And I promised myself that I'd never let anyone that close again. I've known Taylor for nearly five years and we've spent a lot of time together in the last months, preparing for this journey. All of a sudden, I find myself wanting to open that door and let him in. But after all this time, I'm not sure I know how to do it."

I thought that there was something going on between those two. I say "I have never known anyone like that, so I have no idea how to respond. There are only a few men in our town who are of age and not already married. And none who are open for me, for only a warrior would be suitable. Many of our young warriors have joined the king's warband and no longer live with us; others died in battles against the Sea-wolves. Men are allowed a second wife, but not the daughter of a chieftain; she must be a first wife. So I too had resigned myself to being alone. I don't know; maybe things will be different now."

"We will not be here forever" Robyn replies "You know that, don't you? One day, we will have to go back to our home."

I know but I still give a bit of a shiver at the thought. I don't want them to leave.

"Are you cold?" Robyn pulls out a blanket that was behind her back and wraps it around both of us.

I feel like a small child again, thinking back to the times when I was sick and my mother did the same thing. I curl up beside her and in the warmth start to relax. But, before I can drift off to sleep, I have a question. "How can they see rain far away at night?"

"Who told you that?"

"The Captain and Martin. Just before I came down here I wandered up to the room with all the glass, and they showed me that there is rain coming, that they could see it as a yellow blob."

"How to explain. It is called radar and it sends out light that you can't see, but it can. Then it sees what is out there – how far it is and how fast it is moving. From what it learns it makes a picture that we can see. It can see at night and through rain or fog. It also can see further than we can with our eyes, so it can show us rain that is now far away but is moving in our direction."

"Oh." I think that helps. I don't really understand though. How can there be light that I can't see, but this radar thing can? I can feel Robyn tapping on her little box as sleep finally overtakes me.

Voices drift through my dreams. And I feel Robyn shake me awake. The sunlight is streaming through the glass and into the room. I'm still curled up beside Robyn, but she's wake and talking to Martin and Don. "Hey, wake up sleepy!" She gives me another shake. "Time for us to get going. The rain went through in the night, and now the sun is out. Why don't you go have a shower and get your clothes on, and then come down to where we eat? I need to get ready too."

I drag myself from my warm and comfortable spot and head back to my room. Yesterday, Luseth, Genovea and I all moved into a larger room with four beds, so that each of us has our own. When I come in, Luseth is still in bed, cradling her broken arm. Genovea is up and ready for the day. When I ask, Luseth tells me her arm hurts, so she didn't sleep much at all. I promise to tell Robyn, because they might be able to give her something for the pain. She just nods and drags herself out of bed.

By the time we get down to the meal they call breakfast, almost everyone else is already there, and they all seem to be in a hurry. Robyn is already almost finished. We don't want to get left behind, so we grab something and start eating. I forget all about Luseth's arm, but it doesn't matter because Robyn and Sandy come over and ask. Sandy leaves to take care of her while Robyn explains what is happening. Today is a market day. Little Bird sees the merchants gathering in Wynt's marketplace. There don't seem to be many Roman soldiers wandering around, but plenty of others are coming in from out of town to trade goods. She hopes we'll just be a few more strangers in a town full of them.

Then there's the weather. There's more rain on the way and Robyn wants to get into the town before it hits. She says she doesn't want us to show up before the king looking like a bunch of drowned rats. So while we finish eating, Robyn disappears to get ready. We're to meet her at The Bird as soon as we are done. Luseth heads back to bed – now that her arm isn't as sore, she just wants to sleep. The rest of us – Genovea, Bledwyn, Marcelus, and me – all gather together at the back of the boat, then find we are not quite sure what to do. John, Andrew, and Trace are all there, busy getting ready to leave. We wind up standing by the wall, trying to keep out of the way.

Robyn soon shows up beside us. She holds up a small green, soft object that looks like a little pillow. "We also have these for you, in case we get caught in the rain." She opens a little slit in the side and turns it inside out to reveal a thin coat, with a hood like I've seen Druids wear. "You can open this and put it on – the rain won't get through so it will keep you dry. The green and grey colors make you hard to see in the woods, too."

She takes it, quickly folds it back into itself, and closes up the slit. I can see now that there is a little tab that opens or closes the slit. Then she shows us how to fasten them to our belts, so that our hands are free as we walk.

Then she hands the bow and arrows to Bledwyn "These are weapons you earned the right to carry." He can't hide his smile as slings them over his shoulder.

Michael, Lance and Kelly are here now, dressed in the same green and brown patchwork as Robyn, so we climb into The Bird and fasten ourselves into chairs. Taylor is already inside. Trace climbs into her seat, and starts to work. I can see Bledwyn watching her, like he's trying to follow what she's doing. I can't even begin to imagine what she's doing or why it is so important, but I know now that when the noise starts, The Bird is waking up. And when it gets much louder, we are about to start flying.

I watch as the boat drops away and we turn toward the land. I know it would take half a day for me to walk from here to home, then another day to get all the way to Wynt. In no time, we drop toward the ground. I hear Robyn explain that the ground looks wet from the rain ,so Trace will stop just above the ground and we will jump down, just in case it is too soft for the weight of The Bird. The door slides back, Robyn jumps first, then Michael; I follow next. It's only a short distance to the ground, but I manage to fall forward when I land. I'm not hurt, but get my hands covered in mud and grass.

Robyn pulls out a piece of cloth and gives it to me to clean myself. "We can't have you meet the king with dirty hands." I wipe off the mud while the rest of them are jumping to the ground. Hopefully, I'll find some water before we get to the town; my hands are still quite dirty.

As soon as we are all on the ground, Robyn leads us away from The Bird in the direction of Wynt. As we near the edge of the field, The Bird grows louder, so I turn to watch it rise and fly away over the trees. As it disappears and the sound fades, I can hear the sounds of home – there's a beehive somewhere near and the birds start to sing. I realize how quickly I have grown used to being on the boat. The silence, the smells, and the open space of the forest seem almost foreign, yet this is almost my home. How many days have I spent walking through a forest just like this one? Yet, after just a few days, it seems odd to be here in the trees, and I can't quite figure out why. Until I feel the ground move under my feet.

"The ground is moving!" I shout.

Robyn doesn't seem too concerned. "That's just because you've been on the boat for a while, where the ground does move, as the boat rocks in the waves. Your brain has adjusted, and now it thinks the ground always moves. It isn't, it just feels like it is. In a few minutes your brain will figure out that it really isn't moving, and you'll be okay."

I'm not sure she's right, but the feeling has already passed and the ground and trees around me look and feel pretty solid, so maybe she is telling the truth. I decide that the ground really isn't going to swallow me up and that I can manage to walk without falling, so we follow the path into the forest. Robyn leads, with Bledwyn right behind her; I come next, with the rest following. Michael is in the rear. I hear a constant stream of voices in my ear; I'm tempted to rip the thing out so I can hear the birds and listen for threats in the area. There could be people in the area and there are certainly animals. There are wolves, bears, and wild boar to avoid. Not many, but enough that it pays to stay alert and listen. They are all big enough that I can hear them coming and climb a tree or go the other way before they get too close. But today, I won't hear anything until they are right beside me. I even hear Martin's voice and I know we left him back on the boat. Then I see Robyn stop and raise her gun. Bledwyn sees the movement and readies his bow, too.

I hear Robyn speak in her language. I understand some of what she says. I hear Michael's voice and then in Latin she says. "There is an animal nearby. It's not big enough to be an adult bear; could be a young one or maybe a wild boar. It looks like it will cross in front of us by about sixty paces. I want to be ready, just in case, but Michael assures me most animals will avoid a group this size."

I pass the news on to Genovea and Bledwyn. Then there is silence. I forgot that Little Bird is watching for us so we don't need to rely on our ears as much as I do when I am alone.

I feel a movement beside me. Taylor is ready with one of his boxes that will remember what we see. No one is talking now; even the birds are quiet. In the silence, I can hear the rustle of the breeze in the leaves, the buzz of insects, and the occasional snap of a twig in the distance. Like most forest paths, this one is narrow with dense brush on both sides. It is pretty straight for about thirty paces, and then it bends to the right and out of view. If something comes this way, we won't see it until it is right on top of us. Robyn and Bledwyn are side by side, both partly in the bush. Bledwyn is on the left, so will see anything coming before Robyn does. Michael has moved up, and is standing almost even with them, but in the bush off to the side. Bledwyn has an arrow loaded and his bow drawn, ready to fire. Robyn is looking relaxed, with her gun only partly raised. I hear Martin's voice; Robyn tenses and raises her gun the rest of the way so she is ready for whatever comes.

I see the shadow of a big dark shape coming along the path in our direction. I peek between Robyn and Bledwyn as a wild boar rounds the corner and comes directly at us. Only once have I met a boar in the woods when I was alone. I heard it coming, so I climbed a tree and watched as it sauntered on past. This time, I'm not sure I have time to get up a tree, so I don't know what I will do. Before anyone else reacts, Bledwyn's arrow leaves his bow. It catches the boar in the shoulder, but is not enough to stop him. Enraged by the arrow, he breaks into a gallop in our direction. In the second it takes for Bledwyn to grab another arrow, I hear Robyn's gun crack, then a second shot comes from Michael. The boar stumbles and falls, skidding to a stop maybe ten paces from us. It lies still, and Michael takes the lead as we slowly approach the beast. Bledwyn's arrow is still sticking out of it but the beast doesn't move when he reaches down and removes it. I know then that it is dead.

I can see two other holes in the boar – one in the head, just a little above the eyes, and a little right of the middle; the other is in the chest just inside the front left leg. I realize both Robyn and Michael hit it too. Poor beast didn't stand a chance. I'm not sure how I feel as I stare at it lying at my feet with blood oozing out of the wounds. I respect the animals of the forest and don't like seeing them killed. On the other hand, this one would have hurt us if we hadn't stopped it. We could never have all made it out of the way in time.

Now the talk turns to what to do with the carcass. We could leave it for the forest animals, we could use The Bird to take it back to the boat, or we could bring it to the king. Bledwyn argues for the last option since the wild boar has a special meaning to the king. His father, the previous king, was killed by a wounded boar during a hunt. The young prince was at his side and promptly killed the boar with a single spear-throw before turning his attention his fallen father. The procession that returned home that night was both sorrowful and jubilant. Sorrow for the fallen king was mixed with praise for the vengeance wrought on his killer by the son. In our tribe, kingship does not always pass from father to son, for the son has to earn the right to lead the people. If he fails in that quest, they will choose another. This was many years ago, before I was born. Cydyrn was young at the time, and unproven in the minds of the warriors. But after his triumph over the boar there was no doubt that Cydyrn would be king. The same boar who took his father's life also gave him the throne.

All these years later, he still sees the wild boar is both a good and bad omen. The boar remains the symbol of his reign, but also serves as a reminder of his father's death. He could interpret it is as either a boon or a bane depending on his mood and what other omens he has seen or heard recently. In the end, we decide to take the boar with us. If we arrive and present him with the boar, Bledwyn is sure he will take it as our acknowledgment that he is as king. Since he no doubt knows of our presence and strength, Bledwyn thinks he may fear that we are here to conquer his lands and people. The gift of the boar should ease his fears. Robyn insists that we tell him it was Bledwyn's arrow that felled the beast, because he is known to the king and his loyalty is unquestioned. The rest of us, he doesn't know and may well suspect our motives in presenting the boar.

But now, how do we carry it? It will take four or five strong men to carry and we are only half way to Wynt. I hear them talking about using the chopper – the word in their language for the bird we fly in. I don't know how that will work since there is no place here for it to land, but Robyn explains it has a rope they can lower between the trees. They could attach the boar to the rope and The Bird will fly off with it.

In the end, they chose a different method, something they called a travois. Michael is carrying a small axe, which he uses to cut a number of poles from small trees. They lash two long ones together at one end. Then they spread the other end of the poles just wide enough apart to hold the boar, and use shorter poles to make a platform. Another short pole near the end of the long ones completes it. They roll the boar onto the platform and lash it there. Then Lance and Bledwyn pick up the other end with the short pole, and they walk off, dragging the boar behind them. The path is a little narrow for the two men to walk side by side, but both are strong and they manage to push their way through.

My foot is getting sore. The path is level, and it really isn't very far – I've walked far further in a day many times in the past. But even though the path is smooth, I stumble and twist my ankle a couple of times. Once, I nearly fall, but Kelly is beside me at the time and catches me. I don't think Kelly knows any Latin, because Robyn had to translate when he helped me before. But I remember a word in English from my lessons with Robyn and Max.

"Thanks," I say, but softly just in case I got it wrong.

I see him smile, so I think I got the right word. I smile back. I wonder about Kelly since he is a healer too. All the men I know are either warriors or peasants who care for our herds and crops. Men aren't healers in my world, but he is. Maybe in Robyn's world there are more men who are healers. Kelly seems old enough that I think he probably already has a wife. But then I think of Robyn and Taylor and how old they are and neither of them is married, so maybe Kelly isn't either. These people do marry late, so here is a man who is a healer who just might not have a wife. I don't know how to ask him, but I'll have to ask Robyn sometime.

It seems the path goes on forever, but it really doesn't take long before we come out onto a wider road. Robyn tells us this is the road that runs from Wynt to Tordur, then on to the north. Bledwyn isn't too sure that we are on the right track, for he does not remember this place from his previous trips. I trust him because he has been to Wynt several times before and Robyn never has, so I'm a little worried. But before long we round a curve and he recognizes the open fields in front of us. The rain that threatened earlier moved off and the sky is a clear blue, with the morning sun and still air promising a hot and muggy day. Men and women are already at work in some of the fields, pulling weeds. Others are leading flocks of sheep and goats in the direction of Wynt. I look to the right and see the walls rising on the horizon only a short distance away. My first sight of Wynt is disappointing. I was expecting massive huge walls, but they are no taller than the ones at home. And the surrounding ditch is no wider than ours. The gates do look strong and are flanked by towers for defense but today they are standing wide open welcoming visitors to the market. A couple of Cydyrn's warriors are standing here, watching those entering from this direction.

I am surprised to see ahead of us only two groups driving flocks and three or four individuals carrying burdens, all walking in the direction of the gates. I expected there would be many more people on the road.

Bledwyn reminds me that this is the back entrance into Wynt, that more people will be arriving through the main gates. We are so close, but we are going so slowly! Finally, I can't stand to wait any longer, and without thinking I break away from the rest and run forward. I hear Robyn's voice in my ear, but I can't understand what she's saying so I continue my run. In no time I step through the open gateway and into the crowds, the noise, and the stench of Wynt.

Chapter 15.

When Muirenn sprinted ahead, my first instinct was to stop her. Or at least, try to stop her. Instead, I asked Max if he had her on Little Bird. He did, so I let her go. I feel a little like an over-protective mother keeping remote watch on my teenager during her first solo trip to the mall, but I need her. I did tell her we could keep track of her and hear what she says, but I doubt she's thinking about that right now. I'm a little surprised that Genovea didn't follow her, but she's walking beside me, wide-eyed, and looking more than a little afraid. Of course this is not her place. It is the main center of Muirenn's tribe, and as a member of the tribal elite she sees no reason for fear. Genovea is from a different tribe, and even though her language is similar enough that they can understand each other, her accent will give her away. I noticed a few differences in the pronunciation of some words and I am sure the native speakers will instantly pick up on them.

"You can stay with me," I whisper.

She gives me a smile that speaks her mixed feelings. Once again, I feel like a mother. I suddenly realize her mother was probably not much older than me. In this time of short lives, most women become mothers in their mid-teens. So if Luseth was the oldest, then their mother could have been just over thirty when she died. For the first time ever, I feel old. Which is a little strange, since I won't actually be born for another two millennia. But I reach out and grab Genovea's hand as we walk through the gates and enter the market.

Bledwyn immediately takes the lead and walks up to one of the guards. Speaking in his own tongue, he states "I am Bledwyn of Cynbel, of Tordur, here with warriors and friends who recently helped us to drive a large force of Sea-wolves away from the King's shores. We come bearing a gift for Cydyrn, king of our people. Lead us to him."

The two guards eye the boar, and hold a hurried, whispered conversation between them.

"Who are these people with you?" they ask Bledwyn "and where are they from?"

"They come from across the great water to the west, beyond the land of the Irish. They arrived in a great boat, and have a steed that flies through the air spewing fire on their enemies. This is Robyn Hood, their chieftain."

I step forward at the sound of my name. About this time, a breathless Muirenn arrives. She heard Bledwyn's words through her earpiece and decided browsing the marketplace could wait until after we meet the king.

"This is Muirenn, my younger sister," Bledwyn adds, gesturing toward her.

"Follow me," says the older of the two guards.

He leads us into the town but before we reach the congestion of the market, we take a road to the left that skirts behind the buildings that line the market. The buildings here are rectangular in the Roman fashion, but still only one story high. Windows are mere slits under the eaves, just like the hall at Tordur. Pens for sheep, goats, pigs, and poultry line this side of the market. I can see at the further end, there are stalls for other merchants. Before I leave, I'm going there to see what they are selling.

"I can see you looking at the market." I hear Max's voice in my ear. "Women – can't keep away from the mall. Even in the Iron Age."

I might be offended if it was anyone else. But Max knows that it's virtually impossible to drag me into a mall at home. I hate making fashion decisions. I have a couple of favorite stores about where I buy most of my clothes, but I can't stand the idea of spending a whole day searching for that perfect item. It wasn't always that way. Before the accident, Kim and I would happily spend the day at the mall; now the memories are too painful, and the few times I do end up in a mall I usually wind up sitting in the food court, nursing a coffee, and missing her way too much. Not even the passage of years has helped. At least, not very much.

I shoot back, "My interest is purely professional. Besides, I doubt any of them accept Visa, and I forgot to bring cash."

That brings a laugh from Taylor, because he knows why I hate malls, and he also knows his laugh will keep my mind from drifting into a dangerous place. Focus. Follow Bledwyn, I tell myself. We round the edge of the buildings that make up the market, and the great hall comes into view. As we saw from the air, stables and granaries are crowded around it. Beyond it we can see some of the older round huts sprinkled between newer ones. The guard leads us without pause or word into the forecourt before the hall. Like the other sites we've seen, the door of the hall looks to the west, into the setting sun. The hall is on a slight hill, not enough to raise it over the nearby huts, so the view is really of a horse pen and the back of some merchant's home. The hall looks ancient, yet is freshly whitewashed; its walls gleaming in the sun. What we couldn't see from the air is the lower part of the front wall – about the first three feet – made of fieldstone. It looks to be laid with mud for mortar, but it is impressive compared with the wattle and daub walls we've seen on buildings elsewhere. The two carved wooden doors fill a doorway that's at least nine feet high and seven wide. The doors are not large or decorative compared to the ones that will grace manors and cathedrals in later centuries, but they are by far the most impressive that we've seen on this journey. I turn to Taylor to ask if he can be sure to shoot some footage of them, but I see he's already at work and way ahead of me, as usual.

The guard takes us to two others standing by the doors, and explains who we are and our mission. As he leaves us to return to his post, the wardens open the doors and motion for us to enter the dim interior of the Great Hall of the king. When we have passed through the doors, they swing shut with an ominous thud. I glance over my shoulder to see there are more soldiers within the hall. They position themselves in front of the door; giving the clear message our departure may not be as simple as our arrival. I am tempted to reach for my rifle, to be ready for action in case we need to fight our way out, but I don't want to call attention to the fact that it is a weapon. The guards obviously can see and recognize Bledwyn's bow, but can't be certain about anything else that we carry. I wonder if their action in blocking the door was intended to unnerve us into revealing our secrets. I don't show any concern, continue to walk at the same pace, and hope the rest of the team does the same. The fact that Bledwyn is allowed to keep his bow is encouraging. But then a bow is not a weapon for indoors. Neither is a rifle, for that matter.

After the brightness of the day, it takes a few moments for my eyes to adjust to the dim interior of the hall. It consists of a single large room with a great central hearth, and a raised dais at the far end. The fire on the hearth is low and gives little light, for the day is already growing warm. The only light comes from the smoke hole in the roof and the line of narrow window-slits. A few tables and chairs line the side walls, but the middle of the room is free from furniture. The floor is red Roman tile, the walls white, and the ceiling is the underside of the thatched roof blackened from smoke. The raised dais holds single large chair flanked by a side table. The chair is of a dark wood, deeply carved with decorations that we still identify as Celtic. The front legs are covered with the intricate network of the endless knot, seen so often on ancient monuments.

I cannot see more detail of the throne because it is occupied. King Cydyrn looks to be about forty – for some reason I expected him to be older. His brown hair and moustache have just a touch of grey around the edges, and his lined face reveals a life filled with care. He wears a dark green cloak with subtle embroidery around the edges and held by a brown leather belt. The golden torc around his neck clearly identifies him as the king. His brown breeches are tucked neatly into the tops of tall leather boots. A long sword in a scabbard and round shield lean against the side of the chair. The table holds a goblet of bronze and an iron dagger. He looks to be deep in thought as he pays no attention to us as we cross the floor.

As we approach the throne, Bledwyn takes the lead. Kelly and Lance stay back with the boar; the rest of us follow Bledwyn around the central hearth, keeping a few feet behind him. Yesterday as we were planning this mission, Bledwyn explained the presence of women in the group is a good thing, because it means we are not here for a fight. No one in this land brings women if they are expecting trouble. Sure enough, when he notices us in the team, he sits up and actually pays attention.

Bledwyn again speaks first. "Greetings Sire. I am Bledwyn of Cynbel, of Tordur, here with warriors and friends who recently helped us to drive a large force of Sea-wolves away from the king's shores.

We come bearing a gift for you, a boar that attacked us on our journey this morning."

"And who are those with you? Let them speak," he replied.

"I am Muirenn, sister to Bledwyn and daughter of Cynbel, chieftain of Tordur, and your servant."

I speak next. "I am Robyn Hood, from far to the west. I speak little of your language."

"I am Genovea, from the north. Robyn and her people also saved me from the Sea-wolves. My sister was wounded in the attack and is now in their care. We plan to return to our home once she is able to travel."

Bledwyn now speaks again. "The others come from distant lands, and do not speak our language. Taylor and Michael are standing with us, while Kelly and Lance are standing by the boar."

The king sits in silence, considering our group. "Bledwyn give my greetings to your father. I intended to come in your direction earlier this spring, but have had many cares here and have been unable to make the journey. Your father has been remiss in not telling me his daughter has grown to be such a fine young woman. Indeed, it shows that it has been far too long since I ventured to Tordur, or I would have seen her with my own eyes."

"Genovea, I gather you are from beyond the borders of my realm, in the land of the Trinovantes. There has long been a great traffic between our peoples and you are welcome in my house."

He then switches to Latin. "Robyn Hood, I have heard rumors of your arrival on these shores. I learned you speak some Latin, so we will converse in that language. I had hoped that we would meet. Maximus has been here and spoke to me of his talk with Cynbel. I am most interested to hear more of your story and why you have come."

I now step closer and stand beside Bledwyn. I feel like I should bow, because he is the king of this land and we are merely sojourners, but Bledwyn warned all of us against any such display. Cydyrn believes that those who come to with words of flattery and grovelling submission do so because they want something from him. He distrusts such people and has little patience and even less respect for them. It is those who look him in the eye as they speak who are most likely to earn his trust. So I look into his blue eyes and speak directly to him.

"We come from a land across the water far to the west, beyond the land of the Irish. We arrived in a boat that currently rests at anchor near your coast. On our first day here we came across Muirenn, daughter of Cynbel, injured on the road, and cared for her. We also found the town of Dubri-tun near the borders of your realm besieged by Sea-wolves; Saxons I believe from their ships and appearance. We have with us a great bird, which we use as a steed to carry us through the sky. It is also a weapon, for it can rain fire and destruction on our enemies. With its help, we drove the Sea-wolves from the gates of Dubri-Tun and away from your shores. They will not return."

"Defeating those who come to plunder is not the reason we came. We are scholars; our passion for learning brings us to your realm. We know something of the Romans and their ways. The little we know of your people comes from them. So we come as friends to learn of your people, your language, and your ways. Tordur's reputation as a center of healing reached our ears, so we brought some of our own healers to both learn and teach. So far, our healers have been occupied with healing the wounds of those injured by the Sea-wolves. We hope now for a time of peace, so that we may exchange knowledge and hospitality with those we now consider friends."

"We are concerned the Romans may be planning to attack your city, and wish to offer our assistance to you in repelling them, so that our friends remain safe."

Cydyrn takes a few moments to look into our eyes before he replies. "We have a treaty with the Romans. I have no fear that they will attack us. So we thank you for your offer of assistance, but it is not required. But there is something else that I would ask. I spoke with Maximus at length a few days ago on his return from Tordur. He has no plans to attack us, but he has heard there is land further to the north, land that has few inhabitants. That land is thickly forested, so has plenty of wood for building. Soldiers have established an encampment in the area, but Maximus wants a fortress and a city on the coast where there is a harbor, so his boats can bring men and supplies to this planned encampment. I want to encourage them in this, for I believe a Roman garrison on the coast may discourage the attacks of the Sea-wolves, and so will help to keep my people safe."

"I have heard there is such a place not far beyond the borders of my land, where there is a fine harbor with a river for water, and high ground nearby for defense. Perhaps you know of this site?"

I do. I first visited the area during my time driving the back roads of East Anglia, and found a tiny coastal hamlet that was once a thriving city and boasted a fine harbor in the mouth of a river. Then erosion erased the harbor, changed the course of the river, and sent most of the town to the bottom of the sea. Today, the village is little more than a museum of artefacts from the distant past and a pub.

We sent a drone over the site and found no signs of permanent occupation. There are paths, so people may travel through there, probably hunters or fishers. But no one lives here. Like with Tordur, the people moved inland and away from the dangers of the coast. The harbor looks spacious and sheltered – the best available for miles along the coast. Captain Johansen wants to make a trip up the coast soon to check if the water in the harbor is deep enough for our ship. Our drones aren't equipped to map water depths – we can only do that with the sonar onboard the ship. If so, he would like to anchor there, where we are more sheltered from the weather. He also wants to be closer to shore. Some of the crew members haven't been off the boat in the nearly two weeks we've been here, and they're getting a little stir-crazy. If we can move to a more sheltered place close to shore, they can spend more time on the land.

"Maximus wishes to visit the site, to see it with his own eyes before seeking the permission of his superior in Londinium to send the force northward to build and garrison such a place. However, he is not able to devote the three weeks or more such a trip will require until later this summer. That may make it too late in the year for his men to construct a fort before winter arrives. He has heard of your bird, and mused that perhaps you could carry him to the site faster than would his horse. I must admit that I would be most happy to have Romans busy building a fort far from here, rather than camped on my doorstep.

Keep them busy, for if they remain idle for too long they may forget their treaty."

I carefully form my reply; I don't want to get too much into the details of time travel here. "I know of such a site. We have seen it from our bird and plan to take our boat there so we can learn the depth of the water. We have room to take you and Maximus with us, and can bring you back here in a single day." Really, we could make the entire trip by air, but I want Maximus to see our ship – just in case he has any ideas of launching a naval attack against us, I want him to see what he's up against. Okay, I admit, I'm also showing off a bit.

The king adds a question. "If the harbor is too shallow for your boat, will it be of use to the Romans?"

I reply, "Yes, it may well be. Our boat is much larger and needs deeper water than those of the Romans. But we will find out exactly what the bottom looks like. We can see below the water and can tell them if it is safe and create a map of any rocks or other hazards." I don't explain more, and the king doesn't ask; our ship draws just over twenty feet; the largest of the Roman merchant boats draw only eight feet fully loaded.

Meanwhile, Martin has been keeping me posted on the happenings in the courtyard; what he sees is confusing me, because it is so at odds with the conversation in here. A group of guards have gathered just outside the doors. Their deportment and manner does not look like an idly curious group waiting to get a glimpse of strangers from a distant land. They are facing the doors, with spears at the ready. By their dress, the soldiers are Brythonic, not Romans.

I decide to address them with the king. "I see you have many armed men gathered outside the doors of this hall. You might want to call them off before we leave. I would hate for any of them to get hurt because of a misunderstanding."

Cydyrn smiles for the first time. "Your concern for my men is most gratifying."

"Let us now present to you the boar we brought."

I then switch to English and press my talk switch. "Guys, bring up the boar." I say, just above a whisper, barely loud enough for the king to hear. Of course, he has no idea what I said, but he's smart. When they immediately start bringing it forward, he realizes that I signalled them. He just doesn't know how.

When they get to the front, I speak again. "I can see many scars on this old one, so I think he's been hunted before, and got away. He's terrorized your people, hasn't he? Perhaps you've hunted him yourself? This wound here," I say pointing to the wound from Bledwyn's arrow, "should have stopped him, but he didn't even slow down. But look at this one," pointing to the bullet hole just above the eye. "When you hunt boar, do you aim for the forehead? No, because he can see your spear and dodge it and the skull is thick and strong, so even if you do get a hit, your weapon may not penetrate. But here, we have weapons that made this hole, and this one through the chest, all the way to the heart."

Pointing at the shield beside the throne, leaning against the wall, I add "I could put a hole right through your shield and through anyone standing behind it, no matter how good the armor they might be wearing. As could any of the other warriors with me. Do not make the mistake of underestimating us."

"But enough of talk of fights, weapons, and wounding people. We are friends, we will help you with the Romans, and there is no need for violence between us. Call your men to take this boar to the cookery that they may share in it. And send word to the people of the forest, that the boar who has been menacing them is now turning on a spit for the table of the king."

The tension that was building in the room eases. Cydyrn motions to a steward I barely noticed who leaves his spot in the shadows of the corner, and comes to the King. They have a quick, whispered conversation. The steward then motions two of the soldiers guarding the door forward. A quick conversation and they move to take the boar from Lance and Kelly. I move in their direction, and am standing by the hearth when they hand the boar over to the soldiers, who then leave. That is when several more soldiers enter in their place.

The tension is back, but I turn and face Cydyrn. "We will now take our leave, and will return tomorrow with our bird. We will be outside your gates in the field to the west of your wall late in the morning. Today, we would like to visit your market before we leave. Do you want us to call The Bird, to have it come here so you can see with your own eyes today, or shall we wait until tomorrow?"

The attack comes before he responds. I hear the chocked-off start of a cry from my left. I am just turning to see what is happening when I feel arms around me. Don't these guys have any other tricks than grabbing women from behind? This one doesn't have any better luck than Bledwyn had when he tired the same thing. Much worse luck, actually, since when he lands, his leg hits hard on the corner of the hearth, right on the edge of the line of raised stones that keep the fire in place. It doesn't take a medical degree to see that leg is broken. But I'm not worried about him right now; I have my rifle out, safety off, and am looking for the source of the scream. Taylor's eyes are huge with terror; I see an arm around his neck and a hand against the side of his head – the warrior could snap his neck in a second. They are near the far wall – just far enough that I can get a shot away. My bullet hits just above his left eye, and he drops like a stone leaving a spray of blood, bone, and brain on the wall behind him. Taylor hits the ground and rolls away from the body; he looks to be okay.

The scream came from Genovea. Another soldier has her, hand over her mouth. I can't get a shot off; they're too close, not even twenty feet away. But he doesn't know that. He saw what happened to his two mates already, and is backing away from this deadly woman. Since I can't shoot just yet, I take a quick glance around the room. Bledwyn and Muirenn have been herded to the front of the room, and are standing between two guards between me and the king. He's using them as human shields.

Kelly and Lance are surrounded by four more guards over by the door. They don't seem to be threatened, and I'm pretty sure they can take care of themselves; both are armed, and Lance is a decent shot, so I can ignore them for now. *Where's Michael?* Now I spot him, crouched by the wall behind Genovea and her captor, knife in hand. *How did they miss him?* He's about six foot, three and well-built, with that rugged, outdoors look you expect from a forest ranger, so he's a little hard to miss. I'm glad they did, because we've got this soldier surrounded. Without changing my expression to give any hint of what I see, I return my attention to Genovea. I now take a step, looking like I'm trying for a better shot, but really to push them toward Michael. That's a mistake, because one of the guards by the king follows the movement, and spots Michael in the back.

"Behind you," he shouts to his comrade.

The man glances over his shoulder, sees Michael, and releases Genovea, pushing her away as he very quickly backs away from her. As soon as she's free, she runs toward Michael and I know she's safe, so I swing my attention back to the front. I am furious with the king that his men attacked us under the guise of friendship, so I'm ready to fire when I face the king.

He has pushed both Bledwyn and Muirenn aside, and is standing between them with a look of complete shock on his face.

I hold my fire as he speaks. "I wanted to know if you were real, to see how your men would respond to a sudden attack. Would your men number their foes first or act first? We need people of courage on our side. I couldn't believe that a people who carried no swords, spears, or shields could defend themselves, let alone help protect us against the Romans. I had to test you and I must admit that I did not expect you to react with such speed or with such force. I am sorry, but until I saw with my own eyes I did not believe the stories I heard. Since you are strangers in this land, I could not fully trust your words. Now I see that if anything, you understated your strength."

"I'm not looking for a fight with the Romans. I now know having you on our side could give us hope, yet I believe ultimately the Romans will prevail. You will not always be here, and I worry for not only myself and my people, but the children who will come after me and their children. The lesson they taught the Iceni is not lost on me: if we fight and lose, they will utterly destroy our people. No, I will honor my treaty and will keep the peace with these people. So, I accept your other offer to lead us and the Romans to the harbor you have found."

For a few seconds, everyone stands frozen in silence, waiting for me to respond. I did it again – killed someone without giving them any chance to realize their danger and back away. Unlike Michael. The one he targeted is alive and unharmed – and so is Genovea. I left one wounded, one dead. And Taylor didn't need the trauma of seeing a man get his head blown off literally within inches of his own.

I deal with the situation the way I usually do – ignore it and hope it goes away. "I am honored. We will return tomorrow, two hours before noon to pick up you and Maximus for the journey to the harbor."

As I bow and turn to leave, I press my talk switch and peak in English. "Martin, what can you see out there? We're all okay, but leaving behind one dead plus we have one wounded to tend to. Bledwyn told the soldiers in the yard to go prepare for a feast. Are they leaving?"

"Most left and are returning to their huts. There are three kind of milling around, looking like they are not too sure what they should be doing. Two are armed with spears, the other has a sword. All three are standing in the shade of the stables, about fifteen meters from the door, on the right as you exit. I don't know if they're a threat or not, but keep your eyes open."

"I doubt they'll stick around for long. Can you make sure the rescue basket is in The Bird and get over here? We've got a nasty broken leg for Sandy to deal with, and the courtyard here is pretty tight for a landing."

"Kelly already told us. Jack's already on the way with an ETA of fifteen minutes." Jerry's voice breaks through. I should have known Kelly would be on top of things.

The anthropologist in me is fascinated by the difference in the treatment accorded Muirenn and Bledwyn as members of status in the tribe, and the rest of the team. It wasn't lost on me that they were pulled aside and were not part of the test. Maybe they weren't really human shields to protect Cydyrn. The test was for the outsiders and the attack was directed us. Interesting that Michael was ignored. *I wonder; did they just lose track of him, or did they not see him as a threat for some reason?* Could be that between the darkness and the distraction I created, they lost sight of him. His African-American background gives him dark skin, and there isn't much light in here. It certainly couldn't be that they didn't think he was a threat – he is the biggest member of the team and his build reveals his great physical strength. I'll have to think that one over later. But now the challenge is to get the wounded man on board the chopper and the rest of the team to the landing zone. The courtyard is clear, but the marketplace is crowded with merchants and shoppers. I'm guessing that will change quickly when the chopper arrives. I'm not keen about flying here, but we have no choice. Kelly tells me it's a serious fracture and carrying the man back to our drop-off zone is not an option. The plan now is to load him and Kelly with the winch from the courtyard, and then Jack will set down in a landing zone (LZ) they picked out in the field outside the main gates to board the rest of the team. Martin doesn't see sign of soldiers in or around the market, so we should have a clear run to the LZ. That doesn't mean they aren't there, but I'm betting even Rome's elite forces will clear out when Jack arrives on the scene.

I turn to check on the wounded man, but I stop when I see Genovea standing to the side staring at the dead man who had Taylor by the neck before, eyes full of tears.

Pointing at him, she says "You killed him! And you would have killed the man who had me if he hadn't let me go. Why? He's a warrior, guard to the king. I'm just a peasant girl, who doesn't even belong here. Why do you care more about me than this man?"

How to answer that one in a way she'll understand? And in a way that I can live with. I know why I'm so protective of these girls, but when I stop and think about it as an anthropologist, her confusion makes sense. Her cultural perspective sees a strong warrior in the prime of life as contributing more to the survival of the tribe than a girl who tends crops.

I take a deep breath and answer. "When I was about your age, I was hurt badly some men. Because you are my friend, I don't want the same thing to happen to you. I also see in you the potential to be far more than a tender of crops. You are smart, confident and you have a way with words that people notice. You are strong in your own way; you can change your world for future generations in the way a mere warrior can't."

There's more I want to say, but the distant thump of the approaching chopper gets me off the hook for now. I'm glad that Jack is at the controls, because his fire-fighting experience makes him our best pilot for rescue work. Don and Jerry are onboard to man the rescue line. Lance and Kelly can manage on the ground and with two at each end, everything should go smoothly. Once the patient is on board, they'll send the line back with a harness and winch Kelly up. The rest of us will run to the landing zone and board there. I doubt we'll need to dodge crowds in the market, because the chopper flying low overhead will send them scurrying for cover.

Just before we leave, the king speaks up again. "I am told your dragon breathes fire. Is that true?"

News travels fast. I guess he heard of our defense of Dubri-tun, but still doesn't quite believe it.

I reply, "Yes, it is true. But only when we want it to."

"I would most like to see that. Until tomorrow then, farewell."

Everything moves fast now. Doors open and the team heads out as Jack brings the chopper to a hover as close as he can to the middle of the courtyard so he doesn't blow the thatch off all the surrounding roofs. Michael, Taylor, Bledwyn, and Genovea head through the doors. Michael and Bledwyn will help with the stretcher; Taylor is there to get some footage of history's first helicopter rescue. And Genovea won't miss this for anything. Muirenn – *where's Muirenn?* Ah – I see her. She is watching Kelly.

Kelly is still inside, caring for the man. He was knocked out when he landed on the stone floor and became pretty combative when he started to gain consciousness, so Kelly had to sedate him so he could immobilize the leg and prepare him for transit. It takes only a couple of minutes before Michael and Bledwyn come in with the rescue basket. Kelly supports the leg as Lance, Michael, Bledwyn, and I all line up to roll him smoothly into the basket. Then he gets goggles and hearing protectors before we belt him in. All four of us wheel the loaded stretcher across the floor of the hall, then carry it the over the soft ground of the courtyard to the waiting cable.

Just as he is disappearing into The Bird, a group of four women come rushing through the swirling dust toward the hall, hair flying from the intense downwash, terrified by the hovering chopper, but coming forward all the same. One looks to be a little older than me, and from her dress; I guess she is someone of status. *The queen?* Two others both look to be somewhat younger than her. The fourth is clearly younger than me and shares my red hair – the first redhead I've seen here. I like her already. She looks to be crying and in shock, too. Of course, their eyes could be just watering from dust kicked up by the downwash, but I'm pretty sure there is something more. I follow them into the hall, where they quickly demand to know what happened. One, the redhead, runs to the body of the man I shot. Uh-oh. Probably her husband. I can't take my eyes off her. Clearly now, she's a lot younger than me. Twenty at most. From what is left of the man's face, I guess he was young too. Now I know those tears weren't just from the dust.

Now what? Forget the fact that it was me who is the cause of her grief; she's just another young woman who's had her life torn apart by a death. I know something about that. I'm half aware the other two women are standing in the room, looking around, confused. Someone else is there with them now – Muirenn; she's hit her talk switch so I can hear their conversation. I don't know if it was by accident or design, but I'm glad she did for I learn from their talk that the red-head is in fact the wife of the dead man.

Never before have I had to face the family of someone I killed. Genovea is beside me watching – I'm pretty sure she's made the connection, because she can hear, too. This means I can't just do what I really want to do and slink back into the darkness and leave her to be comforted by someone else. *Why did she have to arrive before we cleared out?* I swallow, pop out my earpiece so I won't be distracted, and step forward.

Her full attention is on the corpse in front of her, so she doesn't notice my approach and jumps as I lay a hand on her shoulder, then turns and looks to see who is touching her. She sees my face and my hair and slowly rises to her feet, turning to face me. *Does she know it was my weapon that led to her husband lying here with half his head missing?* I fully expect her to hit me or worse, when I see a half-smile cross her face through the tears. When she throws her arms around me, I am so shocked that I almost fall over. She starts speaking in a language I have never before heard. It sounds like the Brythonic tongues I've started to learn; the tones are similar, but I can't make out any words. It doesn't help that she speaks very rapidly and barely above a whisper.

Nevertheless, I return her hug before responding, intensely relieved that she hasn't tried to kill me in retaliation for dispatching her husband. At least not yet.

"I'm sorry, I don't understand" I say in Brythonic. On a hunch I add "Do you know Latin?"

She does, and she quickly tells her story. Her name is Ahntya, and she's originally from Gaul. Her family, workers in cloth, followed the Romans to this island when she was a young child. She often came to the market here with her father to purchase raw wool and cloth for them to work into garments. On one of her trips, she met a warrior from the town, and the rest was history. She knew from her parents there were others with red hair in Gaul, but had never seen one since coming to the island until today. So she naturally thought I was also from there and spoke in her native language, hoping I would understand.

I am not ... but I know someone who is. "Come with me." I tell her. "We have a man from Gaul with us."

She nods yes and breaks off the hug just as Muirenn arrives with the other two women. They are wife and sister to the injured man. The sister's husband recently died, so she is also dependent on him. They won't be left behind so we will fly them to the ship to be with him. But that creates a problem – the chopper won't fit fourteen people plus the stretcher case. Some will need to stay behind and get picked up later. I reluctantly reinsert my earpiece and join the conversation. *I want to stay and explore the town a little, but if I do, will everyone be able to communicate?* We have four languages represented in our little group now and I am usually called on to help translate. Max assures me that he will help out so they should be okay. If they need my help, I'll be on the radio. Yeah right, so I'll be the one trying to be inconspicuous while I wander through the market wearing strange clothes and talking to myself!

We all run through a marketplace that is now completely barren of people. toward the gate and the LZ. As we run, I catch glimpses of terrified faces peeking out from behind doors and shutters. Of course, we can't run fast enough to keep up with the chopper, so Jack has it on the ground and is doing his best to look bored by the time we show up. On the positive side, there is no need for crowd control. Everyone who wasn't already under cover has scattered at the sight of this huge, noisy flying thing, just above their heads.

Muirenn, Taylor, and Genovea decide to stay behind with me, so after we help the rest of the team climb on board, we back away so Jack can take off. He'll be back in about an hour, so we get to browse the marketplace while ignoring Martin's inevitable comments about turning women loose on a shopping trip.

At least Taylor comes to my defense. "Martin, be nice to her. Just remember what happened to the last two guys who pissed her off," he chips in as we approach the gates.

"I'll keep that in mind."

Yeah, that's me. Violent. Unpredictable. Reactionary. Deadly. So far today I've killed one man and injured another. And it's not even noon. Maybe I am too quick to use deadly force. But now is not the time to second guess myself; we are walking through the main gates of Wynt and into the main street of the market.

Chapter 16.

When I pass through the gateway, I find the marketplace is not quite abandoned. A few brave souls have returned to the street. Merchants are guarding their stock and a few purchasers are wandering around trying to take advantage of the sparse crowds in the hopes of getting a better deal. Others are peering from the doorways of shops, trying to decide if it is safe to return outdoors. Those who see us enter the gate gain courage since we appear to be completely unharmed from our encounter with the dragon.

Along each side of the wide street are the homes and shops of the merchants. There is a bake house, an abattoir, an iron monger, woodworkers, sellers of fabric and pottery, and even a tannery. Down the middle of the street are the sellers of livestock and other goods who come from surrounding towns on market days. I feel more at home here than I do with Robyn and her people. Don't misunderstand – they're really good to me and I like being with them. But I just can't get used to all the things they have. This is much closer to home, where I can speak my own language and people will understand me. Today I just want to fit in and be myself, so I'm wearing my own clothes instead of the ones Michele lent me. Genovea is wearing clothes they gave her, and both Robyn and Taylor are dressed in the green, brown, and grey that helps them hide in the forest. Here they all stick out as foreigners. But this is where I belong, so I really want to leave them behind and explore the market on my own terms.

I run ahead of the others; just inside the gates, I turn and enter the shop of a grain merchant. Bledwyn told me to drop in on this man, for he is well known to our people. Since this gets me away from the rest of the team, it suits me well. Whenever we have extra grain to sell, this is the man we bring it to. Extra grain doesn't happen every year. If the weather is bad or the pillaging from the Sea-wolves or Romans is worse than usual, we may have barely enough to feed our own people and have seed for the following year. Bledwyn thinks this year will bring a fine harvest. So far, the weather has been good, we have peace with the Romans, and Robyn drove the Sea-wolves from our shores. We should have plenty to sell, so the grain merchant will be our friend come harvest.

"Greetings," I call out as I duck through the door. It takes a bit for my eyes to adjust to the inside darkness after the bright sun outside, but I can tell from the sound the room is full of frightened people, even if I can't see them yet.

"Is the dragon gone now?" I hear someone ask. I can't make out the speaker, but from the accent, I know they are a member of my tribe.

"Yes, it is gone." I reply to the room. "It will be back soon, but do not be afraid – it is our friend, and will not harm you as long as you don't get too close when it is near the ground." Not like that might even happen – the noise and dust whipped up by the powerful wind is enough to keep anyone back; even Robyn gives it space when it lands.

Now that my eyes are adjusted, I can see the pale faces staring up at me from under the tables where they are crouched for safety. Slowly, a few crawl out and stretch; some peer out the door to see others safely walking in the market. An older man – I think he's the grain merchant, the owner of this shop – is not so sure. "How do you know it is safe?"

"I am Muirenn of Cynbel, chieftain of Tordur. The dragon belongs to friends of ours; they ride it almost like we ride horses, and I often accompany them. With it they drove the Sea-wolves away from our shores just a few days ago. They have also taken my brother Bledwyn and me to visit the large boat where they live. Tomorrow, they will take King Cydyrn and Maximus to see the site for a new town the Romans want to build on the sea coast."

My name means nothing to him, but I see a flash of recognition cross the face of the merchant when he hears the names of my father and my home.

"I know your father, for we have often done business in the past, when the gods have been good to you and the harvest fruitful."

"I came to see you; we hope for a good harvest this year and may well have grain to sell. Bledwyn asked me to tell you that we see you as a friend and will come to you first."

"Give my thanks to your brother, and greetings to your father." He replies. "The Romans are bringing more troops to our land, so each

*year they need more grain. As you can see, my stock is nearly gone."
He adds pointing to the empty grain bins behind him. "I will sleep
better tonight knowing that your father thinks so highly of me, and
your prospects are for a bounty this year."*

*"Right. Go have a nap." I mutter as I turn to leave. All the grain
merchants are the same. At this time of the year, they have nothing in
stock and prices are sky-high if we come looking to buy. They promise
that come harvest, they will buy everything we can supply. When the
time comes, they will have full bins and will only be able to offer a
token amount for our produce, because they don't have anyone buying
and they don't know where they will put it until they do. According to
Bledwyn, this merchant is actually slightly better than most – he will
at least give us a reasonable price after the usual complaints and
excuses.*

*I have ignored the voices in my ear – Martin and Robyn are talking
back and forth, but now that I am back outside, I pay a little more
attention. Just as I spot Robyn across the market, I hear her call to
me. They are going to wait a bit before The Bird comes back for us,
giving us more time to explore.*

Excellent.

*I quickly step into the shop next door before the rest of the team spots
me. Too late – Genovea follows just behind me. I don't want her to
embarrass me – I actually want to pretend I don't know her, but she
isn't going to let that happen.*

*"Hi Muirenn," she says, looking me right in the eye. "The market is
getting crowded again now that The Bird is gone. Maybe since it
didn't harm anyone, they won't be as scared when it comes back to
pick us up."*

*No way to ignore her. At least she doesn't stand around with her
mouth open in awe like I expected her to. But then, she's seen so much
in the last few days, I guess this really isn't that impressive.*

*This booth sells fabric, and I've never seen so much in one place in
my life. Maybe a few days ago, I would have been amazed.*

183

"A few days ago, this would have seemed extraordinary." She says, echoing my thoughts. "I might have stood in the middle of the room with my jaw hanging open. Now, after days of flying through the air, meeting the king, and all the rest, this is kind of meh. She said this with a hand movement.

"'Meh.' What does that mean?" I'm a little annoyed that she uses the words she's learned from Robyn's people so freely. But I'm also a little jealous that she's picked one that I haven't.

"I heard Michele use it. It means 'this does NOT impress me much'."

Meh. New word. I like it. But I'm not about to admit that in front of Genovea. But I guess I can let her stay around me. At least we can talk without having to translate everything. And she isn't wearing the same green as Robyn and Taylor. She's wearing sort of a short coat that almost matches the color of her eyes and black breeches. I have to admit, it is an attractive combination. And I bet these people haven't seen fabric in that color before.

Once again, my eyes need to adjust to the dim interior. Most everything we wear is wool, leather, or fur. The wool is mostly woven at home or one of the settlements near us. The leather and fur comes from the animals we eat. Furs are for winter when we need the warmth; wool for the rest of the year. Leather covers our feet and is sometimes worn in the seasons where it is neither hot nor cold. We leave the wool natural or dye it with colors from plants – muted browns, reds, greens, and blues. The Romans have introduced new fabrics – linen and cotton that are cool in the summer. Some settlements have started to grow flax and weave linen, but cotton has to come from far away, so is very dear. The Romans also brought new colors, but even they don't have a green like Genovea is wearing. And I have never before seen fabric that is so black either. This should be interesting

The faces I see in the shop show the expected mix of expressions. Fear mostly, but also some wonder. I'm officially envious now; the wonder is clearly directed mostly at Genovea. I guess I should have expected it, given what she is wearing and the fact the people here know fabrics.

"Hi." I speak up and take matters into my own hands. "The dragon has left. It will return, but will not harm you. It is only coming back to give us a ride home." There! That should give them something to think about other than Genovea's clothes.

It does, for a short time. But once the people who sought shelter in the shop get over their terror and return to the street, the merchant switches his attention back to Genovea.

"What is it that you are wearing? I've never seen anything like it? What is it made of, and how did you get that color?"

Genovea speaks up "It came from the far west, across the great water and belongs to my friends, the ones who ride the dragon. They let me wear it because it is the same color as my eyes." She flashes a smile that nearly fills the room. "I do not know what it is made from, but it is so soft, and it stretches – I haven't worn anything like before. Here, feel it," she adds, stretching out her arm.

I think I might be sick.

"These breeches also stretch; they are so comfortable to wear." She puts her foot up on the table that serves as a counter so that can be felt, too.

They also reveal every curve of her body. She definitely has the full attention of the man behind the counter now. The woman – his wife I presume – is trying to decide whether to be curious at these strange and wonderful clothes or to be angry at this little flirt.

I guess my feelings must show, because when she looks at me, the smile drains from her face.

"What did I do wrong?"

Oh great. She's going to cry.

"Come, let's go outside," I say as I grab her arm and drag her out into the street. The street is crowded now with people. I'd really like to hand her over to Robyn, but I don't see her and I'll probably get *dragged into translation services anyway. I can hear her sniffling, but she's managing to keep the tears in; my anger is fading a bit. I decide I don't really want to scold her in the middle of the street, so I take her to the side of the shop we just left and lean her up against the wall. I'm deciding what to say, but don't get a chance.*

"Muirenn, I'm sorry! I know I offended you, but I didn't mean too. Since I met you, I've looked up to you so much. More than Robyn sometimes, because I can talk to you without stumbling to find words that we both know. I know I'm just a peasant and you are the daughter of a chieftain – until a few days ago, I'd never been past the fields that surround my home. There's so much that's new and amazing between flying through the air, meeting the king, living on the boat and all the rest - I would be totally overwhelmed without you. You are so strong!"

Before I can react, she throws her arms around me, buries her head on my shoulder, and starts sobbing. She's right – this is all so new and overwhelming, maybe I should be more gentle with her. Now I can feel tears filling my eyes. I'm not going to cry, I'm not going to cry. "I'm not ...," I tell myself. In the nick of time she pulls herself together and settles into a quiet whimper.

I decide now is the time to speak. "You practically threw yourself at that man. That makes you look like a common slut – no woman of quality will do that. Not only that, but his wife was standing right beside him."

"I'm sorry. It's just that I can't face spending my life tending crops and weaving cloth. It was bad enough before when I only dreamed of life beyond our fields. Now that I've seen what is outside, the thought of going back and getting stuck there is even worse! In my world, the only way out for a girl is to marry one of the merchants who come through. We're not on a main road and we are not wealthy, so we have few visitors – mostly the same merchants who come each year to purchase our cloth or sell us the few goods we can afford.

"Robyn and her people will leave one day and go back to their home across the sea – that magical other world where they live. Just from the little they've let me see, I can't imagine staying here. I hope they'll take me – maybe both of us if you want to go too – home with them. But maybe they won't – maybe they can't, like in the stories where the

immortals can come to our world, but we can't go to theirs. I don't know. I'm just so afraid that I'll have to go back home – we're so small and forgotten that we don't even have a name. Or maybe I'll wake up in my bed and find out this is all a dream. So when I saw the merchant, I just had to try my best."

Something struck me in her words, so I reply "What about Luseth; would you leave your sister behind?"

"We talked last night. She just wants to go back home. Living on a boat, flying through the air, and all the rest terrifies her. She would never choose to go with them. She wants to get home before her baby is born. Sooner or later, I will have to say goodbye to her or give up on all my dreams. Home is so familiar and comfortable, and it means more to her than any adventure."

I can hear sadness in her voice, but something more. Anger? Not quite – more like distain that Luseth would rather stay home where she feels safe than to experience the world. Part of me understands her attitude – part of me wonders how little it would take for her to turn her back on men or anyone else who threatens her dreams for that matter. She scares me just a little.

I start at the sound of a voice in my ear – I forgot about my earpiece. I hear Martin speak and Robyn reply; other voices come on. I hear Robyn conversing with someone else in Latin, and I wonder who until I remember Ahntya, the woman who came from here who speaks Latin. Good – now I am not the only one who can translate for them. I wonder how long she will stay with us.

But now, I want to see just as much of the market as possible before The Bird comes back. There is an iron monger next. I'd know the smells and sounds of a forge anywhere.

"Genovea, let's skip this one, and check out something else. I can show you a forge at home."

Next to that is a bake house. We head in there in the hope of escaping the stench of the animals and the tannery. It's not a lot better inside, but the aroma of fresh bread does help mask the stench. We watch as *the baker pulls some bread fresh from the oven and dumps it into a wooden bin on the counter in front of us. Several other people rush in to buy the warm bread, pushing us back into the corner. I stare at the disappearing bread and notice how hungry I am at the exact same time I also realize that we need money if we want to buy some. And of course, we don't have any.*

Very rarely have I handled coins. My father has a bag full, which he keeps hidden under his bed. He taught me the values of the various coins and what each will buy, so I recognize the coins the people are paying and a sesterce is about right for a loaf of fresh bread. Not that my knowledge does us any good here and now so we turn toward the door just as Robyn comes in.

"I thought I would find you two were in here."

I wish she hadn't come in. I want to fade into the background today, but I can't with Robyn here. She's just so obviously doesn't belong. But then Genovea isn't any better – her clothes stick out as much as Robyn's. I want to get out of here, but Robyn is blocking the doorway and Taylor is right behind.

"Let's get some bread to take back to the boat. And maybe eat some on the way."

Maybe I will stay then, a little longer. It seems odd that those from the other world would use our money, but she pulls out three denarii for a dozen loaves of bread and sticks them into a fabric bag. One she breaks into four and hands a piece to each of us as we walk out the door. I didn't know that Robyn had any money – she's never mentioned it, but I guess the subject never came up. I shouldn't be surprised, I guess. She has everything.

But still I speak up. "I didn't know you used money in your world."

"We do. It just looks very different from your money, and the merchants here would be most unlikely to accept it. I sold a piece of iron to the ironmonger next door to get this money. If you want, I can show you what our money looks like when we get back to the boat."

"Yes, please. That will be wonderful," comes from Genovea.

But now I hear the distant thumping of The Bird and look around at the people in the market. Most look scared, but not everyone is running for cover like they did this morning. A few are staring at the sky as we calmly walk out the gate, eating our fresh bread as we leave the crowds of the market behind. A few others even stand nearby and watch as The Bird settles to the ground in an open field. One is a girl about my age, dressed in the clothes of a merchant. A few weeks ago, I might have been jealous of her, but today I feel her jealousy as I step away from the wall and boldly walk toward The Bird. I see her through my window, still standing there watching us as we lift off and fly in the direction of the boat.

Chapter 17.

Day dawns, and it promises to be a hot one. I'd like to plant the team on the beach and let them relax, but we have a promise to keep. Honestly, I'd like to plant myself on the beach today. I didn't sleep much last night so this morning I'm exhausted. And this time it wasn't dreams of death and fire that kept me awake; I kept thinking about today and wondering how it will play out. Maybe later this afternoon we will have a chance to relax, but not for a few hours at least. Shortly after 9:00 am, we take off to pick up Cydyrn and Maximus at Wynt. As soon as we leave, Captain Johansen will take the ship north toward the harbor that is our destination. The journey will take him a little over two hours, so we should catch up just as he approaches the entrance. We will land on the ship and sail into the harbor, watching from the deck or mission control – the Captain won't allow any extras on the bridge during such sensitive maneuvers. Not the king, not the tribune. No one who is not on-duty crew. Only when the anchor is dropped and the engines are shut down will they finally be welcomed to that sacred place.

Marcelus is looking very un-Roman now, sporting a new haircut courtesy of Michele and the start of a beard. Dressed in jeans and sweatshirt that is pretty much the uniform of most of our crew, he fits right in. For some reason, he is managing to pick up English with a distinct Australian accent, so Michele is teaching him all the Aussie slang she knows. He is so much part of the crew that it is hard to remember he's only been with us for such a short time. He usually doesn't wear his sling anymore, but I know that arm still hurts a lot sometimes. There's not much chance of Maximus will recognize his missing soldier, they met only a couple of times, and never in a memorable way. Just to be safe, he'll confine himself to Mission Control and stick to English for the day.

Taylor, Bledwyn, Muirenn, and Genovea are all on board the chopper for the trip to Wynt. Trace is at the controls, since she is our most experienced over-water pilot. We don't expect trouble, but I am armed just in case, and we are all wearing body armor. Of course, we also have our rockets. I think we are ready for anything.

Anything, except for the spectacle we see as we fly over the walls of Wynt toward our landing zone! There must be five hundred people lined up against the walls and along the line of trees surrounding the field. In the middle is a large pile of wood – there's no mistaking it for an unlit bonfire. I can see the king and Maximus standing side-by-side front and center, bracketed by soldiers holding staffs with banners hanging limp in the calm.

It takes Trace about ten seconds to understand the set up. "They want us to light the fire. I'm not at the right angle, so I'll overfly the LZ and come around for another approach."

Recently, we've been giving people turns riding shotgun in the right front seat on flights over secure territory. This morning was Muirenn's turn – if it was a wide open field with no people around, I would let her fire a rocket. But with so many people nearby, a miss could lead to a lot of people getting badly hurt.

"Muirenn," I call over the intercom. "They want us to light the fire. I need to sit where you are to make the dragon breathe fire. I'm coming up to switch places with you."

"Can you show me?"

I thought she'd say that.

"It takes some practice, and there isn't time to show you. You can watch."

Reluctantly, she climbs out of her seat and lets me slide in just as we are passing the middle of the field. People aren't running for cover today – they are standing, looking up expectantly at us. "Trace, line me up at fifteen hundred meters, I'll fire at a thousand." I want a little extra time to be sure of my aim.

I feel Muirenn lean against the seat back as Trace makes the turn toward the target. Heads-up display is on; I select incendiary, and flip off the safety. When the fire swings into view, the rangefinder shows fifteen hundred and two meters – I knew she'd nail the distance. I hold the aim just above the base of the woodpile and watch the range count down. As soon as it reaches a thousand, I fire the rocket. Trace banks to the left and prepares to land away from the crowds. The trail of white smoke leads straight to the fire; I can see the rocket hit, the wood fall over from the impact, and the blaze take hold as the wood ignites.

By the time we touch down, the fire is fully involved, and people are running toward it with more wood, and what looks to be food – including the boar we shot yesterday. So we just lit the fire for their feast!

Now I can see the banners carried by the heralds standing beside King Cydyrn, spread out from our downdraft. They are green, emblazoned with a red dragon. Those by Maximus also have dragons – green on white background. They look new – *have we given both groups a symbol to rally under?*

As Trace powers down, the king and Maximus slowly approach the chopper with their retunes. Bledwyn and I jump out to welcome them. I have no idea what the protocol is for meeting a king and a tribune, so I let Bledwyn take the lead. Cydyrn does not go for ceremony.

He comes bouncing up like a little kid. "I can't believe what I just saw! It was a stream of smoke, right into the wood then a flash like lightning and 'poof,' the fire appeared. I never imagined that dragon fire was like that. As you can see, I have adopted the dragon as my symbol. Today, you have given my people confidence that I am doing the right thing by treating with the Romans. If the dragon is on my side, my people will trust that I have great power and strength – and maybe wisdom too."

No doubt Maximus and his legions will remember the dragon is on Cydyrn's side. That should offer him some protection from them changing their minds about the peace treaty. Once he sees our ship, I hope he will be even less inclined to launch an offensive against either us or our friends.

I get a close look at Maximus for the first time. He is short, but very muscular. His closely-cropped hair is mostly grey; with his weather-worn face, I put him well into his forties. He has the carriage of career officers everywhere – and apparently every time – that comes from long years of carrying out orders and expecting their orders to be carried out. I can see that he is used to living rough, but also enjoys the comforts and respect that come with the job. I'm pretty sure ceremony will be wasted on him. He's here to do a job. I'm good with that – ceremony was always wasted on me, too.

"Welcome. We have room for both of you and two of your men. Let's get going so we can have you back in time for the feast." We could actually take a total of six, but the last two would be in the jump seats at the back, which are not very comfortable for someone's first trip in a helicopter.

Maximus and Cydyrn each select one companion. They climb aboard and we get them strapped in. Window seats so they can get a good view. Trace is powering up when I slide the door shut, and lifts off just as I slip into my seat. Our Bird is military throughout, so not exactly luxurious. Even so, I can see them touching everything in reach – I'm glad I didn't put one of them in the front. I do notice Cydyrn's eyebrow raise when he spots Muirenn sitting up front beside Trace. He obviously sees that as a seat of honor. I bet he'll be even more surprised when Genovea is there on the way back to Wynt this afternoon.

Trace takes a route that avoids most towns or settlements. We want to keep the fear level for the people here as low as possible – but we aren't exactly quiet and in the clear skies, there is not much we can do to hide. Occasionally, we overfly an open field and sometimes spot a few workers running for cover.

The exception is Tordur. Because they know us, we fly almost directly overhead, know that instead of fear, our presence will bring security to them. It also happens to lie on a direct line to the coast. Once we reach the water, Trace banks left and heads north, keeping about a kilometer off-shore.

The last time I made this journey it was by car. It was about two hours from my base, but I got lost, so it took me the better part of a day. I wound up getting dinner in a manor house, turned hotel, just a couple miles from the museum. I'm told Charles Dickens wrote *Great Expectations* while staying here. I'd have loved to have stayed the night and maybe get some inspiration from his spirit, but alas, I had to get back to base by midnight. I had to be content with the rack of lamb. It was awesome.

Today, it is less than ten minutes from the time we reach the coast until we spot the north-bound wake of Voyager. There's a pretty good chop in the North Sea today, but Trace doesn't miss a beat as she brings us in for a perfect landing on the moving deck. I watch our guests as she matches the ship's speed and times her descent to the roll of the ship. Cydyrn is excitedly watching out the window – I see Maximus is watching too, but without the king's visible wonder. Maximus would definitely be the better poker player; he keeps his emotions well hidden.

After we land though, he can't hide the awe in his voice as he observes to his companion. "There are no oars, and no sail, yet we are moving fast and into the wind. How?"

"Just wait." I tell him. "Now that we have landed, our Captain will show you something of what we can do."

He hasn't seen anything yet. Captain Johansen slowed the ship to just five knots for our landing – that is about the top speed a Roman ship powered by oars can achieve over short bursts. Now that we are aboard and the helicopter is secured, he can open her up to our 22-knot, long-range cruise speed. We can go faster, but it isn't worth it for such a short journey.

"Helicopter is secured for cruise speed," Andrew's voice comes in over my earpiece.

"Let's go to the front deck, so we can see the harbor as we approach."

With that, I lead the way along the passageway to the front deck. The front deck has always been my favorite place on a ship. In part it is the anticipation of watching the destination draw closer, willing to get there sooner – more of my ADD. It is also the thrill of the wind, and the spray – especially on days like today, when the wind sends the spray flying just enough to feel without getting me wet. It brings back memories of summer holidays, riding the ferry to the island my parents loved so much. Kim and I would be out front from pretty much the time we boarded until the order came to return to our car as the ship prepared to dock. I force that memory from my mind – it's too painful.

I can feel my energy rising as the ship's engines rev up and I feel the deck under my feet pick up speed. As I burst around the corner of the superstructure, an enormous wave breaks on the bow, sending waves of spray over the railing, pretty much drenching all of us in icy North Sea water. YE-HAW!

I lean into the wind and am running forward. Once I reach the middle of the deck I stop and turn. Our guests hang back, not quite sure they want to follow this mad woman onto the pitching deck. "Come on!" I shout waving them forward, and forgetting my Latin for the moment.

Cydyrn is the first to step forward; of course Maximus and the rest have to follow. I can see they are having trouble – but then they have only been on a ship like this for about five minutes and haven't got their sea-legs yet. So I have pity on them, and walk over to the railing, holding on as I make my way to the point at the very front of the ship, and stand with my arms spread, feeling like Rose in *Titanic*. When I feel someone beside me, I turn and am hardly surprised to see Genovea standing on the bottom rung of the railing, leaning over, with her face into the wind. Maybe we're related.

I'd love to stand here all day, but I have guests to attend. As I reluctantly turn toward the group hovering just in front of the bridge – the driest part of the deck, I grab Genovea's hand and lead her away from the rail. Just as we turn, another massive wave breaks, drenching both of us in freezing water. I guess we deserved that.

What I didn't need was Martin's voice in my ear. "Hey, is that water cold? When you come in, don't go dripping on our nice clean floors."

I'll drip wherever I want to drip. At least I left my rifle on the helicopter and my sidearm and electronics are protected in water-resistant cases.

But now we are closing in on the harbor – I can feel the ship slowing as Patrick eases back on the power – so there is no time to go in and get changed. I push my wet hair behind my ears and slosh over to the rest of the group with Genovea trailing behind.

"We are getting close to the harbor – you may have noticed we are slowing down and the land is getting closer. Soon we will be behind the headland that will protect us from the waves and much of the wind. Then you will be able to stand at the front and watch without getting wet. If you prefer, we can go inside, where we will be out of the wind and can also see some things that you can't see here."

As soon as I say 'out of the wind part' it is totally clear what they want, so I lead them all inside and up the stairs to Mission Control. I'm really tempted to give Martin a big, wet hug when I see him. But I don't. We pull up the live feed from Little Bird, circling overhead at ten thousand feet on one of our large screens, and the forward looking sonar on the other.

We are still too far out for the sonar to get a good image of the channel – the water here is over three hundred feet deep – so I shrink the image to only part of the screen and bring up the visual from the mast-head camera. It is gyro-stabilized, so the image is rock-steady, even though the ship is still rolling in the waves. Now I can describe what we are seeing.

The overhead view shows a cliff a couple of hundred feet high on the landside, sloping down to the north and the banks of a river estuary. Below the cliff is a wide gravel beach that curves out in the south. North of the river is a headland that tapers down to a long, curving spit that protects the harbor to the north and east. The entrance is to the southeast, well protected from most storms. The estuary, with shelter from the cliff to the south and the headland to the north, offers protection from almost every storm.

The sonar image gives a three-dimensional map of the sea floor. It is smooth, with no dangerous rocks or shallow bars to endanger ships. The depth through the entrance channel is thirty feet at high tide – more than enough for even our ship. Low tide will be a different matter, although the harbor basin is deep enough, we won't be able to get over that bar when the tide is out. There is another bar near the river mouth that we can't pass, but will not be an obstacle for the Roman ships with their shallower draft.

It takes some time for Maximus to understand what he is seeing – the actual bottom of the sea, so I get up and explain, pointing out the features, zooming in. I think he gets what I'm telling him, but I'm pretty sure he doesn't totally believe it. On the other hand, poor Cydyrn is totally lost – this is too far beyond his experience to even make sense. He's just sitting there like he expects to wake up and find it all a crazy dream.

I'd love to keep the ship here where the crew can enjoy time on the shore and in the water, but that bar at the entrance is a problem. High tide is almost on us, and Captain Johansen warns us we have less than three hours before we need to be back into the North Sea – or we will be stuck here for about eight hours. Too bad. Between the sheltered cove and the river flowing in, the water should be a lot warmer than the stuff that soaked Genovea and me not long ago. And the whole area around here appears to be uninhabited, so shore time should be safe. Besides, the drone found signs of an abandoned settlement nearby which I want to check out.

But Maximus is convinced this site will meet his needs, so now he needs to convince the governor in Londinium that this is the place for a settlement. Then he needs to direct people back here by land and sea with men and materials for a town. We can help him there. Don has already run the photos from the drone through our mapping software and printed off the results on our plotter.

"Maximus," I tell him, "we have some maps we can give you. One shows the harbor and immediate area, the second shows the larger area of the coast and further inland. You can see here the road to the north that runs nearest the coast. The one showing the harbor gives the water depths at low tide – your navy commanders will appreciate that knowledge. These are in meters; each meter is about two cubits. The road distances are in miles, so your men should be able to easily find this place." The numbers were easy. Fortunately Steve installed a converter to Roman numerals before we left home.

I hand him two copies of each map, which in his mind, is a gift beyond value. *How do I explain that Don generated them in a couple of hours this morning and let them print while he was eating lunch?* I don't think I will say anything – let him owe me. He unrolls one – the map of the larger area – and starts to study it. As he looks and realizes the depth of detail, I can see a tear start to well up in his eye.

"Who did this? Not only have I never seen a map like this, but I have never even imagined that one could exist. How do create such fine letters and precise lines? And what is it drawn on? I don't think I have ever seen any material like this before?"

He hasn't – I can guarantee that. Polyester film is one thing the Romans didn't invent.

"Don made the map with a machine that can draw the lines that you see. The material is something that we use for special documents. It is expensive even in our world, but is also very durable. I hope they serve you well."

We couldn't invite a king to our ship without giving him a gift. "Cydyrn, we also have something for you. This is a drawing of Wynt from the air." Don stitched together a set of high-res shots from Little Bird and printed them out at maximum resolution. Not only are the people visible, some can be recognized. I point out Ahntya walking across the courtyard toward Cydyrn's great hall, her red hair gleaming in the sun. I didn't point out the other redhead in the picture, the one dressed in green and just inside the east gate. The photos were taken yesterday morning as we arrived in Wynt.

The king is speechless as he looks at the print, staring at the details. "I've never seen anything like this. It's amazing. Maybe I can show it to people and they'll actually believe that I've ridden a dragon through the air."

I stare at the image of Ahntya. Last night, I got more of her story. She speaks both Latin and the Gallic language of her home, but since she grew up living mostly among the Romans, her Latin is even better than mine. Even though she married a man from Wynt, she learned little of their language. He too spoke Latin learned through his dealings with the Romans, but most of the natives of the town much prefer their own language. She struggled and tried to learn, but for some reason it didn't come easy for her and the other people were of little help – most couldn't see why she couldn't speak like they did. Since her husband was frequently away on the king's business, she found herself very isolated and she felt trapped. Even though he was good to her, he didn't understand her struggles. And they both found their command of Latin as a common language may have been enough to foster a romance, but was inadequate to allow them to express the issues they faced. The fact that she failed to produce a child for him did not help matters.

Then she saw me and was overjoyed for she hoped I could understand her and her language – then was devastated to learn that I couldn't. But she had hope again when I told her I knew someone who could. Then she saw her husband lying on the floor and knew the rumor that brought her and the other women running to the hall was true – he was dead. Grief and shock at his loss was followed by relief at her new found freedom, followed in turn by guilt at her relief. Then came the glimmer of hope that she had a way out of the trap. Then came the news there might be someone she could truly talk with. No wonder she wanted to return to the boat with us.

Turns out Marcelus came from the same region as her family, so they speak the same dialect. Even though they both found their command of the language a little rusty, it soon came back. People don't quickly forget their cradle language. Things got a little tense when he told how he received his injury – that it was I who wounded him. She came to me, asking how her husband died. I finally had to admit that I killed him to protect Taylor.

I knew Taylor was in shock yesterday, but he hid it well in the market, chatting happily and capturing stills and video as we ducked into various stalls. As soon as we landed, he disappeared into his room without a word. Alone time is his way to handle stress. He came out maybe five minutes before Ahntya came to talk to me. He saw the interchange, and even though his Latin is pretty much non-existent, he picked up his name and the glances in his direction and guessed the gist of the conversation.

Ahntya understood. She didn't get angry and slap me across the face, which is about what I expected. Instead, she went over to Taylor and wrapped her arms around him and broke down in tears. Taylor hesitated – mostly out of shock I think – then returned the hug. It didn't take long for the tears to spill out of his eyes, too. Marcelus explained to me that in their beliefs when a warrior is killed in battle, if anyone is touching them at the time they die, his spirit enters that person. In a sense, he isn't gone – he becomes united to that person. Taylor, in this case. So Ahntya is now linked to Taylor.

Marcelus went on to explain that usually this person is another warrior who was there in the battle. In such a case, she comes under his protection. He will take her and any children into his household and she will become his wife.

"What happens in this case? Not only is Taylor no warrior, but he doesn't exactly have a household." Waving my hand to indicate the ship, I added "This is about as close to a home as he has."

Marcelus looked a little perplexed as he thought back, "I don't know. I can't remember ever hearing of such a thing happening." I suppose not.

I thought back to my studies. Many tribes from around the world have a similar custom, so the family of one who dies in battle is protected and provided for. But I have never heard of what happens if the one who has the responsibility – or the right – does not have the ability to care for the widow. I expect she becomes the responsibility of his extended family or even the community at large.

"I guess we are her family now." I mused. "She stays with us for the time being." I don't want to think of having to bring her back with us. Convincing Muirenn and Genovea to stay behind when we leave will be difficult enough. Ahntya will be one more complication.

I know Taylor has no intention of ever settling down and marrying anyone. That is something we have in common, but for different reasons. He doesn't want to be tied down. I don't want to let anyone get that close only to lose them. But I had to bring him up to speed.

"Taylor, let's chat." I pulled him to a corner of the room away from the rest of the crowd.

Ahntya followed us, not wanting to let Taylor out of her sight – or maybe just not sure what else to do. Her presence bothered me a bit – I don't know why since she doesn't know a word of English.

"Looks like we have another stray. This one followed you home." Taylor has been giving me a hard time about the people we've picked up, telling me the strays are following me home. Now it's my turn for payback. Then I repeated what Marcelus told me.

"So what do you think we should do?" he asked. "I am in no position to look after a wife."

I told him my idea – that we explain to Ahntya that since Taylor can't support her, the whole village will band together and help. Ahntya caught her name, and realized we are talking about her. I could see her looking back and forth between Taylor and me as she tried to follow the conversation. So, I switched to Latin and told her what Marcelus explained to me, and asked her if she knew what happens in this case because he didn't. She didn't know either, so I explained how our community would help her.

Last night I put her in the spare bunk in my cabin, thinking that she might be afraid being left by herself in such a strange place. We didn't get a lot of sleep because she kept talking, asking questions about our team, and the Voyager and our world. She also told me a lot about her life. Her dream: get back to her family in Londinium and start her life again there. If they will take her back. They did not approve of her marital choice, and have not spoken with her since the day she moved to Wynt. As far as she knows, they haven't even visited the market. Her father is a pretty competitive businessman and Wynt is an important market for the entire area, so he has most likely been there. If he was, he didn't bother to look her up. Even when she did finally run out of questions and drift off, I didn't sleep. I lay awake wondering what we are going to do with all these strays.

But now April comes up to me, bumping me back to the present. "Captain, the Captain is ready to welcome the visitors to the bridge." *Why is it only the ship crew on the team call me "Captain" I wonder?* To everyone else, I am just Robyn.

We gather Cydyrn and Maximus with their aides for a tour of the bridge. I can hear Maximus gasp when he steps through the door and sees the vista from the bridge. Unlike Cydyrn, he has been on a ship before in his journeys, so he had some expectations. We just blew them all out of the water. When I show him the sonar display, it makes more of an impression than seeing the same image on the wall in mission control. Even though the ship is not moving, he can see the image and compare it to the coastline visible through the windows, and he makes the connection. Radar is a little more difficult, until Captain Johansen switches to the shortest range and highest resolution, so the outlines of the nearby cliffs are fully visible. Then he gets it. So when I tell him we can see the land that clearly at night or in fog or rain, his eyes get big. He tells us of some terrifying moments he's had caught in fog while trying to cross the channel. They arrived in one piece thanks to a lot of skill and more than a little luck. Now I can see him thinking.

It is after we leave the bridge that he asks me the question. "Could you come to Londinium with this boat?" He further explains, "I need to travel there to propose we build a fort here and use this harbor for our expansion to the north. I've only met the new governor once since he arrived on this island, and we have yet to learn to trust one another. We spoke of the need for new cities in the north for both trade and defense. He failed to see the importance of such a move. I believe your maps will help to convince him of the merit of my suggestion. He is also a busy man with many responsibilities, and it is difficult to command his time; however, with your boat and dragon, we most likely will get his attention."

Yes, we will get his attention. No doubt of that. We'll get the attention of everyone in the whole town – and completely terrify them most likely. But I must admit, I want to see London. We've taken pictures from the drone, but it's not the same as actually being there and walking the streets. The question is when to go. The day after tomorrow is the summer solstice celebration at Tordur – not only have we promised to be there, but I wouldn't miss it for the world. Based on what Muirenn and Bledwyn told me, I'm thinking not much will get done for a couple of days afterward. A lot of mead and food will be consumed that day. It turns out the Romans have their own celebratory plans, so we agree to pick up Maximus and three others at Tordur, five days from now. Cydyrn will not join us – I get the feeling he doesn't really enjoy flying and he was looking a little green when the ship was crashing through the waves.

Out of sympathy for him, we take off for the return flight before the ship leaves the calm of the harbor. Besides, there is a feast waiting, and we don't want to be late.

Chapter 18.

Oh, my! Was that fun! And the food was so good. Yesterday we returned to Wynt with the king and Maximus for their feast. I like the food on Robyn's boat, but this was so much more like home. There were some other girls about our age, daughters of warriors and merchants, who showed Genovea and me all around the town. We got to search through the market stalls we missed the day before and see inside some of the nicer homes. It is even bigger than I thought from my first visit. There are a lot of houses and stables past the great hall that we only got to see for the first time today. Then we settled down to eat.

The Bird made two trips, so lots of people from the boat could come. Michele and April stayed with us as we enjoyed the feast and then as we again explored the town once we were stuffed full. April is only a little older than me. Like most of the people on the boat, she's been trying to learn my language and about my life, just as Luseth, Genovea, and I try to learn about theirs. It seems strange how different her life is from mine. She lives in what she calls a small town, right on the coast. I asked her if she is afraid of raiders, but she says no. There isn't even a wall around her town. Her father Barry used to work for the Coast Guard which has boats that protect against invaders. She says he mostly wound up rescuing people in boats who got into trouble out in the water. That was a long time ago, before she was born. After she came along, he got a different job that let him spend more time at home with her mother and her.

When I asked about how small her town was, she told me only about two thousand people lived there. Two thousand people – I've never been in a town that big, but she calls it small. That is even bigger than Wynt. Maybe I'll get to Londinium someday and see what a real city is like. She tells me about this place called school that she went to almost every day. I'm not sure quite what she means, because it seems like there is more than one place with the same name. But I guess it is a building where lots of people can gather, like our great hall. When she was little, she went to one close to home, so she had to walk. When she got older, she had to go further so she got to ride in one of their wagons – one big enough to carry lots of kids.

She told me that she went there to learn things.

"What kinds of things?" I asked.

"Things you need to know in our world. Like how to read and write, to begin with. Then we learn about history – what happened in the past – plants, numbers, about the land we live in and all kinds of things. Most people go nearly every day from the time they are about five years old until they are eighteen – some even longer, so they can learn even more."

She then told me that Robyn, Don, Max, and Michele all still go to school. That must be why they know so much.

As for April, she spent most the time she wasn't in school on her father's boat. From the time she could walk, she loved being at sea. Her father would let her watch, and sometimes let her help. When she got older, she worked on other boats whenever she could. Her plan was to join what they call coast guard, like her father did, so she could help protect their land from invaders and rescue people. But, when she was sixteen, her mother got sick and died, so now that it was just her and her father, she decided to stay close to home for a while. They worked together even more, but were looking for something different when the chance came up to join Robyn.

"It sounded like a big adventure, and would get dad away from our home, where every person and every place is another memory of mom. I hope it gives him a new start."

I'm not quite sure what she means and when I try to find out more, we run out of words.

So I asked Michele about her school. I know my jaw dropped when she told me there are about twenty thousand people there. I didn't understand all the words she used, so I tried to guess her meaning. I just decided she must mean that many live near her school when Genovea asks the question that is on my mind.

"Do you mean that many people live in the town?"

"There are more in the town. The twenty thousand people who go to my school are there to learn. You've seen pictures of how big the place is – I live with Robyn."

Oh, yes, I forgot. Then something else came to my mind. "But you're not sisters. How is it that you live together?" In my world, a woman lives with her family until she marries, then she lives with her husband and children. That is the way things work. There is only one woman I know who doesn't. Cyreena's husband died when she was still young, before she bore any children. Now she lives with her sister and husband – and their eight children. She's a healer and has often taught me when my mother was busy.

One day when we were walking in the woods, gathering plants, I asked her: "Why have you never married again? I know there are men who would take you – I've heard them talking around the fire. Some have asked you, but you refuse."

She gave me a smile before answering, but I remember thinking there was some sadness behind her eyes. "I've been there once, and I just can't imagine doing it again."

"Was it that bad?" I've heard some men are ill natured and take out their anger on their wives. It doesn't happen often because in such a small community as ours, it's not something that can remain hidden for long. When something like that does happen, some of the older men from the settlement will take the man for a walk in the forest. If the woman's father or uncle is living, he will take the lead. If not, or if she is from a different town, the lot falls on the chieftain. I only remember my father ever having to do that two times in my entire life. I don't know what was said in the forest, but never again did that man mistreat his wife in any of the cases I ever heard about.

"No, it wasn't bad," she said. He was very good to me and we had a joyful few months. But then he got sick and I watched him die. Here I am, a healer, but there was nothing I could do for him. He died just before my sister was about to give birth again, so I gave myself to helping her to forget my grief. I just never moved on from there and now I can't imagine starting again. Besides, I enjoy my life as it is."

At this point, our conversation moved on to the plants surrounding us and which ones are best to treat a fever. And I wondered if I could ever be like Cyreena. Except I don't even have a sister I could live with.

Michele's response to my question jolted me out of my thoughts. She laughed. "I grew up far away from where we live, and I never had a sister – just a little brother who tormented me. He's still at home with my mom. Most my family are still there, but I moved away so I could go to the school. I didn't even know Robyn when I first arrived, but she had what I needed – a place to stay that was cheap and close to school. When I found out who my new roommate was, I was so scared of her. In High School we watched the film Taylor made about her in Afghanistan and I'd seen her in the news. Now she was living just down the hall from me. That was a couple of years ago. Now we're friends."

"Can we see that film?" *Luseth spoke for the first time today. I'd almost forgotten she was with us.*

"I'm sure there's a copy of it here, so yes. Robyn doesn't like watching it – too many bad memories for her. But we can find time when she's not around or busy doing other things."

Luseth looked to her sister for a translation of these words – I guess she hasn't learned the new language as quickly as the rest of us have. Of course, her wounds have kept her less active than us, too. So that may be the reason.

"There are so many people in your school. How do you keep them all straight in your mind?" *I can't even imagine that many people all together in one place. I felt completely lost even in the crowd surrounding us at the feast.*

"Most I haven't even met. People are there learning different things and really I only know those in the same classes as me. Even then, most of them I just know to say "hi." There are only a few who are close friends. Kind of like here where there are all kinds of people around, but just the five of us are together, walking around, and ignoring everyone else."

Genovea cocked her head and looked at Michele like she was trying to work something out in her mind. "With all those people, you must know many men. Why is it you have not found one who will marry you?"

More laughing from Michele. "Maybe I haven't found anyone I want to marry! In fact, who says I even want to marry at all? In my world, a woman doesn't have to."

Really? I'm not sure I want to marry, but in my world that is not really an option – not for the daughter of a chieftain, at least. Every girl is expected to find a husband within a couple of years after becoming a woman, but a few manage to put it off a little longer. In my case, even that is not an option. Already my father has reminded me that if I don't choose soon, he might have to make the decision for me. I don't think he will – at least not yet, but he could. I bet things are not like that in Michele's world.

"Could your father make you marry someone?"

"No. He wouldn't even if he could. In fact, I'd be surprised if he showed up at my wedding. Just before I left to come here, I sent him a message to say I was heading to Europe for the summer. He never even replied."

All three of us were confused now. I guess it showed on our faces because she quickly explained. "You have seen the little boxes we use to send messages to each other? I used mine to tell my father I would be away. We call that a 'text'." Michele went on to say, "Usually when someone gets a message, they send one back to let you know they read it. He didn't. I know he got it, but just didn't bother to reply."

I didn't know what to say; I can't imagine my father not caring about me. I remember when I was really young coming up to him as he was standing talking with a circle of his men. When he saw me, he stopped, knelt down, and picked me up so I could be part of the conversation. I don't remember what was said and I'm sure I soon got bored, but I do remember feeling so special because my father included me with the big people. That was far from the only time he made feel that way. I always knew I was his special girl. And because of his status, everyone else in Tordur also showed me respect.

"What about the guys on the boat? Would you marry any of them?" I asked.

"They are all a little old for me." This came from April. "Michele, I've seen you and Kelly together a few times. Anything special happening there?"

I admit – I want to know the answer to that one. Kelly's a healer, and it crossed my mind that just maybe he might marry me so I could leave Tordur and still be a healer. Maybe I could learn more from him.

"Maybe. I don't know. It's fun for now," she said, "but we aren't really serious. He just doesn't see the value in all my education. He took a two-year program at a community college to get where he is and thinks that is all that's needed. He can't understand why it's so important to me, and why I'm willing to take so many years to get where I want to go."

"Taylor?"

"Oh, I'm pretty sure his heart is focused on Robyn and has been for a long time. She just doesn't know it yet."

Our conversation drifted off to other topics as we wandered, relaxed by the amazing food and the casual simplicity of our talk. Soon the shadows grew long as the sun made for her bed in the west and I found myself back in The Bird, staring out the window as the land dropped away for our flight back to the boat.

We're all totally exhausted from the day. As soon as we land on the boat, Luseth heads off to find Sandy to get something for her pain. Michele and April disappear someplace, leaving Genovea and me alone. We are still too excited to think about sleep, so we so we wander toward the front deck of the boat. It's a gorgeous evening and it seems too nice to be inside our rooms. But as we head in that direction, I spot someone with red hair through an open door, sitting with her back to us, as she stares out the window toward the land.

Thinking it is Robyn, we pop in to say 'hi.' Only when she hears us and turns, I see it's not. It is Ahntya.

"Come sit beside me, for I am lonely. You speak the language of Cydyrn's people." I'm not sure if that was a question or a statement.

"I do." I reply. "I am from Tordur, less than a day's journey from Wynt. I also speak some Latin that I learned from the Romans and am learning the language of Robyn's people."

Genovea adds. "I am from a small settlement to the north, beyond the borders of Cydyrn's realm. Our speech is very similar."

"How did you two come to be with these people from the other world?"

I relate the story of my rescue and the defeat of the Sea-wolves, then Genovea tells of our meeting on the beach. She asks many questions about these people from the other world which we answer as best we can. Questions like where they came from, why are they here, and how do they do all these amazing things.

She picks up a garment from beside her and puts it in her lap. I recognize as a coat I've seen Robyn wear. She's running the fabric through her hands.

"Robyn handed this to me this morning when it was a little windy outside. It's so soft and light – but it's warm and keeps the wind out like leather. I've worked with fabric all my life and have never even heard of or seen anything like this before. I asked Robyn how they make this fabric, but she doesn't know. She said she bought this at a market near her home. They buy all their clothes come from markets and very few people in their world make their own clothes. I find that hard to believe. But then I look at this tunic and I can imagine those who make it would be reluctant to reveal their secrets."

She spoke slowly. She seemed distracted, staring straight ahead through the window at the distant shore.

"Robyn told me what happened in the hall; that Cydyrn had his men attack the guests who came in peace. But they fought back and my

husband died as a result. Cydyrn made it out to be all a misunderstanding; that he didn't intend to hurt anyone. I don't believe him. I think he fully intended to defeat and humiliate this woman who claimed to be a warrior. Once he realized that he couldn't overpower and intimidate Robyn, he changed tactics and enlisted her help to impress the Romans. Then he threw a big feast to impress her and his people, even though we are only days away from the solstice and another huge feast. It doesn't make sense, but that's what he wants and he gets his way because those around him are terrified of him.

"I haven't trusted that man for a long time – one minute he's your best friend and the next he's your sworn enemy. Then he's your friend again. You never know which Cydyrn you will face from day to day – or what he will do next. He thinks because he's king that no one can touch him. He thinks he has power, but doesn't realize that as soon as the Romans tire of him, he's done. They will crush him like a bug under their feet. I just hope when they do decide they've had enough, he doesn't take many of his people down with him.

"We talked of leaving. My husband didn't trust the man either. But he felt loyalty to his king, so he stayed. We could have left and gone back to my family. I'm sure if I told my father that he was right and I was wrong, he would welcome me. At least he would welcome the opportunity for more profit. I spent enough time in the market that I know where the best weavers are; we could buy direct from them and sell in Londinium – bypass the market in Wynt and others like it.

"Now my husband is dead and I am free of the place. I should be grief-stricken, but feel only relief. I am sorry that the fool I married had to pay such a price in return for his loyalty, but he knew the risk and that was his choice. The one who was injured in the attack and his women all want to return to Wynt. Let them. I have no interest in seeing that place again. I won't even return to get my possessions, for everything I had reeks with memories that I choose to leave behind."

"What will you do now?" Genovea asks.

"Find something to eat and then get some sleep."

I know from the look on her face that wasn't the answer Genovea wanted or expected, but with it, Ahntya seems to come alive. For the first time, she turns and looks at us sitting beside her. She gives us a quick smile as she jumps to her feet and wraps the coat around her shoulders. "I still get lost in this place. Can you take me to where they have the food?"

As we head back downstairs to the mess room, I realize just how tired I am from the day. I'll be glad to reach my bed – but first I think I'll get something to eat, too.

Chapter 19.

We arrived in Tordur a couple of hours before sundown the evening before the summer solstice. During the previous days, I spoke at length with Bledwyn and Muirenn about the coming celebration. They explained that sometimes a Druid or two will show up a couple of days before and lead the people in the sunrise ceremony at the nearby stone circle. Those years when no Druid came, most people would still trek to the circle to watch the sun rise just in case a Druid made an appearance there. If none came, it would be an ill-omen, not catastrophic, but certainly worrisome. And anticlimactic, for there would be no ceremony, as no one else would dare enter the circle, and the invocation and sacrifice can only be done from in front of the lone standing stone in the center. Even in normal times, most avoid the area, skirting around the hill if they must go that direction. Young men sometimes enter the circle on a dare or spend the night in the nearby woods. But never, ever would they enter the circle at sunrise or sunset without a Druid present. And most certainly not at sunrise on the solstice, for it is then that the veil that separates this world from the other is at its thinnest.

In their beliefs, during this time-between-times, the barrier between this world and the other world – the spiritual world that is the home of the mythical beings that make up their pantheon of gods and spirits – is most easily penetrated. According to Bledwyn, the ancient circle of standing stones marks a doorway or portal between the worlds. It marks a place where the barrier is particularly porous; a place where otherworldly beings sometimes enter this world or it may even be possible to cross over to that other place. It is a place of great power, but also of great danger. Wynt, they explained, is also located at a doorway to the other world so the people there don't have to travel to a special place. And since it is the residence of the king, there will always be Druids for the solstice.

Druids are the educated class in this culture. They are both the religious leaders and valued advisors to the kings and chieftains. They are believed to have a connection to the spirit world which gives them a deeper understanding into this one and even allows them to see something of the future. That belief gives them great control and power over the military and political leaders who seek their advice.

Or did. The Romans recognized the power these men wielded, so late last year they invited them all to a gathering and there slaughtered them. Only the few who failed to hear – or heed – the summons managed to escape. I haven't told our friends from Tordur yet that this is the reason no Druids have shown up for the solstice celebration. These men were special – respected and feared – but some were also trusted friends. I don't think the news they are nearly all dead will be welcome in either Tordur or Wynt.

We on the other hand are other-worldly beings; denizens of the spirit world. That's what Bledwyn called us; he still believes that. Earlier today as we were planning for tonight, he called me "Queen of the Otherworld." At first I thought he was joking, but then I saw the look in his eyes – he wasn't. Fear is what I saw in his eyes – and maybe a little respect, too. It actually took me aback a bit.

I did manage to get out "I'm not a queen. I am not even the daughter of a chieftain. I was about to add "just another person," but I stopped myself; that wouldn't be exactly true. I don't know what I am, but I'm not ordinary. Considering the number of people I've killed over the last three weeks, it's a very good thing there are not more like me.

But this evening, I get to lay aside the warrior and take up the role of anthropologist. I even changed out of my green fatigues for the occasion: khakis, blue top, and a grey hoodie to top it off. We've gathered around in the great hall. Most of the gang is here. Of course, all our strays came; none wanted to miss the festivities. Kelly, Michele, Lance, Taylor, Max, Don, and Trace are all here, too. Ahntya is here with us, but we took the injured man, his wife, and sister home to Wynt this morning. We didn't spend much time there, but it was long enough to pick up the oddly subdued mood: for the first time in memory or legend, no Druid arrived there for the solstice.

Here in Tordur, the mood is not quite as depressed. They know how to celebrate the solstice, no matter who does or doesn't attend. Besides, when you have guests from the other world, who needs a Druid? As darkness falls, we all gather around the hearth in the great hall. The night is warm, so the fire is low, leaving the entire room in deep shadow until we break out some solar-charged LED lanterns that fill the room with a soft glow.

"What are these?" I hear someone ask, pointing to the lanterns.

"They gather the sunlight during the day, and give it back at night" I find myself answering.

The stunned silence that follows gives my mind time to wander. Maybe Bledwyn is right – maybe we are from another world, where there are dragons, and iron floats on water, and people can see what is far away, talk to each other over a distance, fly through the air, and all sorts of other things that these people couldn't even imagine before we arrived. We also came here through a doorway that no one has ever seen. And we even can store sunlight in a box. No wonder they think we're magical. I guess I should have expected such a response.

Cynbel's voice pulls me back to the presence. He speaks of the Earth and Sun, how the sun is drawn between her lover in the far south and her duties in the north. Each year, her lover draws her to the south and she leaves her duties, her people, her children behind in the cold and dark. In mid-winter, she reaches the arms of her lover, and then remembers the people she left behind. She then leaves the south and begins the long trek back north, bringing warmth and light to her people. But all that time, she pines for her love left behind in the south. When she reaches her home in the north, and rises in the morning over the markers her people have placed, she knows her warmth and light are enough, that they will survive for another year so she can return south to her love.

So they thank her for returning, and gratefully release her so she can again begin the long journey to the south, back to the one she loves.

I sit listening, fascinated. It is an amazing myth, one that has been lost to science ... until now.

As the night darkens, the stories continue. They will continue through the night. Some people drift off to sleep for a while, but always several people are awake and watching. Just after three by my watch, the first signs of night fading appear in the east. Those on watch break off the current story and awaken the rest. Those of us who are making the trek drag ourselves to our feet, bundle on clothes to protect against the pre-dawn chill, and gather at the gate. Those who are staying behind will prepare the feast later in the day. We offered to bring food, but Bledwyn explained that to do so would be an insult to the people of Tordur. The food served at the solstice is a point of pride, and to bring our own would imply that we didn't think they would have enough.

Cynbel and Gwyn take the lead with Bledwyn, Muirenn, and I immediately behind him. The rest of the group trail behind in a tight pack so they don't get lost in the dark and thick, pre-dawn mist. Of course, all our team have night-vision goggles, but we are running without a drone. We raised Martin, but Jack had a busy day shuttling us between the ship, Tordur, and Wynt; he is still dead to the world. Jerry is flying one further west on a special project. Our other drone pilots are all here on the ground – that is a first. I was a little surprised when Trace asked if she could join us, until she reminded me that she hasn't taken a day off in the three weeks we've been here. She just needed to get away and do something fun for a change.

It only takes an hour for us to walk the distance. When we first set out, I feel a little tense since I am walking blind into the unknown. The route is not the familiar road that leads to Wynt, but is a little-used path extending straight west from the gates across the fields and into the forest.

Just before we clear the fields and enter the forest, Michele comes up and touches my arm. I jump and just about scream. I'm glad I didn't; a scream would not have enhanced my otherworldly reputation. Okay, I am more than a little tense; I'm wound tight.

"Hey, don't worry. They're just plants. I'm here to protect you," she whispers in my ear.

"Thanks. Glad to know we have a botanist to beat back the evil trees," I retort. "I'm more worried about what else might be out there."

But the journey passes without incident. Once we are in the forest, in spite of the darkness and the mist that thickens to full-blown fog, I start to relax and enjoy the peaceful silence broken only by the sound of about a hundred pairs of feet on the soft ground and the occasional word spoken in a soft voice. Even our feet don't make much sound. Most of our people are wearing hiking boots with rubber soles, while the people of Tordur wear soft leather shoes that make almost no noise as they walk. The fog seems to absorb the little sound we do make, so I find myself walking in solitude, and for once I actually feel at peace. As the light grows, I even take off my night vision goggles. I'm little nervous that something will happen, but the only excitement occurs when a fox crosses our path. That apparently is a very auspicious omen.

The stone circle stands on the top of a low hill. As we climb through the fog I think that this sunrise will be most unimpressive, if we can see it at all. But as we near the top, we rise above the fog and are faced with a clear sky, pale in the northeast, darker to the west. The circle is not made with massive stones like Stonehenge; these are only about four feet tall. Almost without knowing it, I step between two of them and enter the ring. As I do, I suddenly feel all alone. Ahead of me I can see the stones that form the far side of the circle; behind them is a wall of fog. Directly in front of me is a single stone that marks the centre of the ring. I glance behind me to see a row of faces lined up a respectable distance outside the circle; no one follows me – not even my team. I'm here now, so I bravely walk toward the center. Here in the open, the grass grows tall, reaching nearly to my waist, so it is more like wading than walking. Between the tall grass and the dim light, I don't see the man until I stumble against him.

He is lying on his side, facing away from me. For a second, I think maybe he is dead, but then he grunts and casually rolls over onto his back as he gains consciousness. As soon as I realize he is alive, I back out of easy reach and draw my 9-millimeter. My other hand reaches for the flashlight I added to my gear for this night mission. He opens his eyes and sees my silhouette against the sky as I am raising the light in my left hand. I hear the grass rustle as he suddenly moves, like he might be reaching for a weapon, but I can't see him. He knows I'm here, so there is no point in trying to hide; I switch on the light. His right hand flies up to protect his eyes from the sudden blaze, and I can see that it is empty. He is half sitting up, with his weight on his left arm, so both arms are occupied and he is not an immediate threat.

In the light, I can see he is an older man, dressed in the manner of a Roman merchant, but in clothes that are worn and soiled, as would be expected from someone sleeping outdoors on the ground. I can see now that his hand holds a silver chain with some sort of medallion hanging from it. The medallion has some sort of symbol on the face, but I can't make it out from this angle. Most likely it is a charm or talisman to keep him safe. I can also see a bundle on the ground that must have been beside him as he lay sleeping; a rolled up cloak served as a pillow.

Considering his Roman dress, I try speaking to him in Latin. "Who are you, and why are you here?"

He responds slowly, as if unsure of the language. Or maybe he isn't quite awake yet. "I come from far away, and am here to purchase tin to ship back to Rome. Recently I learned the authorities in Rome are arresting many of my people, so I decided not to return there until it is safer. I heard there were a people living to the east of this island who fought against the Romans a year or so ago. I thought to seek them out, for I might be safe with them for a while. Late yesterday I climbed to the top of this hill to see if I could see a settlement nearby where I could seek lodging. I could not, but chose to spend the night here for wild animals seldom enter circles of standing stones."

"You are traveling alone?" I ask.

"Yes. No one else wished to join me on this venture."

"The tribe you seek lived north of here. The Romans defeated them last year, and few now remain in the land. The people in this area are at peace with the Romans, and are unlikely to offer sanctuary to a fugitive from Roman justice."

"I have done nothing to harm the Romans, nor have I offended their laws." He is quiet for a moment, then looks at me and asks, "Who are you and where are you from? I have never before heard an accent like yours, nor have I met anyone who holds a star in her hand."

I think about the dozens of people behind me listening to my words who are convinced by their chieftain and his son that we are from the other world. I don't want to blow away that conviction and undermine Cynbel's position with his people, but I don't want to outright lie either. "My name is Robyn. I come from another world, a world far different from this one. We have a steed that flies through the air; we can see things that are far off; and even hold the light of a star. We are not here to harm you, but have come to join our friends as they celebrate the solstice. Join us, and you will find them hospitable hosts."

I flick the safety on as I lower and holster my gun. I don't think I'll need it just now. With my right hand now free, I offer it to the man on the ground and help him to his feet. I hear gasps from the people behind me as they see him for the first time. My mind is full of questions. *Is finding a man in the middle of the circle on the morning of the solstice is a good omen or a bad one? Do they know? Has something like this ever happened before? I'm sure it must have a powerful meaning, but will they know how to respond in the absence of a Druid?* I guess the girl from the other world is the best one here to make that call.

"What is your name?" I whisper as he stands to his feet.

"Symeon."

Symeon – Simon in English – is a name of Hebraic origin, from the eastern Mediterranean. "You are a long way from home," I reply. "Almost as far as I am."

I flick the flashlight off – now that he is not in the shadow of the grass and in the rapidly increasing light of day, I no longer need it.

"Come, bring your bundle and let us leave here. Sunrise is not far off and the people may be frightened if we remain within the circle."

We walk to the line of stones that mark the edge of the circle and the line of faces watching us. and as we approach the stones, I see sunlight reflecting off them. The sun has risen, we were in the circle, and we survived. I have no idea what these people will now think of me or the man beside me.

We walk between the stones, and I turn to see the sunrise. It is then that I notice the shadow of the stone in the center of the ring falls directly on the spot where I stood. Now I feel a shiver down my neck. The people will see the significance of that. Already they are looking at both of us with a level of fear that I haven't seen before. *What do I do now?* I don't want to be their Queen of the Otherworld – I just want to learn all I can about them. I want them to trust me, not worship me.

I have an idea. "The sun must be pleased that so many came to welcome her today. See, she trusts you enough to give you another guest to share your feast." There, it is the sun's doing that this man is here, not mine. We'll see if that works.

Cynbel says a few words of welcome to the sun, adding "now we thank you for your trust in granting us another guest for our feast."

So far, so good.

We all troop back to Tordur in the light of the newly-risen sun. As we cross the fields and pastures, before we reach the walls, I can already catch the aroma of cooking. Oh, I am hungry. I haven't eaten since yesterday afternoon, and even though it isn't yet five in the morning, that seems like a long time ago.

The gates open wide as we approach, and we enter into the hectic bustle of cooks preparing the feast. I try to keep out of the way, but I really want to see what it takes to prepare a major meal for a hundred and fifty or so people during the late Iron Age. Wow, what a spectacle. There is a full ox, a pig, and I think maybe a deer, all roasting on spits. Over the roasting meat and the smoke from the fires comes the aroma of bread baking in the oven. I see heaps of greens and fresh herbs, pots of stew or soup, and foods that I can't identify. There are vats that I am pretty sure must contain beer and mead – and yes, even a couple of Roman amphorae which just might contain wine.

Muirenn leads me into the hall with all their other guests for the honor of celebrating the feast with Cynbel and his family. Even the sick and wounded in the room are clearly honored guests this day, for they receive the food and drink before anyone else. Why not – they are the paying customers. We are served next, then Cynbel's family, and then down through the hierarchy of Tordur. The food is good, but I have to admit, it doesn't have the familiar flavors of home. This is a time before spices arrived in this part of Europe. Even salt is almost unknown. But as I eat, and take in the flavors of the herbs, I come to appreciate the way they subtly blend together. I could get used to this.

It is a noisy crowd, and I found myself seated between Michele and Symeon. Apparently, because I found him within the circle, Symeon is now somehow my child, so we belong together. He is not young, but not as elderly as I first thought. I learn that he is about fifty years old, and has made the trip to the Roman province of Britannia many times, following the tin trade – a trade he learned from his father, who learned it from his father before that. As I guessed from the name, he is Jewish and lives in the town of Joppa when he is not in the far limits of the empire.

We speak of his journeys. He usually travels by ship to the south coast of Gaul, then by land to the Channel and across to the Roman harbor at Londinium. His shipments of tin go home by sea – around Iberia and through the strait of Gibraltar, and then on to Rome or whatever other city he believes will earn him the best price. He doesn't relish the danger of long voyages across the open sea, and doesn't spend any more time on the water than absolutely necessary. On the other hand, shipping by sea is much cheaper than carting the same load over land. So the tin goes by sea while he travels over land. We discuss the tribes in the area, and the few sizable towns that might offer him safety. As we talk, he considers altering his plans.

"Perhaps the rumors I heard are untrue ... or at least greatly exaggerated," he muses.

In turn, I tell him of our journey across the ocean, from the distant west, far beyond all sight of land. And that we live on a ship that is anchored away from the land and we fly out to it – I don't think he believes me on this one. I then tell him something of our world, and our plan to visit Londinium in a few days. And that we are at peace with the Romans, but only after we chased a patrol of their horsemen home. That seems to get his interest a bit. Maybe it is the alcohol he has consumed or maybe just the fact that he speaks no Brythonic and the warrior seated on his other side speaks little Latin, but he becomes most interested in our conversation. About an hour into the meal, he reaches into his bundle and pulls out a bronze goblet. It is about the size of a wine glass, decorated on the outside with some beautiful chase-work and a green enamel band. I pick it up – it is heavier than I expected. The chase-work is in the classic Celtic endless knot – beautifully done.

Cam Clark

"Isn't it beautiful? My father had it made in Londinium many years ago to celebrate his first shipment of tin. When he died, it came to me."

"The chase-work is amazing." I reply. "This is enamel?" I say, pointing to the green. "I didn't know they did enamel work in Britain."

"It was made by an artisan who came from Athens with the Romans. He did the enamel, but a man from here did the engraving following their traditional designs"

I carefully trace the pattern with my finger, amazed at the precision of the design of interwoven lines. "Do you know which tribe this man was from?"

"No, I don't think my father ever knew. He spoke mostly Greek, so probably did not speak directly to the man."

He pauses for a bit before continuing, as if considering whether or not to tell me something. "You say you are here to learn about the people. There is a story about this cup that may interest you. It happened about thirty years ago, when I was still a young man and traveling with my father. In the spring one year, we found ourselves in the city of Jerusalem. As Passover was near, we decided to stay in the city for the celebration. While in the city, I fell very ill – so ill that I was expected to die. It was serious enough that my father purchased a tomb for me. That year there was a particular excitement. A man who had attracted a following as a healer and prophet – a leader and revolutionary whom many felt would deliver us from Rome. Through a connection in the city, my father met the man, invited him to the place we were staying. He spoke to me, touched me, and immediately I started to feel better. Within a day I was up from my bed.

"We wound up celebrating Passover with this man. That day, my father loaned this cup to him for the ceremonial dinner. After the meal, he picked it up and likened the wine inside to his blood, predicting that soon it would be shed. He then passed the cup on to each person at the table; it then was passed around the room. Each took a sip, and there was still plenty left when it reached me.

"His words that night were prophetic, for his blood was spilled soon enough. He was arrested that very evening. The next day, this man was tried, condemned, and crucified. His body was laid in the tomb my father purchased for me. I am glad to say that I did not need it.

"We thought that was the end of it, so we packed up to leave for the coast. Before we could leave, word came that the tomb was empty. Most people believed his friends stole his body, but I was with them and knew they were as surprised as everyone else. Then, one evening we saw him – met him, talked to him, even touched him in that very room where we celebrated Passover.

Very soon afterward we left the city, and it was years before I learned more of what happened. From those few men and women, a movement has grown and it now spreading across the entire empire. The authorities have tried to suppress it, arresting and killing men, women, and children, but it continues to grow. To protect ourselves, we adopted a symbol, by which we may know one another."

He reaches under his tunic and pulls out the medallion I saw this morning. I see now that it is a round bronze disk decorated with a ring of the same interlocking lines as on the cup. In the center is a clear space, decorated only with the simple outline of a fish – the earliest symbol adopted by Christianity.

My mind is spinning. Growing up, once in a while we went to a nearby church – Christmas and Easter mostly. Jon's family was much more involved, so sometimes he dragged me out to other things. I was never quite sure what I believed and never felt that I fit in there. After the accident, they offered their building for the funerals and provided luncheons afterward on back-to-back days. They wouldn't accept any money either. But after the funerals it didn't take long for the people to disappear into the woodwork. One girl invited me to a special July 4th event and picnic, but the memories of the place with three caskets lined across the front were far too fresh, so I declined. After that, I never heard from her again.

Kate switched to a mega-church on the east side of town. I went with her a couple of times, and found it an impressive show, but felt so overwhelmed by the sheer number of people that it wasn't much fun being there. I never really took it very seriously – I thought it was a bunch of old legends and myths which might have some basis in fact. Kind of like the Robin Hood legends.

Of course, I've heard the legend of the Holy Grail from the time of the equally legendary King Arthur. Never, ever did I once even remotely consider the possibility that there could be any truth in those stories. Yet if what Symeon says is true, and I have no reason to disbelieve him, then what I am holding in my hand is the Holy Grail. As an anthropologist, I am intrigued by the story, and would love to learn how it morphed into the Arthurian legends set some four centuries from now. I want to talk with Symeon more and find out all I can about his story and this cup.

"I think when we leave here you should join us on our boat. We have things you may wish to see, and can take you to Londinium. I don't think you need to fear the Romans when you are with us. What is more, I think you will find our boat far more comfortable than those you have taken previously in your travels."

"Thank you, my lady. I accept your offer."

He now turns to the serious business of eating and drinking, so I turn to Michele. She's been unusually quiet.

"You seem to hit it off with Symeon," she whispers in my ear. "The guy beside me speaks only Brythonic, and my vocabulary of about six words ran out pretty quick. That cup looks cool."

"Here have a look." I reply, handing it to her. "If he is telling the truth, you're holding the Holy Grail. Don't drop it." In the years I've known her, I don't think I've ever seen Michele at such a loss for words as she is right now.

"I thought that was just a legend made up in medieval times," she finally gets out.

"So did I. I put it down as fiction, but his story has the ring of truth. So what now?"

"Hey, just in case the legend is right and drinking from this cup does lead to endless life, I'm having a drink!" Michele says as she reaches for a pitcher of wine.

"Worth a try. I can guarantee you that if drink from that, you'll be alive almost two thousand years from now."

"Been there, done that," she replies with a laugh, just before she chugs the contents of the cup.

As she refills it and passes it to me, I explain to Symeon that it is an old tradition in our land, without going into more detail. As I take a drink, I notice Taylor quietly filming us in the background. I wonder how long he's been there. *Did he capture the exchange between Symeon and me?* Michele refills the cup and takes it to each member of our team. Of course, Genovea wants in on it too, so I give her the same explanation I gave Symeon.

"But why this cup? Why not any of the others on the table? Does it have to do with you finding Symeon in the stone circle?" Her questions tumble out one after the other.

"It is that cup – there are strange legends woven about it." I reply.

"Why was he in the circle? Did you know he was there? You went into it alone. How did you dare to do that?"

"I didn't know he was there. He found himself in the area as night fell, and thought it would be a good place to sleep. He is from far away, and does not fear the power of the circle. For me, remember I am from another world. The circle has no power over me."

"Oh" she stops to think for a bit. "You can see in the dark and what is far away. How is it that you didn't know he was there?"

"You know it is our birds that let us see what is far away. One was on the boat, while the other was far to the west, looking the celebration at another circle; one that exists in our world." I requested that we overfly Stonehenge to see what is happening there. We got some amazing shots of it rising through the mist. The ring is almost as ruined now as it is in our time, and only a small number of people gathered around for the solstice.

"So neither bird was where it could see the man. And I wanted to see clearly in this world, so I wasn't looking through my world, where I can see in the dark and even see people who are hidden." Then I add, "I was so surprised when I stumbled over him, I nearly screamed." I know that last comment will harm my reputation as the queen of the other world, but I am already so tired of trying to live up to that expectation. Let them think what they will.

The dinner eventually comes to an end, and we all gather around the hearth in the hall, telling stories, drinking, and listening to the falling rain that started sometime while we were eating. I start to drift off – between the lack of sleep, a huge meal, and consuming a rather large amount of alcohol, keeping my eyes open is a major challenge.

Then I start to hear voices, and it takes a bit to realize Martin is talking to me. I manage to get to my feet and wander to the doorway so I can talk without disturbing those listening to the current story. "The weather is closing in, and it looks like it will last for the rest of the day, we might not be able to get The Bird off the ground until morning. You guys okay there?"

I look back into the room. Trace is telling a story about flying over the gulf on the edge of a hurricane. Muirenn, Bledwyn, and Luseth are all tripping over each other as they try to translate, much to the delight of the listeners. Genovea is – *where is she?* She's with Taylor, learning how to manage the video camera. Marcelus and Ahntya I can see outside, standing in the shelter of a hut, talking quietly with each other. It looks like a romance may be blooming there. Kelly – I hope no one gets hurt, because he's passed out at the table.

"We won't run out of food, that's for sure. The beer and mead should hold out too, although Kelly is making a valiant effort on that end. We should survive."

When I quietly let our team members know that we won't have to leave tonight because the weather is too thick for flying, I find that no one is in a hurry to get home. It's a win for everyone.

Of all the people in the room, I think the happiest is Muirenn's and Bledwyn's mother. She is sitting at the edge of the firelight, watching her two youngest relate a story about dragons flying over the sea in a great storm to reach their secret source of fire – they are changing it a little as they translate, much to the delight of each other. I skirt the edge of the group and come beside her. Up close, she looks younger than I expected – then with a shock I realize she could be just a few years older than I am. People grow up fast here. Her oldest is Gwyn. He may not even be twenty-five yet, and if she was Luseth's age when he was born, she's in her late thirties. Closer, I can see the wear of a hard life. People also grow old fast here.

"Those two are amazing," I say as I sit down at her side. "Thank you for letting them join our team. We have learned so much from them, but I feel bad I haven't had time to sit down with you until now."

She turns to me and smiles as I add, "they are teaching me your language."

She looks younger when she smiles and the creases in her face smooth away. She replies with a gentle voice. "I owe you for the lives of both my children and many others as well. Today would have been much sadder had you not driven the Sea-wolves from the walls of Dubri-tun. By now, they would have been here. We would perhaps have little reason to celebrate and little to celebrate with, had you not come to our aid. For me, I have no doubt that my children are alive because of you."

I learn her name is Sibernne. After we talk a while, she drops her bombshell.

"The Romans have talked to Cynbel about leaving Tordur and moving to the west. They found a spring where the waters are hot and healing at a place they named Aquaesulis where they want to build a place of healing and for us to move there. While it is further from the coast, it is on a river, so there is easy access, but I am not sure we would be better protected from the Sea-wolves than we are here. I want to stay here, but Cynbel thinks the Romans are really telling us to move, and they will move us by force or destroy us if we try to stay. But if we follow them, we would earn their favor and their protection."

"I think Cynbel knows them well," I reply. "I doubt they will take 'no' for an answer. I know this place they speak of. There is a hill that is easy to defend, and the Romans will build a strong wall for protection and station a garrison there. The river mouth faces Gaul, so is less exposed to the predations of the Sea-wolves than you are here. That city will be safe for many lives of men."

"You give me peace. Cynbel is ready to agree to Maximus' request. I think the Romans are already building there, and we will move in the autumn after we have harvested our crops." Then she adds, pointing at her offspring in the center of the crowd, "they don't know yet. Please let me tell them in my own time."

I agree, and our talk wanders to other topics. The day is growing old before we come up for air.

Chapter 20.

We spent the night after the solstice celebration in Tordur because Robyn told me The Bird doesn't like to fly in the rain. I'm glad we stayed because I had a lot of fun. It was so good to back home with my friends and family. I must admit though that after a chilly and damp night sleeping on a cot in our hut, I will be glad to go back to the warm dry bed on Robyn's boat. This morning dawned clear, so The Bird came to take us back. Now, we are flying back to the boat. Symeon, the man Robyn found yesterday in the stone circle, is with us. So is my mother. She talked with Robyn for a long time yesterday and now she wants to see the boat with her own eyes. She won't stay long; tomorrow we will take Luseth back to her home and my mother back to Tordur. Last night, Luseth decided she wants to go back home. Her arm is now better and her baby will soon be born; she wants to be home when that happens. I understand– where a baby is born is very important, for that place is their home for life. Even if chance or choice leads them to spend most their time elsewhere, it is always that place where you were born that is where you really belong.

I don't know what happens to people who are born on a boat – is it the boat where they belong? What happens when the boat moves? Do they belong anywhere? I don't know anyone born on one to ask. Maybe Robyn knows. I always thought my mother was so old, and Robyn so young. Yet she tells me they are not far apart in age. Perhaps in Robyn's world, they age differently than here. Robyn tells me she is still considered young in her world, while here my mother is growing old. I guess people in the other world live much longer than in this one – maybe they live forever.

I thought my mother would be terrified of flying out to the boat, but she wasn't. "I always dreamed of flying with the birds and seeing what they see. Now I have," were her words when we reached the boat.

We spent a day and night on the boat. My mother spent much of her time with Sandy and Kelly – learning some of their healing secrets. Robyn and I were both there to translate – at least I helped to translate, but I was really there to be with my mother. I didn't realize how much I missed her until I was back in Tordur. So much has happened since I met Robyn that I almost forgot what home is like.

That was yesterday. Earlier today we took Luseth back to her home, dropped my mother at Tordur, and then picked up Maximus at Wynt. Now that it is evening, we are sailing down the coast to the great Roman city of Londinium, the home of the governor of all this land. Symeon is with us – he knows people there who he wants to see. Maximus wants the governor to meet Robyn and show him the site for another town he selected further up the coast. Me, I want to see the big city. So does Genovea – she refused to stay with her sister at the expense of missing Londinium.

Bledwyn is pretty excited too – he is looking forward to meeting the governor. He thinks maybe the Romans will have a place for him, something that Tordur can't offer. I hope so. In the last few weeks, he has grown in my estimation. No longer is he just Gwyn's shadow; he is nearly as fluent in Latin as I am now. He is even learning to read and write it. When he stood before the gates of Dubri-tun to free the people from their terror, and again when he spoke before the king, he showed a confidence and authority I have never before seen in him. Maybe it was always there, but I just couldn't see it because I was always looking at Gwyn or my father.

We spent most of the day resting, recovering from the feast yesterday. As evening approached, we raised the anchor and headed south. Robyn wants to arrive in the dead of night, when most people will be asleep. She hopes this way they won't be as terrified by this strange boat approaching as they would be if we came in the middle of the day. Hopefully when they see us in the morning already at the port, they'll realize pretty quickly that we mean no harm. Robyn also told me that the tide will be just at its peak as we arrive. She explains that when the tide is high, the water in the river will be deeper making our journey safer.

The light is fading, but we can see the shape of the land to the west as we head south. The night is warm and still, so most of the crew is outside. Some are talking quietly; others are just sitting in silence as they watch the distant hills glide by. Inside the boat the lights give a dim red glow, like inside our hall on a winter night when the fire is low. Outside there are no lights at all, so no one will see us from the shore.

I want to stay awake all night and watch as we come to Londinium, but in the end I just can't keep my eyes open and I fall asleep with my head on Robyn's lap.

I awake to the sound of voices. "Hey Muirenn! Wake up sleepy, or you will miss the excitement," Bledwyn calls out as I open my eyes and try to focus. The sun is up and I am lying on a bench on the rear deck of the boat. I roll over and find that we are at what can only be Londinium! From here I can see a wall of buildings lining the river bank. They are square, as big as our great hall at home, but with red roofs. Beyond them are more buildings, with one that looks to be huge towering over the rest.

Now I sit up so I can see better. Further down the river I see the burned-out skeletons of several buildings. As I look around, I see many more signs of fire: blackened timbers rising above scorched walls. There is also a lot of building, with the light tones of newly-hewn wood and stone, in contrast with the burned remains. On the higher ground further from the river, I can see signs of a substantial stone wall under construction.

When I look down, I see the buildings are set back a bit from the bank of the river. Here and there, boats are tied to the bank. I always thought Roman boats were huge, but now I find I am looking down into them, at the clutter of cargo and supplies that fill their hold, and realize just how big this boat is when compared to them. There are two boats tied to the bank beside us and they look so small. Together they don't even reach half the length of ours. No wonder the space between the buildings and along the river is filled with people come to see this wonder that arrived in the night.

Robyn is standing at the rail with Maximus, Bledwyn, and others I can't quite see. Maximus is shouting something to men on the nearby boats – I can see men working on one and it is starting to move. Looking straight down, I see a stair on the side of our boat leading down to the water. Funny, I've never noticed it before. Lance and Andrew are standing at the bottom of the stair with a rope and as the moving boat comes near, they throw the rope to the men in the boat. I see now what they are doing. The boat will fill the gap between ours and the one tied to the bank. We will be able to walk across the two boats to get to land. I watch as they maneuver the boat into position and tie it fast.

Robyn comes over to me. "Maximus is going ashore with your brother now to set up a meeting with the new governor. While they are gone, we will welcome aboard the captains and owners of the two boats beside us which we are using as a bridge. We will give them a tour and a meal; later we will go ashore to meet the governor and see the city. Come, stand with me."

We watch as the three troop down the stairs and climb across the boats to the shore. Now a group of six men come the other way, climbing up the stairs to reach our deck.

"Welcome to the Voyager," Robyn tells the men. "This is our Captain, Patrick Johansen. He does not speak your language, so we will translate for you," she adds pointing to herself and me.

We take them first to the bridge – the room I first saw that night I couldn't sleep. I'm glad Robyn is there to translate, because I don't know many of the words Captain Johansen uses as he describes the workings of the boat.

"How does it move?" one man asks. "I see no oars and no sail, yet you tell me that you could reach Rome from here in less than five days. With good winds we might make it in twenty-five days, but thirty is more common."

In response, the Captain leads us to a door that I've never before noticed. When he opens it and the lights come on, I gasp at what I see. The room is huge – it must be as big as our great hall at home. We are standing at the top of a set of stairs that lead way down into the depths of the boat. I see several huge blocks of grey metal and lines of all different colors that lead in different directions. The room is filled with a rumbling sound that seems to come from everywhere.

"When we need to move, we burn oil in these metal blocks we call 'engines'." Robyn explains, pointing to the two largest blocks near the far end of the room. "The fire turns special oars under the back of the boat, which move us forward. Since we are not moving, the fire is out. This one here," she adds pointing to a nearer block that is smaller,

but still big, "powers all the lights you see on the boat. Most the sound you hear is coming from it. It is also cooking the meal we have ready for you, so I suggest we go and eat."

Good idea. I'm hungry.

Just after we finish eating, Bledwyn's voice tells us Governor Petronius will see us if we come now. It takes me a bit to realize just how much has changed in the last few weeks: Bledwyn is far away, yet hearing his voice in my ear seems normal. So is my ability to reply to him. Before we met Robyn, I couldn't even dream of being able to do that. But he can talk to us, so we gather as a team, lead the sailors back to their boats, and climb across to the shore.

The walk to the Roman barracks is an adventure all its own. I've never seen so many people or buildings before. Most of the buildings are like the ones we saw in Wynt – some are even two stories high. And instead of the thatched roofs of home, most have red tile roofs. At least, those that aren't burnt out shells have red roofs. Robyn tells me the town was burnt by the Iceni last year – what we are seeing is the damage from that attack. It looks like pretty much everyone who is not down at the riverside staring at our boat is hard at work repairing the damage: men and piles of supplies are everywhere. The pathways are full of carts carrying stone and timber toward the places they are working. I am soon so lost in the twists and turns of the roads that I realize I have no idea how to get back to the boat.

"How do you know where to go?" I ask Robyn as we dodge out of the way of another cart. Before we left the boat, I kind of mapped out in my mind how I thought we could get to the barracks, but the maze of winding streets we are walking has me hopelessly lost.

She shows me the tile she carries. I forgot about that. "Little Bird is high up above us. Here are the streets. These red dots are us and that lone dot here is Bledwyn. We just need to connect the dots. We cross here and take this street – it will lead us right to him."

We turn to a new street where there are fewer signs of damage. Here the shops are open and people are walking, looking at the shops, stopping to stare at the strangely-clad group heading toward the

Roman barracks. There are ten of us: me, Robyn, Genovea, Ahntya, Kelly, Michael, Taylor, Marcelus, Lance, and Don. I find myself walking beside Don. We talk for a bit as we walk. My English still isn't very good, but I find out he has two sisters – one older than him and the other younger. I guess he doesn't see his family very much, for they do not live nearby. There is a gentle sadness in his voice when he speaks of them, and somehow I get the feeling there is something more than just distance that keeps them apart. He smiles a bit when he tells me that his younger sister called him just before he left to come here and they will get together when he gets back home.

As we walk, I tell him of my dream of finding a man who will let me continue as a healer. Once I thought it would have to be in Tordur, but being with these people from the other world has opened my eyes to other possibilities. "I don't think I'd go to the other world even if I could. It seems so noisy and busy – and dangerous. Far different from how I ever imagined it to be. In all the stories, the other world is much like this one, but I guess the stories are wrong. But maybe the Romans have healers. Do you know?" I ask.

"They do have healers," he answers. "Maybe you will find a home with them."

I feel a little hope rising in me to replace the fear and doubt which has followed me for years. Maybe there just might be a place for me in this world. I walk on in silence until we approach the gates of the Roman garrison.

"Bledwyn" I hear Robyn say. "We're here at the fort and will be come through the gates in a few seconds. Tell Petronius we have come."

Don quietly tells me, "now the governor will think he has some special sight or knowledge since he knows exactly when we will arrive. I think it will raise his stature with the Romans."

We walk through the gates that are standing open, past the guards and enter a large open square completely surrounded by red-roofed buildings. Most are two stories high, some even three stories – I've never seen buildings that tall before. Taylor is using his cameras to remember what they look like, but the rest of us walk across the open courtyard without a pause and without looking around. Even in this area, I can see signs of fire that have not yet been repaired.

Directly in front of us, I see Bledwyn come through a doorway in the tallest part of the whole fort. In front of the door is a large platform reached by several steps. Maximus and two other Romans are with him. I don't know why I am anxious, but realize as I walk through the gate, I am chewing my lower lip. Maybe it is the memory of what happened the last time we did something like this. But Robyn doesn't hesitate as she leads us up the stairs toward the men at the top.

After the usual greeting, we enter through the doors into a large room. Petronius is seated in a chair against the far wall. Another man is standing at his side.

As soon as we enter, Petronius speaks and gets right to the point. "I hear you helped Maximus find a location for a new harbor up the coast for us. He told me you gave him some highly detailed maps of the land and even of the harbor itself so we know there are no hidden rocks to endanger our fleet. We are most appreciative. I agree with his assessment and have given permission to establish a harbor and a town we will call Aborgium. We will need someone to lead this town, someone who knows the land and the people – and is loyal to Rome. Maximus suggested Bledwyn and I have no reason to alter that. Cydyrn's realm will increase to include the new lands, so Bledwyn will continue to be under his oversight.

"I also hear that your sister is here, one of the healers which have made Tordur so famous." I can feel my face blush as he continues. "We found a place with a hot spring of mineral water to the west of here, and are building a new place of healing there in keeping with our traditions. We have asked Cynbel to move his people there so that you may add your healing skills to the value of the waters. He has not yet given a decision, but I hope he will soon. As it happens, Finanius is the tribune in charge of the three hundred troops that will be leaving soon to build and defend the settlement. I hope that meeting him might allay any fears you or your father may have about our intentions."

I turn my attention to the man he indicates. He's shorter and stockier than most of the Romans I know. I can see brown hair peeking out from under his helmet to match his brown eyes. As I look closer, he seems young to be a tribune – no more than thirty at the outside. Of course the only tribune I know is Maximus, and he is my father's age or older. I guess I just thought that all of them were his age.

But – the people of Tordur moving? It is the first I've heard of it. I can't imagine my father doing such a thing. But for me, it sounds like the answer to all my dreams. Maybe in this new place I can find a husband and continue my work as a healer. "I do not know my father's thoughts on this matter. I know it is not a decision he will make lightly, but will carefully weigh the options to choose what he believes is best for his people. For me personally, the decision is much easier, for I am only the daughter of a chieftain, and have not the responsibility that is on his shoulders. I will move to this new place of healing, bringing such skills as I have."

Maximus looks to me with something that I think is respect. And maybe a little sadness. "Please grant my request to not tell your father of this decision until he has made his own. I wish him to decide on behalf of Tordur, and not be influenced by your choice. We spoke long on this matter a few days before the solstice, and I know that you and your future weighs heavy on his heart – more so than with Gwyn or Bledwyn. You father deeply loves you, Muirenn, and I think if he knew your decision, he might move the entire town to keep from losing you."

I am shocked, to think that my father might value me more than the rest of Tordur. I never even considered such a possibility. Now I find myself fighting back tears as I answer to him "Of course I will honor your wishes."

My thoughts are all in a whirl and the rest of the meeting is a bit of a blur to me. I remember hearing Robyn release Bledwyn from her service so that he can lead the people in the new settlement the Romans call Aborgium. The construction of a fort there by men under Maximus' command will begin immediately. They hope to get the walls up and the barracks built before the weather gets too cold and wet in the fall. Bledwyn will ride with them and seek to gather people from the surrounding area to populate the new town.

I remember Genovea pleading with Bledwyn, "don't forget my people. They have so little, but are hardworking and loyal. They can offer so much."

I think ... "looking out for her people, like any good leader." But that pulls me up short – she's not a leader, just a peasant girl from a tiny settlement of farmers and sheep herders. Then I think of me, planning for only myself and leaving the care of the people to my father and Gwyn. But then, the people of Tordur have a Cynbel and a Gwyn to look out for them – they don't need me. The people of Genovea's settlement, too small to warrant even a name, only have her. I can't help but thinking how fortunate they are. Maybe I should stop thinking of her as 'just a peasant girl.' She is standing before the governor of all Britain, and a Queen of the Other World without fear and pleading for her people. Maybe she really is something more.

"Her town was attacked by the Sea-wolves; many of their crops were destroyed, their herds taken, and their people killed." Bledwyn directs his words at Petronius. "They are, as Genovea has stated, a hard-working people who are also weavers of some repute. Even so, they may have trouble feeding themselves this winter."

Then to Genovea, he replies. "I thank you for reminding me of your people. I will most certainly visit them and invite them to move to the new city."

But now I turn my attention to Finanius, the tribune I will join in this new town. "Have you been to this town before? Is anything built there yet?

"I have been there, but nothing is built yet. The area is covered in trees, with just a small clearing at the spring. No one lives there, but there are the remains of a few stone dwellings so I think people lived there in the past. The first thing we will do is clear some land and use the trees to build a fort to house the men and provide protection. The river it is on can be navigated by large boats, but is many miles from the sea, so we don't think we need to worry about invaders. But we want to be prepared."

"Once the fort is built, we will start to work on the bath itself. There is a road being built to the site, but is not yet complete. There are parts of the path which are not suitable for carts so the tools and supplies we need will go by boat, while the men will walk. Stone and wood are plentiful, so we will use what is already there. The road will be complete by the time we are building the bath, so will be able to bring more material from here over land."

"What about the hall for those who need healing?" I ask.

"There will be lodging rooms at the bath, and some wealthy individuals will build villas for their own use or to rent to those who can afford the price."

"Where will we live?" I ask. Then I add, "... the people from Tordur?" so he doesn't think that I am asking only for myself.

"We will build housing for them in the fort. Once the bath is complete and the area is safe, some will want to build homes outside the fort. I am sure your family will have quite a nice villa. The area is beautiful, much hillier than it is here and well forested."

"What do you mean by a 'bath'?" I ask. "I have never heard that word before."

"It is a building with large pools of water where people gather to relax in the water. Some go to get clean, but mostly it is a gathering place. Of course, the bath we will build will also be a place for people who are ill to immerse themselves in the healing mineral waters. There is a bath here in London that you may want to visit while you are here. I can take you there if you wish. Would your companions like to go too?" he adds, looking at Robyn.

"Yes, some of us will want to come."

By the time we finish with Petronius, Finanius tells us it is too late to go to the baths. "By this time of day, they will be crowded. It is better in the morning when there are fewer people."

So in the morning, Finanius comes to the boat with three other men. We give them a tour of the boat and a meal before a big group of us troop off to the baths. The sun grows hot in the narrow, noisy, dirty, twisting streets that Finanius leads us through, so by the time we arrive at the large building housing the bath I am hot and dusty, and looking forward to clean water. And that is in spite of the shower I took this morning.

"Get a basket and put your clothes in it," Finanius tells us. "Some people wear a toga in the baths, but most don't. Once your clothes are in the basket, give it to the attendant. She'll give you a tag on a ribbon you can put around your neck. When you are ready to leave, give your tag back to get your clothes. In Rome, most baths are open to only men, with women allowed in the morning. Out here in the colonies, we are less formal and allow anyone to come at any time."

As we strip down, I notice a mark on Robyn's shoulder for the first time. It is shaped sort of like one of the shields the Romans use. Above it is a bird with spread wings, in the shield are stars and some strips of red. Below are some symbols – I recognize them as the ones the use for words, but don't know what they mean. I have learned how to speak their language, but Robyn is mostly teaching me to read and write Latin. She said I should learn what will help me the most here in this world. I guess I have to agree.

"What is that?" I ask her.

"What is what?" She asks in return.

"That mark on your shoulder."

"Oh, my tattoo? I got it when I was fighting in Afghanistan – Parthia in your language. The words at the bottom are the name of a friend who died there to remind me of her and what we were fighting for."

"You were in Parthia?" Finanius asks. "I didn't think anyone came back from there."

"Not everyone did" Robyn replies. "But both Taylor and I were there and managed to get back home." There is a sadness in her voice as she says this. Taylor hears his name and comes over. Robyn throws her arm around Taylor's shoulders. "Yeah, we survived."

Finanius wants to hear more, but Robyn clearly doesn't want to talk about it. Finally she says "Come back to the boat this evening, we will show you something of what it is like. Then, maybe you will know. The world we come from is very different from this one."

With that, he leads us into a room with a large pool of water. There is a carved head at one end with water pouring from the mouth and into the pool. Surrounding the pool, on the walls and ceiling is beautiful stone that is mostly white with green and grey streaks running through. It's also carved into statues and columns and all sorts of amazing shapes.

"The stone is called 'marble'. I am amazed at how much there is here – and the beauty of the carving. I didn't expect it here so early" Robyn says mostly to herself. She adds louder "Finanius, this is beautiful. With all this stone, I bet it survived the burning by the Iceni, or has it been rebuilt since then?"

"There was some damage, but it wasn't even finished when they came through. Most the marble arrived after the revolt was put down."

Only a couple of other people are in here. There are steps that lead down into the water – we climb down them. I find the water isn't very deep – only up to the middle of my chest, but it is cold!

"This is the cold room. I like to start here to get the blood flowing. We won't stay long. Then we go to the warm room. The pool there is larger and will probably have more people." Finanius tells us.

He is right. There are nearly twenty people here – men and women in the pool or relaxing around the edges. The water is also much warmer. We stay here for a while, the he leads us to the hot room, where the pool is smaller, but the air in the room and the water are hot. Even the floor is warm under my bare feet.

"There is a fire to heat the water and warm the air that flows under the floor," Finanius explains. "At Aquaesulis the water comes out of the ground so hot that we won't need to heat it for the hot room. We'll mix in cooler water from the river for the warm room."

After the hot room, we return to the cold room for a while, and then return to where we first entered and collect the baskets with our clothes. Finanius gives us each a large cloth from a pile stacked on a table to dry ourselves before we get dressed. He explains that usually we'd have to pay for using the baths, but he knows the man who manages it and he allowed us to use it for free today.

"Tell your friend he has our thanks," Robyn speaks for all of us. "Bring your friend around to our boat when you come. We won't use our big bird while we are here in Londinium – it would scare too many people. But we will give you both a good meal and a ride on the river in our small boat. You will go faster than you've ever gone over water in your life."

It doesn't take much to convince Finanius' friend Antonius to join us. Since the day is still young, we take a winding route back to the boat. Taylor keeps taking pictures of the city while Robyn keeps referring to her tablet so she knows where we are. At one point, we stop along the stone wall being built to protect the city. Robyn gets Taylor to take several pictures covering a long length of the wall, the workmen who are building it, and their tools.

As we walk, Robyn explains "In our world, Londinium is a great city. We are taking pictures and marking the locations of exactly where we are so when we get home we can match what we see here to what exists in our world."

"Why do you want to do this?" Genovea asks.

"We want to collect as much information as we can while we are here. There are people in our world who want to learn more about this one and we want to do everything we can to help them find traces of your world that remain in ours. Parts of the wall we saw today still exist in our world, so we hope our pictures help identify other sections of the wall. We might even be able to match the pattern of the stones with what can still be seen today."

"Oh," I answer. I still don't really understand why they are here and am not sure what more to add.

Genovea keeps asking, "Can't other people just come to this world and see it for themselves?"

"No, it is not easy for us to come here. Most people don't even think it is possible to travel between this world and ours, so we are not sure if people in our world will believe we actually made it here. And we don't know that once we leave here if we will ever be able to come back. So we want to collect as much information that might be helpful to other scholars in our world. I admit, I also want to be sure we are believed when we tell people we were here. Before we leave, we will try to leave something behind where it will be found by people in our world, so they will know we were here."

"What will you leave?" I ask.

"A small box with some of our pictures and a copy of my notes," Robyn says to me.

"Where will you leave it?

"Tordur. Inside your father's home, under the floor near the wall just inside the sleeping area. I spoke to both your parents when we were there – they agreed we could dig up a bit of the floor. And there is room to leave a copy of your notes, too. If you want."

I respond with a bit of a blush "I've started to write down all that has happened since I met you, to practice my writing and so I remember everything. It isn't very good, but I want to keep it with me."

I didn't know that she noticed my writing.

"I will show you how to make a copy – then we both can keep it."

I think that sounds good and I give her a smile.

Genovea isn't done yet. "Why don't you just take some of us home with you? We could tell everyone that you were here!"

"I don't think it would be fair to do that. Our world is complex and can be dangerous. You would have a lot to learn. And there would

be no promises that we could ever get you back here. You might never see your family again."

Now Taylor speaks up. I can actually understand most of what he says now. "Come on. *Genovea has been chased by a whole boatload of Saxon invaders. Muirenn by a patrol of Roman soldiers. Both have stood before a king and the governor of all Britain. Now they've seen a whole world they never imagined existed. Think they might be able to survive high school?"*

Robyn gives a quiet laugh. "It would still mean taking them from everything that they know and everyone they love. And Muirenn, you have already promised to go to Aquaesulis."

Genovea looks like she's trying to come up with another argument, but they arrive back at the boat before she speaks again.

After we eat lunch, it is time to get ready for the promised boat ride. It takes some work to convince Finanius to put on the soft coat that Robyn wants him to wear.

"Can you swim? If you happen to fall in, this will keep you afloat until we can get you out. I wear one. Lance will wear one. If you want a ride, you can wear one too. I don't want to have to tell Petronius that we lost his favorite town-builder at the bottom of the river."

He reluctantly puts on the coat and heads down the stairs to the boat.

I'm watching closely as they climb down into the boat. I know what to expect, but they don't.

"It is a sort of cloth," *I respond to the questioning looks they give when they step into the boat and find that it is a little soft.*

"How does it move?" *Antonius asks.* "Robyn said we'd go upstream, yet the tide is flowing out, so we'll be against both the current and the tide."

"You will see that I told the truth," *Robyn says as she steps into the boat.* "Lance will take it a little slow until we get past the bridge, then *he will give us a ride that you won't soon forget," she adds, pointing to the large wooden bridge that extends all the way across the river a little way upstream from us.*

I can see why we stopped where we did. Our big boat could never get past that structure. We are far too tall to get underneath the roadway. I have only seen one bridge before – the one the Roman's built near Wynt. I thought that was impressive, but it has nothing on this one. It is so long across the river – far wider than the river at Wynt. And this bridge looks to be wide enough for about six horses to cross abreast. But it is close to the river so not even the Roman boats can get past with their tall masts.

Antonius begins to talk. "We built that bridge a couple of years ago and many workshops moved to the other side where the land is cheaper. Many Britons live there and others from elsewhere in the Empire, but few Romans. There are tanneries, weavers, iron-mongers, woodworkers, brewers, and many more artisans over there. Nearly everything we need can be made right here. Most food and other supplies come down the river from the forests and farms further inland. We are quite self-sufficient in our little corner of the Empire."

"Last year the Iceni wrought much destruction on both sides of the river, but many of the workshops survived – or were quickly rebuilt. There is talk of building a wall around the settlement on that side of the river, but it may not happen. We are at peace with the tribes living there, for we have brought great prosperity to them."

He looks like he is about to continue, but Robyn pre-empts him. "Sit down, grab the ropes and let's get going." He does as she suggests, and the rest follow her example, except Lance who is standing at the wheel he uses to steer the boat. Once he even let me try steering. We didn't go very fast, but I took it all the way from the shore out to the big boat.

Knowing what is coming, I glance at the crowd watching us from the shore. Sure enough, some of them jump at the rumble and cloud of smoke that comes from the back when Lance starts the engine. When we start to move, Genovea can't resist turning and waving at the crowd. Why not? I join in, too.

Once we are clear of the boats by the shore, we pick up some speed and head to the middle of the river and the bridge.

As we approach the bridge, Finanius turns to Robyn "When I saw a boat with no sails or oars, I didn't believe that it would move faster over the water than any other boat I've been on. But, you spoke the truth – I have never before ridden a boat this fast heading up the river."

Now we are almost under the bridge. "Hang on! It may be a little rough under here. Once we get to the other side, you will see what I really meant."

Robyn is right. We bounce a bit as we go under the bridge. You can see the water swirl as the current takes it around the bridge piers, creating waves that toss the boat around. But as soon as we clear the bridge, the water gets smooth again and I hear the engine pitch change, the nose of the boat rises, and we start to fly up the river. The warehouses and workshops that lined the river below the bridge soon give way to the villas of the wealthy, then the fields and settlements of the farmers and fisher-folk who dwell on the shores of the river.

"We're getting close." I hear Lance's voice in my ear as the engine noise dies to a dull murmur.

"We saw something this morning that I think deserves a closer look. That is the real reason for this trip today," Robyn tells me as she gets up to stand beside Lance. "There is a small settlement here, and it looks like they are in trouble with a contagious disease, possibly cholera. There are at least three bodies visible and those are the ones we can see. There are some still alive, but they don't seem to be moving much. At least some that are still living are children – hopefully we can save them. That is why both Kelly and Sandy are here."

"Kelly and I are going ashore first to be sure it is safe. The rest of you can stay on the boat for a few minutes. Okay, Kelly, let's get suited up."

They take off their jackets for the boat and pull on white garments that completely cover them. They add gloves and masks that cover their faces. Robyn carries her gun, while Kelly has a white box. I look at them, and think how those people will be so scared when they see those white shapes approach them.

"I want to go with you." I find myself saying.

"We only have two of these suits. Until we know why they are all sick it might not be safe – you could get sick too. Sandy and Kelly think it is most likely cholera – if so, we will know quickly and you will be able to join us."

I can see the roofs of several huts just over a slight rise from where the boat is beached – it is not very far away. Suddenly, I am afraid. "Is this safe here? We are very close."

"The wind is behind us. If there is anything in the air, it will blow away. You're safe. I hope I am," Robyn replies as she steps onto the ground with Kelly trailing behind.

With that they walk up the rise and disappear down the other side. It doesn't take very long before I hear Robyn's voice. "It is cholera for sure. We have six survivors, so can use some help. Everyone who is coming ashore put on gloves and masks, but you don't need these suits."

Sandy gives us each a pair of gloves and mask and shows us how to put them on. I hate the mask! It feels so strange, trying to breathe through it. But I leave it on. Then she has us each carry a box toward the settlement. There are a dozen or so small huts in a rough circle, surrounded by only a low fence that is already falling down in places. Kelly and Robyn are already at work. One young woman is lying in the open area in the middle of the circle, near one of the huts. They are carrying someone else from a hut to lie beside her. Two children and an old man are together by another hut, but I know by looking they are beyond all help.

Sandy kneels down by the woman – I think she might be dead too, but she moans slightly as Sandy sticks one of her metal pins into her and connects a bag of water. I've learned they believe that if people don't have enough water in them, they will get sick. So the first thing they usually do is give them some. But Robyn explains it isn't just water, there is medicine in there to help them get better. I think that it better be pretty strong medicine if it will help this woman. I've seen people who look like her come through our gate, and it never ends well for the patient. But I watch Kelly and Sandy work on her; not knowing what else to do, I hold the bag that Sandy hands me, just like I remember Robyn doing when we found Luseth.

By this time, Finanius and Antonius have joined us. As they help carry the sick, Sandy moves from one to the next, doing the same thing. Genovea helps hold the bags up, but as soon as all the sick are moved out, Robyn takes out her knife and starts to work on the wall near the woman I first saw. As soon as she gets a stick worked loose, she takes a bag from my hand and hangs it from the stick and quickly moves on to the next patient. When my hands are free, Robyn tells me to watch the patients.

"If one stops breathing or anything changes, tell Sandy immediately."

All of a sudden, I feel terrified by the idea of being responsible for these people. "If something happens, what do I do?" I can hear the rising panic in my voice.

"Just shout Sandy's name, she'll come. Or Kelly." With that, Robyn moves on to free Genovea from holding her bags and I squat down beside the woman. In the dirt on her face I can see the dried tracks of tears, and I wonder about the bodies stacked on the other side of the settlement. Her father? Maybe her children. And now she's lying here dying and I don't think even these people can do anything to save her. I wonder if she knows they are trying. I reach out to brush the hair from her face and gently stroke her cheek as I watch her chest rise and fall.

"What is your name?" I whisper.

She doesn't answer. Instead, her chest stops moving and I see her relax, and I'll never know her name.

But I remember my instructions. "Sandy!" I shout out.

I don't know what to expect. Maybe that she'll wander over and take away the bag; maybe drag her over by the others. That's not what happens at all. Both she and Kelly come running, carrying boxes.

"She's not breathing." I get out. "She's dead." My voice catches.

But they're not paying attention to me. Kelly has put a sort of mask over her mouth and nose – I see the mask is connected with a tube to a round metal container. Sandy rips open her already tattered dress and takes two small flat objects from her box, holding one in each hand. I'm trying to understand what is going on and creep closer when Sandy places both these objects on the woman's chest, and shouts something. I scream as the woman jumps in a way no dead person should, then gasp as she gives a little cough and starts to breathe again. Tears start to rise in my eyes as I realize she isn't dead any more.

In the last few weeks, I have seen and done so much that I never dreamed possible. Flying like a bird for instance. Or learning to write. But never, ever did it even cross my mind that I would see someone who was dead be brought back to life. Just as I am thinking that maybe I'll learn her name after all, Robyn comes up to me.

"You saved her life!"

"You are from the other world! You even have power over life and death. She was dead! I know what it is like. I've seen people die before, and I watched her die. And now she's living again." I can feel myself starting to tremble out of fear and the enormity of what I have just seen. For even as I speak I realize the truth. "You even have power over death."

Robyn looks me in the eyes, and I stare back into hers. "Sometimes we can bring them back if we reach them quickly enough. Not always. Often the injuries are too severe or it takes too long for people like Sandy and Kelly to reach them. Then they die and we can't bring them back." I can see tears in her eyes, and I remember her telling me that her family all died.

"Is that what happened to your family?"

"Yes. They were all too badly hurt to be saved. Will you watch her, in case she tries to die on us again?" I nod, and Robyn stands up to leave. "I have to help with the others."

I focus again on the woman lying before me. She's resting now, breathing easily. I can see her breath slightly fog the mask she's still wearing when she breathes out – as she breathes in, it clears and I can see her teeth through her slightly-parted lips. The light breeze flips open her torn top exposing a breast. I'm sure she's recently given birth and was suckling a baby and I wonder again what happened to her child.

Genovea comes over with some bed clothes gathered from a hut. "Sandy said we should cover them to keep them warm." I take one of the heavy woven blankets and spread it over her. "Robyn and Sandy are trying to decide how to get all six back. There are too many to fit in the boat at one time. So do they make two trips in the boat or use their bird. Sandy wants to use The Bird, but Robyn doesn't want to scare the people of Londinium. I think they will get Bledwyn or Marcellus to warn the people about The Bird and bring it for the sickest."

I look at the sleeping woman at my feet and think that she should get to ride in The Bird. After all, she died today.

"How long she will sleep?" I wonder aloud. "If she wakes up in The Bird – or even on the boat, she'll be totally terrified."

"They gave them something so they will stay asleep. That is what Sandy told me. I need to go and cover the rest," Genovea says as she moves on to the others with her pile of bedding.

The woman is resting easy, so I get up, stretch, and look around. The first thing I notice is the bodies that were across the settlement are gone. I quickly count those stretched out on the ground, thinking maybe they called others back from the dead. But no, only six are here. I see Lance come out of the hut furthest away from me, one that is set a little apart from the others, carrying some sort of red box in one hand. Robyn comes behind him, and they both hurry a distance away before they turn to watch. Through the open door I watch as a fire quickly blooms and grows to fill the inside. In no time it bursts through the thatch roof, sending out a column of smoke and a cloud of sparks.

I keep watching as the roof collapses into the hut and the fire dies down. They must have put the bodies in there before they set fire to the hut. We usually bury our dead in the ground, but sometimes when there are many at once, we burn them. Just like the people of Dubritun did with the Sea-wolves. I guess Robyn's people do the same thing.

As I watch the hut burn, I hear in the distance the approaching thumping of The Bird. Before long I see it flying low over the trees that line this part of the river, keeping under the clouds that have moved in since this morning. As it approaches, I make my decision. I want to learn how to bring people back from the dead. If I join Finanius and the Romans at their new city of healing, I may find a place where I belong; I may even find a husband. But I will never again see what I saw today – and I will never learn how it is done. I am staying with Robyn's people and will convince them somehow to take me back to their world.

The bird touches down behind me in a clearing just outside the circle of huts. As soon as it is down, the action on the ground starts. Bledwyn, Marcellus, and Michael all come running from The Bird, carrying cots for the sick people. We all help to carefully transfer each one to a cot from the ground where they lie; then carry them to The Bird.

After last one disappears into The Bird, Robyn comes over to where Genovea and I are standing. "We won't have room for everyone in The Bird, so only those needed to care for the sick will fly. The rest of us will ride in the boat. Muirenn, Sandy wants you in The Bird. Come on Genovea, we are heading back in the boat."

With that, I climb into The Bird. I'm a little scared. This is the first time that I've been around these people without Robyn nearby to help translate. But it turns out well. It is only a few minutes before we land on the boat; then I help unload the cots. I follow Sandy, thinking we will head into her room and care for the sick people. We don't. Instead we head to a shower room.

"We need to get cleaned up, so we don't get sick or make them sicker. So let's get to work."

I agree that we were both a little dirty, but I have never been through such a thorough cleaning in my life before. We take off our clothes, shower, and then wash our hands until I think my skin will come off. Then Sandy gives me some clean clothes. Only then do we head into the room with the sick people – 'patients' I hear Sandy call them. Kelly and April are already in there working on them.

"Roll up your sleeve." Sandy tells me. "Like this," she adds, demonstrating what she means. "We each will get some medicine to protect us in case we were exposed to their sickness."

I do what she says, and Kelly picks up a clear, round thing filled with liquid and a fine piece of shiny steel at one end.

"We need to clean you first," he says, ripping open a little pouch and pulling out a small cloth. Clean me? I've never been so clean before in my life, and he wants me even cleaner. It is wet and cold where he wipes my arm.

"Hold still."

I feel the prick as he sticks the metal into my skin and watch as he pushes the end of this thing, sending the liquid into my arm.

"All done," he says as he pulls it out. I can see now the metal is hollow, so the liquid flows through the middle. And it is pointed at the end so it will go into my skin. "That should keep you from getting sick from these people."

He then does the same thing to Sandy, then Sandy repeats it with him.

Now that we are clean, we all help to get the patients onto beds from the cots and get them settled in.

"Some may start waking up soon. I would like you to be here when they do. Why don't you go get something to eat and come back when

you are done?" Sandy says to me. "Kelly, you go too. We can handle them for now."

I suddenly realize I am hungry – and thirsty.

As we are eating, I start asking Kelly questions. "What is the medicine that you gave me?" "Why is it so important for us to be so clean?" I don't understand most of his answers, but I do see that there are tiny animals – far too small to see – that get into us and make us sick. The cleaning washes them off our skin and the medicine kills them.

"How do you know, if you can't see them?" I ask.

"We have a machine that lets us see them."

I should have guessed. They have a machine for everything. But now I am curious. "Can you show me?"

And that simple question launches me into a whole string of new experiences. Sandy teaches me how to use a microscope and I actually see vibrio cholera, the bacteria that nearly wiped out an entire settlement. I spend most of my time in the clinic, helping the patients, asking questions, and learning as much as I can.

The patients we rescued recover quickly. Rosathe, the woman I helped save, woke up early this morning. I have to talk to each one, to tell them what happened and that they are being cared for by people from the other world – right in the middle of Londinium. Rosathe tells me that her son - only a few weeks old was among the first to sicken and die. She fought to save her other son and her husband. After they both succumbed, she took ill, one of the last healthy ones in the settlement. They had been there for two days, too sick to care for themselves when we found them. In the end, her brother and her husband's sister were among the six who survived.

I learn that they raised crops, fished, and made charcoal that they sold to iron workers in Londinium. It was a hard life – they didn't have much land and found what little they could grow was often wiped out by floods or stolen before harvest. And now Roman villas are springing up along the river and they fear soon the land they do have will be taken from them.

"But now, I can't imagine ever going back, not with only six of us."

Bledwyn! Where is he? He needs people for his town. These are people who are looking for a town. He went into town with Marcelus and Ahntya, but I think he'll be back soon – probably just in time for the next meal, knowing him.

Sure enough, when I come down to the mess room with Genovea and Rosathe to get some dinner, Bledwyn is there gathering food. How does he know just when to show up?

After we eat, we can finally sit down and watch the movie Robyn promised Finanius, so he could learn something of the land they spoke of this morning.

Robyn brought our guests up to speed. "We told you the boxes Taylor carries remember what they see and hear. This is how they show us what they remembered. What you will see is the land that you know as Parthia, which we call Afghanistan. In our world, it is a land in the middle of a deadly war where there has been much destruction. I will try to translate the words you hear into Latin so you understand what you are seeing."

With that, the wall lights up and the first images appear. I recognize that face! It's Taylor. I turn to Robyn.

"Is this the one Taylor made?"

"Yes."

I'm so excited to actually see these images, but I find it hard to understand some of the words, so I listen to Robyn instead.

"This is for people who have seen many images of the war, but have never been to Afghanistan. Taylor is here to make the film about how we are trying to help the common people whose lives have been uprooted. You can see here the homes and markets that have been destroyed in the fighting. Each damaged building represents multiple lives torn apart – dreams crushed; loved ones killed."

She falls silent as we travel down a road through the city. I have never seen a place like this. Everything is brown and dusty with few trees. So completely different from here that I wonder how the people live. Most of the buildings look to be intact, but here and there I see damage – some places have holes in the walls, others are totally destroyed.

"Most of the people who live here are not involved in this fight – our fight is with a group which took over several years ago and our mission is to eject those invaders and return control to the people of this city. Trying to root them out has taken many years and cost many lives. Those left behind often are living in desolation, having lost family and home in the fighting. My mission was to work with these people, to help get them re-established and give them hope. This is one of the women of the city called Kabul."

I see the face of a pretty young woman with black hair, brown skin, and brown eyes. She wears a red shawl that's wrapped around her head, so just her face shows. Now the camera backs away from her so we can see more, but I keep staring into her eyes; they look so sad. As she gets further away, her eyes get smaller and I finally turn my attention away from them. I see now she is wearing a dark blue dress and sitting on a chair in front of a dusty wall. Her lap is occupied by a young child wrapped in a cloth that was probably once white but is now stained.

I watch as she looks down at her child and pulls the clothes away. I can see she's worried about her child, but it doesn't look sick. It looks up at her with eyes just as dark as hers.

Then Robyn speaks. "This is Fatima the day we first met. When she came, she had no home, no money, and no food. She came because she saw us as her only choice to get food and safety for her son."

I watch as another woman comes onto the screen. She's dressed in clothes the color of the sand and wears a shawl on her head similar to the other woman. Most of her face is covered, but when she turns to face us, I instantly recognize her eyes. They are the same ones that looked at me when I was lying on the road that day.

"That's Robyn!" I exclaim.

"Yes that is me." I can hear her voice crack as she speaks those words and I wonder why.

I continue to wonder why this bothers her so much, as we watch Fatima and her son get food, and a new place to stay that looks even nicer than the room I share with Genovea. We watch as she attends a school and gets money. She tells us that she feels happy and safe in her new place. Robyn tell us that she's sad that she will have to leave Fatima behind soon, because it is time for her to return home. But she's sure Fatima will be okay.

Then we watch as Fatima goes with her son into a marketplace. Taylor tells us that we can't follow her because it might be dangerous for her – the enemies might see us paying her special attention and harm her in response. So we watch her disappear into the crowd. Then there is a flash of flame, followed by a loud crack. Smoke and dust billow from the market as people run out into the street. We follow as Robyn and several others run toward the site of the fire. I see many people wounded – others take care of them, but we keep running. We find Fatima's son first. Then Fatima herself a short distance away. Both are covered by blood and look to be dead.

Robyn told me that most of what we see on the screen is like a story – people really aren't hurt or dead. Just like how horrible things happen in stories, but no one is really harmed, it is like that with what we watch. But I can tell by looking at Robyn and Taylor that this was real – their friend really did die. And now I know why they both hate watching this.

Chapter 21.

We spend ten days in Londinium. During that time, we have a steady stream of visitors to the ship, while the crew takes full advantage of our presence here to spend time wandering the city. Even in the first century, London is a maze of narrow, winding streets. Only the area around the governor's villa and the barracks has streets that are anywhere near straight. That didn't keep us from exploring; just about everyone on the crew got lost at one time or other and needed help getting back. I think I'm the only one who never had to call for a drone to locate me and have Martin give me directions back to the ship. This is fortunate because I know he would have never let me live that one down. Not that I will let him forget the time he got so lost that even with the drone we had a hard time finding him. Just how does one cross a bridge and not even remember it? Of course, he did manage to find a tavern, so that may have had something to do with him getting so completely lost. A few of our team sampled the local brews until we rescued the cholera victims. Then most decided they would stick close to home for their food and drink.

The six people we rescued from the settlement on the river – Michele tagged them 'the survivors' – have all recovered. Most keep a pretty low profile here – intimidated by the city and buried in their grief. There were about thirty in the village before the cholera struck, so that's an eighty percent mortality rate. It would have been one hundred percent if Don hadn't spotted them on one of his survey runs that morning. Rosathe, the woman Sandy and Kelly resuscitated, is a little more outgoing than the others. This is fortunate, because since word got out of her return from death, she has been very much the center of attention. I blame mostly Antonius for wild-fire speed that the news spread. The baths are the center of news and gossip in any Roman town and he took full advantage of his position to share – and no doubt embellish – his eye-witness report.

Rosathe, on the other hand, has no idea how to handle her new-found celebrity status. "I can't stand this. So many people! People I've never met before always pushing against me, touching me, asking me to bless them. I was happy in our little village by the river. Sometimes I just want to go back home, but I can't. The people who made it home aren't there anymore. And I don't think I could ever feel safe there again. I am glad that we are soon leaving here with Bledwyn to his new town by the sea. I've long heard of the sea from the men who buy our charcoal, but never imagined that I would ever get to see it for myself. I hope that once we get there, I can go back to just being Rosathe instead of this goddess everyone wants to touch."

We were walking along the quay that lines the river when she said these words, enjoying a clear and warm morning before most people are up. It is the only time any of us can get any peace, here most of all. But all of the crew experience the same thing now. It was bad with just the Voyager sitting in the river, but when we had to use the chopper, things got a whole lot worse. Now everyone knows that we have a dragon – a dragon that is totally terrifying and makes a tremendous noise, but rescues sick people so can't be all bad. I think some of the people half expect it to burn down the city one night, in spite of all our efforts to convince them it is completely safe. Ahntya has tried her best – she actually knows some people here so has more influence on public opinion than the rest of us. Now, I think they accept it as their friend and we are probably the reason behind London's choice of a dragon for its city symbol.

Now we go from symbols to saints: Symeon found his reception here somewhat different than he expected. He had a touch of the flu or something when we arrived, so didn't get out to meet his friends until after we rescued the survivors, so the news of Rosathe's resurrection preceded him, and it didn't take long for them to connect him with us. Quickly they divided into two camps: those who figured we performed a miracle and should be accepted as saints or something similar, and those who thought it must be the work of demons, and therefore we should be avoided at all costs. It is a very confused Symeon who comes stumbling back to the ship long after dark following his first visit ashore. He finds Taylor and me in Mission Control, cataloguing photos and planning our journey for the next day, just like any good London tourists.

"How did you do that – raise Rosathe from the dead? Was it by God or by devilry?"

Oh boy, how do I answer that one? Not sure how "medical science, a couple of highly trained professionals, some advanced equipment, and good timing thanks to an alert Muirenn" fits into his "a or b" concept of reality. I would turn to Taylor for help here, because I know he'll come up with a snappy answer, but his Latin is still pretty basic, so he just sits back and watches.

"God," I blurt out, being pretty sure the other option would get me into a whole lot of trouble.

"How can I trust your answer?"

"Aren't you really looking for an answer you can give to your friends that they will believe?" I'm stalling for time here. My knowledge of Christian theology is pretty basic. I did take a comparative religions class in my second year university, but I don't remember much. Since the day of my family's funeral, I have a hard time believing in a loving God who sat by and did nothing as my whole family died in the crash. And that was before Afghanistan.

"First I want an answer I can believe."

I search my fading memories and come up with an idea. "Isn't God the source of life? If so, Rosathe is alive, so her life must be from him. Am I right?"

"That may be true," he admits.

I hate theology, and would normally run from an encounter like this, but as a researcher, I also want to learn more from this man, and am now gaining some confidence. "Why do you doubt? Who other than God would want Rosathe to live?"

"I heard that a magic box was used to restore her to life. None of us have ever heard of God needing a magic box."

Ah. That is the source of his distress. At least we are moving away from theology and getting closer to my comfort zone. "There is no magic in that box, but I am not surprised that one who doesn't know its secrets would think there must be. You have seen many strange things – how we fly through the air, make light without flame, see things that are far off, and many more that must seem like magic, yet only this bothers you. Why is that?"

"None of those things have power over life and death. This box does and that makes it different."

"The box only holds our secret for starting someone's heart. The heart is critical to life – when it stops, you are dead. But this box can sometimes restart a heart. It doesn't work every time – it did with Rosathe. It didn't work when my whole family died." That last sentence came out with more venom than I intended.

"So she looked like she was dead, but you were able to keep her from dying? Using the secret in your box?"

"That's right – she was mostly dead." I reply, suddenly thinking of Miracle Max in The Princess Bride. That was one of our favorite movies when we were young; we watched it time after time until we knew virtually every line, and I'd go to sleep dreaming of finding my Wesley. I'm pretty sure that my parents deeply regretted that Christmas we got that movie. Yet dad gave Kim the nickname of 'Buttercup' and would even sit down and watch it with us. Of course, I never got a nickname. Ever. With my name ... I didn't need one.

Great, now I'm thinking about my family and the accident just before bedtime. I know what is coming. Sure enough, in my dreams I keep stumbling into funerals. I try to get away, but everywhere I turn – a park, a down-town corner, and finally my own yard – there is another one with mourners and a casket. I finally escape from the one in my own yard and run to the street, only to come face-to-face with the flaming wreck of our SUV. I wake, drenched in sweat, throw on some clothes, and stumble to the sitting area just outside my cabin. It must be a couple of hours later that Taylor finds me on a sofa, legs drawn up to my chest and arms wrapped around them. I'm barely awake, but afraid of what I will see if I close my eyes. So I just stare straight ahead, and don't stir when he comes over and plops down beside me.

"Hey, girl. What ya' doing still up?" he asks in an unnecessarily cheerful voice.

I tear my eyes away from the blank spot on the wall and turn to him. A trace of a smile crosses my lips – Taylor's enthusiasm is so infectious that I can't help myself. "I could ask you the same thing.

But you should know me well enough by now to know why I am awake."

"Dreams again?"

I silently nod as he slides closer. Taylor is amazing when I am in a mood like this. Most my other friends – even Don or Michele who also know me well – will try to talk me out of it. Taylor knows better. He just puts an arm on my shoulder and silently sits, watching me. I feel so useless and weak that I am still haunted by something that happened over ten years ago, but I am and I can't stop it. Taylor's about the only one I know who doesn't tell me more-or-less to just get over it. He sits in silence, and after a few minutes starts gently whistling bits of random songs in my ear.

I can't help but smiling in spite of my mood. Slowly I find myself relaxing and the next thing I know it is morning. Taylor is out, cuddled up next to me and curled up next to him is Genovea – she obviously found us sometime in the night. I can see her sleeping there – her long dark hair is loose. Recently she's taken to wearing it in a braid – either Michele or April taught her that. In her borrowed clothes, she could easily pass for one of the kids in my freshman anthropology class. The more I get to know her, the less I look forward to having to convince her to stay behind when the time comes for us to leave. It isn't that I don't think she could handle the complexity of our culture – I am pretty sure she can. She's smart, confident, and socially adept. Steve has been teaching her the basics of our technology, and she's making remarkable progress for someone who only started learning to read a month ago.

I can't just tell her "No, you're not up to it." I don't believe that, and neither will she. *How do I convince her that this is her time?* I'm hoping that when she sees Luseth's baby she will decide to stay here in this world. Deep down, I know it is a long shot that the baby will change her mind, but I am out of ideas. What's more, I wonder if I should convince her to stay. When I think of the opportunities she would have in our time compared to what she has here, maybe she should return with us to the 21st century.

I see she's now awake, and staring at me with her amazingly intense eyes as if she's reading my mind.

But she just asks, "Are we going to take the sick people to Bledwyn's town soon, now that they are better?"

It was Muirenn who thought of resettling the survivors at Aborgium and convinced Bledwyn that it was a good idea. Bledwyn didn't take much convincing since he is a totally freaked out about not having enough people. And this is a great idea. These are river people, fishers, and charcoal burners. They can fish in the river that meets the sea there, and the Roman garrison will bring the need for ironworkers, and ironworkers need charcoal. They should fit in well, it will give them something to do and contribute to the success of the town. Importantly for them, it will give them a new start at life in a place that isn't filled with painful memories and hopefully isn't contaminated with cholera.

We still hope to convince some of the people from Genovea's home to move too. Bledwyn needs lots of people.

"Yeah, tomorrow we will leave and take them to their new home. The first troop of soldiers should be hard at work there now, building the fort, so they should have a place to live. Then we go back to your home and try to convince them to move too. And see if your sister has given birth yet."

Genovea responds with, "I just hope she will come with us. I don't want to leave her behind."

I was afraid of that: she has no intention of being left behind in this time when we leave, and I'm not sure that I blame her. Symeon is another story entirely. He's trying to decide whether to stay here in Londinium or travel north with us. Apparently the situation here is not nearly as dangerous as he feared – his friends were quite surprised when he related the rumors he'd heard. But he still wants to check out the northern part of the country, so he's been back and forth several times in his plans. Finally, as we are preparing to leave, he comes aboard.

"I finally decided. I'm getting to old for this constant travel and for sleeping out under the stars. My daughter's husband will take over my tin trade, and I will settle in this new place. I'm sure there are opportunities for experienced traders in the new town, and the advantage goes to whoever gets there first."

So we gain one, but we lose two. Marcellus and Ahntya left this morning: they plan to return to Gaul. Ahntya learned that her family moved back there a year ago and she wants to find them. A friend still in Londinium tells her that her parents came to greatly regret the words which drove her from their home, and according this friend, they will warmly welcome her back into their lives. Marcellus needs to start a new life far from here, where he won't be recognized as an army deserter. The fact there is clearly a mutual interest between these two no doubt played into their decision. Last night we threw a big party for them, gave them some gifts and wished them well on their journey. And now they are gone.

Before we leave, we have one last task – to take on a load of building materials for the new town. We pulled the chopper into the hanger, freeing up the deck for wooden beams, bricks, ironwork, and amphorae of cement. The Romans provide a legion of slaves to help with the loading, but even so, it takes the better part of a day. Slowing the process is Barry's careful supervision. He makes sure everything is balanced and properly secured so it can't shift and endanger the ship. We let him. It is a short trip and the weather is fine, and ... this ship is the ticket home for all of us – we can never forget that.

The journey is perfect – it's a beautiful morning just before sunrise as we cast off from the port and head down the river against the incoming tide. In spite of the early hour, a large crowd of the curious gathers along the riverbank to see us off. Captain Johansen can't resist an audience, so he sets their ears ringing with an extended blast on the ship's horn. Ha! Those lazy ones who didn't bother to get up to see us off don't get to sleep in after all. The Roman sailors think we are nuts for leaving when we do – they would wait to take advantage of the outflowing tide to help carry them to the sea. But their boats only draw about six feet of water so they don't have to worry about the bar a couple miles downstream. We do. Captain Johansen times our departure so that we reach there at the peak of the tide, leaving a good four feet of water under our keel as we cross the shallowest point.

We journey north on calm seas and under clear skies. At least the seas seem calm from our vantage point. About halfway up the coast we pass a fleet of four Roman merchant vessels heading in the same direction. I stand at the rail watching them pitch and roll in the swells that look so tame from ten meters up. Down at their level, the waves are sending spray over the gunwales and I watch fascinated as the sailors climb the rolling decks to manage the sails. I know these boats – they left Londinium a full two days before us, headed for the same port. We will get there before nightfall this evening. They have two more days ahead of them if the weather holds. I keep watching as long as they are in sight, fascinated at the courage and determination of these men who brave the seas at the outer limits of the known world, in wooden boats with no compass or any other navigation tools apart from their own eyes.

By the time we arrive it is getting too late to unload our cargo before nightfall, but after we anchor in the harbor, the tribune leading, the construction troop is welcomed aboard. He seems a little out of sorts, and it doesn't take long to find out why. Just a couple hours ago he received the dispatch informing him that we were coming, and he thinks it was delayed on the way. He calms down after we finally convince him that we only left Londinium this morning, so the dispatch riders were doing well to beat us. The good meal we give him doesn't hurt his mood either.

At first light, we start to unload. The water close to shore is too shallow for us, but we have a plan. We run a line from our derrick to a tree near the shore to create a zip line. In no time a steady stream of materials are running from our deck down to the shore – much to the delight of the soldiers who don't have to row boat after boat out to our side to ferry our load to the shore. They just have to unload and stack the materials on shore.

We are almost done when the accident happens. Andrew is helping to secure a large beam to the carrier on the line. When he raises it with the derrick winch, one end gets caught. He keeps pulling, the stuck end breaks free, causing the other end to swing fast and hard. It catches him in the head, knocking his hardhat off and sending him flying. Kelly and Sandy both materialize out of nowhere and quickly spring into action. I help as we carry him down to the sick bay, and it's clear his injury is far beyond what they have the equipment or training to deal with.

"We need a neurosurgeon – someone who can handle a traumatic head injury. We can sedate him and try to keep him alive for now, but he won't last long without a lot more help than we can give him here."

It's a very subdued team that finishes unloading. We had planned to show the Romans the other use for zip-lines, but no one is in the mood, so we just pull the line in and gather in Mission Control.

It's Max who finally speaks. "It's not safe yet for us to take the ship back through time, but we do have plan B."

What we've always called 'Plan B' is a small, one-person time machine in the hold of the ship which can take someone back to our time. We brought it so in an emergency we could send someone back home to bring a spare part or a rescue team. It never even crossed our minds to make it big enough to return home with a critically injured patient. We believe that being physically smaller and with far less mass, it is less likely than the ship to be affected by the ripples we left in the space-time continuum during our journey out. That is our hope – I still don't fully trust the math behind time travel, even though it has worked so far.

Max explained his plan. "I can take it home and come back with one that can carry Andrew, so we can get him to our time and the emergency care he needs. I hope. If something happens and I can't get back, Don can get the rest of the team home. I just can't sit here and let Andrew die without making the effort."

No one else has a better idea, and no one is about to prevent Max from leaving since that would mean certain death for Andrew, so we work fast to get ready for the trip. We already planned the site for launching the time machine – the one spot on this island we know hasn't changed from now until our own time. We load the chopper with the large box that contains the time-machine into the chopper and take off for our spot – Stonehenge. It's a small crew on board: Max, Don, me, Taylor and Michael. Jerry is at the controls. I'm not quite sure how she managed it, but Genovea is with us too.

I spend the flight alternately staring out the window and staring at the blue box strapped to the floor in front of me that will take Max home and if all goes well, will bring him back.

"If you can't get back within a few hours of the current time, there is no point in coming – Andrew will be beyond anyone's help." Sandy told him before we left.

I try to blink back the tears that are rising in my eyes. I can't say that I am particularly close to Andrew, but he is part of the team – the team I helped to put together and brought to this place. I personally approved Andrew for the team, so I have to accept responsibility for his injury – and maybe his death. The team I'm supposed to protect. Now Max has jumped in to put his life at risk to attempt a rescue in a machine we've never tested over this span of time. Max I do know. I'm one of the very few around him who know is reputation with the girls is just an act that he's perfected over the years to hide the truth he still fears to expose. He's gay. He told me once that his father is so viciously anti-gay that if he ever came out, he would never be able to go home again.

"I get along great with my mother and both my sisters – I can't lose those relationships. I'm sure they are the reason I like hanging out with girls. So I keep my relationship with Don a secret – he's pretty low key anyway, but since his family is almost as bad, he's okay with us keeping it quiet. So we go through life as roommates." I still remember his words that night they told us girls. I'm fighting back the tears as I think of him risking everything to try to save a guy he really doesn't know all that well.

Genovea sees my distress. She doesn't try talk over the noise of the chopper. She just unbuckles her seatbelt and quietly slides into the seat beside me. As she snuggles as close as she can, I can't help but smile as she looks up at me – jade green eyes peering out from under an army green helmet that's just a shade too big. I put my arm around her shoulders and she just sits quietly until we land on the plain just outside the circle of standing stones. The stones look about the same as they do in our time: a few of the smaller stones are standing now that will have fallen in two millennia, but the giant bluestones are lying in the same positions they will be in the pictures I took during my visit here. They don't look quite as worn, but even now this is an ancient monument isolated in the middle of the plain. We place our box just outside the inner ring, close enough that we know the land won't be disturbed. Don and Max hug and share some quiet words; then he climbs into the box and shuts the door. We stand with our backs to the chopper and watch while it stands against the ancient stone looking like a refugee from a Dr. Who episode.

Max explained his idea to make it look like the famous T.A.R.D.I.S. from the series. "It makes sense – anyone who sees it in our time will think it is just a prop. Besides, it appeals to my sense of humor."

Suddenly the box appears to rotate and shrink to a single vertical line. Then it's gone, without a noise or a flash. Suddenly there's nothing but some flattened grass and a slight ozone odor. I feel Don lean against me, and hear his sobs in my ear. Put my arm around him as Taylor hands him a tissue. I reach for one, too. I'm going to need it.

It is just after three when Max sets off. We agree to wait for three hours for him to return, but wind up staying longer, knowing that our departure from here will condemn Andrew. Max is not our worry. He has a radio that can easily reach the Voyager from here and we will to leave a capsule here containing a messaging device we can update remotely. If Max makes it back here anytime during the rest of the mission, he can dig it up and contact us. He'll be okay. Still, I sit in the open door of the chopper staring at the empty space formerly occupied by the time machine long past the agreed time. No one else seems in any hurry to go either. It is finally nearly 8:30 when the radio crackles to life with the news we've all been dreading.

Andrew is dead.

We bury the capsule beside one of the large fallen blue stones and lift off for home without any more delay. Genovea again takes the seat beside me – but this time she promptly falls asleep so I ride in silence, staring out at the green countryside passing beneath us in the dusk.

Chapter 22.

This morning we buried Andrew on the top of a hill overlooking the sea he loved. We all stood in the drizzling rain while Robyn and the Captain both spoke some words before they lowered the box containing his body into the hole in the ground. As soon as the team finished filling in the hole, Lance starts to shuttle the team back to the ship. I stay and watch as John and Michael lay a heavy flat stone on the ground to mark the location. I watched last night as they made the stone by mixing a coarse gray powder with water and poured the resulting mass into a mold. John made some letters out of wood and we pressed them into the soft material to spell Andrew's names. Beneath it we put some numbers. I don't really understand what they mean, but I learned they are another kind of symbol they use. Each day gets a number, and anyone who sees that number knows exactly what day they mean. Because these people are really concerned about remembering when things happened, including the day everyone is born and when they die, the first number is the day Andrew was born and the last is yesterday – when he died.

By morning what they called a 'grave marker' was as hard as stone - and as heavy as stone, too. I tried to lift it, but couldn't. Even John needed Michael's help to carry it to the boat and then up the hill to the grave – it is that heavy.

Andrew MacQuaid. Born: 1985-08-05 Died: 0064-07-04.

All Robyn's people are deeply saddened by Andrew's death. April, Michele and Steven all seem broken even more than the others, but I don't understand why. When someone dies, they pass to the other world. I thought these people were from the other world, so doesn't Andrew just wind up in their world – no different than Max will be when they sent him back yesterday? Genovea noticed the same thing, so we find Robyn when we get back to the ship.

"You two are very observant to notice. No, people who die here don't come to our world. Even in our world, people die, and no one knows for sure what happens after that. But people live longer than they do here, so Michele and Steven have never had anyone close die before. April and Andrew had a romance going – they kept it so quiet I don't

think anyone knew. I thought I knew April, but even I didn't have a clue until last night when she came to me in tears."

I can't imagine a world where you can live for years and not know anyone who has died. People die all the time here. Babies die, children die, adults die. My best friend died of disease; a young warrior who I might have married was knocked from his horse during a hunt; another friend's baby died not long before I met Robyn. All since the last winter solstice, and that doesn't include those who came to us too late seeking healing. It hasn't been a good year. Then I remember I probably would be on that list if it Robyn hadn't found me on that road. That thought makes me more determined than ever to know their secrets, and I won't leave until I do.

I speak up "I want to know your secrets, why your people live so long. How you can sometimes even bring back people from the dead. People here die and I'm tired of not being able to do anything about it, of having to just sit back and watch it happen. I don't care how hard it is or how long it takes – I want to know."

I'm almost shouting now. "Don't tell me you won't take me!"

Robyn looks at me with a half-smile. "I thought you were going to join the Romans at their new town to the west."

"I was until I saw Kelly and Sandy bring Rosathe back to life. We can't do that. The Romans can't do that. But you can, and I want to know how."

"If that is what you want, you will need to learn many things that most girls your age already know. Things like how to read our language, for starters. We better get to work. And remember, if you travel with us, we might not be able to get you back here. Max went to try to get help for Andrew – he didn't make it back. You probably won't either. We don't even know if we can get back home – no one has ever tried it before and something could go wrong. Be sure this is what you want."

I just look her in the eyes. "This is what I want."

"Tomorrow morning, we will go see Genovea's home." Now Robyn looks at Genovea. *"I hope you will choose to stay here, for this is your world. If your choice is to come with us, you need to understand that you face the same challenges that Muirenn will. Don't let Muirenn influence your decision."*

"I decided to stay with you on the day we met on the beach. I haven't changed my mind."

"I'm sure that is true. But I don't think either of you begin to realize how hard it will be to fit into our world."

I think about her words before I reply. "It scares me to leave, but having seen a bit of your world, it would be impossible to stay here and not spend the rest of my life wishing I had the courage to go. Genovea feels the same way."

I'm surprised when Robyn laughs at this. "I understand. I made the choice to come here, knowing full well if I didn't, I would regret that choice for the rest of my life."

Early in the morning we leave the ship for the flight to Genovea's home. I'm looking forward to seeing Luseth – it has been nearly a full moon since she returned home. I find myself wondering how she's doing and if her baby was born. With a start I realize that when I leave this world with Robyn, I won't ever be able to see my family again or find out anything about them. My resolve wavers for a bit, but by the time we touch down in the field beside the settlement, I am sure. The shocking news we get as soon we enter the gates makes me even more certain.

Luseth is dead.

It wasn't an easy birth. She was in labor for a full day and in the end she lost a lot of blood. The baby – a girl – was finally born dead, and Luseth soon followed her into the other world.

Genovea doesn't bother to stay any longer. She just turns without a word of parting and returns to her seat in The Bird. I can't say I blame her. We have to stay a little longer so that Bledwyn can make his pitch to the gathered people, to convince them to join him in his new town. Most agree. After the devastating attack from the Sea-wolves, the idea of living under the protection of a Roman garrison sounds very appealing. Even though the weather has been nearly perfect this year, the damage to the fields was greater than they expected, and food this winter will be scarce. The option of food and protection in return for help in building and populating this new town sounds like an attractive alternative to their present vulnerability. Even so, some are not so sure they are ready to leave and start a new life on the coast.

Elsidd is the one who sways the majority. He knows Bledwyn so his words carry a lot of weight with the people, and in the end they agree to move to Bledwyn's town just as soon as they have gathered their meager harvest. Bledwyn hoped they would come earlier, to help with the construction before winter sets in, but the people would not budge – their faith was in the beans and barley in the fields, not in the promises of the Romans or even those of my big brother. From what I saw of their fields as we flew over them this morning, I think I'd trust Bledwyn. But I can't blame them – they've lived here for generations and change is hard.

Nevertheless, it is a disappointed Bledwyn who climbs into The Bird for the quick trip to Tordur. It still seems like magic that we can travel through the air so fast. It would take me a full day to travel the distance by foot. Now, even though the morning is already growing old, we will still arrive well before noon. As we near home, I stare out the window as the familiar landscape passes by and feel a twinge of guilt at the thought of leaving my parents and this place behind as I travel with Robyn to her world to learn their secrets of life and death.

It is only after we land that and I have a chance to speak to my family that I learn their news – all the people are leaving Tordur and moving to the new Roman town Finanius is building far to the west. My mother explained to me. "There will be new buildings with roofs that don't leak in the winter rains."

This was always her only complaint –during the long rainy nights of winter, the rain would get in through the smoke holes in the roofs, leaving puddles on the stone floor of our hall and turning the dirt floors of our homes to mud.

She continues. *"They will build baths; there will be a wall and troops for protection; we can learn from their healers and maybe find new cures. And the Romans have money."*

Then Gwyn adds. "There is good building stone in the area, so they will need stone-working tools from our iron workers. The land is good so our herders and planters will have plenty to do. There is fish from the river, and plenty of game in the nearby forests.

It is my father who gives the rest of the story. "The Romans invited us to make the move, and as much as we love it here, we decided keeping on good terms with them is more important. Like it or not, we rely on them for protection and much of our income. I know your friends saved us from the Sea-wolves once, but they won't be here forever. The next time, it will be the Romans who will save us."

"The barley will be ready for harvest about the time of the next new moon. As soon as have harvested it, we will pack up and leave. The wheat will be later – the people of Dubri-tun will harvest it for the Romans promise to provide us enough for the winter."

"What will happen to the town after you leave?" Robyn asks from behind me. I turn, startled, not realizing she was behind me.

My father responds. "We'll do what we always do it we abandon a fort – we have a ceremony where we return the land to the gods then burn it to the ground. After we have removed everything of value."

Now it is my turn. I tell them about Rosathe – how she was dead, and is now alive and healthy. "I want to learn their secrets – I want to learn how to bring dead people back to life and I can't do that here. I am going to the other world with Robyn. She warned me that once I get there, I might not be able to get back to this world. But I'm determined to do it."

My father spoke again. "I suspected as much. Go with our blessing as we have Cydyrn's blessing in our decision. I reminded him during my last visit to Wynt, he had a surprise for me. His bard sang a new song, the tale of Bledwyn and the Dragon, how Bledwyn the brave saved his people from invasion by the Sea-wolves, with the help of a great warrior who came from the other world on the wings of a dragon. I hope you can hear it before you leave."

My mother silently envelopes me in a hug, soaking my shoulder with her tears, which gets me crying, too.

"I always knew this day would come, when I would have to say goodbye to you. I had hoped our move to the new town would let you stay for a while, but since you tell me otherwise I am torn. On one hand, I am not ready to give you up, and I will deeply miss my youngest – and my daughter. But to think that you are going to the other world – where people fly through the air and do all kinds of amazing things – even to the point of raising the dead. That is magic – the making of tales and legends."

I finally get some words out. "I still sometimes think this must be a dream, that I'll wake up and find myself in my own bed with the morning sun peeking through the cracks in the wall. I am already learning to read and write in their language – the language they call English. I already understand most of what they say, even though sometimes I have trouble coming up with the words when I try to speak, but I'm getting better every day. They have these magical drawings on the wall that move and talk. They sometimes tell it to help us learn to read better – Genovea is learning too. I think she talks even better than I do."

Chapter 23.

I am sitting at a table in the mess room twisting the lid of a salt shaker off and on – off and on – trying to keep my hands busy in the hopes that I might just make it through the next two hours. This is the day we have to bury Don.

We knew that one of the risks of time travel is exposure to disease, so everyone got a full suite of all the available injections for travel to the developing world before we left home. Of course Lance and I both got the complete military set of immunizations; Taylor did too before his trip to Afghanistan. For the three of us it was only a few boosters. The others didn't have it so easy. Sandy also brought a good supply of antibiotics and antivirals, so we thought we'd be safe. Such was not the case.

Michael was the first to get sick. He woke up in the night with a high fever, aches and pains, so went down to sickbay to be nursed by Sandy. She was pretty sure it was the flu and he would be fine in a couple of days. She's always been right before, but not this time. Not only was he worse in two days, but others on the crew were also showing symptoms: April, Kelly, Don, Steve, and Trace all went down over the following days. Symeon also soon showed symptoms – the only one of our strays to get sick.

By this time, Sandy was pulling her hair out trying to figure out what these people had.

I remember the morning all the healthy ones gathered in Mission Control to hear her thoughts. "It's contagious – I know that. It looks like a virus, but I don't know yet what it is. Until we know, all I can do is treat the symptoms. I don't know yet the mode of transmission or how long the incubation period is, so I don't know who else might have been exposed. I think we should give everyone an anti-viral injection – maybe it will help us fight off whatever this is. We can't handle any more sick."

I'm the first to roll up my sleeve. I hate needles. I never liked them, but since the accident they remind me too much of my stay in the hospital and what happened just before that. The longer I have to wait, the more nervous I will get and I can't afford to show any weakness – not now.

Taylor comes up to me as I rise from the chair, next in line for the injection. He says "You're brave today," with a hint of a smile. He knows I'd rather do pretty much anything other than get a needle.

"I know the longer I wait, the harder it will be."

"You're not one to stand around and wait for things to get worse. I know that. Just like at Wynt when we were attacked. I was angry at you for acting too fast – I thought you should have waited longer to see if there was any other resolution before pulling that trigger. But deep down I know something really bad could have happened fast if you didn't act when you did."

"In that second I had to decide, all I could think about is that if I didn't act and something happened to my best friend, I'd never forgive myself. I had to save you."

"Thank you. I couldn't say that before now because I just couldn't get over the ick factor of having his head blow apart right there beside me. I still gag at the memory of having to wash brain out of my hair."

That hug he gave me – right where I got that needle in my arm – felt so good. Then he had to let go, and get his own shot.

It was the very next morning that Michael broke out with the distinctive pustules and Sandy learned the identity of the mystery virus: Smallpox.

Since it was wiped out in the 1970s, smallpox vaccinations were discontinued so most of the team carried no immunity. I'm pretty sure it was included in our military injections just in case it was used in a biological weapon, so Lance, Taylor and I were all safe. The older members were vaccinated as children, and none have come down with the disease. Some of the others managed to escape too: Michele, Candice and Francois are all totally healthy.

Muirenn and Genovea are also unscathed. Is it the luck of the draw or do they have some immunity? I'd like to know the answer to that question. To find out, we visited Tordur a couple of days ago with pictures of our patients. They know the disease – most years they get a handful of patients, usually foreigners or children. Right now they have two patients – one a Roman merchant, the other a child from a nearby settlement. That's more than usual for them, but given the highly contagious nature of the disease, we're surprised they don't have more.

Sandy wonders if most the population has resistance to the disease, because there is no historical trace of the disease in Western Europe until about the 15th century. Her theory is vaccina – the related virus that gives immunity to smallpox and was the origin of the word 'vaccine' – could be endemic to the area. If so, most of the population will have resistance, so it is mostly children who have not yet been exposed and those from other lands who are susceptible. Our team for example. Even though the disease is uncommon, it remains deadly. April was the first to succumb, leaving Barry broken in his grief. Symeon died two days ago, and yesterday it was Don. This morning Trace breathed her last. Kelly, Steve, and Michael are all recovering nicely.

I can't say that I knew either April or Trace well, but Don's death is a blow. I can't imagine breaking the news to Max – they've been together for so long, always afraid, always living behind masks, always waiting for the right opportunity to come out. Now the chance is gone forever. Maybe the chance has been over for a while – we don't know where in time Max is – maybe he made it home safely, but couldn't get back for some reason, but maybe he didn't. I hope he did.

What would really thrill me would be to see him walk through the door right now. Because now we have a huge problem: we lost both our time travel experts. Between Martin and me, I think we know enough to enter the right parameters that should take us home, but I'm not sure we know enough to recover if something goes wrong. Maybe I'm over-reacting. If the geo-locking fails, by the time we realize it we will be somewhere in outer space and already dead. If it takes us to the wrong time, we just wait it out for the ripples in space-time to settle down and try again. We've got plenty of supplies: food, fuel, and weapons. Even our medical supply room is still well stocked – Sandy made sure we have plenty of everything we might need. Except smallpox vaccinations. And a neurosurgeon. Everything else we have. We should be okay – it just might take a little longer than we planned.

As my thoughts turn to Sandy and how fortunate we are to have her, she comes in and plops herself into the chair opposite me, her face revealing the stress and exhaustion of the last few weeks.

"Muirenn's keeping an eye on the patients. I really hope she does get into medicine – she has a good instinct for it, and will act quickly when needed – like at the cholera village. She knew Rosathe was dying and reacted quickly enough that we saved her – she didn't have a clue what we could do, but she still did exactly the right thing. She's so eager to learn everything now. She's even trying to work her way through a biology text. She does surprisingly well until she comes up against anything to do with numbers. They still confuse her."

I respond with the fear that's on my heart. "Are we doing the right thing, taking them with us? They don't really have a clue what they are facing. They're both bright teenagers, but stuff we learned as toddlers and take for granted, they know nothing about. Numbers and basic math is just one example. There are so many others. Neither one knows their true age or their birthday – Genovea is probably fourteen or fifteen, , Muirenn might be sixteen. Do we just turn them loose in high school without giving them the grounding in how to navigate teenage society?"

"You're sounding like a mom," she replied. "In Genovea's case, I think the bigger concern is how to prepare a high school for her. I'm convinced she'll have every teacher and most the kids wrapped around her little finger within a week."

I laugh, and add, "She'll earn enemies soon enough, though. I may need to give her some martial arts training first. She already has Lance teaching her some fighting skills, so she won't be totally defenceless. Between that and her incredible eyes, yeah she'll be more ready for high school than I was."

Sandy smiles, but it's a sad smile that soon fades. "I need something to eat, and then I'm getting some sleep. I can't remember ever being so exhausted before. These past weeks have been hell – I'm just glad that it didn't spread further; I don't think I could have handled any more patients – or deaths. Five dead in less than a month when you include Symeon. I was so sure everyone would come home just fine, and the worst I'd have to deal with would be a cut finger – or maybe a bruised ego. Oh, speaking of Symeon, before he died he said you were to have this, the wooden chest that never left his side."

With that she opens the bag at her feet and places on the table between us the small wooden box Symeon showed me the night of the Solstice celebration at Tordur.

"What is in this?" she asks. "I never saw it open, but he seemed to think you would value it."

I pull the chest to me and spin it around so the simple clasp faces me. I can feel my hands shaking as I undo the clasp and lift the lid. Inside is the cup I remember, carefully wrapped in a piece of cloth. I unwind the cloth and set the bronze goblet on the table just as Taylor wanders past.

"Behold the Holy Grail – at least, it is if Symeon was telling the truth."

Taylor plops himself into the chair beside me, quickly recognizing the cup standing on the table before me. "What's this – getting your legends mixed? Never heard of Robyn Hood being the keeper of the Grail?"

"I can't imagine why Symeon wanted me to have it. Why give it to me? Why not one of his friends in Londinium? If he trusts me to keep it, why not trust me to deliver it to someone?"

Taylor gives me an answer. Two answers, really. "Perhaps he trusted you more than the others to keep it out of the hands of the Romans. I mean, this ship is right now about the safest place on the planet – there is no one out there who has much chance of successfully attacking us. Or maybe he knew that we can hardly enter Londinium unnoticed. All of us are far too well known – so if we visited one of his friends to deliver the Grail, we would inevitably draw the attention of the Romans. They might start asking questions and cause them trouble. Either way, he decided to entrust it to you."

It is then that I notice the note tucked against one side of the chest. It clearly is new, for it is modern paper he could only have got here. I open it and read the words, translating into English as I go.

This cup must not fall into the hands of the Romans. I feel that so strongly that it greatly influenced my decision to travel to the north with you. I intended all along to request that you take it with you when you leave this world, for I don't believe that anywhere in this one will remain safe for long. I told my friends before I left that I intended to send it with you. Now that my days are short, it is time to confirm that decision.

Keep it safe, and remember me.

Peace.

"So what do I do with it?" I ask mostly to myself. "I can't exactly take it home and expect to be believed. The Grail legend has always been assumed to be a much later addition to earlier tales. Most scholars think it's from the twelfth-century or so; that it was created to help justify the crusades. I don't think anyone seriously believes there is any truth to those legends at all. Now I have this cup that he claimed is the Holy Grail and absolutely no way to prove it. I don't plan on tarnishing my research and career by announcing to the scientific community that I am the keeper of the Holy Grail."

Taylor adds "I guess the theory that drinking from it gives everlasting life doesn't hold up – it didn't work for Symeon."

Michele wanders over and takes the final seat at the table while I am thinking out loud. "Yeah – and we can't use our eternal youth as evidence – time travel kind of screwed that one up."

I give them all a bit of a smile – it's about as close as I can come to a laugh today. "We might need a little miracle right about now. Max is gone and now that Don is dead, we don't have anyone who really knows how to get us home. I think Martin and I learned enough, but we won't know for sure until we push the button to take us home."

Time travel isn't just punching a date into a keypad and pressing "Go." There are twelve non-linear parameters to calculate and enter; getting one of those even slightly wrong will have a huge impact on when we wind up. The big unknown for us is the impact of the ripples in space-time created by our own outward journey or Max's return. After he left, Don started the calculations to adjust for the distortion, but I don't think he was fully satisfied with the results. He got sick before he could verify his work. Now he's dead.

For the first time in this expedition, I'm scared that we won't make it home.

Chapter 24.

It was Francis who saw the light from the flames in the night and alerted Robyn's people on the Voyager. The sound of Little Bird taking off into the night woke Genovea, who in turn woke me. We threw on some clothes and went upstairs to Mission Control to investigate.

We didn't even get that far when we met Robyn running the other way. "Tordur is burning! Come! We are going to see what happened and help out your people."

I think I screamed – I don't really remember the next few minutes. My next memory is sitting in The Bird with Genovea beside me, looking at Robyn's tablet, trying to spot my family in the pictures, and thinking they were forever getting The Bird into the air. I don't even want to put on my armor coat, but reluctantly agree to wear it when Robin threatens to leave me behind if I don't. It's so uncomfortable and heavy – I hate wearing it. When we finally take off, I just stare out the window and watched the light grow with the coming of dawn, my mind racing in the terror of the disaster unfolding ahead.

"What happened? How did it start? Is anyone hurt or worse? Dead? I'm pretty sure I can see my mother standing with a group of others outside the fort, but there aren't nearly enough there – it doesn't look like even half the people who live there. Where is everyone else?"

I can feel the panic rise as we clatter low over the trees, watching the orange glow grow in the sky and not knowing if it is from the fire or the approaching dawn. Suddenly, I see the glare from the sun behind us, the trees drop away and we fly through an explosion of sparks as we come directly over our hall.

It's too much for me; tears are running down my face as The Bird settles on the field at a safe distance from the walls. I can feel Genovea beside me move to put her arm around my shoulders, but I don't want comfort right now – I want to know what happened and if my family is okay – so I push past her and rush the door, jumping to the ground right behind Robyn.

The smoke from the fire mixes with the morning mist to create a thick, swirling fog that stings my eyes and makes it hard to breathe. The lights on The Bird illuminate the air around us, piercing the half-light of dawn and surrounding us with an intense, bluish glow as we walk toward the competing orange from the flames. I feel Robyn tense and raise her weapon beside me as we both catch sight of a shadow walking in our direction through the fog.

"Muirenn! Robyn!" I hear my mother's voice, and I break into a run as I recognize the figure coming toward us.

I crash into her, wrapping my arms around her to keep us from falling. Her tears soak my shoulder as they wash tracks in the dirt and soot that covers her face. She quickly explains what happened during the night. It turns out, in spite of his earlier words, Cydyrn was not happy about their decision to move at the behest of the Romans. He came just after nightfall with his war host. The watchmen on the walls recognized them and opened the gates to let them enter. As soon as they were inside the walls, my father came forward in greeting – unarmed, for he did not expect treachery from the man he recognized as both king and friend. But as he approached, Cydyrn's dagger flashed and my father fell at his feet, blood pouring from the slash across his throat. Gwyn was right behind him and sprang into action. He was better prepared than my father; his sword slew two of Cydyrn's chief warriors and wounded a third before he was overpowered and fell beside his father. Cydyrn's men then kindled torches and set Tordur aflame, driving the inhabitants out into the night, killing those who got in their way.

"He knew you would come and is ready for you,." she tells Robyn. "He sent me to tell you his men have the rest of our people just outside the wall. He is challenging you rescue them – if you don't, his men will kill them."

Robyn steps back a few feet, leaving me with my mother. I can't ignore the quiet voices in my ear, so I whip out my earpiece so I only hear my mother's voice.

"He's dead. They're both dead. And we have no home. I know the Romans are building a new town, but will it be ready before winter? All our food, my plants. Everything is gone."

My father is dead? And Gwyn? I made the decision to leave, but Tordur is still home – or was, I think as I look over my mother's shoulder just as a section of wall collapses into a cloud of sparks and flame. It isn't anyone's home any more. I'm so choked up that I can't even sob. So I put my arms around her and we stand in silence for what seems like an eternity. Tears are running down both our faces, soaking each other's shoulders.

I'm so totally focused on my mother that I don't even realize Robyn is back beside me until I hear the sound of a foot stepping on a twig beside me. Then she starts to speak and I jump. "We have a plan to get the rest of the people away from Cydyrn and his men. Michael and Jack are with The Bird – there are about twenty men headed toward them in two groups. I don't know if they will try to capture The Bird or cut off our retreat – in either case, those two know what to do."

"For the main group, Lance and Genovea are quietly circling to the far side, armed with this." She holds up a gun that looks different from any I've seen before. It is big enough that I could almost stuff my fist into it, but shorter than her usual weapon. "It's called tear gas and makes everyone's eyes sting and water so much they can barely see – far worse than the smoke in the air. Cydyrn's men are gathered around the outside of the Tordur people. Most are close to him with the rest in two groups between the people and the forest. Our two are just on the edge of the forest where they can't be seen, but the men are well within range of the gas. They also have little balls that make a bright flash and a loud bang. They won't cause harm, but are certain to disorient the men for a few seconds. I'll take out the men around Cydyrn. When we gas them they won't be able to attack your people – they'll be too busy trying to get the gas out of their eyes. Your people will be impacted too, but they're further away so it will bother them less than Cydyrn and his men."

She hands each of us these things they call masks to protect our eyes and mouths. "When I start shooting, put on these on right away. They will keep it out of your eyes so you can see and you'll be able to help your people get away."

With that, the three of us walk together up the hill through the fog to where Cydyrn is waiting. I stick my earpiece back in so I can hear her words.

"Well, if isn't the great one from the other world," Cydyrn shouts as we draw near. "Maybe I can't harm you, but look what I can do to the people you claim to protect. I burned their town and now you can't stop me from killing them as you watch."

I gasp at the thought of watching my friends and family die, but Robyn seems untroubled. "If you did that, there would be nothing to stop me from killing your men and burning Wynt to the ground before you could ever reach home. You know I can kill, and you also know our bird flies faster than the swiftest horse can gallop and spits fire as easily as you breathe. The men you sent to attack it – you should call them off before they get hurt."

Just as Robyn pauses for a breath, I hear the distant crack of guns coming from the direction of The Bird, followed by cries that I know are coming from his men.

"It sounds like it is too late for that. You should know by now that we can see through smoke and mist; the dark of night offers you no protection. We know where your men are. Tell me, what is it that you want from me? Perhaps you can still escape the trap you set for yourself."

"This is my kingdom. I can't have a bunch of my people pack up and follow after a pack of outsiders, taking all their wealth and stores with them. I won't allow it and there is nothing you can do to stop me. If you try to kill me, my men will turn on your friends. I will do as I wish, and I wish for you and your friends to know they cannot forsake me without paying a very high price."

Robyn laughs at this. "If you let them go, no further harm will come to you or your men. You speak of paying a price, so will I. If you refuse, I will make sure you regret this day for the rest of your life. You or your men hurt any more of these people, and I'll make sure you never again wield a sword or walk a step without pain as a reminder of this day. Make your decision quickly."

Cydyrn replies. "Why should I trust you? The truth is, I don't. Yet I have no argument with you, so I intend no harm to you. Nevertheless, I am glad you are here to watch as I exact retribution. Know that there is nothing you can do to stop me."

With that, he motions to his men who arm their bows and raise their spears as the turn to face the people crowded behind them. Only his personal guard remain passively facing us.

"I told you that I don't trust you. These men will make certain of my safety."

"Genovea, Lance. Now!" I barely hear Robyn speak even though she's standing right beside me.

Far on the other side of the field, near where I know the rest of Cydyrn's men are standing, I see two bright flashes of light followed by loud bangs, reminding me of the time lightning struck a tree just outside our walls. The men in front of us are momentarily distracted as they turn to see what is happening. In one smooth motion, she reaches up and pulls her mask over her face as she raises her gun. I pull my mask on in time to see her fire, not at the men, but at the ground in front of them. Black objects hit the ground and start to spew a dense white cloud. Instantly, there is pandemonium as the men drop their weapons and start coughing. Most drop to the ground, some run away. One man, standing off to the side, keeps his feet and his wits. I see him turn to face us and raise his spear. I try to shout a warning, but Robyn already sees him. She raises her gun and fires, hitting him square the chest with a canister just as he throws. He goes down and the spear goes wide, whistling by and sticking into the ground far behind us.

Now Robyn drops this gun to the ground, and raises her rifle as she stalks to where Cydyrn lies on the ground. "Get up you coward."

He scrambles for his shield and manages to get it between Robyn and himself by the time she's standing over him.

"Do you think that will save you? You don't learn very fast. Get up and call your men off while you still can."

I hear the cracks of rifles in the distance, and know the attack is continuing elsewhere.

"Call them off while you still have men to lead."

I can see tears streaming out of his eyes as he glares at us over the top of his shield and tries to control his coughing enough to point his sword in something reasonably close to our direction.

"Are you going to tell your men to drop their weapons, or do you need more convincing that resistance is futile? Perhaps I should start with you?"

He finally manages to control himself enough to spit out, "I'm not afraid of death."

"Oh, I have no intention of killing you. That would just turn you into a hero, worthy of song. I will hurt you so badly you become an object of pity. Or perhaps ridicule."

I could tell her that Cydyrn won't back down. He knows that Robyn holds his life, so if she spares him, he will owe her a debt he cannot ignore. Just like Bledwyn, he will be bound to her. And in front of all his men, too! There is no way he out for him. Just as I am about to tell Robyn this, I catch sight of a movement off to the side. One of Cydyrn's men has gained his feet and is preparing to launch a spear in our direction.

"Robyn," I cry out in warning.

She turns toward me, away from the flying spear, so I do the only thing I can think of and run toward her, pushing her out of the way. Then I scream as I feel the spear catch me in the side. The force of the blow knocks me to the ground, and my side feels like I've been hit by a hammer, but the spear bounces off the hot, heavy armour she insisted I wear this morning. Even as I roll to see what is going on, I silently promise to never again complain about this weight on my shoulders.

I see Robyn regain her balance, swing and shoot the man who threw the spear, and quickly turn her attention back to Cydyrn. A breeze has picked up and blown away the fog and smoke, so the men are starting to recover, but I'm sure Robyn knows that now. She does – without further words she fires into the ground about a foot from Cydyrn's head, blasting dirt and grass into his face. Then she shifts her aim to his groin. I sit up to see as he tries to shift his shield to protect himself.

"Guess where the next one is going? And that shield won't help at all. Get up now and order your men to back off or I will drill you in the dick."

It doesn't take long before he thinks this through, and gives up. He lowers his sword, drops his shield to the ground beside him, and manages to roll over onto his hands and knees. He still doesn't have the balance to regain his feet, but uses one arm to drag his sword over so he can lay it at Robyn's feet. I expect her to kick him in the face. That's what I would do, but Robyn does something else. She reaches down and takes up the sword from the ground and turns the hilt toward Cydyrn as he cowers like a condemned slave in front of her. With her free hand, she pulls off her mask and speaks to him.

"I won't kill you. I'm tired of killing. I need you to look after these people instead of fighting them in a battle you can't win. The people of Tordur made a wise and difficult choice to follow the Romans. These conquerors will be here for many generations and those who learn to work with them will thrive. Those who resist will be wiped away without mercy. Don't expect me to seek victory over you or to steal your kingdom. I will soon be gone. Before the harvest is gathered and the rains of autumn come, I will return with my people to our own world. Your reality is a Roman world. That means change for you, but not all change is bad. The famed Pax Romana will give you peace and prosperity for your people.

"Take your sword and lead your people."

With that she reaches down and pulls a shocked Cydyrn to his feet and presses the sword into his hand.

I look to see the fighting has stopped. Those of Cydyrn's men who are near us are gathered in a silent cluster watching his defeat and restoration. Those further away are moving in our direction, heads down, eyes still teary from our gas. I see now. He placed scouts off to the side where they could see everything and signal to the men in the groups at the rear. The scouts missed the worst of the gas, but could only watch as their plan fell apart. Now they are leading their comrades to join Cydyrn in his defeat. But, he's still alive. My father and brother are dead because of him, and I can feel the heat of rage rising as I stand watching the scene before me. Bledwyn is far away – there is nothing he can do. My mother – she's a healer, not a warrior. No one else can step forward and avenge their deaths. I know what I have to do.

Robyn and Lance taught me how to shoot, but I'm not very good so I'm not even carrying a gun this morning. Genovea is way better than me, and Lance has spent time teaching her even more while I was busy tending the sick. Now she's a pretty good shot, which is why she helped Lance out on the far side of the field this morning. And I know she is carrying a handgun. I know what I need to do. As soon as I spot her headed in our direction, I make a beeline toward her.

"Lend me your gun." I demand.

She hands it over without a word. I check it to be sure there is a round in the chamber and the safety is on before I stuff it down my pants and drop my shirt down to cover it. I don't want Robyn to see it, because I know she'll try to stop me. I also pull out my ear piece so I'm not distracted by the chatter and no one can tell me to stop.

"Thanks. I need to do something. I'll be back shortly."

She knows what it is.

"Want me to help?" she asks. "I'll keep Robyn distracted if you want."

"Yeah, that would be good. I don't think she'll be happy about this, but I have to avenge my father. And my brother."

So Genovea takes on Robyn, talking excitedly about her part in the defense of my people, but I don't listen. I go around them and head toward Cydyrn. He's managed to regain his feet, but I think his eyes are still stinging because his head is bowed and he's looking at the ground. The remaining mist is on my side too, so I'm only six feet from him when he realizes I am here and looks up. Good, I want him to see what's about to happen.

I slip out the gun and click the safety off before I speak. I don't think he knows who I am yet, but he soon will. Last night we watched a movie on the boat, partly about a guy who spent his entire life tracking down the man who killed his father. Now the man who killed MY father is in front of me, and I can't resist using the one line that was said over and over again. Of course, I translate it into our own language so he's sure to understand.

"Hello, my name is Muirenn of Cynbel. You killed my father. Prepare to die."

With that, I raise the gun as fast as possible, but Cydyrn was just as fast with his shield. I fire anyway, hoping the bullet would miss the shield, but it doesn't matter. It goes right through and hits him in the chest, causing him to fall backward. I walk toward him and kick the shield out of the way. Then I just about lose my breakfast when I see the bloody hole the size of my fist. But I manage to hold it down. He's still breathing and trying to fight his way back to his feet, his eyes burning with anger, so I step forward to finish the job. I send a second bullet right between his eyes, the light in them goes out, and he slumps to the ground. As he dies, the heat of my anger fades, and I lower the gun which is suddenly too heavy for me to hold.

Then I look around. All of Cydyrn's men are staring at me as I stand over their fallen king. Most of them are fingering their weapons like they are not sure whether to throw them to the ground and bolt or continue to fight. Behind them, Lance, Kelly, and Taylor are leading the refugees from Tordur in the direction of Dubri-tun. I feel movement behind me, and glance over my shoulder to find Robyn and Genovea standing behind me, rifles at the ready.

I glance at Genovea. I'm shocked at what I see. She looks just as serious, just as determined as Robyn does. She looks taller, too. I *think maybe she's standing on a high spot, but when I glance down, I find that she's not. She's taller than I am. And she looks dangerous. She's dressed in the same dabbled green that Robyn wears and the solid boots of Robyn's people instead of the soft leather ones of our people. Her rifle is raised and her long hair hangs from under her helmet in a single black braid. With the remains of the smoke and fog swirling around her, she looks like some strange being from another world. Which stops me short, because I realize she soon will be from another world. So will I.*

Now Robyn speaks. "Enough men have died today. Take your fallen king and return to your homes before more of you join him in his folly."

One man raises his spear as if to throw it, but I hear a shot ring out, and he drops it as he cries out in pain. I see his right arm turn bloody just above the elbow. Then I realize the shot came from Genovea.

"Nice shot!" I hear Robyn call. "That will slow him down for a while, but he'll recover in time."

Now the men are looking toward one another, looking confused and lost as they try to decide which one is going to make the call to fight or retreat.

Finally one says, "Let's go home."

He turns and walks away across the field in the direction of Wynt. The others begin to follow and within a few minutes all we can see is the backs of Cydyrn's men as they make their way home. As they leave, they stop to gather the fallen. One died and three were wounded before the gates of Tordur, with two dead and five more wounded on the attempt to attack our bird, so it does not take long for them to leave. Soon, only the body of the king is left.

"Will you leave your king?" Robyn shouts after one of the last men to remain on the field.

"This was his fight, to feed his pride. It wasn't ours. We had no argument with these people or their chieftain. Good men died, and

more were wounded on this fool's errand. It is fitting that he lies here alone."

With that, he turns his back and stalks down the slope to join the others. Robyn walks to the body lying there, takes the torc off his neck and hands it to me. She keeps his sword and the remains of his shield. Then like his men, she turns her back and walks away.

We hurry to catch up with the others, who are now gathered near the chopper. Kelly and the healers from Tordur are treating the wounded while Lance is keeping watch for stragglers. I hear Robyn speaking and wonder why her voice is so distant when I remember that I pulled out my earpiece before I shot Cydyrn. I feel around my shoulder until my hand catches the wire and quickly stick the end back into my ear. The voices come through clear now and I learn what Robyn and her people are planning.

They will fly all the wounded and ill out to the Voyager tonight. The able-bodied will walk to Dubri-tun and stay there for a few days. Martin says there is a mounted Roman cohort on the way here – they must have seen the fire – they will meet Cydyrn's men on the road before long and get the news from them. Robyn thinks they will be here before noon, so she wants to wait for them. She's hoping it is Finanius with news that Aquaesulis is ready for the people, so they can move to their new home.

I learn that I'm to go back to Voyager with my mother and the wounded because my skills as a healer and translator will be needed. But I want to go to Dubri-tun – I don't want to go play translator on the ship. I have family there and all of a sudden I don't want to leave this world forever without seeing them again. But Robyn assures me I'll have my chance in the days to come. The plan is to take all the survivors from Tordur out to the Voyager, and carry them around this island to their new home. It will be a few days before we leave, so that once the ashes of Tordur cool we can see if there is anything to salvage. I have time to visit Dubri-tun, so I reluctantly agree to the plan. I hate being a translator.

"After we take them to their new home, what happens next?" I ask. "Will we come back here?"

Robyn responds, "No, it is time for us to return home. From there, we will sail straight west and return to our own world and time. Are you still determined to come with us?"

I don't even pause for a second. "Yes, I'm coming with you. Is Genovea coming too?"

"Of course I am. Why would I want to stay here?" I hear the note of disgust in her reply.

I never really doubted it, but wanted to hear it for sure. It sounds strange; I'm scared to go through with this. I know if I leave I can never return to this world, but knowing that Genovea is coming too makes me just a little less terrified. When we first met, she was a peasant girl who was afraid to sleep by herself. How she has grown in these few months and not just in height. Today she faced twenty or so warriors by herself without flinching. And she's going forward into the other world without fear, without doubt and without once looking back. I wish I was like that. But I decide to do the same, and without another backward glance at the ruins of my former home, I stride down the hill toward the people gathered around The Bird.

Chapter 25.

The past week has been wild. The night of the fire at Tordur, it started to rain. For three days it poured, extinguishing any remaining hotspots and turning the entire site into a great soupy mess. It also kept the chopper grounded – the low ceilings and high winds made flying too dangerous. Even the drones stayed on board. For two days it was too rough to even launch the boat, so we were stuck on the ship with the thirty extra people we rescued from Tordur. Most are recovering from minor burns or other injuries, but none have ever been on a boat before and most are at least a little seasick. The three with more serious injuries are having an even rougher time. We have a broken leg, a nasty burn, and a dislocated knee. The constant movement of the ship doesn't help any of them feel better. But Kelly and Sandy have done as much as they can.

Of course, not everyone was in any condition to eat, but enough were that Candice needed help in the kitchen. It was so weird to see John's massive bulk wrapped in an apron flipping burgers at the stove while swaying with the ship. He's actually not a bad cook – and a decent dancer, too. But the storm reminds us that it is time to leave. This storm is just taste of what the North Sea can deliver come winter. The equinox is nearly here, days are getting shorter, and we're ready for home. We just have to get there.

Before Max left, he and Don shared a little of the operation of the time machine with Martin and me, so we are not running completely blind, but the calculations are complex. *If Don wasn't comfortable with his results, then what chance do we have?* We just don't know enough to know whether we are right or wrong. But we don't have any choice, so we'll give it our best shot and hope it works. It might take us a couple of tries, but that's not the end of the world. We still have plenty of food, water, fuel, medical supplies, and ammunition. We can do it – we can get home. I keep telling myself that a thousand times a day. Now that the storm has finally blown itself out, there is nothing to stop us.

We met up with Finanius the day Tordur burned and learned that the people can move to Aquaesulis – there they will find shelter from the coming winter and food to keep them alive. Those who are able will drive the herds that escaped the fire over land to their new home. Little was saved of their crops for the year, but they recovered considerable iron and money from the ruins. They'll load the animals with what they have. Those who are not needed for the cattle drive will come with us. They'll be okay.

We helped the people salvage the town. The bodies of the fallen we laid in the remains of the great hall. *Cydyrn?* We dragged him into the far corner and dumped him into the remains of the latrine. That was my idea, because I know that area will eventually be excavated – if his bones survive they will tell quite the story for the archaeologists. We only had time to bury Cynbel and Gwyn – side-by-side they will lie where they fell just inside the gates.

I worry. I have a lot of people counting on me – I guess it's not just up to me, but I still feel responsible. I chose the destination time for this trip – and pushed hard to come here during our planning meetings. I didn't stop Max from trying to go back to save Andrew – and Andrew died anyway. So did April, and now Barry's broken heart is on my hands. Don died. And Trace. Every single person who is dead or missing I personally recommended for this mission. If we do make it home – correction: WHEN we make it home – it will fall on me to break the news to Max that Don is dead. I know I need my full wits for the coming day, but the bottle of scotch on the table beside me is a lot emptier now than it was when I set it there.

Now Taylor walks in and plops down on the couch beside me. I try to hide my thoughts from my face, but he knows me far too well.

"Robyn! Not everything is your fault! This trip isn't a failure – you gave every one of us the chance of a hundred lifetimes. We all knew it would be dangerous. You rammed it into all of our heads long before we signed up. We knew some of us might not make it home, but we chose to come anyway. In fact, we knew there was a chance none of us would get home. Knowing that, we still jumped at the chance, trusting ourselves to the entire team. From the very first day, we achieved far more than any of us dared to dream for. You led us directly to our target site. We saved lives here, gave hope to any number of people and we've experienced so much over the last four months. I'd do it again in a heartbeat – and so would everyone else on this ship. We all owe so much to you and your leadership. None of this would ever have happened without you."

In response, I think I manage a bit of a smile. "Thanks for trying to help. You know that whatever you say, I will still try to figure out what I could have done differently to save those people. Even Cydyrn – I knew Muirenn would try to kill him, but I didn't do enough to stop her. I figured that since she didn't have a gun there wasn't much she could do. I didn't think she'd get her hands on one so quickly – I misjudged both her and Genovea. Could I have done anything? Should I have done anything?

"Then there's the trip home in a couple of days – have I done absolutely everything possible to get us home in one piece? I've racked my brain and can't think of anything else I can do, but I'm still second-guessing myself."

He doesn't answer my questions. He changes the subject. "Do you have your stuff ready for the cache?"

We planned from the very first to leave a cache containing a record of our presence that we hope will survive until excavated by archeologists in the twenty-first century. The stainless steel and fiberglass box we prepared is standing open on my desk. Everything for it needs to be done tonight. Tomorrow morning, it gets closed and sealed with another layer of fiberglass. Once that sets, the whole thing will be encased in two heat-sealed layers of heavy plastic film. At sunrise the following morning, we will bury the sealed box in the ashes of the kitchens at Tordur, in the area scheduled to be excavated the summer after we return – an area that appears to be completely undisturbed from this time until then. Then we will shuttle the Tordur refugees out to the Voyager and sail around the island to the Severn estuary, transferring them to Roman boats for the short journey up the Avon to their new home. Then we head out to sea and make our voyage through time and return home. That is, if nothing goes wrong.

Originally, we were going to bury the box in a spot in Cynbel's hut that should be safe. Now that Tordur is abandoned, I'm less worried about it being disturbed and will go for the place where it will be found soon after our departure. Just in case we don't make it back. Then people will know what happened to us. Etched into the cover are instructions to send it to Kate. If anyone can recover the data we will leave, it is her. No doubt whoever finds it will assume it's a recent contamination and will fire it to her immediately, demanding an explanation.

I quickly reply to Taylor before my thoughts turn back to worry. "Almost done. I just have to finish today's entry in my journal. Muirenn and I finished her part this morning, so I'm the only one holding up the show. Are you ready?"

"Yeah. I dropped the disks with both video and stills on your desk just before I came in here."

It's funny – I find it easier to relax when he's around, so I lean back and kick my feet up on the coffee table. "Hard to believe the summer is already over and in just a couple of days we'll make our jump back through time. So much has happened – we've seen so much, learned so much, and met so many people – years from now I wonder what I'll remember the most."

"I know what I'll remember."

His voice is so serious it catches my attention and I turn to face him. Our eyes lock and I hear him speak one word.

"You."

"Don't say that. You know what happens to everyone who loves me. They die. And the last person in my life I want to lose is you." I can barely get the words out past the sob that is rising in my throat. Damn, I shouldn't be afraid, but I find myself terrified that whatever I say will be exactly the wrong thing.

Taylor responds, and that saves me from my own words. "You are so worth the risk."

I suddenly feel extremely vulnerable and completely safe at the same time. Am I confused, or just tired of being lonely? Maybe I'll work out the answer later, but for now I don't care. I just lean toward him with my eyes wide open. I don't know what I'm expecting when our lips touch, but it's certainly not the faint but distinct flavor of the ash from Tordur that I can taste on his lips. I don't care – mine probably taste about the same. I forget everything – my worries, my sorrows, my fears – as fold myself in his arms. I least I won't have to speak anytime soon.

When we finally do come up for air, Taylor is the first to speak. "Are you drunk?"

I'm so shocked by the question that I actually answer it before I can think of a suitable retort. "I just had a little, but not enough to get drunk." I try to focus on the bottle and guess just how much I drank, but it's a little fuzzy. Maybe I drank more than I thought.

Then he notices the cup standing on the table beside the bottle. "Are you drinking scotch out of the Holy Grail? I'm not sure whether that's being brave or a fool."

Then he adds. "Did you save any for me?"

I decide to have some fun, and get a little payback for calling me drunk. "Yeah" I slur. "Th' bottle's over there." I add, waving my arm in the general direction.

"You are drunk. I'm getting that bottle before you knock it across the room." With that, he reaches across me, grabs the bottle and takes a slug, then places it on the floor beside him and out of my reach.

I'm suddenly annoyed at him, so I respond with "You didn't have to ask if I was drunk. Did you really think I'd kiss you if I was sober?" I regretted the words as soon as they leave my mouth.

I watch his face fall. "Actually, I did." He mutters. In one smooth motion he rises, drains the dregs from the Grail, grabs the bottle, and turns toward the door. "I'll leave you to sleep it off. Meanwhile, I just might go get drunk myself."

With that, he's gone before I can think of a way to retract my words. Or that it was the alcohol talking. *Why can I say now?* I don't know. I take the now empty cup from where Taylor left it on the table and feel its weight as I repeatedly trace the engraved lines with my fingernail.

I guess I fall asleep because the next thing I know the rising sun is shining through the window. I carefully unwind myself from the corner of the couch and return the cup to its box in my room before I head down to the gym to clear the cobwebs out of my hung-over brain with some exercise.

I can't decide. I don't want to let anyone through the walls of protection I've built around me – not even Taylor. Not even now.

I hit the treadmill and somewhere around the 10k mark, consider that we might all only have a couple of days. If our navigation system fails, we're dead. It's that simple. Martin thinks there are enough backups and fail safes that we don't have to worry. He's probably right – if the system has the slightest hint that something is wrong it will stop the time transfer before we separate from the Earth. I hope so. I still worry. Max's trip might have caused some ripples in space-time that we didn't adjust for. We might have miscalculated something or even made a stupid typo. So many things could go wrong. I'm taking so many risks anyway that I finally decide I might as well take just one more.

I head to my cabin for a shower and change before searching out Taylor. It doesn't take long – I find him in the mess, dishevelled, eyes bloodshot and staring at a large cup of coffee like he fully expects it to attack him at any moment. Otherwise the place is empty. I can hear Candice banging around in the kitchen, but no one else is in the room at this hour.

"Ouch. Did you finish off that scotch last night or did it finish you?" I ask, sliding into the chair beside him.

He doesn't even try to look up. "I seem to remember putting up a good fight, but I'm not sure who won."

"By the looks of you, that bottle came out on top." I plunge ahead before I can chicken out. "Last night I said something really mean to you, but I didn't mean it. That was just me trying to be funny and failing miserably. Instead of getting a laugh, I hurt someone I care about deeply." I see by the look on his face that my words are just not computing, so I shut up, and kiss him. And I don't mean a quick peck either. By the time I stop he's fully grasped the meaning of my words. Just to be sure, I whisper in his ear. "This time I'm sober – I'm so beyond excuses and my stupid walls; I want you to know I'll never let you go."

He manages a bit of a smile as he takes my face in his hands. "You sure know how to get a guy's attention. And since I've been trying to get your attention for – it seems like years – I really wish I wasn't so hung-over right now." He gives a gentle laugh, but I can see tears in his eyes.

I can feel the tears in my eyes too. But before they can spill over, I change the subject. "No offense, but you look like you need to drink that coffee instead of just staring at it. Then maybe go grab a shower. I'll meet you out on the deck in an hour."

With that, I give him a squeeze on the shoulder as I rise and head for my room. For the first time since the accident, I am at peace. I even find myself humming some old love song as I spend the hour finishing my journal and copying it to the archival solid-state drive for the cache. I'll drop the whole thing off with John on my way out to the deck.

Who knows what the next few days will bring, but today my future is bright.

Postscript.

The contents of the container marked Site 9; Sector R19; Level 7 submitted to this office for analysis and data recovery were badly damaged in spite of the protective packaging. The seal on the container was intact, so there was no penetration of water or other contaminants. Even so, both the container and contents show signs of considerable corrosion of the metal components and degradation of the plastic to a far greater degree than I have seen previously. Samples have been sent to our materials lab for analysis. I will forward their findings when available, but am issuing this preliminary report in response to your urgent request.

The box contained two archival disk drives and a solid state drive. The disk drives were unfortunately virtually unusable. Less than two percent of the data could be read and I was only able to recover twenty partial images. Copies of the images are attached to this report as Appendix A.

I had much better luck with the solid state drive. The encapsulated silicon memory chip was intact. I was, therefore, able to extract and recover the single document file that it contained. From the contents of this document, it appears this artifact is contemporary to the site and not recent contamination as was supposed. A printed copy is attached as Appendix B.

The document explains why my name and address were engraved on the artifact. It purports to be from my good friend, Dr. Robyn Hood, who was on the research vessel Voyager when it disappeared without a trace nearly two years ago. It claims to have been placed there by her in the late summer of AD 64, just days after the site was abandoned. Based on the condition of this artifact, I have no basis for disputing this date or any of the information contained in the document.

Kate Smith
Data Recovery Specialist
Department of Information Technology

More Information.

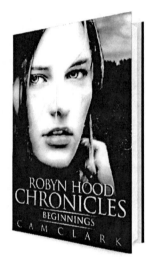 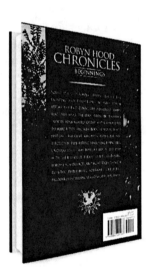

To learn more about **Robyn Hood** and **Cam Clark**, and for information on the next book in the *Robin Hood Chronicles* series, please visit the website:

www.CamClark.com

Acknowledgements

First, I would like to the friends and family who suffered my absence, but were not allowed a peek into this work while it was in progress.

Thanks to Leigh St John for her encouragement and unmatched assistance in helping me through the publishing process.

Also to Leslie Flowers, my amazing editor, who turned my manuscript into something so much greater. And also delivered so many positive words to me. Thank you my friend.

Finally, there is the Sunday Brunch Bunch, and that day the talk turned to time travel. That got me thinking…

CPSIA information can be obtained at www.ICGtesting.com
Printed in the USA
LVOW07s0332210616

493438LV00021B/217/P